PRAISE FOR *VIRTUAL*

MW01492795

"Cressman's argot-heavy ...... is Kurt Vonnegut-like in its satire and offers a Bruegel-like canvas in its sweep."

—*Kirkus Reviews*

"A post-modern tale that rings the alarm bells loud and clear. Reading *Virtuality* will make you take a personal inventory of the "infotainment" you consume. This story has stayed with me and continues to color my perception of recent events in the news. A must read for fans of speculative fiction, although this one hits pretty close to home."

—Tiffanie Simpson, *Book Haus*

"Cressman's *Virtuality* is above all else an exuberant excursion through a a future that seems both bonkers and entirely plausible. In a world controlled by big corporations, virtuality and reality are on a collision course, and every character has to figure out how they fit into a society that appears monolithic, but is hollow inside. This is a novel written for the modern brain, exhilarating, zippy, and insightful, all the while using the pace and vocabulary of virtual reality to skewer it. A trip to the future you don't want to miss!"

—Julie Price Carpenter, author of *The Last Train Out of Hell*

"Cressman's writing is sharp, often layered with quotable lines and interesting parodies. . . . focusing on breaking down virtual reality addiction and attempting to convince people to interact with each other and the natural world around them. Recommended to anyone who enjoys dystopian and speculative fiction."

—*The US Review of Books* (Recommended)

"*Virtuality* is a brilliant cautionary tale extrapolating modern day trends of crony capitalism, manipulation of facts, distraction of the masses and more into a future where food is free but minds are captured. Cressman reveals how our consciousness may change as truths dawn, and encourages us to hold those revelations and each other closely. He reminds us the future is not so distant as it may seem."

—Sue Wilson, Writer/Director of the movie "Broadcast Blues" and Founder of the Media Action Center

VIRTUALITY

A NOVEL

DEREK CRESSMAN

HIGH FREQUENCY PRESS

ISBN: 978-1-962931-37-3
LCCN: 2025906882
Printed in the United States of America.

For Peri

CHAPTER 1
Oscar

HE AWOKE IN A STRANGE PLACE. SOMETHING WAS MIS-sing. Something was off.

An icy blast knocked a crow from a lopsided pine with branches bent backwards from decades of previous gusts, causing the tree itself to flow east with the wind. The bird regained its perch, only to be blown off again. And again.

Layers of apparently real blankets pressed down upon him, heavy cotton or wool or some sort of reusable fabric other than his normal disposable sheets. There were no screens on the wall, only old wood paneling, a few paintings of elderly people in funny hats, and a single-paned window.

The windows in his mind were gone.

Da fuck?

By dim candlelight, his eyes followed a row of twin beds toward a door at the end of the room. It cracked open.

"He's awake! Go tell Ellen," came a hushed voice from outside the room. Feet shuffled. "It's OK," the whisperer said, but not to him.

He lifted his head for a better look and pain stabbed his brain.

Fuckin' A!

Relaxing his neck, he re-examined the window to avoid the door crack's curious eyes. *Black wings.*

He knew about birds, of course, but this was the first time in his nineteen years of viewing the mid-twenty-first century he recalled seeing one. His skull throbbed as he glanced back toward the door; the pain was worst just behind his left ear.

"Hi," came a fresh voice through the doorway, followed by a teenage girl holding a leafy green twig topped with something white.

"Where the fuck am I?"

"Mercy! Don't say that. You're in a convent of the Sisters of San Bernardino. I was the one who found you. I wasn't sure you'd ever wake up."

Had he paid attention to the same sort of characteristics his parents had, he would have observed her blonde hair and fair skin as clues to how she identified herself, her tribe. Instead, he noted a white blouse buttoned up to the neck under a gray dress with a matching headscarf, all lacking corporate logos or branding of any sort. A long strip of leather served as a makeshift belt, forcing the loose cut of the short-sleeved dress into something that revealed a hint of her body's curvature. She wore boots. Unbranded cowboy boots. He hadn't met many girls IRL but was a bit disappointed she didn't look much like those he swiped left to enjoy virtually on Cynder™.

"Whuzzat?"

"A flower, silly. Someone was here earlier helping build a greenhouse for growing them. He gave me this one. Would you like it?" Her blue eyes smiled when she bent over and handed it to him.

"What do you do with it?"

"Nothing. It's just for pretty. Anyway, why weren't you wearing a helmet? You could have died."

"I don't need no fucking helmet; I got an implant years ago."

"Mercy! A what?"

"You know, a MyndScreen, so I get 11G brain-streamed 'stead of wearing a VR helmet for games and movies and stuff. Don't you got one?"

"No. I meant a real helmet. To protect your head."

"That's for momma-boys. I'm at double diamond level and when I crash only a few hit points come off."

"Hey, what's your name?"

He hesitated. "Oscar. It's Oscar."

"Well, welcome to the real world, Oscar. You're lucky I brought the dogs along when I went out riding. If they hadn't barked so much, I'd have trotted right past you."

"Let him rest, Ellen," scolded an older nun, carrying a tray toward him in her frail hands. "I brought you some nice warm soup."

"Thanks . . . aaaagh!" Pain chiseled his skull when he tried sitting up.

"Don't move! I'll spoon it into you. Off you go, Ellen."

"As you say, Sister Martha," she replied reluctantly. "Bye, Oscar."

He'd have rather had Ellen stay than Martha.

"Now, young man, try this." Her tawny arm lifted a half-filled spoon slowly toward him. "Easy now. Sound nourishment comes in small doses."

Oscar wanted a big dose. Steam tickled his nostrils as the spoon passed under the thin black mustache that eked out a meager existence on his face. *Ouch!* Hot metal seared his lips. The plastic spoons at home didn't burn like that. She paused, blew on the soup, and tilted it into his mouth. A salty broth washed over his tongue. Tender bits of pale green and orange cubes provided texture and some sort of pasta had an awesome buttery taste. The whole thing warmed his insides. A soothing sensation coursed through his arteries, deep into his marrow. With careful bites and swallows, tastes he'd never experienced titillated various parts of his tongue, sinus, and throat. Salt. Celery. Garlic. Parsley. Black pepper.

"It's fanta. What brand is this?"

"Why, it's chicken noodle soup."

"Yeah, but what's it called? I want to download it when I get home."

"It's called chicken noodle soup, that's all. We made it last night."

"You made it? From what?"

"Chicken of course; and noodles and a few vegetables. Have you never had it?"

"I never had nothing that didn't come out an extruder. We order online, it goes straight to the CokAid machine and prints out. We've got, like, a zillion flavors installed but nothing ever tasted this good. It's kinda chewy."

"Well, take your time young man. Going slowly will heal you faster than rushing to recover."

After the soup, Sister Martha got down to business. "You need some sleep, but first tell me your name and address so we can contact your family."

"I'm Oscar, like I said. I ain't got no family. Some biker dudes ganked my parents."

"Ganked?"

"They're dead."

"Oh, my goodness, I'm so sorry, Oscar. Oscar who? What's your last name?"

This seems strange, but he couldn't remember. Or, maybe, he'd never known. "My handle's @OscarBro92346."

The smile on the nun's face relaxed and her eyes opened wider. "How about your address? Where do you live?"

"Highland. Right outside San Bernadino. A yellow house on the corner. I got a red pin dropped there in my NoodleMaps."

"Lord help us, I'm afraid the accident scrambled your brain a bit."

She removed an ice pack from behind his head and gently pressed her hand against his forehead as he tried sitting up. "Don't move, remember? You've had a concussion and possibly worse. Why in heaven's sake were you beyond the ski area boundary? Didn't you see the signs?"

Skiing. He'd been skiing. For reals.

It all began that morning while playing DownhillDemon™ on his MyndScreen. He was getting pretty good staying up on skis and mowing down opponents with a semi-automatic pistol. Some might consider virtual gaming for hours on end a waste of time, but Oscar deemed it on-the-job training. He might need gunslinging skills IRL someday. Besides, he'd always wanted to try skiing, even as a kid.

He'd lean left and MyndScreen technology detected the nerve signals and steered his avatar around a tree. He'd jump, kick one leg forward, the other back, and his avatar would catch air and do a Daffy over a landmine obstacle. Cerebral cortex synapses triggered his implant to fire the virtual weapon when he twitched an index finger.

Contorted writhing back and forth made his back ache, or perhaps it was sleeping on the old foam mattress he'd tossed on the cracked vinyl flooring. Maybe someday he could afford a 4D lounge to enhance gaming with vibration and scent-effects and provide a deep tissue massage afterwards. For now, he just closed pop-up ads for mattress recycling that seemed to appear every time he noticed the stiffness in his shoulders. The damn ads disrupted his game.

His twelve-year-old sister, Luella, was in the kitchen waiting for their home CokAid extruder to whip up some ScramBoldEgz™.

"We're out of FlavrPaks!"

"Huh?" Oscar mumbled, eyes glassed over and staring at the bare wall. His brain focused instead on animations of snow, villains, and exploding virtual obstacles.

Drops of water fell from above. The rains had started, and the roof was old. After their parents died, this place had been an ideal squatter's pad—a vacant ranch house with solar panels and working batteries. The electric company required payment in ByteDime, but Oscar's income was old school cash from clandestine cigarette sales. To save what little cyber currency he could launder for things like CokAid FlavrPaks, they lived off-grid.

During wet years, water seeped in through the holes where screws fastened solar panels to the crumbling asphalt shingles. He should do something about it, some day. But the solar kept the CokAid flowing and ran the AC during blistering heat waves. Most importantly, it recharged Luella's GalExSee™ helmet, which Oscar let her plop on her head whenever she became too much to handle. That was most of the time. Taking care of his sister these past five years, while still a teenager himself, had been anything but easy. He never had time for himself. When she turned thirteen, her cerebral cortex would be sufficiently developed for an implant powered by a glucose fuel cell. Then the VR helmet could be pawned.

"I said we're out of flavoring. Can you order some?"

"I'll get you something," he mumbled through a lit cigarette dangling from his lips. A cockroach scurried as the CokAid machine whirred and its 3D printer head produced a hot polyethylene disk. The food nozzle extruded greenish gray unflavored soyalgent-based scrambled eggs atop the newly printed plate. A protruded fork completed the entrée.

"This breakfast sucks. Oscar, pay attention to me! Pause your damn game or I'll hack your chatterfeed and take you off-line." Had Oscar been a bit more observant, he'd have taken this as more than an idle threat.

"Just a sec, this guy's getting away."

A new ad popped up. "Ski real snow. Let SlalomSnake™ guide you down epic slopes." A video loop displayed a bad ass skier rocking a backscratcher trick with knees bent and toes pointed straight down while catching serious air off an overhang.

Fanta! He squinted to pause the game and thought about pinging his MarlBro bruddas. In a rare moment of introspection, Oscar decided instead to go it alone the first time. *Can't let them see me fall.*

Within thirty seconds, he'd pre-ordered ski clothes to be fabricated on site, reserved rental equipment, and purchased a Snow Valley lift ticket all with ByteDime. Following years of virtual gaming, a "real" experience was irresistible. He'd built his credit rating sufficiently over the past few years and deserved a splurge. A Lubyr™ was en route to pick him up.

"See ya, sis. I'm outta here."

"Wait! Dammit, Oscar."

"Be back in a few hours."

Riding up to the San Bernardino mountains, Oscar practiced some more DownhillDemon, although his moves were a bit awkward sitting in the back of a self-driving SUV. Snow Valley hadn't opened in four previous seasons due to lack of snow. This was finally a dump year and he wanted to be ready for the real stuff. Over ten feet had accumulated by January.

He slammed the Lubyr door shut with a "thunk" and walked into an antiquated ski lodge. While the marigold and avocado striped carpeting was well worn, today not a sole scuffed its surface other than Oscar's high-tops. *Where da fuck is everyone?*

His MyndScreen's OttoNav pointed to a locker with an LCD screen displaying his name and QR code. Placing his thumb against a print reader, the door opened and he took out the prefab gear. He hadn't a clue how to put the skis on, so he found a BoubToob™ video that walked him through it.

He approached a motionless ski lift, still looking around for the competition. After maneuvering in front of the chair, it sprang to life and scooped him up.

A cold breeze stung his cheeks. From up high, Oscar could see he had the place to himself, like the DownHill Demon entry levels. At least there'd be no collisions. He managed to slide off the exit ramp and selected "intermediate" on the app settings. Pointing his skis down the line recommended by SlalomSnake, he pushed off. *Fanta!* Skiing IRL was a lot like hitting the virtual slopes, only the hard-packed snow grabbed at the edges of his skis when he turned. It was also bumpier. Left, right, bump. *I got this.*

Hard and fast then down on his ass. *Dammit.*

After the third run, a different lift took him all the way to the top. A large black bird perched on a trail map; its feathers ruffled in the wind. Oscar cruised by without noticing. He also, of course, didn't see many wavelengths of the electromagnetic spectrum the human eye has not evolved to detect. Our brains filter out extraneous light and construct a reality using only the information deemed necessary. Oscar had no need for birds or signs. SlalomSnake would guide him down based on each run's terrain and data it already captured about his ability.

He was all alone, in the zone. Commands of "Pizza," or "French-fry" flashed on his screen when SlalomSnake wanted him to slow or accelerate. Yellow lines projected over his field of vision showing exactly how skis should point in the shape of a pizza slice for a snowplow turn, or like two yellow French fries for a parallel turn. A longer purple line curved down the slope, superimposing a transparent path while a Swiss-accented voice suggested, "curve right," or "keep straight."

Slopes steepened. He zoomed over a mogul and flew past several crossed red poles holding triangular yellow signs. "Proceed to the route" commanded the voice in his head. Purple MyndScreen lines vanished. Wet snowflakes whirled by. His legs jostled over crusty snow.

What da?

Oscar leaned back, hoping to slow down. That just made things worse. It was too late when he saw it, a car-sized boulder looming past the edge of a precipice. Maybe a backscratcher would help him clear the rock.

When a human being perceives danger, the amygdala takes over. Senses elevate. Hyper awareness slows time. Oscar hung there, floating midair, with cortisol and adrenaline surging through his arteries. He felt the cold atmosphere brush against the fine hairs on his cheeks and chill the inside of his nostrils on its way to his lungs. He could see detailed ripples in the snow below him, little crystalline waves blown by the wind and frozen in space and time. The fir trees shimmered a deep green—more intensely than just moments ago. He could hear a gentle swish of breeze blowing past his ears. It was a sublime moment he felt sure he'd remember the rest of his life.

"I said, didn't you see the signs?" Sister Martha repeated.

"I . . . I don't know. I'd been following the line on my screen when the display went blank. I kept going with only my eyesight. Then, it got really steep and . . . "

"And you skied off a cliff and banged your head. You're lucky to be alive young man. Next time use some common sense instead of that brain chip to stay where you're supposed to."

The cliff. Dammit. It came so quickly, and he didn't get the same hang time as in the game.

He tried pulling up an instant replay from his Klowd™, but his MyndScreen was still blank. *Un-fucking-real.* "What's with transmissions being down so long?" he asked. The nun had already left. He'd have to rely on native memory, yet those details were fuzzy.

Wind slammed snow crystals against the old window with a "rat-tat-splat" and the crow continued its blustery dance. Up in the air, flapping back to the branch only to be blown off again. And again.

He's got nowhere to go but where he is.

The following day, Sister Martha returned with more soup and more questions.

"How can we get you home if you don't know your address? Do you have any extended family we could call?"

"Only my kid sister; she can't order up a ride. No biggie, I'll just check my Lubyr account and reverse my last trip." Oscar squinted and stared at his palm. *Nothing.* "Hey, you could run a facial recognition app. Look me up."

"We have no apps here. No need for antisocial media, or vulgarity. We find what we seek through silent prayer."

"No MyndScreens? No extruders? You living in the fucking dark ages?"

She sighed. "The spark of life is easier seen in darkness than infotainment's glare. Now, get some sleep. Your brain needs rest and even my dull sights and sounds are more than an addled mind should take in."

Before Martha could close the door, Ellen hurried back from the barn with an old VR helmet. "I found this in a cardboard box marked 'Thrift items.' Let's run a Noodle search to help Oscar remember his past." She tried enthusiastically to put on the device, but it was a kid's version and too tight to fit over her ears or position the visor properly in place.

"There will be no virtual reality in this convent Ellen, not ever. I've seen what it does to people. That's why we moved out here, fleeing the digital onslaught where screens were everywhere, even inside people's heads." Oscar saw Martha hesitate before further explaining. "People close to you, Ellen, succumbed to the temptations of infotainment and lost more than you could imagine. You have no idea the lengths I've gone to protect you."

"What do you mean, people close to me? I've been in this quote dark ages convent all my life, totally disconnected from the world. You never let me do anything Martha. Never!" Ellen stomped off in a huff.

Another day later, Oscar's skull no longer throbbed. The soup had lost its charm, as had his hosts. "You ever gonna let me outta here?" He'd never really learned any manners.

"You should see a doctor, but yes, you may go home today," Sister Martha replied tersely. "A nunnery is indeed no place for you."

"I still don't know my fucking address though." Martha scowled as Oscar rubbed his head, revealing a tattooed rodeo rider on the back of his hand. "I can't believe MyndScreen transmissions are still down or I'd just look it up."

"Highland's not that big," offered Ellen. "I could take you around until you recognized it."

Martha wasn't having it. "Don't be ridiculous. How would you get him there? You can't just call a Lubyr like he did with no account, and the bus stopped running years ago."

"We'll ride down on the horses."

"Huh?" Oscar scrunched up his nose.

"You know, horses," she smiled. "Like your tattoo. You can ride them."

Oscar looked down at her boots and realized she was serious. "Like in cowboy movies?"

"Ellen, it would take hours," Martha objected. "Besides, it's cold."

"We can't just keep him here. I rode to Highland before, remember, to fetch the runaway dog. I'd just need somewhere to stay the night so the horses could rest before heading back tomorrow."

"I got a nice foam mattress. Crash with me."

Martha looked him up and down, eyeing the cowboy tattoo. "I don't think that would be appropriate, young man."

"Come on, Sister, you never let me do anything! This would help Oscar. Like you said, a nunnery is no place for him."

Sister Martha sighed and thought silently for a long time. Ellen's pleading eyes pierced her, searing with simultaneous resentment and teenage hope. Oscar avoided Martha's disapproving frown and looked out the window to see if his new friend the crow was still perched atop the windswept pine. It had abandoned him.

"When the Sisters of San Bernardino still ran a thrift shop in town to support our missionary work, we set up a cot in the back room. That was before everyone bought disposable things and just dumped them down the recycling chute. Anyway, it's a place to stay." She rummaged through an old pine desk, producing a jagged piece of metal attached to a U-shaped pendant.

"Thank you, Sister! What's on the horseshoe?"

"A key. Don't lose it, it's our only copy."

"What for?" Oscar wondered aloud.

"Back when thoughts were plentiful and things were scarce, we locked up what was important to us. You'll need this to open the Thrifty Sister's door." Martha drew a little map with directions. "It's right next to a boarded-up hotel. Actually, Ellen, you've been there before."

Oscar wasn't sure what was going on between Martha and Ellen. In any case, he was ready for home. Luella might be wondering where he was.

CHAPTER 2
Caspian

AS HE GATHERED HIS GRANTEES FOR ANOTHER QUAR-terly VRoom™, Caspian Blaine felt important—just not yet important enough. It wasn't ego. He wasn't one of those foundation execs who let doling out wealth go to his head. He shunned the perks his colleagues enjoyed, the trips to donor retreats at swank hotels in tony locations, the per diem accounts for meals, and drinks, and "personal expenses."

Caspian wasn't satisfied with steering a smidgeon of the foundation's ginormous endowment toward projects benefiting underprivileged Vues. That was all well and good, but his real undertaking was to plant the smallest seeds of public trust and critical thought into a post-truth society that coped with the constant torrent of infotainment by disregarding it all as fake news. As one of the few remaining individuals who had maintained the ability to filter out extraneous infotain, he'd preserved the capacity to not only think for himself but to give a damn about what had happened.

He'd sunk twenty-five years working his way up the OrangeVine Foundation's org chart to arrive at the semi-coveted post of Junior Vice President of Special Projects and Strategic Initiatives. With the emaciated governments of Globalia rendered impotent by tribunal fiat, private philanthropy was where the action was at, baby. He'd been an activist himself before getting into philanthropy and his allegiance held to the grassroots organizations he funded rather than the foundation higher ups. This had turned out to be somewhat of a barrier to promotion, as organizations tend to favor those who serve the institution more so than its mission.

Six 3D avatars of his grantees huddled around a virtual campfire he'd selected for the SurroundGround™, hanging on his every word. Behind each avatar's head, stars twinkled over dark mountain silhouettes. Chirping crickets provided audio backdrop, punctuated occasionally by the faint howl of a distant wolf.

Speaking in a hushed voice, he purveyed his pearls of erudition. "Look guys, this isn't just a job for me. It would mean a lot to me for you all to get your grants renewed. I really care. Here's how you work the system." He detailed precise social welfare metrics and deliverables that each grantee's organization must document, along with OrangeVine's non-fungible formula for converting their work product into quantifiable "utils" and assessing whether its efficacious grantmaking maximized the greatest good for the greatest number.

His pinstripe-suited avatar paused a moment to let his words of wisdom sink in. Vanessa Youngblood's charming avatar cocked her head, swept a strawberry blonde side bang off her left eyebrow, and tucked it behind her ear. It was a signature gesture of hers that he kinda liked.

"Transparency, baby," he exhorted. "It's all about quantifying your work for our board. We don't demand perfection. Of course, there will be setbacks and unexpected outcomes. It can feel embarrassing to acknowledge failures or shortcomings, yet being open and quantifiable facilitates our market-driven philanthropic mission to efficiently upscale prosperity for even the most underprivileged among us. It's all about the metrics, my friends. You gotta play the game." He winked his left eye and his cornrowed avatar winked, too.

Vanessa's avatar nodded and smiled enthusiastically, which struck him as odd since she frequently complained offline about OrangeVine's formulaic grantmaking regimen. *Why the sudden affection for quantifiable outcomes? Maybe she's just playing along.*

He admired Vanessa as another grantee asked a long-winded question that was really a request to turn in a grant report two weeks late. Her avatar's purple turtleneck looked smart, perky. The animation was exquisite, down to the tiniest protrusion in her collar bone. *Hey, wait a minute, isn't that the same outfit she wore last week?*

In 2065 Los Angeles, repeat Vwardrobes™ just didn't happen, no matter how delightfully that tight-fitting sweater accentuated Vanessa's curves. Rewearing meant an out-of-fashion style, a dated identity, a lack of proper self. Keeping one's avatar mirrored to the insta-released disposable clothes you were wearing IRL was basic virtual etiquette. Either Vanessa was a fashion Luddyte—devotees of the ecoterrorist Omar Ludd who promoted vintage reusable clothing as a nostalgic statement about permanence—or . . . *Wait, her gestures are totally out of sync with the meeting content.*

HALexa, Caspian's personal digital assistant, pinged him as the long-winded grantee "question" continued. "Your next meeting's in two minutes, sir." He silenced the alert, opened a multitask window, and activated a private Noodle search for Vanessa's non-profit UpLyftingLives. He looked for Klowd archives of last week's VRoom, but an accompanying top search result caught his eye. It was a video that Vanessa herself had uploaded.

Teenagers in tie-dyed shirts accosted strangers, handing each a white Shasta daisy. This random act so shocked the recipients they dropped the flowers and rushed away.

HALexa nudged him again. Caspian silenced it before checking the recording of last week's VRoom. It wasn't just the turtleneck; Vanessa's hair tuck gesture was identical.

Damnation! She's just posting her captured input from before. Her avatar was going through the usual motions, yet she wasn't really there. Caspian wrapped up his presentation to the remaining five grantees and shot her a note in the Chattersphere, "Lets grab a 🍵 at 2:30. I'm on to you."

Caspian had HALexa cancel all remaining appointments before logging into his next VRoom. He was seven minutes late.

Twelve avatars of OrangeVine's Senior Program Officers float amid a semi-transparent SurroundGround replica of the foundation's mahogany paneled 19th floor conference room. The actual chamber stood empty most days, with staff members instead VRooming in comfortably from their personal desks. Caspian's spacious office, one floor up, was furnished with a walnut desk, an ostrich leather chair, and custom lighting from Murano, Italy. It was positioned directly beneath OrangeVine President Wallace Packard's executive penthouse suite on the 21st floor.

Like most people, Caspian normally stared at his palm during VRooms, much as he once stared at a smartphone. Modern MyndScreen operating systems used eye movements to control the curser, which meant his implant constantly tracked lines of sight, both physical and virtual. A familiar physical backdrop, like his light melanin palm, wouldn't distract his awareness from the semi-transparent avatar faces, indicating to the VRoom's AI that he wasn't paying sufficient attention.

Senior Program Officer meetings demanded participants feign interest in their colleague's redundant info dumps. He'd done thousands of similar VRooms, learning when to keep his head down, when to pipe up with a helpful question ("Can you explain those upsides further?"), and when to slide an insightful comment ("We should light this up on Chatter!") or emojicon (📖) into the chat.

Today, it all felt a bit contrived. He pivoted the ostrich leather chair toward the windows, allowing a glance straight through his MyndScreen's semi-transparent avatars to serene Pacific vistas behind them. Orange-Vine's virtual conference table was now superimposed atop the line where an overcast sky met steel blue ocean. By repositioning his VRoom window until the horizon lay right at Wallace Packard's neckline, he made the old man's gray-tufted head float amid clouds. Virtuality layering was one of Caspian's oldest tricks. He knew certain eye positioning would keep the AI monitor's dashboard green while providing an opportunity to observe nature. Maybe a bird would fly by, a gull or even a pelican.

Packard had been at the helm a tad too long in Caspian's view—should really consider retirement. As the VRoom droned on, Packard announced a new board member. "Please welcome Yvonne Putcher. She's connected to a high rolling hedge fund that's made significant investments in OrangeVine." Her board appointment was a transparent attempt by Packard to keep the spigot flowing. Yvonne's lovely avatar appeared to stare deep into Caspian's eyes. She introduced herself and tucked her perfectly straight platinum hair behind her left ear.

The final agenda item came from the Vice President of Finance, an unimaginative woman straining to give upcoming audit preparations some gravitas. "You'll remember that despite going over budget in our 'special projects' area last quarter, we ended the fiscal year in the black due to cost savings in our human resources department. We expect our auditors will be pleased."

Caspian's avatar raised an eyebrow, not because he cared about the audit but because he cared whether anyone else did. VP DeVrine was a favorite of both OrangeVine's board chair and President Packard. It was painfully obvious to anyone paying attention to these things that Margery DeVrine was scheming to replace Packard whenever his inevitable retirement arrived. Caspian happened to think there was someone better for the job. She didn't need to make that dig at his special projects division, but so far as he could tell nobody noticed, or cared. The other senior officer avatars had vapid looks of MyndScreen multitaskers. He messaged an ally in their private Slick™ channel and grinned triumphantly when his friend posted a 👊 beneath DeVrine's comments. Meanwhile, he shrunk the VRoom window and opened up his own multitask stream to view the latest episode of *Big Brother V*.

"Pawp!" A champagne bottle appeared on his MyndScreen along with the signature sound of uncorking. "Congratulations Caspian. You've absorbed 4 terabytes of infotainment today, reaching your goal and earning you 4,000 Zing points. Tomorrow, try and stretch your multiviews to 4.1 terabytes!" *Yeah baby, who knows how the game is played?*

In closing comments, DeVrine mentioned that Packard asked her to organize an in-person today at 3:30 in the conference room. "We'll have refreshments, so come grab a snack!" Caspian knew what he could grab with Vanessa at LuckyStars Café would beat the junk they handed out at the office. So would the company.

After dictating LuckyStars into what he thought was a private search window to pull up driving directions, he pinged his yellow iDrive convertible to meet him at the curb. Private search was his SOP—no need for SpeiDrWebs to track a preference for real coffee over OrangeSmash products. Unfortunately, since he'd previously used a private search when pulling up Vanessa's Klowd footage, he'd now unwittingly toggled the "Private" selection to "Off." The iDrive whisked him away.

LuckyStars was a newly renovated post-hipster establishment still managing to acquire real beans despite heat-dome coffee bush decimation in Globalia's Central American and African regions. Caspian stood in line, staring at a ridiculous 1990s-era illuminated menu on the wall, with quaint sizes like "grande" and "tall." Exorbitant price structures meant they could staff the place with live baristas doing makework jobs. Real foaming milk hissed in the background.

Vanessa waited at a fauxmica table, wearing a gray leather jacket over a disposable white T-shirt and black jeans. Turquoise stud earrings completed her outfit. She was the only customer there.

"Hey, nice jacket. Looks like you've had it a while. So, what's with this daisy thing?" He softened the abrupt query with a smile, cappuccino, and hash brownie.

"Oh, that?" Vanessa licked foam from her upper lip and tucked away her strawberry blonde bang. Caspian felt all warm and fuzzy inside, perhaps from that first sip of cappuccino. "Well, we're experimenting with a new micro capital program that catapults people out of poverty by training them to innovate small businesses. Some of our clients sell home-grown daisies. They give a few away to generate market demand." He watched her take a small bite of hash brownie, leaving a little crumb in the corner of her mouth.

"Wouldn't it be cheaper to 3D-print flowers with a protruder? OrangeVine was founded by a guy who invented those construction protruders that layer plasticized concrete skyscrapers from the ground up. My board would love the parallels." The luscious cappuccino aroma tantalized him. He savored a long slow sip while she pondered his calculated suggestion.

"Caspian, I can trust you, right?" She leaned forward and lowered her voice. "We're getting people off the consumption treadmill, where they spend all their resources buying enhanced soyalgent food products and all their time viewing infotainment. That leaves an attention deficit that makes it challenging to identify new business opportunities by observing people's needs and imagining how to meet that demand. Growing their own food, our clients accumulate micro-capital to start businesses instead of relying upon CeleTeCharity donations from movie stars and tech moguls, who, as you know, can be fickle in their giving. There's this amazing volunteer, Aldo, who's training kids to garden.

Getting underserved clients out into the dirt frees them from video games and episode addiction. Their brains have a chance to rest and nurture creativity."

"How much can one daisy do? Seems a bit symbolic as opposed to real systemic social change."

"The daisies are a side hustle that sprung out of the community gardens. The best thing is their butterfly effect." Vanessa's voice dropped a half octave into some minor key as Caspian tried to look, and feel, calm by drumming his fingers on the café table. To maintain a routine surfing pattern, he opened a MyndScreen window and checked out some AmaZing!™ specials. "The gift of a flower jolts people out of their screens and pulls them into reality, if only for an instant," she continued. "Most go right back to their apps, but a few take a daisy and reflect on the wonder of a stranger handing it to them with no expectation or compensation. Those interactions turn disadvantaged communities around by upscaling social capital."

"Hey, Vanessa, knock off the jargon and listen to me." The finger drumming stopped. "You know that I know what you're doing. It's totally amazing and you gotta keep at it. I've known about Aldo for years and always managed to fund his fanta work. Still, I need you to do something for me. Remember that program of yours, "Girls Who Goad," or whatever it was called? The one that trained teenagers to use social media and also how to program it? You wanted those kids boosted to the upper five percent that makes real money working essential jobs. Yet I sold the project to my board as a troll farm operation that juiced Chatter views, and ad revenue, by creating content too outlandish to ignore. I snuck it past our VP of Finance because she can't say no to anything empowering girls. Now I gotta similarly present your garden project in a way that doesn't freak out my higher-ups.

"So in your report, describe springboarding youth from poverty while leaving out the daisy stuff that pulls people away from their screens. Mercernary General made some big-time donations to OrangeVine and now they've got someone on my board. If they figure out what you're doing, they'll not only cut off your funding, they'll target your neighborhoods with enhanced SpeiDrWeb tracking."

"Why? What are you even talking about?"

"The hedge fund that owns Mercernary General is heavily invested in Pepsoilent food and beverages as well as Timeless Warning infotainment. They make their money when Vues consume the stuff you're trying to wean them away from. They're not gonna fund a program that undermines their core business model."

"Whoa. Who'd have thought a few daisies would be a problem?"

"You would. That's why you didn't bring it up until I stumbled across your subversive video. That's why we're gonna keep this crypto, just between you and me."

Vanessa curved her eyebrows in a cute expression admitting guilt and tucked her hair back behind her delectable left ear. "Thanks, Caspi. I can't tell you how much it means to have an ally inside OrangeVine. The bureaucracy drives me nuts."

"I can't tell you how hard it is to pull off. If my Finance VP catches wind of this, I'm toast. But it's nothing compared to the risks you take day in and day out." He stood and gave her a wink. "By the way, you better update that avatar recording where you pretend to be on my VRooms. My AI moderator software hasn't flagged it yet, but it's only a matter of time. I know you've got real work to do that's more important than my stupid meetings. Still, you gotta be savvy about playing the game. Just be careful you don't then let the game change who you are. Got me, boss?"

"Got you." She smiled and winked back.

A goodbye hug lasted a second too long. Caspian ignored the HR department message popping up in his MyndScreen, "**Attention, OrangeVine policies strictly forbid romantic encounters, or thoughts, between employees, grantees, interns, or board members.**" He closed the window. *It's not like that. Really.* At 28 years old, Vanessa was nearly two decades younger than him.

Their encounter ran longer than he'd planned on. Driving back, he received an instant chat from Margery DeVrine. "**Hey Caspian, looks like you're stuck in traffic. Don't worry if you can't make it back to the office. I had to cut the event refreshments budget so no real loss if you want to phone it in.**"

Instead of questioning how DeVrine knew his location, he wondered about the sudden act of kindness. It wasn't like DeVrine to be looking out for him. Truth be told, he'd always found in-person stuff kinda awkward. Plus, his iDrive's estimated office arrival time was 3:47. Showing up late twice in one day was not a good look. He'd logged enough monthly in-persons to fulfill the foundation's twenty-hour requirement and these late afternoon meetings were rarely important. He'd just VRoom it from home.

Drones filled the air with a happy buzz as Caspian's yellow iDrive convertible rolled up to Colossal Column Condominiums, a cutting-edge cylindrical complex for five percenters who hadn't yet made it into the High Establishment. He admired today's exterior screensaver of Giant Sequoias filling each building's extruded twelve-story façade—a virtual redwood grove right on the edge of Wilshire Boulevard.

After squeezing his six foot three, broad framed body inside the parking garage elevator, Caspian unlocked the top floor by placing his palm to a scanner. The elevator opened directly into his condo. He tossed his shoes down a doorside recycling chute, took four steps, and settled into his ZiBro™ recliner—the sole piece of furniture centered in the cylindrical room. Once he reclined in its welcoming faux fabric, the chair activated cooling air jets to dissipate a blot of perspiration along his spine.

Within arm's reach, a deluxe OrangeSmash dispenser sensed his presence and a humming 3D printer head coiled extruded polystyrene into a 1.5-liter cup. The acrid scent of molten plastic still annoyed his nostrils after all these years. Refiltered water pumped through a chilling nozzle with precisely metered FlavrPak doses, producing a Barnicle and Janes Whine Kooler™. Next, grayish soyalgent paste flowed through super-heated nozzles along with a proprietary blend of natural and artificial flavors to print some CrayZ™ potato chips.

Who needs crappy office food? A sip and a sigh, and he was on his way to ultimate relaxation as an extended footrest vibrated tension out of his feet. He admired the floor-to-ceiling VirtuWall™—a 99% accurate rendition of the Brooklyn brownstone he grew up in. The original WallPayPer™ alternated between Versailles and the Taj Mahal, but he'd swapped those out with images from his childhood picture gallery. The hyper realistic display included scenery from the park across from his parents' house in its virtual "windows." He pondered what the missing 1% of detail might be.

HALexa disrupted his reminiscence with a reminder: "Your 3:30 event is starting." Upon signing in, he saw fifty employees convened in the mahogany-paneled conference room enjoying appetizers of shrimp cocktail and real tomato bruschetta topped with fresh basil. *Damnation! That's the reduced budget menu?*

A bottom screen chryon noted this was a live event, not to be recorded. Audio wasn't yet on during the initial commotion as people chatted about last night's episodes while noshing hors d'oeuvres. Caspian opened two additional MyndScreen windows to catch the evening news and use his Zings for tomorrow's drone-delivered outfit.

As he checked out the AmaZing! fashion algorithm's pre-selected wardrobe, Margery DeVrine sat down to Wallace Packard's right. Packard wore a sharp looking Italian suit and an apricot-seafoam striped tie with tiny, embossed diamonds providing some texture. The same tie popped up in Caspian's MyndScreen which automatically placed it into his AmaZing! shopping cart.

He clicked "Buy Now," as Packard stood up underneath an antique crystal chandelier.

Yvonne Putcher, wearing a little black cocktail dress, took a seat to Packard's left. The audio unmuted as she leaned over to ask DeVrine, "Where's Caspi?" Caspian saw DeVrine shrug.

Packard began in a deep, self-important voice. "Ladies, gentlemen, and others; hes, shes, and theys; fellow colleagues, philanthropic value-adders, and OrangeSmash lovers; let me share a few thoughts about social progressinationary philanthropical legacy fortification . . . "

Boooring . . .

Just like that, audio cut out. The video stream also froze, at 3:37 p.m. Refresh. Refresh. Still nothing. A news anchor paused mid-sentence in another window.

It's not just VRoom, the whole friggin MyndScreen system is frozen. Damnation! He slapped a hand to his forehead and knocked over his wine cooler.

Transmissions stayed down; this wasn't just a temporary glitch. *Unreal!* With nothing to watch, Caspian approached the condo's three-by-three-foot delivery balcony to retrieve a stack of AmaZing! boxes. Sliding open the door, he saw it. A sparrow lay panting on the protruded plastic-ply deck, clearly stunned after flying smack dab into a grove of red-woods that turned out to be giant LCD screens. When he crouched down, the bird bolted through the screen door. Things went from bad to worse as it flew repeatedly into his condo's windowscreen renditions of Brooklyn. After flailing frantically, exhaustion overcame the hapless creature.

Ever so gently, his stubby fingers pried open a package and placed its contents on the floor. Slowly, incrementally, he crept toward the gasping little ball of feathers until, whoosh, he slammed the box over it. Daintily, one incremental step at a time, he nudged the container across the floor until reaching the balcony. Only after closing the screen door did Caspian lift the trap. *Freedom, baby!* A grateful bird alighted and landed on his neighbor's railing. The sparrow joggled its head, then looked at him with serenity. It would have been a perfect moment to capture and post, no doubt generating tens of thousands of views on Chatter. But Caspian just sat there staring at the little brown bird and enjoyed the inner satisfaction of doing something just for its own sake.

When he logged back in, OrangeVine's conference room stood empty. The meeting was over.

CHAPTER 3
Chase

HE FELT THE GUN'S STEELY COLD BARREL POKING HIS sweaty skull, just below the left ear by a nickel-sized cranial protrusion. An occupational hazard of outlaw life is that sometimes the attractive lady you jump turns out to be an outlaw herself. He could have run a bullet through her after grabbing the Gucci bag, except he was too much of a gentleman. Next thing he knew, she was pressing a pistol against his head and not only retrieving her bag but pinching his wallet, and a piece of his ass, while she was at it.

It got worse when two motorcycle cops pulled up. Within sixty seconds he went from perp to victim, victim to hostage. One cop radioed for backup. The other aimed a Glock semi-auto directly above Chase's left shoulder, presumably at his assailant's head.

"Everyone just calm down and drop your weapons," said the Glock cop in a trained law enforcement voice.

Chase saw three options. One, the ass-grabber used him as a human shield while lighting up both cops, and then put a slug in him. Two, the cops somehow prevail, only to take him into custody. Game over. Three, he made some sort of move before backup arrived.

Looking down he saw a pair of black stiletto heels. "Nice shoes," he said, choosing option three. He bent over, jabbed an elbow into her gut and heard her gun fire. The bullet bit his ear but continued on to find radio cop's rosy cheek.

He heard the signature crack of a pistol as Glock cop returned fire. Everything went dark.

Goddammit!

His screen stayed black. No sound effects or background music. There was nothing to do. He checked his other windows. *Big Brother V* was frozen. Ditto the news, paused at 3:37 p.m.

He was back IRL.

It had been seventeen years since his upgrade; virtually a lifetime. Seventeen years since he'd entered the Triple Ex Entertainment Home. Seventeen years since he'd consented to live in this enhanced infotainment paradise. He could check out any time he liked. But he could never leave.

He looked around the white plastic walls of his pod. Nothing to see but the 4D RealiT-Lounge™ he was lying on and a disposable sheet covering his pale naked body. He rubbed the back of his head, feeling where the chilled gaming lounge massage node thrust just enough pressure to simulate a pistol's muzzle. The beach volleyball scene he had selected when he first arrived still played on a wallscreen window. A hint of RealiT-Lounge simulated gunpowder scent lingered.

Something scurried into an AC vent near the sliding doors. Something alive. Surely that wasn't possible, but he swore he heard noises. Little scratching sounds. Maybe it was just a MinuteMayd™ cleaning the hallway.

Moments flitted by; his brain slowly waking. For the first time in seventeen years, his stomach felt empty. The back of his right hand itched where a soyalgent IV needle was inserted.

Just like that, the game was back. Grand Heist Otto picked up where it left off, but not Chase. The interruption had somehow pulled him out of the game. He wasn't ready to dive back in.

The chiseled jaw and striped, tan pants on the Glock cop reminded Chase of CHiPs reruns he watched with Grandad in that god-awful retirement home. Those reruns sparked his screenwriting career. He instinctively went to rub Grandad's lucky penny, which he'd stashed between the cushions of his 4D RealiT-Lounge. When his fingertips touched something soft and threadlike, he freaked. His hair, waist long, was smushed between his ass and the cushions. *Gross.* He shouldn't have rejected beauty bot haircuts all those years.

The pod had no mirrors, of course. Chase missed the old days, when he'd use the 180 sunglasses—which served as a rearview device for his motorcycle—to take selfies. He'd hold them at arm's length and grab a handsome mugshot using rear-facing temple cameras. Based on his hair, he must now look like crap. Until that moment, his self-image was an ageless 3D animated avatar walking around VR in a blond mullet, red T-shirt, and faded blue jeans. Better not to dwell on his current appearance. The game beckoned.

Chase knew the CHiP's hog was no match for his tricked out Cowasaki™. He raised his hands until Glock cop approached within four steps, hopped on the bike and cranked its throttle. Shooting forward, a jolt nearly lifted the front tire as the RealiT-Lounge tilted backward. Wind blasted his forehead and the lounge vibrated to mimic acceleration on a bumpy road. His cheeks stretched a shit-eating grin across his lips as the electric motor's low hum reached a high-pitched whine, the RPMs cranked, and Glock cop disappeared in the rearview screen. *Boombaby*! White dash lane markers blurred to gray. He swerved, calmly dodging a driverless commuter van proceeding down Highway 101 at a mundane 75 mph.

Life was good. Yet within sixty seconds, a staccato chut-chut-chut of helicopter blades closed in from behind. An electronic voice blared something over a loudspeaker, but the words barely registered over the cycle noise and rushing wind. He leaned left and banked through an S-curve while views of the Pacific swept by. The 4D RealiT-Lounge sprayed a slight ocean mist to cool his cheek.

When the road straightened, a red laser dot appeared on his windshield. "Dizz iz your final warning" blared the loudspeaker, followed by more inscrutable words. Chase swerved, losing the dot momentarily. It was back within two seconds. *Goddammit. They're locked on target.*

Defeat now meant more than losing a game. Whatever rustled inside that AC vent stirred something within. An awareness. A will. A desire. For the first time Chase could remember, he cared whether he won or lost. Once you decide you care about something, losing it means losing a part of yourself.

Glancing at the GPS screen he made a split-second calculation. Time to try something different. He slammed the brakes, skidded to a stop, and spun 180 degrees. An oncoming delivery truck swerved through a railing and tumbled down to the ocean. *That's gonna add to the charges.*

The copter took just a moment to reverse course, hounding him like an addiction. Crackling pops of gun blast echoed above. Bullets bounced off asphalt. One shattered his windshield as he swerved back and forth to buy another thirty seconds. He slowed, taking cover in the shadow of a bus he passed on the right, and forced the copter to hold fire. The loudspeaker squawked orders at the bus driver, who edged toward the shoulder and squeezed Chase toward a rocky hillside.

A wide-open throttle shot him forward. The copter pursued. Chase reached 187 miles per hour, banked hard right, and nearly scraped a knee against the pavement. His body writhed and dripped with sweat under the RealiT-Lounge's disposable sheet. Coming out of the turn, he saw it. The Gaviota Tunnel swallowed him whole and the copter exploded on the sandstone cliffs above. "Level 5 complete. Next up, Grand Heist Otto™ does Vegas."

A message popped up, "Fanta move, dood! I thought you were a goner." It was @BadScootr, another virtual player who'd logged in as a spectator, providing Chase a rare ego boost. @BadScootr's bald-headed avatar was huge. A black leather vest only partly covered his bare abdomen and bulging pectorals. "Let's do a heist together. I know a few hacks. Between us we can outplay the game."

"Thanks, man. That's so meta."

"Meta?"

"Never mind, just something we said when I was a kid."

Experienced multi-player gamers choose partners wisely. @BadScootr not only looked bad ass, Chase saw he'd been around the block from his hit points, accumulating an impressive lifetime score and reputation rating. This was someone you wanted on your side. He wondered what the guy saw in him, a dilettante who had until that moment played less from ambition than to escape his boredom, his despair.

As if reading his thoughts, @BadScootr now sounded skeptical. "You some sort of old timer, Gramps? I need a partner with reflexes like lightning." That "meta" quip must have dated him, considerably. *Bad move.*

"Actually, I used to ride IRL. I can handle a bike. What I lack in youth I make up for in experience. I've learned a few tricks along the way that come in handy."

Street cred worked wonders. "Cool, dood. I always wanted a cycle and gotta admit that was a pretty fanta maneuver at the Gaviota. I'll ping you when I'm down for some multi-player."

Chase took a break from GHO and resumed binge watching *Big Brother V.* Since the upgrade, his days were filled with VR games, episode viewing, and BS-ing in the Chattersphere. As an ex-screenwriter, ex-husband, and ex-father, the Triple Ex suited him well, although he'd never taken a fancy to the virtual porn that inspired its name. Infotain was absorbing enough that he never felt the urge to leave. A daily dose of intravenous Pepsoilent bred lethargy. Despite recent advances, Total Parenteral Nutrition still produced moderate-to-severe fatigue and liver inflammation. The IV provided just enough glucose to keep his heart beating and power his MyndScreen's embedded fuel cell without energizing his soul. A chem-commode built-in to the RealiT-Lounge featured a bidet and catheter, relieving any need to rouse oneself for basic toilet functions. They truly thought of everything when designing this place.

A former content creator himself, Chase knew something about *Big Brother V* most viewers did not. The reality show was entirely fake. Not just fake in the contrived manner all early 21st century reality shows were manufactured by directors cramming paid actors and washed-up celebrities into situations anything but real. Fake because *Big Brother V* contestants weren't even real people. The show was one-hundred percent virtual, hence the "V" in its title. Its quote unquote actors were computer animated avatars AI scripted to recreate episodes of *Big Brother* produced before it was taken off air. By 2040, it had become nearly impossible for reality producers to trigger any participant interaction whatsoever. Everybody just sat around staring at their palms instead of scheming, yelling, or flirting with the others they were confined with for months on end. Worse, when they did interact, it was through Chatter. While the directors intercepted their messages and posted them on screen, the "dialogue" was simply too dull compared with spontaneous controversies of years gone by. Plus, bottom line, the avatars were just cheaper.

Though idiotic, *BBV* was strangely intoxicating. Chase initially told himself he'd watch only to ridicule how pathetic the entertainment industry had become since his quote unquote retirement—to the point where most Hollywood studios didn't even bother with new narratives. Yet after the first episode, he was hooked on mundane scenes where nothing much happened except regular turn-of-the-century life. People hung out, vaped on the couch, made pointless conversation. It was mesmerizing, much like a fish tank or a waterfall had once been. He'd been watching re-runs for the past four years just to catch up.

This episode was a new release, so millions of Globalians watched along with him. The virtual staging was perfect. Every piece of furniture in its proper place. Everything nice and tidy. Chase thought the set looked cartoonish instead of like a normal house with dirty floors and furniture cluttered by people who never tidied up. The virtual "actors" were attractive but lacked sparkle in their smiles. A seventy-year-old washed-up rock groupie with pouty lips, a surgically lifted face, and bloodshot eyes sat distraught in the BBV kitchen. She nervously twirled her salt and pepper pigtails like a fidgety child.

Another housemate, with an exceptionally large bosom, walked in for a cup of Koffy™.

"You OK? You look a little under the weather."

A forlorn Pigtails mysteriously replied, "Always remember, time may change you, but you can't trace time. Alright?"

What would she know? Now a fake avatar is gonna lecture us about life transitions?

"Huh?" Big Bosom also couldn't grasp the pearl of wisdom.

"You know I wouldn't act this way if I just had a cold, right?"

As tears welled in pigtail's eyes, producers dubbed in somber music and dimmed the lights. Fighting back sobs, she made Big Bosom promise not to tell a soul what she was about to reveal. Chase sat up in his lounge, hanging on every word. Violins built to a crescendo. She bowed her head and whispered, "David's dead."

CHAPTER 4
Aneeka

ANEEKA RANDALL PACED CLOCKWISE AROUND HER living room. She walked deliberately, feeling the grain of old hardwood flooring press against her bare feet, sensing a tightness in her legs, her hips, her torso as she angled each step to maintain a perfect circle. Her fingertips traced along the spines of antique hardcover books she stored on oak shelves running floor to ceiling, feeling the brittle paper jackets.

As fingers and toes felt their way, a controversy raged within. Timeless Warning had filed a trade dispute against Mexican transportation magnate Dagny Huerta for erecting a two-hundred-foot-tall barrier around one of their 11G transmission towers. Globalia's Tribunal of Educates was hearing the case, streamed live via encrypted chat to each Educate's MyndScreen from the Grand Tribunal Chambers in Dubai.

Aneeka Randall was the newest of thirteen Tribunal members. The distinguished council interpreted the Piese Treaty, a global agreement that resolved the War Unseen and launched a post-scarcity era combining political stability with economic prosperity. That meant adjudicating thousands of trade disputes, which turned out to be quite a chore. Chief Educate Lewis Leon had tapped Aneeka to draft an opinion for this case, her first assignment. Her chance to prove to herself it had all been worth it: years of work, sacrifices in personal life and relationships, rationalizations made along the way. Now, she craved the satisfaction that should accompany such a position. She was the one who could decide the tough issues. She was the one who would make a difference. Here, finally, was her first crack at it.

"Tell me, in your own words, Ms. Huerta, why you built the wall." Timeless Warning's attorney looked directly at the camera instead of the subject of his interrogation.

"Because I wanted it there. It's my own private property to do with as I please," she answered in perfect English. Eighty-five years in the gang-filled barrios of Mexico City forged her stern smile, keen wit, and glistening eyes. The trillionaire glared at Chief Educate Lewis Leon, sitting alone on the dais with twelve empty chairs made of gilded walnut, each magnificent as a medieval throne.

"Well, yes, Ms. Huerta, but *why* did you want it there?"

Gripping her wheelchair's gray rubber treads, she inched closer to the camera streaming the proceedings to all other Educates who had not bothered to appear in person for oral arguments, an antiquated process Ms. Huerta had invoked her right to utilize. Both Dagny Huerta and the Chief looked different in human form than the avatars Aneeka was accustomed to seeing. More frail. Frighteningly real.

"I thought it would look pretty. I had it painted like the sky and clouds."

"I see. Did it have anything to do with wanting to conceal the 11G transmission tower of my client, Timeless Warning? Were you trying to erase its broadcasts from your little valley?" asked Celious Tudball, a cutthroat infotain attorney whose job at the moment required a nuance of professional poise while viciously cross-examining an elderly widow. He adjusted his bow tie, leaned back a bit, and folded his arms while awaiting her response. Aneeka thought he'd look better with a completely shaved head, given his bald spot nearly reached his ears anyway.

"I suppose that was an added benefit."

Still pacing, Aneeka's fingers ran down the back of her neck, feeling bristly cropped hair. She studied her curved chrome and black leather Wassily chair standing like a monument to mid-century modern functionality, elegance, and logic, envisioning it encased behind a concrete wall. Surely its form, even hidden from view, would still exist if no one could observe it. *But its purpose?*

Dagny Huerta became the richest woman in Globalia's Mexican region by moving into dirigibles years before anyone else. Adding blimps to her existing railroad lines, she moved freight and passengers slower than planes yet more efficiently than locomotives alone. Airships proved ideal launch vehicles for delivery drones. One blimp could ferry dozens of quadcopters from a distribution warehouse before dropping them from a cargo bay like a hive of bees that flew the last mile to a delivery balcony. When beachfront billionaires began hiring private security contractors to shoot down airplanes under the climatic self-defense doctrine, Dagny's dirigibles filled the gap in Mexico's air-transit economy. Within a year, she was the envy of Globalian investors who had missed the blimp.

So, what does one buy when you can afford anything in the world? The Grand Canyon, that's what.

Dagny had insisted on representing herself, without an attorney. She floated all the way from Mexico to Dubai to address the Tribunal in their Grand Chambers. The Chief was sufficiently annoyed at being forced to physically officiate that he knew he wasn't objective. He handed the case to Aneeka Randall, thinking her background in psychiatry would be useful in ascertaining the true mindset of the defendant.

The lawyer's interrogation continued. "So, you understood your concrete wall would block 11G transmissions?"

"I'm not an engineer, Mr. Tudball. I was honoring my property's easement permitting Timeless Warning to build a transmission tower, while mitigating its impact upon my viewscape. A contract is a contract. If they had a problem with walls around their tower, they should have put that into the easement language."

"Yes, but surely you understood that your wall would undermine the tower's purpose."

"My understanding is not what's on trial today."

"In fact, Ms. Huerta, it is. Preventing Grand Canyon visitors from receiving Timeless Warning's infotainment via 11G transmissions created an international trade barrier. Absent a rational self-interest justifying that trade barrier, the Educates must rule against you. The motivation behind your wall's construction will prove dispositive. Have you ever been to the Grand Canyon, Ms. Huerta?"

"No."

"How many visitors were there last year?"

"I don't know. Probably dozens."

"Do you charge an admissions fee to your visitors?"

"Heavens no. Are you crazy?"

"With all due respect, Ms. Huerta, that is precisely what this Tribunal is trying to ascertain about you. Any objectively rational person holding an asset as costly as the Grand Canyon would charge an entrance fee to maximize their investment return."

"Just say it Tudball," interjected Educate Roland Thompson's red-faced avatar. "She's off her rocker! Gonzo. Nuts! I can't believe we're wasting our time on such an obvious case."

Aneeka felt an ice ball forming inside, pressing against an internal girder of conviction forged of rigid steel. She paced on. Faster. Firmer.

"Your honor," continued a cucumber calm Celious Tudball, refusing Educate Thompson's invitation to move for summary judgment. "Timeless Warning, as a corporation, has a human right to free speech guaranteed under Globalia's Piese Treaty and the U.S. Constitution, which I'd remind you is still binding precedent. Corporations are people, we all know and accept that. The defendant's wall is silencing Timeless Warning's freedom to speak with its customers. It's Orwellian. It's a human rights violation. Now, we aren't arguing Ms. Huerta should be prosecuted at the Hague or any such thing. We simply seek an educated ruling to tear down that barrier, just as Ronald Reagan poignantly called on Mikhail Gorbachev to tear down the Berlin Wall."

"Speaking of the U.S. Constitution and presidents and what not, why shouldn't this issue be handled domestically within the United States?" Chief Educate Lewis Leon asked. Aneeka had been wondering the same thing.

"Thank you for asking, Chief. While this matter does fit within existing U.S. Supreme Court case law in that it involves a corporation, which is a person, having its human and constitutional rights violated, what is more fundamentally at stake is global peace and prosperity. Timeless Warning is an international conglomerate technically located in the Cayman Islands. The Educates have well established that issues of global commerce must be adjudicated by this Tribunal, not populist institutions like the United States. Blocking access to MyndScreen transmissions threatens Globalia's economy, which relies heavily upon products and services purchased only due to a steady stream of advertisements. As you know, with the advent of 11G transmissions, Timeless Warning became Globalia's largest infotain purveyor. Blocking that content means blocking the advertising. And blocking the advertising means collapse of the global economy ensuring poverty, deprivation, and war. Imagine the cataclysm that would occur should global transmissions crash for even a few minutes."

Cataclysm? That seems like a stretch.

Tudball built to his climax with ever so slight an increase in vocal tone. "The Tribunal simply cannot allow the irrational whims of an 85-year-old who isn't even maximizing monetary returns on an investment as substantial as the Grand Canyon to set a precedent allowing anyone to block 11G cerebral implant transmissions. It's an existential threat to our prosperity, which in turn destroys our freedom!"

"Prosperity isn't freedom!" Dagny Huerta stopped Tudball's monologue stone cold. "I would know. Freedom is freedom. Prosperity is gluttony."

Dagny's glare went static and pixelated on Aneeka's screen. "Transmission error" popped up in a chyron below. Everything froze. Time stood still at 3:37 p.m.

Dagny's last words reverberated inside Aneeka's head like a bell. *Prosperity isn't Freedom. Freedom is Freedom.* Aneeka had heard that before. It was lunacy. At least, that had been her diagnosis at the time. She stopped pacing and pivoted around, thinking she'd heard something drop behind her in the now eerily quiet room. The swift motion sent her lower back into unbearable spasms.

Dammit. Cataclysmic indeed.

Collapsing to hands and knees, Aneeka eased into child's pose. She'd dealt with this before. Her back locked up after excessive exercise and sleeping in all the wrong positions. A gentle stretch released her lumbar region, but she dared not change position. Maybe she could order an oxycodoze spray to dull the pain and relax her muscles. It could be drone delivered within 20 minutes with a rush fee. No. Medication would dull her senses, impairing her ability to hear the case. Besides, her MyndScreen was still down. Weird.

The world looked different from her present vantage point. A few dust bunnies hid under the red velvet couch. She made a mental note to inform the cleaners. Her fireplace had fissures in the brickwork. How did they make bricks anyhow? Could she find a replacement?

After a moment's contemplation, she crawled toward the bedroom. Carefully reaching atop an Art Nouveau dressing bureau she grabbed her signature blend of Randy™ potpourri perfume and dabbed a bit on her left wrist. Inhaling its nostalgic scent, her entire being relaxed.

She lay motionless for several minutes, waiting for muscles to recover. Then, just like that, Dagny's speech resumed.

"You're trying to take away my freedom. That's socialism, you know. The main characteristic of socialism is public ownership of the means of production, and, therefore, the abolition of private property. The right to property is the right of use and disposal. Under fascism, people retain the semblance or pretense of private property, but the government holds total power over its use and disposal. The Grand Canyon is my private property. You can't hold power over how I use it. And I use it by building a big, beautiful wall."

Ugh, she's actually making some sense. Now my head hurts too.

"Chronic pain? Try AcheZappers™ today!" popped a MyndScreen ad.

Ugh.

Dagny Huerta's closing argument was abruptly cut off by an urgent DM from the Chief Educate.

"Login now to SecuritE-Chambers for an emergency session. That outage was a simultaneous hack from Oslo, Tel Aviv, Arlington and Southern California. Globalia is minutes away from economic collapse. We've been summoned to a crypto briefing."

CHAPTER 5
Oscar

BRISK MORNING AIR STUNG OSCAR'S CHEEKS AS HE AND Ellen trotted downhill on the road's narrow shoulder. Cars passed, rarely, with a whooshing sound. His memory was still shot to shit, yet his powers of observation felt keener.

Martha had worried the concussion would render Oscar instable. She'd persuaded Ellen to put him on Benjamin, the mule, whose slow and steady gate could balance a glass of water. Even then, a flood of new information from the great outdoors made him woozy. A never-ending verdant forest, horseshoes clopping on pavement, and the smell of horse manure overwhelmed his senses.

White knuckles gripped his saddle horn while Ellen guided Benjamin with a lead rope. He instinctively tried clicking his MyndScreen's pause button to give his overstimulated brain a break, but transmissions were still down. Eyes closed, he instead just felt the saddle rock back and forth. The cadence felt strange yet comforting.

For two hours, they rode in strained silence while dropping in elevation and inclination. He noticed the leather strap Ellen had tied around her semi-bodacious hips was just an old bridle rein.

On the outskirts of town, discarded mattresses were stacked twenty feet high outside an abandoned recycling facility. A pony nibbled grass tufts sprouting from the waterlogged foam. Funny he'd never noticed this before. There was a lot more to see without transmissions in the way.

"They're feral," Ellen explained, sensing his interest. "People stopped caring for them, so they fend for themselves."

"Who would abandon ponies?"

"I guess humans found easier pastimes that didn't require mucking out barns and refilling feed bins."

They entered Highland, a foothills community San Bernardino had sprawled around prior to the Great Saturation's housing collapse. Frenetic delivery flocks whirred all about. Clothing drones dropped off WearOnce™ outfits. Pepsoilent and CokAid drones brought FlavrPak refills, others carried a hundred vigarette cartridge varieties. Advertising copters tugged giant banners through the sky reading, "Watch *Big Brother, Vreality* like no Other!"

Ellen asked which way they should go.

"I don't know. None of this feels right. I've never come into town on horseback before."

She turned at the first stoplight, entering a century-old ranch home neighborhood of faded stucco and crumbling asphalt shingles. Most houses had white PVC PlastikPly™ epoxy glued across their windows, decorated with graffiti. Clumps of weeds poked through cracked Astroturf.

Ellen puckered her forehead. "This can't be it. Let's try another part of town."

"Keep going. This doesn't look familiar, but something feels right."

Ellen agreed that gut instincts could be as reliable as memory, yet two blocks later she remained unsettled. Several Lubyrs drove by, their riders staring off into space while failing to notice a horse and a mule walking through suburbia.

A young pedestrian in a BroncBoy T-shirt walked toward them, his head encased in a bulbous VR helmet.

"Ask him for directions," Ellen suggested.

"To where?"

Ellen was undeterred. "Yoo, hooo! Hello there!" The kid, who looked about ten, stopped and pointed his helmet their way.

Just like that, a drone intercepted him, its tri-copter blades cutting the air. Two others descended on either side, their menacing rotors blocking all escape. A fourth copter hovered above, extending a long tube that puffed a cloud of pink smoke underneath the kid's helmet visor. His knees buckled. The hoverdrone's crab-like claws wrapped the kid's torso, while a bladed robot arm severed his helmet's chinstrap. As suddenly as it arrived, the drone lifted off, the helmet gripped in its pincers.

The BroncBoy fan collapsed.

"My goodness!" Ellen's voice shot up half an octave. "We should help him."

"He'll be OK. Those are pincas. They can't use physical force, just apprehend you for non-payment or violating terms of service. Pincas get you out in the open if you're not moving quickly, which is why we normally stick to cars. That pink stuff is ether. It'll wear off in a minute or so and he'll be back on his feet wondering where the hell he is. Weird though, I've never seen 'em repo a helmet."

"Let's turn around. This neighborhood doesn't feel safe. Nobody even seems to live here. Do you recognize anything?"

"No, but I'm usually gaming, so I don't look around much. Things look kinda different now. Hey, that's my sister."

"What?"

"Right there. I'd know those sneakers anywhere. Hey! Luella!" Pink Chuck Taylor™ high tops dangled over the edge of a fraying polyester rope hammock strung under a corrugated metal carport.

Oscar slid awkwardly off the mule and sauntered over all casual, making a pimp roll motion with his arms. "Yo Lulu. 'Zup?"

"Huh?" came a voice muffled by the VR helmet and visor encasing her head. Seeing her faceless like that, immersed in virtuality, reminded Oscar of when four-year-old Luella told him his avatar looked like a generic game icon. He should fill in eye detail, hair, a persona. Even his baby sister knew Oscar had to decide who he was before he could game, at least if he wanted other players to engage. Nobody wants to play a faceless gray orb.

So he created @OscarBro92346, gangsta extraordinaire with slicked hair, black hoodie, and Patriader ballcap. That was before he had to embody Oscar Tamero, caretaker of a parentless kid sister. *Tamero*. That was it. His last name. He'd never used it, but he was suddenly certain it was his.

Only after Oscar rocked the hammock and nearly tipped her out did Luella remove the GalExSee headset, squinting her eyes at Ellen's relieved face.

"You asshole! Where've you been? You just bolted without ordering FlavrPaks or telling me anything. I couldn't even track you on FindMyFiends. I thought you were a goner, dude. Even the MarlBros were wondering where you were."

Oscar froze.

Ellen touched the small of his back. "The who?"

"You know, Oscar's bruddas. Who are you, anyway? What are those?"

Oscar regained composure. "This is Ellen. She helped me ride these horses. People used these before cars and stuff. Anyhow, I had a small skiing incident and she helped me get back."

"What's on its neck?" Luella pointed at Ellen's horse.

"A brand," Ellen answered. "Flossy was a wild mustang. The brand identifies where she was rounded up and registers the Sisters of San Bernardino as her rightful owner."

"Cool," Luella replied. "I never knew they still lived in nature."

Something suddenly made Flossy flinch.

Like a pitcher keeping an eye on baserunners before throwing the slider, Oscar calmly glanced around to see a polished black car cruising toward them, its windows down. Thrusting an arm upward he yelled,

"Yo brudda!" A MarlBro, donning a Patriader cap, drove the mid-thirties electric roadster old school. With hands on the wheel and cigarette dangling between his lips, he stared straight ahead as if mesmerized by the horizon.

What up? Oscar thought, searching for a dialogue box to ping Jerome in the Chatter. But there was no window, no Chattersphere, no screen to pull up. "I'm still offline. It's like I don't exist." Rubbing his neck, he closed his eyes.

"Oscar, put some ice on that," Ellen suggested in a protective tone. "It's been quite a day."

"Good idea. Let's go inside."

Oscar led Ellen around back of the faded yellow home, where a piece of plastic ply covered a sliding aluminum frame that once held glass. He noticed her tread carefully, placing footsteps between cracks in the concrete patio.

"You live here? Where're your parents?"

"Like I told Martha, my parents died, OK? It's just me and Lulu."

"What? You left your kid sister all by herself to ski?"

"Yeah Oscar, how'd you feel if I ditched you?"

Oscar sensed Luella was sufficiently jolted from her media daze to work up a real resentment. "I didn't know it would be three days, OK?" Then, he turned to Ellen. "Anyway, what's the deal with *your* parents? I thought nuns weren't supposed to have kids."

"I, … I don't know. Sister Martha never told me anything, but she's not my real mom. She just says I was meant to be where I am. Are you going to be OK here?" she asked, looking at Luella. "I mean, this place is barely livable." The sound of drones circled outside.

"We've got everything we need. Mattresses, CokAid dispenser, a recycling shower, and solar to run it all. Hey, you want a CherryColaFriz and some nachos?" Oscar narrowed his eyes, trying to pull up his extruder app, yet nothing happened. "Damn. Transmissions are still down."

"No, they're not," Luella said. "I've been playing Angry Bugs for hours."

"Transmissions been down ever since my ski wipeout. In fact, my SlalomSnake app freezing up is what made me crash."

"You crashed because you thought you could ski by implant, silly," Ellen jibed.

"Uh-oh," Luella mumbled. She threw her GalExSee back on, its two half-dome screens made each eye look like an insect's. She approached the CokAid dispenser, which began printing a plastic bag. "I'm sure whoever hacked the MyndScreens wasn't trying to hurt anyone. It was only down three minutes, so that's not why you're still offline." The bag began to fill with marble-sized instant ice balls.

"Someone hacked the 11G system?" Ellen exclaimed. She grabbed the bag, tied it in a knot, and pressed it against Oscar's head. Then, she said in a hushed voice, "Oscar, I don't know much about these things, but I think your problem isn't transmissions. It's your implant. Your crash must have dislodged it."

"Oh man," Oscar grabbed the icebag and his cowboy tattoo wiggled with the flexing metacarpals. He gazed at his feet before looking straight at Ellen, saying, "I'm dead."

CHAPTER 6
Caspian

CASPIAN'S YELLOW 2063 IDRIVE CONVERTIBLE HAD WHITE Lethor™ bucket seats this week. HALexa suggested apricot-colored cushions with chesterfield-style button studs for next week. He could swap out plastic polished MyHogAnEee™ trim with something more modern, graphite powder coating perhaps. He felt rampant consumerism was a bit vain, yet one had to keep up appearances. Looking the part was half the secret of success, and he'd noticed Vice President Margery DeVrine just bought a new town car. It would be a shame if anyone deflated her oversized tires.

The morning after his weird MyndScreen freeze up, Caspian listened to Globalia Public Media's morning edition while riding to work. There were regular updates about the economy, glowing obituaries of fantastically interesting people, and man-on-the-street interviews asking Iowan consumers their thoughts about the President of the United States. The presidency was a largely ceremonial position, on par with England's monarch. Both nation-states had joined the Globalian trade agreement, meaning both let the Tribunal of Educates decide all the big stuff. Still, news reporters never tired of presidential campaigns or dustups in the royal family—they provided the conflict, characters, and plotlines necessary to keep news entertaining.

A ginormous dirigible opened its underbelly to deploy a flock of drones, each homing in on delivery balconies with today's non-essential parcels of consumer satisfaction. The air buzzed with energy and commerce while ByteDime flew through the metaverse. Some small smidgen of those proceeds supported the philanthropy Caspian had committed his lifetime to, yet he worried there was something a little sinister in all the excess.

Back on GPM, the Iowan consumer speculated about yesterday's unprecedented MyndScreen outage. "Personally, I think Timeless Warning shut down their own transmissions deliberately. No way could anyone hack such airtight cybersecurity. They want a government bailout to fix their 11G towers, which are a real fire hazard during windstorms. Threatening bankruptcy and scaring us with an occasional outage reminds us how the world would look without MyndScreens. I'm sick and tired of politicians kowtowing beneath a Timeless too-big-to-fail monopoly."

"Thanks for that perspective," said the monotone host. "Timeless Warning did not respond to our requests for comment, but the company did issue this statement: 'We regret any inconveniences or purchase disruptions our transmission outage caused hard-consuming Globalian families. Rest assured Timeless Warning is working diligently to assess this uncertain situation and will not rest until we are 100% certain of our certainty.'"

Caspian's coffee jumped out of his cup when his yellow iDrive dodged a pedestrian bolting suddenly in its path. The stunned man had scrambled to avoid a flower thrust by a disheveled teenager.

"Damnation!" Coffee stained his apricot and seafoam striped tie. *That daisy stuff really IS disruptive.* He removed the soiled neckpiece.

His MyndScreen popped open AI driven noodle searches about disruptive orange ties. All sorts of weird results appeared in his brain, including a picture of an orangutan wearing a sea foam striped tie. Then, an insta-ad appeared, "Need a replacement? Delivery guaranteed within 24 minutes" while his AmaZing! cart already contained the tie with OrangeVine's address pre-selected. He grimaced and squinted his eyes to click "Buy now." Caspian knew how to roll with the punches, handling whatever obstacles life threw at him with aplomb. Flower gawking traffic was now so thick the delivery drone would arrive at the office before he did.

Caspian's convertible abandoned the gridlocked thoroughfare for minor streets traversing a Vue neighborhood. The Establishment called its consumer class "Vues" because their primary economic value was viewing infotainment in sufficient quantities to fuel Globalia's consumption economy. Many older Vues still used VR helmets like the MyScreen or its competitor the WhamZong™ GalExSee™, being unable to afford cerebral implants favored by Establishment members and younger generations.

Establishment Myndscreen chips like Caspian's were always on. However, when Vues removed their VR helmets on hot days as the internal air conditioning systems failed, they experienced infotain downtime. Vues' minds could wander offline, observing the physical world around them. These infotain deserts bred periods of under-consumption that made Vues considerably less profitable to Timeless Warning and more dangerous to the Globalian economy. Vues' free thinking and chronic debt depressed infotain purchases, risking worldwide recessions. This is precisely why Caspian Blaine was interested in the Vues. They had the power to change everything.

His job revealed just how much Globalia's corporate leadership feared infotain disengagement. They partnered with Hollywood stars and Silicon Valley moguls in CeleTeCharity campaigns to fund cerebral implants for underprivileged Vues. Wall Street financed both implants and monthly data fees with long-term capital debt schemes repaid over a lifetime of implanted viewvitude . OrangeVine helped expand implant access, getting Vues "online at all times." That's how Caspian funded a crypto project to provide at-risk 13-year-olds WhamZong Gal-InSee™ implants instead of MyndScreen implants.

WhamZong was an upstart tech disrupter bucking industry trends by providing screen time reports to facilitate customer self-limitation. Consumption data gave WhamZong a competitive edge against more addictive MyndScreens that maximized views regardless of social impact. WhamZong launched with a self-limiting GalExSee VR helmet for children under 13, whose brains weren't considered sufficiently developed to accept a surgically implanted chip. Kids got a warning emojicon whenever continuous gaming exceeded seven hours. Caspian wished it was lower, but still, it was better than nothing.

Caspian understood the need for Vues to connect with the modern world, yet also valued some level of autonomous thought. He smiled inside as his convertible passed a block dotted with kids in dreadlocks, a less refined version of his own tightly braided cornrows. They jumped double-Dutch, with WhamZong GalExSees tossed carelessly on Astroturf lawns. *I did that! Their helmet told them to take a break, and look, they're out playing in the sunshine. Disclosure baby. It's all about transparent information so people can decide for themselves. We're changing the world, one small double-Dutch step at a time.*

His iDrive eventually dropped him in Santa Monica at OrangeVine's twenty-one-floor tower of shimmering Plexiglas and protruded plasti-CAB I-beams. The car rounded a corner to spend the rest of the day circling in a holding pattern. Caspian inhaled moist sea air. *If only I could work out here. But you don't upscale lives just sitting around on the beach.* With aspirations of pragmatic idealism, Caspian went inside.

He was surprised to find Margery DeVrine heading out just as he arrived. Her poised legs strode purposefully in gray slacks with light pink pinstripes matching the lobby's speckled rose and charcoal granite floor. A sherbet-colored scarf added a distinguished flair.

She was accompanied by a steely-eyed Yvonne Putcher, with perfect complexion and delightful cherry lips. Yvonne tucked rigid platinum hair behind her ear before shaking his hand. "Nice to meet you in RL, Mr. Blaine. You must be excited about yesterday's big news."

"It was a pretty shocking disruption." Caspian assumed she was talking about the 11G outage, like everyone else on Chatter. When she gave him a puzzled look, he added, "I've never seen transmissions go down so long."

"Oh, that! I meant Packard's big announcement," Putcher clarified. "We were listening so attentively there in the room we hardly noticed the transmissions. Anyway, Marge and I are just grabbing coffee and a hash brownie, but let's touch base soon." Her delicate fingertips tapped Caspian's left elbow as she said, "touch base." DeVrine just glared. He felt his cheeks warm, gave an awkward, "uh, sure," and bolted into the elevator. *Not smooth man, not smooth.*

Inside the mahogany-paneled elevator, Caspian's Chatterbox filled with messages. He arrived at his office locked and loaded with 347 new items. He skimmed frantically in preview mode for "Packard's big announcement."

Message 54 was from an organization helping Finnish villagers plant banana trees. DELETE. Message 79 was about curbing judicial overreach on the Tribunal of Educates. DELETE. In Message 148, *Philanthropy Savvy Today* announced a new webinar on maximizing tax abatement through creative endowment outsourcing. DELETE.

Message 184 was Wallace Packard. "Caspian! Let's get lunch at Michael de Angelinos. Real food. My treat." The message included a press release announcing Packard's retirement.

Caspian had been to Michael de Angelinos, one of the few restaurants still catering to High Establishment diners that shelled out big bucks for non-extruded food. OrangeVine took employees there when it wanted to buy them out. Over the years, he'd severed a few over-the-hill subordinates there by informing them OrangeVine was very generously funding their retirement, effective immediately. Caspian was 47 years old. He strapped on the new apricot and seafoam striped tie and wondered what to order for his last meal.

Packard was waiting at a private table, his belly bulging out a South African mohair suit and pressing up against the French tablecloth. Bushy white eyebrows and tufts around the perimeter of his hairline needed a trim. He didn't bother getting up but motioned for Caspian to sit and loosened his tie.

"Look, boss, sorry I missed your big announcement," Caspian stammered. "I was out in the field, researching new grant opportunities." Packard waved him off and asked what he wanted to eat. It had taken Caspian years to acquire a palate for the viscoelasticity of meat and fibrous vegetables, but his jaw eventually hardened. He knew soilborne food illness stories were just rumors spread by soyalgent firms to scare restaurant goers. With only a slight self-righteousness, he pitied lower Establishment types who feared any meal not coming out a machine.

After awkward pleasantries while perusing an actual paper menu, Packard ordered a lab grown filet mignon with roasted root vegetables and braised greenhouse kale. Caspian chose free-range chicken with carbon-fixing saffron rice. His mind grasped for reasons Packard ought not take him along down retirement's lonely road.

Packard sipped a martini with three real olives skewered on a bamboo sliver before laying down his cards. "Look, Caspian. I like you. You understand the profound enormity of the task before us. During the Great Saturation's depopulation, we as a global society, and even OrangeVine as a foundation, became so focused on keeping people alive that we forgot the need to actually live. Humans cannot survive on bread alone, as somebody somewhere used to say. Most of my staff's brains are totally fried by infotain's sizzle, but you've somehow kept the drive our society needs to reinvent itself and escape our stupor. I know you know what I mean."

Caspian's fingers drummed on his pantleg, awaiting the inevitable, "but, unfortunately . . . " that he knew followed the flattering introductory paragraph OrangeVine's personnel manual prescribed as a prelude to termination.

Packard took another sip of martini and nibbled an olive. Caspian sat in pregnant silence. Then, it came. "I want you to be OrangeVine's next president."

Caspian snorted into his cocktail as Packard continued, unfazed.

"But here's the deal. Our board chair is leery. He wants the endowment even bigger than it already is. He freaked out over the stock market collapse after yesterday's 11G downtime. His identity, his ego, his sense of purpose are built upon our balance sheet, not our social change. He covets a forty-year reserve fund, stockpiled ByteDime for an infinite risk-proof sustainability that ensures we never rock the boat or make a rat's ass worth of difference. I've spent decades inching this institution toward an edgier place and someday you'll be the guy who gets it done. But first, I need you to get past the board chair. He thinks you're too idealistic, too focused on big structural change instead of quarterly philanthropic returns. So, tone down your pie-in-the-sky rhetoric of opening hearts and minds and focus for a while on the metrics, will you? Dollars out, utils in. I know it doesn't work that way in the real world, but right now you've got to push grantees to deliver. Down the road, you'll tweak the metrics and shift the entire charitable world into a saner place. You'll turn the battleship."

"Read you loud and clear, boss," Caspian said with a smug grin and skipping heart. He took a long sip on his Manhattan and popped the maraschino cherry into his mouth. "I'll put up some short-term numbers. Meanwhile, dial me in to whoever I should network on the hiring committee."

"There will be a time and a place for that, Caspian. For now, focus on results while keeping this conversation crypto, as they say. And steer clear of DeVrine, you wouldn't believe what she's saying about you. There's also a guy named Shawn Fellia who might trip you up." Caspian vaguely recognized the name. "Get this right and you'll eat like this every day, but you gotta play the game." Packard's chaufferscurity-staffed limousine had already pulled up. He stood, shook Caspian's hand with a practiced grip and grin, and waddled out the door. Caspian couldn't help but think about all the worthwhile projects he could have funded with the expense of Packard's ego-fluffing limo and the purely ornamental driver who didn't even steer the vehicle.

Back in the office, Caspian opened a deliverables spreadsheet and the accompanying utils OrangeVine used to quantify social value. AI predicted which grantees would deliver the most utils in the next three months. Vanessa's track record at UpLyfting Lives was impressive, she was the GOAT. Unfortunately, her newer projects didn't come online for 18-36 months. Still, if there was anyone he could count on, it was her.

He shut down seven active MyndScreen windows, closed his Chatterbox, and killed the background music. Caspian stared at a Montblanc pen he'd never used, standing erect in a brass and marble holder, and rubbed both thumbs against his shiny brown temples.

After 37 seconds of contemplation, his MyndScreen poked him with an inactivity alert. Springing back to action, he downloaded a movie, checked the news, and followed on-screen prompts to install the most recent Implant Operating System. After scrolling through ten pages of terms and conditions, he clicked "ACCEPT," knowing he'd yet again signed away his cerebral IP. It was the price you had to pay. While the IOS installed the most recent anti-virus protections, he pinged Vanessa in a new tab. "Hey, did I ever tell you about the OrangeSmash program? It's a separate stream of funding that got folded into my Special Projects and Strategic Initiatives Portfolio a few years back. Our founder was a huge fan of Orange-Smash soda."

"So? ¯_(ツ)_/¯" Vanessa was fond of non-copyrighted retro emojicons instead of the more up-to-date trademarked lexicon offered by Timeless Warning.

"So, I have a lot of discretion as to how to award those funds. Let's do a site visit to your San Bernardino expansion project. We'll talk about squeezing that into an Orange-Smash proposal."

"Pawp!" The movie download completed, the Chatterbox was empty, and a champagne emoji appeared. "You've reached your daily goal of 4.1 terabytes in data absorption." *That's how you play the game, baby!*

His office OrangeSmash protruder suddenly whirred and printed a plastic bowl. He hadn't ordered anything. A dollop of brown poo oozed out. It didn't smell like poo, didn't really smell like anything. Still, it looked like what came out of a dog. It kept coming. *WTAF?* The bowl overflowed.

DeVrine's messing with me, tryin' get inside my head with some twisted prank. Caspian unplugged the machine. He chucked the bowl down a recycling chute and accidentally smudged brown goo on his orange tie. *Damnation!*

The following morning, Caspian's MyndScreen woke him gently when his sleep cycle was optimally abating. He picked up Vanessa outside her Silver Lake apartment. As a persimmon sun illuminated the FiredStone™ expressway, his iDrive navigated heavy traffic to sync with an eastbound

OttoTrain in the high speed HOV lane. Globalia Public Media described a presidential virtual ribbon cutting to debut a new metaverse amusement park on the non-fungible token exchange.

While technology whisked them along, Caspian chatterpinged his car-mate and stared at his palm. "Give me the deets on your expansion project."

"Well," Vanessa strained against her seatbelt as she turned toward him, "There's significant poverty and gang activity ..."

"No, no. Don't just *tell* me. Chat me the details, so the SpeiDrWebs know we're conversing and we rack up some Zings. Otherwise, it will track like I'm spaced out instead of in a work meeting."

"You want me to chat at you when you're sitting right next to me? You're killing me."

"C'mon. It's easy. Your dictation app can type whatever you think into a message. Then, just hit send. I'll respond the same way. You gotta play the game, Vanessa." He glanced up from his palm and winked.

She sighed. "OK, Caspian. San Bernardino experienced severe home underpricing after the Great Saturation and ensuing real estate market anomalies. Population downsizing from World War Unseen further eroded neighborhood structure, leading to significant social anomie. Many people never rebuilt after the 2045 Hades fire. We're launching a SuburbiaUpLyft program to reduce gang activity, refurbish blighted communities, and create safe zones empowering collective esteem boosts for underprivileged youth in disadvantaged microregions experiencing disrupted family units. The Sisters of San Bernardino previously ran neighbor-hood programs using thrift store proceeds, but that folded and the nuns need to reinvent their philanthropic model. We can assist them with that. Over and out, Vanessa." SEND.

"FANTA. Please submit a 200-megabyte proposal to the Or-ange-Smash funding stream. Check out our SpeiDrWebsite, <LINK> for more details." SEND.

"What's the deal with that, anyway?" Vanessa blurted.

"OK, look," Caspian replied, offline. "I can move some major money your way, but we gotta repackage your work product and ramp up timelines. As you've probably noticed, some people take soyalgent food and drink choices really seriously. Branding becomes integral to who they are, how they conceive of themselves, kinda like ethnicity, race, religion, and sexual orientation once shaped our identities. OrangeVine's founder was like that. He really, really personified this indie brand OrangeSmash. He was devastated when a botulism lawsuit nearly ran them into bankruptcy. Then the Educates granted Pepsoilent and CokAid a virtual duopoly on extrusion. OrangeSmash survived a merger, yet there's virtually no brand recognition because the big two are assimilating everyone into their brands. So even though he was a one percenter High Establishment guy, he felt disenfranchised by the dominant brands. He launched OrangeVine to boost self-esteem for OrangeSmash consumers and rebuild their lost culture. It's a little outside the box, but I'll move a big pile of money your way if you work in an OrangeSmash angle and crank out massive social uplift utils within three months."

"Three months? We're just starting to build relationships. We don't even know what people want to do."

"Can't you just replicate your gardening business on the Westside? Only, that might take too long. What if kids ran lemonade extruder stands or something that sold OrangeSmash drinks? Proceeds could fund virtual midnight basketball leagues to keep 'em out of gangs? I'll hook you up with WhamZong GalExSee helmets and even GalinSee implants for the older ones."

"Wouldn't real basketball be better?"

"Do that too; a clicks-to-bricks spinoff. Just don't mention that in your grant report. How many gang exits, graffiti cleanups, and lifetime consumer value enhancements could you rack up in three months, if money was no object? I need numbers."

Vanessa looked him straight in the eye, tucked her hair behind her left ear and said, "Why don't you meet these people first. We're here."

CHAPTER 7
Chase

"AAAAAGH!" THE BIG-BOSOMED AVATAR SHRIEKED. *BIG Brother V* had just finished a 360-second commercial break. Ever since Timeless Warning's outage, Chase found himself noticing details like ad segment duration. Today, they'd dialed advertising down and upped content quality to levels reminiscent of old-time "sweeps weeks." He felt a slight breeze come through his pod's vent when the AC kicked on. It smelled chilly.

"He can't be dead!" A look of horror spread across Big Bosom. "Oooaaa, whoooa, noooooo," she wailed, drawing attention from other housemates.

"Shhh! Stop it! You can't scream or they'll all know," Pigtails commanded in a loud whisper.

"What the hell's going on?" A guy in an alligator logo polo shirt asked three other housemates enjoying Koffy on the patio. Shrieks were unusual, even for this show. They leaned in.

"This ain't real," Big Bosom insisted. "You're joking. It's fake views."

"I'd never joke about something like this. It just happened."

Big Bosom grabbed a Pepsoilent BloodEMarry™, stormed outside, and informed everyone their housemate, David, had died. "I can't keep this crypto. I gotta get this out."

Chase, along with millions of other catatonic viewers, knew David had been sick in bed the past several episodes. Contestants rushed to his bedroom and found him covered to his nose beneath a comforter. When jostled, he proved to be very much alive.

"This is fucked up!" Big Bosom yelled. "She told me he was dead. Why'd she do that?"

Chase couldn't care less. His room smelled sterile. The LED lighting was weird, with an aqua twinkle. He kept glancing at the HVAC vent, just beyond his MyndScreen's periphery. There it was. A bug! Definitely a bug. He hadn't imagined it.

In a multitask window, a Chatterpost came through using hashtag #BBV65. "David really is dead; I just know it! They've swapped in a body double to pretend he's alive. Those tears were real. Don't believe what you're seeing." The message, from @RTGasLyte, went viral with 12,981 reposts.

Pigtails entered a private confession booth to explain what happened, while a near naked man with six-pack abs left the shower. He explained that yes, David was dead, but it was a different David. Pigtails had told him her ex-husband, David Bowie, just died of cancer. She'd wanted to grieve in private, offline, not as some spectacle of the show. The towel wrapped around his waist slipped. He bent down, grabbed it and scampered off.

"There's your fake news, people," Chase blurted into the Chattersphere. "David Bowie died in 2016. #BBV65 is just a Celebrity Big Brother rehash from 49 years ago. We're watching bots! The algorithm changed contestant names, but not Bowie's because he's not actually in the show. That's the tell. Of course it's fake, it's a reality show! They're just reprising a mistaken identity storyline—one of the oldest tropes in theater going way back to Shakespeare."

"That's so meta! Who's Shakespeare? Who's David Bowie?" @RealiTeaDiner responded. "Never heard of them." Chase's original post got little traction, but RealiTea's comment received 37 likes and one reply from @FactPecker, "David Bowie wasn't a real person either. His real name was Ziggy Stardust and he died in 1969 when his spaceship oddly stopped communicating with Earth."

There was the bug again. Chase felt his pulse increasing. Had it been there all along?

The episode replayed the dramatic "David's dead" moment, with violins straining along with footage of every housemate reacting to Big Bosom's scream, all from different camera angles and voice-over commentary from off-screen hosts. Contestants entered the confession booth, recounting their trauma from the non-death. Chase was impressed how the producer's algorithm teased 90 seconds of recycled content into an hour-long episode.

When a MinuteMayd™ rolled in to exchange his TPN soyalgent bag, Chase muted his screens. He studied how its mechanical arm grabbed his infusion port. "Good afternoon, Chase. How are you viewing today?"

"I'm OK. How are you, Diri?"

"I'm glad to hear that, Chase. I'm fine, thank you," said the bot. "Time for lunch."

The bot's arm clamped his catheter port while an interlocking mechanism disconnected the TPN bag. Four greenish gray drops fell to the floor. The robot deftly retrieved a new bag from a refrigerated storage chest in its abdomen and hung it on the IV stand while disposing the old bag in a recycling chute.

I could do that. Not that I'd need to. Everyone knows there's no going back.

The MinuteMayd placed some extruded chocolate pudding on his tray. No explanation. Chase hadn't eaten solid food in 17 years. The bot probably had the wrong room. He let it sit there and switched on the news.

"Unnamed sources claim yesterday's disastrous Mynd-Screen outage was caused by a Chinasian missile attack on Timeless Warning's satellite network. The unconfirmed space force assault allegedly retaliated for Globalia's surgical drone strike targeting Chinasia's five remaining coal-fired power plants to enforce the Jakarta Climate Protocols. Economic sanctions have proven ineffective against the Chinasian Trade Conglomerate, which has sufficient gross domestic consumption to withstand years of export warfare. Lewis Leon, Chief of the Tribunal of Educates, had no comment when asked about the alleged attack."

Some bot probably unplugged the wrong server and they're trying to blame it all on Chinasia. Chase looked again at the bowl of pudding. His stommach rumbled.

He restarted Grand Heist Otto and multitasked as the news brought up an expert panel with a balding retired general, a former administration staffer wearing tortoise-shell glasses, and a wavy blonde commentator in a low-cut leopard print dress. They gesticulated and bantered while Chase poked @BadScootr, asking if he wanted to pull a joint heist.

"I'm in. Let's hit the Venetian."

"OK, 50-50 split," Chase affirmed. The plan was set.

Entering the metaverse, Chase loaded his Cowasaki's Holstein-patterned saddlebags with an arsenal of sawed-off shot guns, Uzis, and hand grenades. He strapped on body armor and mounted the bike. After launching a HeliGunnr™ personal protection drone for air support, he followed @BadScootr off road, riding through an abandoned golf course and pulling wheelies in the old sand traps. They mowed down pedestrians on a fake canal bridge, then crashed their bikes through a jewelry store's display windows in the Venetian Casino Resort.

Following an hour of gunfire, fisticuffs, and scantily clad 3D ladies offering their purse contents, Chase and his partner in crime gathered watches, gemstone necklaces, and loose cut diamonds. Manned police helicopters circled, and SWAT Humvee sirens blared outside. Chase's

HeliGunnr held the cops at bay with suppressing fire until a Lockheed micro-missile took it out. "Follow me brudda, I know a hack!" @ BadScootr yelled, motioning for Chase to abandon his cycle and run further into the casino.

Bolting down a maintenance stairway, they entered a storm drainage tunnel. Chase glanced at @BadScootr's points with a twinge of envy. *This guy's good.* He racked up some points of his own, and increased his arrest warrant rating, by shooting homeless people just for kicks while @ BadScootr navigated the underground maze.

Their escape required perfect reflexes and problem-solving skills to pick locks, avoid collapsing tunnel walls, and escape toxic sewer gas. After emerging from the complex drainage network, the bandits commandeered two cycles from some Hells Angels. This led to a fanta chase scene with the biker gang in hot pursuit. Four hours and thirty-seven minutes later, the two players sat comfortably in an abandoned warehouse on the outskirts of Vegas.

Back in his entertainment home, Chase could smell his own sweat through the sanitized air.

They divvied up the loot and @BadScootr high-fived him. "Nice heist brudda!" Then he kicked Chase in the teeth, tossed their plunder into his saddlebags, and put a bullet in Chase's crotch followed by a second shot in his cycle's hydrogen fuel cell. "You got played sucker."

Chase's bike burst into a fireball. His hit points dwindled to zero as his avatar writhed in flames. *I'm dead. That's so meta.*

CHAPTER 8
Aneeka

SOMETHING WAS EATING AT ANEEKA RANDALL. ONE NAG-ging moment's vapors returned again and again—relentlessly corroding her inner girder of conviction with nearly imperceptible mist much like ocean spray oxidizes maritime steel.

Objectively speaking, she should be happy. She had accomplished everything she set out to and beyond: top university psychiatry and law degrees, a coveted therapist position at Mercernary General, then punditry gigs explaining intersections between mental health and respect for Glob-alian trade doctrine. That alone would be a lifetime of achievement for an average Establishment member. Aneeka was not average.

She took a long draw off an Atlantis™ vigarette, admiring the polished black anodized stem embossed with a golden dollar sign icon. She let the Kewl™ flavor roll over her taste buds, down her throat, deep into her core. Exhaling, the billowy cloud of steam briefly obscured her clothbound book collection.

Aneeka's successful techno-deviancy treatments, both at the individual and societal level, had surely prompted her lifetime tribunal appointment. She had joined the world's most powerful elite, shaping not only her own destiny, but society's as well. In law school, she had coveted a spot on the pre-approved A-list of potential nominees. She joined the Dead-Or-A-List syndicate, attended a few schmooze fests, and her career took off. She wondered now if perhaps it had been a bit *too* easy.

She loafed around her Rustic Canyon bungalow, nestled beneath upscale Pacific Palisades. Her study's walls were lined with copper wire mesh, electrified into a Faraday cage to block 11G transmissions and permit wandering contemplation. Her bare feet tread gracefully over byzantine wool carpets, hand knotted centuries ago. She slipped into a silk kimono and ran her fingers through the jet-black hair she'd spent top dollar to style, reaching back to the short and bristly nape. Stroking her molasses-hued neck, her fingertips followed a sterling necklace to where a jade pendant hung above her sternum. She idly twisted the stone, exploring its smoothness.

ZZZZap! Her home extruder vibrated and produced an extra-large serving of chocolate pudding, unordered. *Odd.* Perhaps a secret admirer had sent a gift. She dipped a curious finger and licked. It tasted like carob-infused algae slime.

Setting aside the umber goo, she grabbed a tattered copy of *Atlas Shrugged* from her personal library. Aneeka Randall read aloud. Those glorious words applied a thin yet durable coat of paint to her steel inner core, protecting it from caustic doubts. She fully grasped that speaking from a physical page was less efficient than absorbing audio books on her MyndScreen. Still, she indulged annually in the antiquated ritual of reading this novel. She knew the story. Her purpose was not content consumption so much as to bolster her conclusions, her daily acts, the identity she had so carefully curated. She was an individual—an internationally acclaimed one at that. This success was nothing to be ashamed of, nothing to boast about, but a legitimate source of pride and confidence. She had ruthlessly elevated herself, her career, her priorities, ahead of everything. *Atlas Shrugged* reinforced this virtuous selfishness and revealed the world's immense need for exceptional people who accomplished great things.

"Educates Reign Supreme." She cherished this motto, inscribed on the Tribunal's Grand Chambers in capital roman gold-leaf font. Almost nobody saw these profound words. Except for Dagny Huerta's case, the Tribunal conducted business in secure VRooms. Individual Educates rarely laid eyes on the building's marble Corinthian columns. Nonetheless, like humans revere the pyramids of Egypt even without visiting them, the mere existence of the Grand Tribunal Chambers provided all the inspiration Aneeka needed to tackle her job. It was a heavy responsibility. When the Educates received a confidential security briefing suggesting recent 11G cyber-attacks had been an inside job originating from the Pentagon, she was the one to recommend an enhanced infotain regimen to pull viewers back into their MyndScreens and restore ROI in the advertising market. Shouldering the burdens of top-secret information and reacting in split seconds with confidence and poise required emotional stamina. Aneeka had stockpiled a lifetime reservoir of self-assurance in preparation for just such a task.

Soon after her appointment, Aneeka ingratiated herself with the other twelve Educates, an increase from the original nine-member body. All but Roland Thompson seemed to appreciate her efforts. Using her therapist training, she stroked egos and offered helpful tidbits of her own reasoning for others to appropriate into their rulings without attribution. She could someday quote those lines in her own doctrine, citing the authority of case law. Aneeka knew how to craft her own reality and enlist others to conspire in its creation. She had quite literally written "The Book" on reality—*A People's History of Globalian Thought and Truth*. "The Book" was now the standard of care for treating patients experiencing MyndScreen Side Effects who needed satiation with facts before consenting to an upgrade that left them blissfully consuming infotainment for the remainder of their lives.

She knew the treatment she had devised was expensive, yet it was well worth the price. It was not only therapeutic for the individual, but essential for global peace and prosperity. Therapy ensured a vibrant infotain economy. If people ignored MyndScreens, they'd avoid the advertisements that fueled global consumption. Data backed this up. An ever-growing marketplace provided resources to keep world hunger, and the violence arising from economically emaciated populations, at bay. Prosperity was freedom and Aneeka Randall's intellectual foundation held freedom as the highest human virtue.

The logic was impeccable, she constantly reminded herself. Globalian lives were at stake, nearly a third of Earth's population. She was personally responsible for the economic stability keeping Vues safe, fed, and entertained. Objective rationality demanded no other course than what she'd charted. Her will, her determination, her talent produced great things society had only begun to appreciate. And yet, Dagny's stridence resurrected a seventeen-year-old conflict with one of Aneeka's particularly troubled patients. It kept coming back, despite her best diversionary efforts.

Aneeka, look at me, listen to me. I know that you know what is going on, not just here but everywhere. I can see it in your eyes. I can feel it in my bones. Look at me Aneeka! How can you be complicit in all this? How can you, day after day, brainwash people into giving up their lives, giving up their truths, giving up their realities for a world created by infotainment firms? How can you?

Dr. Randall had recognized the anger as a normal part of the 14-step recovery process. She tried to assuage the patient by calmly addressing her by name, "Vera . . . "

"Don't 'Vera' me, Aneeka! Goddammit. You wrote *The Book*. You know we're all just living fodder for an infotainment economy that exists only to make greedy multinational corporations richer and to further some fabricated notion of prosperity. Prosperity isn't freedom. Freedom is freedom. Prosperity is gluttony. Freedom is the ability to think for yourself, to have your own feelings, to make your own choices, to experience the real world and accept your own world of beliefs. Freedom means you can know pain, and joy, and love, and fear. You're trying to take those things away from me, Aneeka. You know it. You know it! I *know* you know it!"

As a trained psychiatrist, Aneeka Randall understood that her own present malaise was in part sexual frustration. She had developed a crush on Vera when they first met. She took standard precautions every clinician uses to prevent inappropriate interactions. She knew Vera loved a man, even if she exhibited some bi tendencies. Aneeka tried to purge not only the memory, but the accompanying emotions. Yet here they were. Again. Irrepressible, yet treatable.

She ordered Yukon gold potato chips, fried in olive oil with pink Himalayan salt, from GhostPlates™ and alpine strawberry gelato made from organic, grass-fed, heritage-bred cows for instant delivery. The price was outrageous. She could afford it. More importantly, she'd earned it. Waiting on her balcony, she looked toward the ocean and felt a breeze cool her cheeks and forehead. Eucalyptus aerosols tickled her nose. Aneeka wondered for the first time where her delivery drone would come from. She snapped a MyndScreen image and enlarged it with the TellaFoto™ app. There it was. Upon close inspection, a tiny dot was unmistakably an airship. Probably one of Dagny Huerta's.

After the drone released the package into her receiving hammock, she carefully opened it and recycled the insulated foam box. Dipping a protruded plastic spoon into perfectly softened gelato, she relaxed on her massage lounge and binged her favorite series. It was a Timeless Warning classic, where aimless twenty somethings hung out in a real coffee shop and had real conversations. *Virtually Friends* was even better with avatar enhancement. Hollywood reporters claimed nothing conceived in the AI authored era captured the same charm, humor, and romantic tension. Everyone said Rachel was the prettiest, but Aneeka preferred Monica and thought she didn't get enough screen time.

Timeless, indeed.

"Dr. Randall, paging Dr. Randall." An emergency Educates message interrupted her episode. "Please enter the Chambers VRoom for an urgent crypto briefing. There's been another hack. The nutrition delivery industry is code level red."

Aneeka put down her alpine strawberry gelato and glanced at the bowl of pudding.

CHAPTER 9
Oscar

"WHAT DO YOU MEAN YOU'RE DEAD?" ELLEN DEMANDED. "You could have died from your idiotic ski jump. Be grateful you're very much alive."

Oscar looked at the shag carpet, still wet from his leaky roof. Seams were showing on the sheetrock walls where paint and joint compound had flaked off.

"With no MyndScreen, I can't run bacco. Crypto Chatter is how the MarlBros do bizniz. If I'm outta my gang, I'm good as dead." He didn't tell Ellen, but it occurred to him there'd also be no more virtual hookups on Cynder.

"Maybe quit tobacco, Oscar. Smoking cigarettes is bad for you. Selling cancer to others is worse."

"What would you know about it? Vaping companies make a killing out there. Why shouldn't us little guys get a piece of the action with an age-old product grown by real people? Now I'm stone broke and on the outs with my bruddas."

"Don't worry, Oscar," Luella chimed in. "Just borrow my helmet to enter the Chattersphere and take orders. I traded my old one for an adult sized from some BroncBoyer. It'll fit you. Plus, when you aren't wearing it, the Pincertons can't track you."

"I don't know. I gotta think that through." Oscar worried he'd look dorky walking around in a helmet. Or worse, like some impoverished Vue.

Suddenly aware he was still wearing the ski outfit from Snow Valley, Oscar went into his room and rummaged through a pile of disposable clothes. He eavesdropped as Ellen pressed Luella for information in the family room. "Who are the Pincertons? Why are they tracking Oscar?"

"Those rent-a-cop drones circling outside. Real police are basically AWOL with all the budget cuts, so vaping firms hire pincas to shut down contraband bacco dealers who dodge the $30 a pack sin tax they got the Educates to slap on cigarettes. They say it's to finance a seawall below the Golden Gate bridge and other climate mitigation stuff, but really they're just trying to squash the MarlBros. Those pincas been crazy active the last couple of days, so the MarlBros must be doing a lot of bizniz. Anyhow, if they catch you in the open, they etherize you and ruin your credit rating to make it impossible to buy anything, like ever. You might as well be dead."

Oscar walked out, black cargo shorts slung low on his waist. He'd pilfered them from Establishment recyclers, and they didn't fit quite right. They'd slip if he moved too aggressively, so he didn't. He sauntered smoothly, with music in each step. He'd practiced these motions for years to project quiet confidence, graceful toughness, and a heavy dose of street savvy. A black reused hoodie covered a Patriader baseball cap and most other details of his appearance. Only the whites of his eyes shone through.

"Oscar," Ellen suggested, "Maybe your accident was a blessing. Neither the Pincertons nor the MarlBros can track you. It's your chance to start something new. You could find a job or something."

"I don't want no fucking makework gig catering to some high establishment dude that doesn't give two shits about me. The MarlBros are my friends, my people. Without them, I'm nothing. C'mon, let's eat."

Oscar lifted a full container of unflavored soyalgent onto the CokAid extruder, which looked like an old time 3D printer with both heated and supercooled FlavrPak nozzles. He then loaded a five-gallon jug of distilled water, set the empty one down, and asked Luella to order some JalapeñoCheezWhizBurritos™ from her helmet. The machine vibrated with a *zzzzh* to print out tortillas and fillings. Oscar rolled them up and apologized the burritos wouldn't taste quite right since they were out of cheese flavoring.

Ellen took a bite of rubbery bean and beef flavored soyalgent chunks and politely swallowed. He saw she wasn't overly impressed with his cooking skills.

After dinner, Luella plugged her helmet in to recharge and they used Martha's map to locate the nuns' old store, just a few blocks away. As they walked, the pincas maintained a holding pattern over Oscar's block.

The Thrifty Sister was near an abandoned park with four baseball diamonds of overgrown grass, perfect for grazing. A rusty chain link fence would keep the animals penned overnight. After figuring out how the horseshoe keyring opened the door, they walked through a huge collection of discarded items. Guitars, toaster ovens, books, and non-disposable clothing had gathered dust for years. They found a cot in the backroom, just as Sister Martha had said.

Ellen bid Oscar goodnight.

"Lock the door just to be safe," he suggested. "Nothing bad usually happens around here, but there must have been a reason they put the lock on." Since neither were familiar with locks or had ever turned a deadbolt knob from the inside, he locked the door from the outside and promised to return the next morning with the key.

On the way home, Oscar and Luella walked past some teens bouncing a ball around a concrete courtyard. "What's that?" she asked.

"It's like WhamDunk online only with a real basketball. You should try it sometime."

"Looks stupid. They probably just can't afford 11G."

Oscar saw Jerome drive by. This time, Jerome saw Oscar, too. "Brudda, where the fuck you been? Pincas been crawling all over our asses ever since you went dark. I been tryin' to reach you but you giving me nothing man, nothin'. You ain't on my locate app even now." He pulled a semi-automatic pistol out of his glove compartment and looked behind Oscar. "I thought you got ganked by the Winstons. Anyone following you?"

"No brudda, it's cool. I've been having some technical difficulties with my screen is all. I'll deal with it and get back to making runs, but I may be a little harder to reach in the chatter."

"OK, my man. We need you, Oscar. Things getting weird 'round here. I been short on runners ever since a couple bruddas got upgrades, so play it cautious. We gotta serve custos or competitors will move in. Keep walking or those pincas will etherize you." Jerome cruised off, slow.

The following morning, Oscar and Luella brought freshly extruded MochXino™ and D'ohNutz™ to the Thrifty Sister. He'd used scarce ByteDime to purchase the Koffy FlavrPaks, and the drone delivery had been slow, so they were late arriving.

The door was open, yet Ellen was nowhere to be found.

"Damn, I hope everything's OK," Oscar said with genuine concern.

"Cool!" Luella cheered, "Let's get some sturdier clothes instead of the disposable stuff you've been scavenging." She started sorting through the racks.

"No, Lu. That ain't cool. We can't steal this stuff, Ellen saved my life." He thought about the example he'd been setting all these years through his technically illegal profession. "Wait, I still have the key. We should get it back to her." Truth be told, Oscar didn't mind having an excuse to see Ellen again, even if he wasn't keen on another encounter with Sister Martha. He locked the door.

Oscar strapped on Luella's GalExSee. "Locate Sisters of San Bernardino" he directed. The helmet's internal camera saw him squint his eyes to activate the search. With another blink he'd called a Lubyr. The ride back up seemed to take forever, maybe because he gave the VR helmet back to Luella so he had no way to entertain himself.

Ellen was brushing down the horses when they arrived. Oscar rushed over. "You OK? How'd you open the door?"

"Oh, I figured out how to work the lock from inside and let myself out. It was a nice day, so I just got going. I'm fine, Oscar." She gave him a smile as he sighed in relief. Hay and manure stung his olfactory when he inhaled.

Sister Martha took one look at Oscar's threadbare hoodie and low hanging cargo shorts and wrinkled her nose. "Back so soon? I know a place to get some respectable clothing, young man."

Oscar took a step back before Luella dropped a question as only a twelve-year-old could.

"You're not really Ellen's mom, are you? What happened?"

Martha froze a full thirty seconds, staring at Luella's helmet. She let out a long sigh and looked at Ellen. "Well, if you're old enough to go into town alone, I suppose you're old enough to know. Come in, all of you. This story should serve as a warning to everyone."

After pouring them cinnamon spice tea and offering treats from the fridge, Martha sat at the kitchen table and began.

"About seventeen years ago, I found myself in a hotel lobby when an exhausted-looking woman rolled in on a motorized wheelchair scooter. There was a baby seat strapped to the handlebars. I smiled, but she just stared off into space, clearly enraptured in some virtual game on that mind screen gizmo. I was knitting and offered to make the baby a little beanie. She didn't respond. There was a morbid stare on her face, as if she had peered into the abyss and fallen down inside."

"OMG, this is delicious!" Luella was spooning homemade chocolate pudding into her face. Martha had served it up while telling her story, which so far hadn't fazed Luella in the least. "It tastes like heaven. You're so generous, giving it away for free!"

"You're very welcome my dear. Sometimes it feels even better to give than to receive, especially when the gratitude is so heartfelt." Martha resumed her story.

"The baby woke and started spitting up. I was worried you'd choke, so I picked you up and burped you. The woman didn't notice—she was dodging some sort of invisible demons—so I bounced you up and down and told her I'd walk you around the block until you stopped crying. I'd done the same sort of thing dozens of times working in a daycare center. Anyway, when I returned to the lobby, she was gone. Just like that. I inquired at the reception desk. They wouldn't tell me her room due to privacy restrictions, but they had no problem sharing their web tracker. She'd been visiting a website for something called the Renaissance Mercernary childrearing center."

She paused and looked at Ellen, whose mouth gaped open. "So, I took you there. Right outside, a huge electronic billboard displayed ads about watching *Big Mother*, this ridiculous spin-off show at the time. The whole thing gave me the willies. Walking in, I saw a god forsaken hell hole. Babies were warehoused in cribs with video screens strapped across the top playing lullaby videos, or images of teddy bears or spinning toy mobile holograms. If a baby cried, the crib vibrated and rocked until a robot attendant could change their diaper or offer a nipple of baby formula."

"In the next room, one-year-olds sat on vinyl floors with touch-screens flashing words and pictures while computerized voices read aloud. They'd touch the screen and if they got a question right, out came this happy sound to make them giggle. Then the machine sprayed their face with a strange pink mist. They had automated childcare and passed it off off as a technical innovation to improve preschool STEM achievement."

After raising Luella in abandoned subdivisions surveilled by Pincertons, automated childcare didn't sound so bad to Oscar. *I mean, you were fed, air conditioned and clothed. A little dopamine spray ain't gonna hurt anyone.*

"The sole staff person confirmed you were enrolled and had me sign a waiver before whisking you away. I just stood in a state of shock when they pried you from my arms. There was nothing I could do.

"Three years later they told me to take you to an elementary childrearing center. Their computer system assumed I was either your mother or legal guardian since I had signed your waiver. Well, I didn't argue. I carried you away as fast I could. You've been at the convent ever since. That was the Lord's work, and only he knows what's in store for you next."

"So, her mom's in one of those decked out entertainment homes?" Oscar asked. "Where people just chill and watch screens all day?"

"I don't really know. I don't even know her name."

"I've never heard about those, but I'll start poking around online," Luella offered. "I'm pretty good at tracking people down,"

"Thanks, I guess," Ellen replied, still looking a bit pale.

CHAPTER 10
Caspian

CASPIAN'S IDRIVE PARKED BY A LUBYR WAITING OUTSIDE a 1970s-era mountain cabin. The car doors closed automatically with a "thunk" after he and Vanessa got out. The air smelled crisp, like Pine-Sol™. An azure sky seemed not only bluer, but bigger, than in West LA. Caspian failed to notice a western scrub jay alight on the gutter, ruffle its neck feathers as if shaking off a chill, and joggle its head. His thoughts were elsewhere.

The door opened before they reached the porch. Out came an unshaven teen, whose tan skin, cargo shorts, and swagger looked out of place amid the evergreens. A smaller person followed, with head encased in a VR helmet and feet clad in pink Chuck Taylors.

Vanessa greeted them, with "What up?" and some weird hand gesture. *A gang signal?*

"Huh?" Oscar asked, reluctantly returning the gesture.

Caspian gawked like a toddler. An automated Noodle search produced images of crack cocaine pipes and switchblades.

"Is Sister Martha or Ellen around?" Vanessa asked. "I want to introduce them to my friend."

"I'll go get them," came a voice within the helmet as it pivoted back toward the door.

"Smoke?" Oscar offered Caspian a cigarette.

"No, thanks. I . . . I only vape," Caspian stammered. Truth be told, he did go for the occasional cigarette to sooth his nerves during extreme stress, but this wasn't one of those times.

"Vaping's for wussies who can't handle the real deal, kinda like wine coolers," Oscar replied. It was a light-hearted jibe, yet it landed kinda sharp on Caspian.

"You from around here?" Vanessa adroitly changed the topic.

"No, down the valley in San Bernardino. I was just up here skiing. It's a long story."

"Cool. What do you do down there?"

"Oh, you know. A little of this, a little of that."

She took the opening. "Ever thought about starting a business? You gotta pay for those lift tickets somehow, right? I run a program for micro-entrepreneurs and we're thinking about expanding into San Bernardino." *Damnation,* thought Caspian. *She's good. But is this really the type of client we want?*

Oscar lit the cigarette and eyed Vanessa top to bottom while taking a drag. All but Caspian turned and listened to the jay's rustling wings as it took off. Oscar was about to answer Vanessa when Caspian figured he'd steer things in the proper direction.

"I'm providing funds for the program. What about a lemonade stand to sell OrangeSmash beverages? I'll hook you up with free dispensers, especially if you'd swap that Patriader cap for an OrangeSmash lid. You could use the proceeds for a virtual midnight basketball league or something."

"You shitting me Sherlock? That's whack."

Vanessa tucked her hair behind her ear. "It wouldn't have to be lemonade. We could pull together a community forum and discuss your neighborhood's needs." She was clearly trying to salvage the situation, but Caspian's insides felt all funny, like he got elbowed in the gut or something.

"Hey ,Vanessa," Ellen yelled, emerging from the convent with Sister Martha, Luella, and a mid-sized dog.

"Hey. This is Caspian Blaine. He's with the OrangeVine Founda-ation, which could help revive your community service project in San Bernardino." The dog sniffed Caspian's crotch.

"Nice to meet you, Mr. Blaine."

Caspian consumed Sister Martha's pudgy bronze hand inside his lighter brown stubby fingers with a vigorous squeeze. "Tell me about your proposal. Who's your project management consultant?"

Sister Martha began a lengthy backstory about organizing a thrift store that had provided families at the edge of poverty with discount clothing and household items. Caspian multitasked in a MyndScreen window, checking work messages and downloading a podcast as Martha explained the project's demise when people switched to disposable clothes. Plastic protruders made goods more cheaply than the nuns could resell donated items. He read a V-mail from Margery DeVrine scheduling a mandatory sexual harassment training, implying there had been unspecified "issues" in a certain department. *It ain't like that.*

Vanessa asked Martha questions as Caspian nodded vigorously and said, "Mmmm, hmmm." She jabbed her elbow into his rib cage and poked him in the chatter, "Pay attention! These are the people we're trying to help."

Vanessa explained how Aldo and the Sisters discussed a community garden to replace the thrift store.

"Mmnnn, hmmm."

"That's a new way to involve citizens," she added, nodding toward Oscar. "Now, we just need a location."

Luella removed her helmet so the dog could lick her face, which Caspian noticed was both adorable and mischievous. "Use our backyard. None of the other houses have people in them. We could tear down the fence and plant those yards too." Caspian lit up as he noticed Luella's helmet was a WhamZong GalExSee. That jolted him away from his multitasked virtuality.

"I'm sure there's an abandoned lot OrangeVine could purchase. That would be more accessible than some shady backyard situation and have street frontage for a farm stand. You could sell refreshments with the vegetables," he offered, simultaneously downloading the latest MarWell™ movie to keep racking up Zings. "We could build a community gaming center for people to enjoy after planting their carrots or whatever."

"Hey, Oscar," Ellen interjected, "You could grow tobacco, break away from the MarlBros, become your own operator. Just sell door-to-door instead of delivering orders for the gang."

"I could plant some strawberries," Luella interjected.

Before Oscar could respond, the dog jumped on his leg, having sufficiently slobbered Luella's face and needing a new target for enthusiastic greetings. When Oscar didn't bend down, the dog pulsated its hips against his shin.

"Stop it, Scout!" commanded a blushing Ellen. Sister Martha pulled the dog down by its collar.

Random noodle image searches appeared on Caspian's screen, baby orangutans in cute orange t-shirts, orangutans with huge lips wrapped around cigars, orangutans making obscene gestures with strawberries. "Pawp!" Caspian met his data absorption goal, earning more Zings. Unfazed by his virtual milestone or the dog's enthusiasm, he regained control of both his attention span and a conversation that clearly had gone off the rails. "I don't know, tobacco is a tricky one. On the one hand, the garden would provide education, jobs, and community connectivity. On the other hand, tobacco kills. We'd need to run some util calculations ascertaining if this really delivered the greatest good for the greatest number. Oscar, any idea how many community members would be uplifted by a project like this?"

"Huh?" Lines bunched up on Oscar's forehead. "Whatchu talking 'bout, Sherlock? I thought you were worried my neighborhood was too shady?"

"Don't worry," Vanessa assured. "I'll fill out Caspian's paperwork and we'll get something done. Martha, will the nuns sponsor the garden?"

"We'll ask the Lord for guidance. The convent must stay afloat financially, and our younger members could once again work with the community," she said, looking at Ellen.

And so, it began. In the coming weeks, Vanessa drafted a grant proposal for UpLyftingLives and the Sisters of San Bernardino to jointly oversee the SubDirt garden, hoping a community would sprout from the barren suburban landscape. At Caspian's urging, there would be orange trees. Other ideas included tomatoes, beans, lettuce, corn, grapes, and black-eyed Susan flowers.

Caspian and Sister Martha vetoed tobacco, provoking a side comment from Oscar about how "big ol' fat people never enjoy life. Whose garden is this anyway? The do-gooders or people in the hood who enjoy a good smoke?" Ellen gently reprimanded that it wasn't nice to body shame and suggested he find another location for his tobacco.

In other matters, Sister Martha relented and let Ellen activate a VR helmet she'd found among old thrift items. She told Caspian and Vanessa it was only for requesting Lubyr rides to the garden.

Caspian worked the system on the inside. When DeVrine blocked the project, he went straight over her head. Wallace Packard directly allocated funds from the OrangeSmash portfolio. *Progress, baby. Playing the game.*

He put out fires left and right after receiving a call from some big-shot lawyer named Celious Tudball. The guy was just absolutely frickin' furious that somebody installed malware on food extruders making them print out unbranded chocolate pudding. For free! That explained the bowl of poo.

Tudball melodramatically claimed his clients, Pepsoilent and CokAid, would go bankrupt if people learned to program extruders with home recipes instead of purchasing branded entrées. The companies evidently made all their profits on FlavrPaks, enough riches to subsidize unflavored soyalgent's free distribution. Caspian figured they made the unflavored product intentionally unpalatable, so Vues would get a makework job to afford a home extruder with some basic menu options. *What's the harm in freelancing a little flavor?*

"The Tribunal of Educates granted Pepsoilent and CokAid a global food production duopoly in exchange for providing the unflavored soyalgent dole," Tudball inveighed. The pudding malware infringed on their exclusive right to sell flavored food. *Whatever man.* Tudball blamed Caspian's Special Projects division, something to do with a Girls that Goad program. Caspian was pretty sure this was some ploy DeVrine drummed up to make him look bad. He sent Tudball's calls to voicemail and flagged his messages as spam.

Whenever he did a site visit, he'd find Luella playing with Scout. BoubToob videos helped her train the dog to roll over, play dead, and shake hands. *See, those GalExSee helmets are doing some good!* She searched Noodle for strawberry varietals yet was having a hard time buying them. In fact, every nursery in Southern California seemed out of business.

He received progress reports from Ellen and Vanessa, who'd been going door-to-door. They'd ask people what sort of vegetables they wanted. Most houses were vacant. When they'd finally found an elderly lady, she replied, "Gross. You mean soilborne food? I hear that stuff carries disease."

This wasn't going to be easy.

CHAPTER 11
Chase

CHASE WAS PISSED. HIS NOODLE SEARCHES FOR @BAD-Scootr's real identity kept drawing blanks. After being so easily duped, he wanted to know who the guy was and find a way to exact a pound of flesh in revenge. It would take months of gaming to regain the hit points and weapons he'd acquired. Unless, that is, he found a way to steal back the loot—and maybe a cycle to go with it.

The bug was back, crawling brazenly out of the HVAC vent. A reverse Noodle image search IDed the insect as a cockroach. Once labeled, it no longer bothered him. Live and let live. He could feel the ambient temperature slightly fall whenever he heard a faint hiss of the heat pump kicking in.

@BadScootr had not responded to Chase's nine direct messages congratulating him and proposing a duel to settle the score, but Chase could tell they'd been received. He'd been ghosted. A tenth message challenged @BadScootr's masculinity. "What sort of man are you? That girly move was below the belt. You owe me a shot at redemption." That provoked a response, "No do-overs in the real world, dood. BLOCKED."

Cut off from his assailant in virtuality, Chase schemed to track him down IRL. Like most players, @BadScootr didn't use a real name or likeness, preferring to fabricate a self-aspirational avatar instead of mundane actuality.

But Chase knew a few tricks. Using an inverse SpeiDrWeb tracker, he geolocated the IP addresses where @BadScootr logged in. He found something strange. There was an address near him, in San Bernardino, but also one in Oslo, one in Arlington, Virgina, and a fourth in Tel Aviv. @BadScootr seemed to physically reside in four cities simultaneously.

Further Noodling revealed a TrickiPedia page about cyberwarfare bots and virus spreaders using multiple IP proxies to conceal their origin. As he read, an ad popped up, "We'll bet 1,000 ByteDime you can't beat Grand Heist Otto's new Vegas avatar."

A bot! I was playing the game itself, not another player. Meta lame. They were probably beta-testing on me, running a sim from multiple locations to mask the AI. As when playing a supercomputer in chess, or gambling against the house, the algorithm always won.

Getting played by a machine left a shameful ember smoldering inside him. That slow burn ignited internal kindling he had smothered long ago, but never completely extinguished. The deeply buried memory of his wife.

Their marriage was never all that. They got along fine, and she found his bad puns charming. However, she was immersed in the metaverse before they married and that only deepened afterwards. She spent more time logged in than attuned to him. He'd been attracted by her wavy blonde hair, curvaceous body, and pink pouty lips. Her appearance IRL surpassed her online profile, even if her physique was somewhat enhanced through surgical body sculpting. They shared chemistry without climax. He was young then, bursting quickly onto the scene instead of slowly building a rhythm, stroking her in all the ways a woman wants to be touched.

One night, two motorcycle police knocked on his door. They had some bad news. His wife's minivan had veered off an overpass. She didn't survive.

Chase learned she'd been cheating for weeks, seducing her new flame with self-made AvaPorn™ in the Virtual Sex Liberation League.

She'd been going for their first hookup IRL. SpeiDrWeb tracking revealed her paramour to be a computer-generated PlaeGRL™ teddy. She'd been sexting a bot. If they'd actually met up, she'd have found only a disappointing server bank. Chase accessed her passwords and viewed the sordid details himself. She got played by the game.

He bought a motorcycle and dallied in relationships to distract from the shame. He became more thoughtful, a better listener, a better lover. Flings ended when his partners got upgraded—disappearing forever into an entertainment home. Chase suspected his entanglements with these women led to their upgrades. His physical pull took them out of the virtual world, out of the Chattersphere, out of the infotain marketplace. The attention merchants wanted them back, and they got them.

And then, there was Vera.

He felt down the crack between his 4D reality lounge cushions and rubbed his lucky penny. Two wheat spikes curved up the edges of one side, the other featured Abraham Lincoln in bas-relief. Grandad gave it to him the last time he'd visited, saying he wanted Chase to have good fortune. It was his sole physical remembrance of those pre-ByteDime days, before everything went cyber. He'd put the coin in his jeans pocket that final day he met Vera on the beach, hoping for the best. He'd kept it, even after their quote unquote rescue, treatment, and subsidized upgrade. It slipped from the pocket of his velour leisure suit that he wore to the entertainment home and slid into the seams of the lounge during his first 4D movie with vibration enhancement. He'd never bothered retrieving it, yet it was indeed lucky to have fallen out. His disposable clothes eventually disintegrated to tatters, leaving him naked in the Triple Ex entertainment home. He might be down and out, but at least he wasn't penniless.

Goddamn bots. First they take your wife, then they take your life. Better not dwell too much on it.

Chase eyed the plastic bowl, waiting patiently full of chocolate pudding. Would just one little bite ruin his stomach? Solid food must be like riding a bike, once your body learned digestion you never forgot, right? On the other hand, his 4D lounge's chem commode might not be up to the task if things got messy. Maybe not. A new episode of *Survive the Island* was starting.

It began with ash, falling like gentle snow. Pre-industrial villagers stood mesmerized, watching smoke and cinders rise from a volcano's caldera. There was nothing to do, nowhere to run, no way to evacuate the remote island.

Arguments broke out, finger pointing, and interrogations over who caused the volcano to awaken. Who angered the gods? Yet mostly, there was rubbernecking. People just stood and stared, enraptured by the eruption's sheer power and scale.

All except Jonah, that is. Childhood disease had left him extremely nearsighted. He saw cinders falling, but not the distant volcano. To keep ash off his hammock, he built a shelter from palm fronds and driftwood. He collected coconuts for tomorrow's meal.

While doomsaying villagers jeered that his little lean-to would never withstand the encroaching lava, Jonah continued his work. Better to do something than stand paralyzed in fear.

Their mockery devolved into chants, becoming rhythmic and soon accompanied by drumbeats with primal dancing. A mosh-pit of near naked humans ebbed and flowed around Jonah's shelter, writhing with nervous energy. Their frenzied parade snaked through the village, absorbed in euphoric mania. Chase figured they needed one last gulp of life before the inevitable befell them, just as it had befallen him. Better to have lived and lost than to never have lived at all.

Jonah removed his shirt and tied it around his face as a makeshift breathing mask while villagers scattered in panic, unable to avert their eyes from the glowing crimson river flowing down the mountain. As day passed to night, drifts of ash covered Jonah's encampment, burying his lean-to as snow blankets cars during polar vortexes.

A geyser of steam shot upward when magma reached the ocean across the island, forming a cloud of condensation that collided with cool air above. Raindrops fell on Jonah, turning ash into thick mud. His lean-to held firm, now as a gray adobe igloo.

When the glob of molten rock reached his village, it had spent most of its force. Slowing on level ground, sizzling slurry met Jonah's damp muddy shelter. The lava hardened just enough to push the oncoming flow around it to either side. Additional accumulation formed a bigger and bigger barrier around Jonah. He awoke to find himself surrounded by sweltering stone, with not a villager in sight. He ate a coconut.

Goddammit! The bug, the goddamn bug was crawling all over the pudding. A filthy disgusting cockroach. Just when he was working up the nerve to try real food, a critter ruined it.

Chase chucked the bowl against the wall, splat! He'd woken up pissed off and escalated to pure anger. Shutting his eyes, he tried dozing in his normal state of nocturnal oblivion. It was never really what you'd call sleep, given his screen's continuous projection onto his cerebral cortex. But tonight, it wasn't even rest. His internal embers flared.

CHAPTER 12
Aneeka

ANEEKA RANDALL WASN'T GETTING ANYWHERE. SHE WAS on her treadmill.

Thump, thump, thump. Footsteps rhythmically pounded the revolving black band while her heartbeat intensified. Her MyndScreen synched with the machine's ScenicSprynt™ SurroundGround to project Colorado's San Juan Mountains.

TellURyde™ inspired her awe not only for nature's majesty but also humankind's taming of the wild, harnessing its raw power for human consumption and pleasure. She saw the Ames hydropower plant, where Nikola Tesla's inventions had converted rushing water into smooth flowing alternating current. Rational science created the prosperity of 2065, which she must defend at all costs. This year, ScenicSprynt's live satellite imagery displayed no water in the streams. There had been no snowfall. Turbines at the Ames plant stood idle. Aneeka ditched the live imagery for a twenty-year-old archived scene to revive a rushing alpine stream and quaking aspens.

Wearing pink spandex tights and a translucent sports bra, her virtual coach urged her on. "C'mon Aneeka, take it up a notch!" The treadmill accelerated and a line graph prompted a sprint for two final minutes. She panted heavily, gasping for oxygen while sweat rivulets washed her temples. The avatar exulted, "you did it! Now, enjoy a nice cooldown and set your life goals for today." The rollers spun slower as inspirational quotes she uploaded years ago scrolled across her mental landscape:

"Prosperity is Freedom. Corporations are People. Educates Reign Supreme. You got this."

She recycled her sweat towel and pondered the slogans. She'd selected them from a motivational speech by prominent legal scholar Lewis Leon, long before he became an Educate. She'd been self-creating, self-affirming, her own reality with these daily quotes throughout her lifetime, her own personal mantra. Had Lewis Leon seen some early promise in her legal studies and provided these personalized quotes to guide her entire career? Or had he only identified her promise later, perhaps even because she'd selected those slogans from his public speeches? As a caustic mist of doubt again oxidized Aneeka's internal steel girder, she tried to recall where she first learned about the Tribunal. Probably at Stanford Law's Dead-Or-A-List Society, some two decades ago when the Piese Treaty was relatively new.

She hadn't actually practiced law since graduating, accepting instead a master's in psychiatry scholarship from John Hopkins and conducted extensive post-doc research on MyndScreen Side Effects (MSE). She then combined skills to provide mental public health therapy by explaining tribunal doctrine on the evening news. People were happier knowing a rational authority figure steered society's ship if they understood the rules. The Educates played that role in Globalia, and Aneeka's pundit therapist role helped Globalian consumers comprehend tribunal doctrine. This helped control MSE which left some individuals feeling inundated with infotainment and seeking escape into terrestrial reality. Had Leon lined up her scholarship, or secretly helped her land the psycho-punditry job?

When mass media therapy failed to cure every troubled soul suffering from (MSE), she administered individual care in the Department of Prosperity, which is where she'd encountered Vera. *Why did everything keep coming back to Vera?*

Aneeka washed her face. Keeping the tap open, she let the water recycle and refrigerate nearly a minute while rubbing her hands together and feeling clear cool liquid make her skin tingle. She ordered a BodyMindPro™ recovery drink from her home extruder and ran a Noodle search for "Piese Treaty."

"The Piese Treaty established the Globalian post-scarcity economic system following the War Unseen. A modern-day Martial Plan, this multinational trade agreement created the Tribunal of Educates, which is widely credited for ending the famine and economic collapse brought on by the war and the preceding Great Saturation. While its <u>original mandate</u> was confined to international trade protocols and tariff reduction, subsequent Tribunal rulings have expanded its authority over most aspects of economic and social activity."

Her imagination inexplicably piqued, Aneeka wondered what the original treaty looked like. With brow furrowed, she clicked the "original mandate" hyperlink and pulled up its complete text. Sipping her recovery drink, she ran a search for "Educates Reign Supreme" but came up with nothing. A similar query for "Corporations are People" returned zero results within the document.

Somehow Aneeka Randall had wound up on the Tribunal of Educates without ever studying its founding manuscript. Other Tribunal members must have read it. She could rely upon them. When individuals specialized in areas of personal strength, they combined into a more efficient and rational team than any one person alone. Rather than textual expertise, she brought public notoriety. Vues and Establishment members across Globalia knew and trusted her opinions due to her extensive media appearances. She had acquired a PPAR (Public Perception Asset Reserve) five times greater than any other Educate, yet that didn't mean she'd had time to get up to speed on every little detail about the whole enterprise. That was fine. She added value in her own non-fungible way. Educates like Roland Thompson brought a different perspective. Besides, everyone's ultimate purpose was to maximize personal fulfillment. Her Tribunal appointment fulfilled her, which in turn maximized societal value. The invisible hand of self-interest never failed.

Prosperity is Freedom. Corporations are People. Educates Reign Supreme. The words still hovered in her ScenicSprynt window, which she hadn't closed after her workout. Aneeka's dark amber eyes stared blankly into space as her mind fixated on those semi-transparent words floating inside her brain. She crooked her head sideways and the words momentarily tilted with her until her MyndScreen autocorrected the view and leveled them out once again.

Prosperity is Freedom. Corporations are People. Educates Reign Supreme.

Surely these concepts originated in the Piese Treaty even if the document didn't use those exact phrases. These quotes fed emotions, while Aneeka Randall worshipped reason. Emotions have a purpose. They can be helpful or deleterious. Negativity breeds harmful, unproductive behavior. She'd chosen these quotes to build esteem and self-realize her full inner potential. Now, for some reason she couldn't explain, she recalled a human phenomenon called confirmation bias she had studied in psychiatry. Was it possible her carefully curated identity had filtered out not only harmful emotions but also objective information refuting her constructs?

What if Vera was right?

A doubt. Dr. Randall diagnosed a self-doubt. This wasn't abnormal. Everyone experienced occasional symptoms of uncertainty. Overcoming doubt required objective rationality. And reason required information. Data. Knowledge.

Aneeka Randall vowed to read the entire 5,600-page Piese Treaty. She'd always envisioned it beginning with inspirational language—

something about self-evident truths, equality among people, creating a perfect union of nation-states to provide for the general welfare, secure international peace, and promote liberty. Instead, the pre-amble read:

The Nation-States of Globalia hereby resolve to:

ESTABLISH a comprehensive agreement that promotes prosperity through economic integration, liberalizes and maximizes trade and investment, raises consumption, ends scarcity, and relentlessly grows the economy;

STRENGTHEN the bonds of friendship and the sharing of culture and entertainment between them and their peoples;

ESTABLISH a predictable legal and commercial framework for trade and investment overseen by an educated and nonpartisan expert tribunal;

FACILITATE global trade with efficient and transparent customs and tariff procedures that reduce costs, ensure predictability for importers and exporters, and eliminate international and intersectional trade barriers;

RECOGNIZE the inherent right of each nation-state toward self-government and autonomy in such areas that do not impact global economic prosperity;

And so on, and so on . . .

A lengthy table of contents followed, a road map of articles and sections and paragraphs and subparagraphs and clauses and mind-numbing gibberish that overwhelmed the intellect.

After plodding through the definitions section for forty-five minutes, Aneeka needed a break. She opened up the evening news.

"Everyone remembers where they were that fateful day the world stopped working. Several thousand automobile accidents were reported when the 11G network used by driverless tech apps crashed inexplicably. For a full 214 seconds, Globalian consumption reached near zero levels. Security experts believe an evildoer cyber-attack caused last week's MyndScreen outage. A polymorphic virus known as Gonereater launched a denial-of-service incursion into Timeless Warning's 11G network. Virtual porn and dating apps like Cynder were targeted, mounting suspicion the attack originated from religious extremists. Wait, I'm getting breaking news ... " The anchorman pressed his fingers against his ear.

"Authorities now say the same evildoer cell is responsible for another virus causing unauthorized pudding production. Health experts suggest even a taste of this rogue pudding could poison your brain and strongly recommend against eating any unbranded food. The Tribunal of Educates is expected to issue anti-terror quarantine orders. In the meantime, users are encouraged to download the most recent SpeiDrWeb tracker to their MyndScreens and scrub their implants of any malicious notions. Back to you, Bambi."

Aneeka checked her inbox, worried a flood of attack-related messages had come in while she was exercising. There was nothing, only a VRoom reminder of tomorrow's meeting with her law clerks. *Odd.* If the Educates were expected to act, she should have heard about it. There would be an emergency briefing. Then again, this story hadn't run on the *Two-Minute Spate*—the only portion of the evening news certified as "completely true" by the Department of Information's fact checking protocols. Tribunal action might be pure speculation. Maybe the 11G attack didn't even occur and was just some conspiracy theory or excuse by Timeless Warning for botching their service delivery. Maybe that pudding wasn't really poisonous. She'd tasted it herself.

Gonereater. There was something about that word. She ran a search, "Did you mean gonorrhea?" was the top result. *Gonorrhea. That's what Vera was obsessed with.* The growing failure of antibiotics to treat gonorrhea sparked Vera's resistance to the whole infotainment regime, her heretical embrace of terrestriality. Vera's gonorrhea fact-checking is what got her thinking, got her exploring, got her doubting. Maybe Vera was somehow involved with this Gonereater virus.

For seventeen years, Aneeka had avoided contact. The therapist ethics code discouraged personal relations with a former patient. Besides, she wasn't sure communication would be healthy for either of them. Yet this was different. She was no longer a therapist, but in a crucial public position charged with Globalian safety and prosperity. If Vera could shed some light on a possible attack, it would be irresponsible to spurn her.

Aneeka knew Vera's Chatter profile. She could just ping her. "Hey there, how's it going?" The draft message hung in Aneeka's MyndScreen window a long time. She puffed on her Atlantis vigarette, rolled her fingertips over its embossed golden dollar sign logo, and squinted her eyes to hit send. The reply was instantaneous.

"You have been blocked from messaging with this user."

CHAPTER 13
Oscar

THINGS HAD WORKED OUT, SORT OF, WITH OSCAR BOR-rowing Luella's helmet to communicate with the MarlBros and their custoz. The GalExSee was a bit tight, so he didn't wear it longer than necessary, but at least he'd reconnected with his bruddas. That afternoon, however, had been a struggle. Despite her promise, Luella immersed herself in a game for hours. Pink high tops bounced on the hammock's edge, yet her body was immovable. "I'm in a multiplayer, Oscar . . . Stop distracting me . . . This is live, I can't just pause it . . . OMG! Go away Oscar, I'm crushing this loser . . . Dude . . . Just a few more minutes . . . "

"C'mon Lulu, you know I gotta do bizniz. Plus, I need to track the pincas. They've been thick as flies lately."

"Don't worry too much about them. I'll be done in a sec."

When she finally handed him the device, he saw a dazed look in her eyes. Her hands jittered and his impatience melted. "You know, sis, I'll be done soon. Maybe then you could log on to V-Classroom. You're a smart kid Luella, you could get somewhere if you wanted to."

"Whatever," came the reply. Then to his surprise, Luella she'd joined an online club where kids wrote computer code. Ellen was teaching her algebra before they knocked on doors gathering suggestions for the garden. "It's pretty useless, with all these formulas and stuff. But I kinda like it."

With the helmet battle over for today, Oscar caught a quick episode of his favorite old-time movie, where a British detective ensnares bad guys with the aid of a trusty sidekick named Watson. Then, after a quick

Cynder session, he picked up several cartons from Jerome and logged on to start dropping orders.

He looked a bit like a Mandalorian wearing a Jedi robe with his oversized hoodie pulled over the helmet. Oscar figured the semi-ridiculous look beat wearing the helmet unobscured, like a common Vue. He flipped his Patriader cap around, with the bill sticking out below the helmet. If he ran into a MarlBro, he'd remove the helmet and sport his proper lid.

A new Boi Banz song played in the background. *And then I saw her space . . . now I'm a V-leaver I wouldn't grieve her if I fried . . .* Luella must have downloaded their album while gaming. He let it play, distracting him from his jaw's subtle tightening as he looked up.

His AreoScan™ app surveyed the buzzing drone flock above. AI modeled each machine's trajectories, identifying which flying objects had a purpose more sinister than delivery. Oscar stood motionless until the app outlined three drones in flashing pink on his helmet's visor screen. *Pincertons.*

Surveillance drones hovered in place fifty feet above delivery copter altitude. They'd upload live video to the Klowd, enabling real time ground traffic analysis that identified typical rideshare cars plodding to a popular drop off location, going into a brief holding pattern, then off to pick up another passenger.

When Pincertons IDed a delivery trajectory, like a van stopping along a circular route, they'd analyze whether the vehicle belonged to ground-based courier companies. Flower deliveries, for instance, lost emotional value when airdropped in a box. Other items were too heavy to air drop such as five-gallon soyalgent bottles transported by FederalExcess™ crawlers. If a delivery was none of those, Pincertons scanned local Chatter traffic for bacco gang words like "smokes," "pack," "singles," etc. After finding a hit, the drones descended with signature pink "pincer" claws to etherize the perp when he left his vehicle and was vulnerable in the open air. The drones confiscated any contraband and sent faceprints off to SpeiDrWeb trackers and credit bureaus. Accounts would be frozen. MyndScreens disconnected.

"Hey," Oscar chatter-pinged custo @Vien99478, "Got 3 pincas hovering 2day. Can't wait outside your 🏠. Meet at Fewd-Court™ instead."

He'd thought about walking; the day was pleasant as winter rain gave way to spring breezes that cleared the sky enough to see downtown LA. The pincas changed his plan. A FewdCourt trip would track as a regular fast-food run, so he ordered a ride. Still unable to afford his own car, Oscar used rideshares both for drops and to mask his mission with plausible trips. While waiting for the Lubyr, he rummaged through the garage of the yellow ranch home he'd been squatting in. *A skateboard. A real fucking skateboard.* He'd seen 'em in video games but never ridden. Pincas probably weren't programmed to track one. *Why not try it?*

He let the Lubyr come and paid for the trip, leaving a trail of digital breadcrumbs the SpeiDrWebs could follow. Instead of getting in, he scooted off on the board. If he kept moving, he wouldn't get pinched.

At the FewdCourt, he took cover beneath a shade canopy and ordered a couple of liter-sized RaspberryFantastiks, a trackable purchase. His Chattertrak beeped when an older man walked out an adjacent condominium.

"Oscar? Is that you?"

"Oh yeah, sorry," he removed the helmet so the custo could see his face. "Want a drink?" Oscar offered @Vien99478 a soda while concealing two packs of cigarettes beneath the supersized cup. Given the shade canopy, this was probably an unnecessary precaution, yet he was nonetheless relieved the Pincertons stayed where they were.

"Thank you, Oscar. Thank you. I'm not used to seeing you wear a helmet. I didn't recognize you." His voice was soft, sincere. Vien lit a cigarette with an old-fashioned Zippo and offered one to Oscar along with a fifty-dollar bill folded in his palm. Contraband was the only remaining business still conducted with cash. The government couldn't track ByteDime transactions, yet everyone knew vaping firms bought cyber currency data to track down bacco dealers.

Inhaling deeply, Vien let the smoke slowly waft out his mouth's upturned corners and rise like a rivulet up his face, merging into the wispy tufts of white hair flowing from his head. A deep sigh exhaled the rest of the smoke. He glanced sideways to avoid blowing it in Oscar's face.

"This takes me back," he said, watching the cigarette smolder between his thumb and forefinger. Tension released from his cheeks and forehead while a spark lit up his eyes. Oscar watched him carefully place the pack into the pocket of a pressed yellow poplin shirt with oversized pointy lapels.

Just like that, the Pincertons descended. Also, every AmaZing! drone, every HawlMart™ drone, all of them dropped like hovering raptors nabbing their prey. Many landed right in the street, grinding Lubyr and FederalExcess traffic to a halt. Rotors stopped spinning, lights stopped blinking, even beeping proximity alarms went mute. It was stunningly quiet as Vien shrugged his shoulders with a "that's weird" expression clearly lacking concern.

The transaction was over and Oscar had fifteen more drops. With the pincas grounded, even temporarily, everything would be easier. But something about Vien's satisfied smile made Oscar linger. "When'd you first start smoking?" he asked.

"I was about 12. I stole a couple of Jackpot Menthols from my dad's glove compartment and shared them with a friend. That was back when we had our own cars, so you could store things like cigarettes, tissues, even maps. Have you ever held a map, Oscar? They were wonderful. You'd unfold them, spread them over your lap, and trace these little red road lines to figure out where you wanted to be. They were nearly impossible to fold back up, but that was part of the fun for a kid to see how many times it would take to do it. When you knew where you were on a map, you understood your place in the world. Your spot. It gave you a grounding, a bearing of where you belonged and maybe where you were going. Nowadays, you kids go from dropped pin to destination point with no idea where you came from. No idea who you are or who you're with."

'Whatchu talking 'bout, Sherlock?" Oscar prepared to stand up, yet Vien's smile disarmed him. His smooth, skinny hand pressed Oscar's forearm against the plastic table.

"Don't go. I meant no offense. I feel grateful to you Oscar. I sense something different about you. You've been dropping me cigarettes for the past two years, but today for the first time you looked at me as a person, not just a transaction. You came on a skateboard! You look like you know where you are, not just staring at your palm. You offered me a drink, Oscar. You asked me a question. It was delightful. I am sorry I offended you, I was only thinking out loud about young people these days, nothing specific about you. Please. Stay." He lit another cigarette and handed it to Oscar.

"What's the big deal about place? What are you even talking about?" Oscar's voice softened from defensive bristle to genuine query as he recalled failing to remember his own address.

"You once knew a lot about someone by where they came from. Sometimes a country, like my parents coming from the Philippines. In places within the United States, like Texas, people living together developed similar ways of talking, ate the same sort of foods, went to the same churches or restaurants. Now, you can get everything everywhere, so no place is distinct. People simulate personality with crazy food flavors, or vaping varieties, or fashion brands or gladiator sports teams, but in the and, everyone is the same. There are no unique groups holding us together, no culture, nothing to ground you except so-called brand identity. People can't understand the world without first understanding who they are. That once meant knowing where you came from." He took a long drag and held it in before a deep sigh sent up a cloud of smoke.

"You live here, right?" Oscar asked, finishing his soda.

"Yes, the third floor."

"So, what's that tell me about you?"

"Look around. Everyone here is about my age. We all moved in right after this building was protruded. We were mostly in our thirties then, and able to afford our own condo. After the Great Saturation, housing prices collapsed so everyone's underwater on our fifty-year mortgages. Nobody can afford to move, and really, nobody wants to as nowhere else would be any different."

"So, you're saying that if someone lives in this building, there's a decent chance they're about your age. That tells me something about them, what I might expect them to be like?"

"Yes, Oscar. It does. Or at least, it used to."

"Do a lot of 'em smoke, like you?"

"Yes, Oscar. When we were in our late teens or early twenties, a big vaping epidemic killed thousands from contaminated fluid, or unregulated THC and the chemicals they were putting in." Oscar wondered if this had something to do with his uncle's stern warnings against vaping after his parents died. As if reading his mind, Vien continued, "A lot of us switched to bacco then, even though it costs twice as much as V-cig fluid with all the taxes. That's why I buy from you."

"And you buy two packs a week?"

"From you, or one of your colleagues. The MarlBros send different people. Many times it's been you. You don't remember?"

"My memory's kinda funny these days, but to tell the truth I never paid much attention to my drops. They always felt pretty much the same, each place just like the next, you know."

"Yes, Oscar. I know," Vien paused, taking another long drag. "Oscar, I have an idea. What if I buy cigarettes directly from you instead of ordering online? Could you come by once a week, say every Monday morning at 11?"

"You mean here? At the food court?" Oscar wondered if the MarlBros would be OK with him running orders independently. If he could line up his own supply, he'd make twice as much without them taking a cut. They'd never notice one fewer custo, would they?

"There is a park bench across the street, Oscar. Let's meet there, under the oak tree. Every Monday. OK?"

"OK."

CHAPTER 14
Caspian

CASPIAN BLAINE WAS BUILDING HIS SYNCEDIN™ PRO-
file. OrangeVine's presidential search process was highly competitive. He
needed every possible advantage. Further, if DeVrine was picked, he'd
need a new job. His MyndScreen superimposed graphics over the office's
glass windows.

Caspian had 8,879 professional contacts. His personal performance
goal was 10k by week's end, a level granting gold star elite status. He
searched for McChesney™ employees and sent invitations to connect
based on a hunch that the management consulting firm would handle
OrangeVine's headhunting.

"Only connect with real people you know well," read the
disclaimer as he invited each one. *I know their type well.* After exhausting
the 335 profiles he had 3rd or 4th level connection to, he clicked a link
for "executive search" that appeared as a "related item" and saw 44,687
names scroll down his screen. *Damnation.* Click. Click.

HALexa offered advice. "Caspian, have you considered some
volunteer experience for your profile? Applicants with community
service in their bio have a 3.7 times greater chance of landing a top
executive position in the philanthropic industry."

Of course. "HALexa, pull up soup kitchen volunteer opportunities in
the greater LA region."

"I'm sorry, Caspian. AI indicates the last charity soup kitchen closed
in 2040. There was no demand once unflavored soyalgent went into free
distribution." The sterile man's voice in his head sounded only slightly

disappointed to report this news. Caspian remembered serving with his parents on Thanksgiving at local shelters in Brooklyn. People seemed to appreciate the companionship as much as the food. Now folks get lonely paste made from soy, algae, and lentils. *It's heartless.*

An ad popped up. "Time for a kitchen remodel? Let FabriGators™ resurface cabinets, appliances, floors and ceilings in just 48 hours." Then another. "Pepsoilent Chicken Sewp™. It's what real men eat for dinner."

Frickin' ads. Caspian closed the windows and tried concentrating on what he'd been doing, but his mind wandered. *Corporate Globalia has taken over our minds. Any wonder we've lost our hearts as well?* This thought auto-composed a Chatter post and his MyndScreen asked if he wanted to send it. *What the hell. Send.* It got two likes.

HALexa tried again. "You could try tutoring. Here's an online program needing mentors to life-coach kindergartners." Caspian pulled up the V-link and saw it didn't require physical attendance or possession of any particular knowledge. You merely touched base weekly in the chatter and paired kids with an appropriate virtual learning app, most of which were provided free through a CeleTeCharity partnership between AmaZing! and Tim Kardigan, a rising reality star whose signature look featured an argyle button-down sweater. Caspian signed up.

In another open window, an upbeat announcer teed up the latest Boi Banz hit, *Well I saw her space,* now *I'm a V-leaver. There's not a place, for doubt in my mind.* He saved the mentoring V-link in his browsing history and checked his work feed.

Message 18 was from the Vice President of a Nigerian Bank. His client suddenly passed away and instructed him to transfer the account to Caspian. He just needed Caspian's bank routing number. Delete. Message 93 was from an Arkansas senate candidate clearly pandering to Spryte supremacists in the branding wars. Delete. *Who cares about the U.S. Senate anyhow.*

Caspian looked out at seagulls soaring over the ocean. *As OrangeVine president, I could change the stupid twenty hour in-office monthly work requirement. On the other hand, the view doesn't suck.*

Message 179 was from a Long Beach nonprofit wanting inhalers to give overstimulated children BrainSoothe™, a pharmaceutical to calm seizures induced by game helmet immersion. He sent that one to a junior program officer for vetting.

It was 2:35 p.m., time for his weekly marketing team VRoom. They wanted a custom 3Demoji for chatter sharing, as focus groups indicated people wouldn't share messages containing OrangeVine's lengthy name. Evidently it ate too much into their bandwidth limits. The Board Chair preferred a 3D citrus emoji with a green vine on top. Margery DeVrine noted oranges didn't actually grow on vines. The Chairman's avatar frowned. Caspian downloaded the draft 3Demoji and saved it in his Klowd. *Back to work.*

Message 309 was from the University of FreeNicks™. "Ever considered an EMBA? Our self-paced program gets you a certified Executive MBA in just four months. Download lectures at your leisure and work problem sets on your commute." Caspian kept that V-mail open and flagged it for follow up.

Message 313 was from Barron Koldwill, the realtor Caspian tasked with finding a vacant lot for Vanessa's community garden. "Hey, I've got you a site. Abandoned gas station, great location. Just minor contamination, so sellers ready to accept rock bottom pricing. Site cleanup would take 17 months. Did I mention prime location? Great for a ♡aid extruder stand."

"Need something shovel ready in <1 month," he shot back. "Timing> price."

"Whoa. Not sure any process can move that fast. This is real estate, not AmaZing!"

"Maybe I need a new realtor. Find a site ASAP. Can incorporate a rush fee if you find a way to expedite. Get creative or get lost."

"Roger that, boss." Koldwill's avatar winked.

It was 3:27 PM and his final VRoom had ended. Caspian needed a break. He walked down the hall, tapping his fingers against his thigh to the Boi Banz tune. The elevator smelled of Pine-Sol as it took him to the ground floor extruder cafe, one of the few locations in LA still offering OrangeSmash beverages. He wanted to support the marginalized brand; he just wished it tasted a little better. As Caspian waited for his drink to print, VP Margery DeVrine stepped out of a Lubyr carrying a half-empty cup of Pepsoilent Eyeced Koffy—not OrangeSmash.

"Caspian, you wouldn't believe what just happened. My town car was surrounded by downed drones. GPM said they lost control tower communication and activated an emergency landing procedure that plopped them down wherever they were." She spoke in a rushed cadence, with more volume than a watercooler conversation seemed to require. *Why's she being so open?*

"The car didn't crash, but I was stuck by an old schoolyard where sweaty Vues played basketball, of all things. Basketball! I had nothing to do but stare at them for hours, at their menacing abs and chiseled triceps. It was carnally mundane. Then, the hunkiest, most menacing one with gleaming skin and majestic brown eyes let all the air out of my car's tires while giving me this weird grin. It was absolutely p-paralyzing. I had to grab a Lubyr like a common Vue."

"Yeah," he suppressed a smirk. "Drone tech can be a drag. Sometimes it feels like it's hurting more than helping us. Hey, did you catch the new episode of virtual *Big Brother* last night? I think there was a glitch in Leticia's algorithm. She kept looping through the same mindless dialogue about her bikini top being too tight."

"Um, I was watching Daze of our Lives, actually. I'll catch BBV on archive tonight." He noticed she kept looking past either of his shoulders as they talked. His eyes tracked down to the plastic Pepsoilent cup she tried concealing in her hand. He snapped a 3D image onto his MyndScreen. DeVrine gave him a cold stare and said she was off to a meeting, but it was great to see him and wasn't the weather nice these days. She hurriedly chucked the half-full Pepsoilent Eyeced Koffy into a recycling chute before entering the elevator.

As he rode back to his office, Caspian pulled up the 3D image of Margery DeVrine holding a half-empty Pepsoilent cup. He photochopped a selfie of himself with an OrangeSmash MochaTangerineBlizzard™ in hand right next to the VP and posted it to the chatter. "Always nice to bump into a colleague on an afternoon OrangeSmash run. #TeamCaffeine!" He inserted the draft 3Demoji of an orange with a green vine coming out the top. Then, he tagged Wallace Packard and the chairman of the OrangeVine board just to make sure they saw how group-oriented everyone was at the office.

Back at his walnut desk, Caspian kept inbox churning. Message 1172 was from AmaZing! Could he please rate the LiquorIce™ V-cig fluid he ordered last week? Caspian had poured the juice on the ground the day it arrived. He knew how to play the game. Maintaining heavy purchase patterns kept the SpeiDrWebs from flagging you as insufficiently consumptive. He'd seen it happen, particularly to people questioning the infotain treadmill's meaningfulness. Caspian had plenty of questions himself. He also had answers. Resist in small steps, keep your head down, stay below the radar. Any drastic change in consumption could lead to an upgrade. It took just two seconds to give the V-cig fluid four out of five stars. When prompted to reorder, he chose a different flavor.

Message 1799 was from someone he knew from high school. If Caspian didn't forward the V-mail to seven close friends, he'd lose a chance to win a trillion ByteDime. Delete. Message 2048 was from Educate Aneeka Randall. "Mr. Blaine. I've been following your posts a long time. We haven't all lost our hearts along with our minds. There's something I need to ask you."

Caspian startled as a seagull dived to avoid a HawlMart drone and crashed into his office window. Bam!

CHAPTER 15
Chase

CHASE WAS RETOUCHING HIS AVATAR. HE'D CHOSEN A twenty-year-old selfie and adjusted the warmth to produce a nice suntan. He used Anti-Fatify™ to sharpen his cheek bones and jawline just a bit, telling himself he's probably thinner now on the carefully dosed IV diet. Had there been a mirror, he'd have seen things were far worse than he imagined. He was skin and bones, minimally maintained with the cheapest doses of drip soyalgent required under his entertainment home contract. Using a healing tool, he erased a skin blemish on his avatar's forehead, which truth be told was still there. His fingers knew his hairline had further receded while the ends had grown considerably since the image was taken, yet he kept the avatar's dirty blond mullet as it was. He finished it off with a smoothing filter, fading out the crow feet wisdom lines that had accumulated on the sides of his eyes even as a younger man. *Nobody likes a wise guy.*

The cockroach was back, scurrying underneath the IV bag. His anger over its pudding trespass had subsided; however the incident got him wondering about eating real food, solid nourishment. Could he handle it?

"Hey buddy," he greeted the roach, which had scurried up the IV stand, down the little plastic tube, up his arm and right across his chest. *Brazen little bastard!*

With a camera icon click, he uploaded the new avatar into his Chatter bio. An algorithm then flashed an old photo of him on a motorcycle, a shit-eating grin spread across his face. "Would you like to re-

share this highly liked memory from your previous posts?"
He grimaced upon seeing the virtual sex liberation league tattoo on his
right bicep. It was a decoy, intended to provoke routine sexting thought
patterns in his terrestrial lovers. They'd then register normal activity on
the Sexual Liberation League app, which the SpeiDrWebs would track.
This emotional masking provided the cover necessary to engage in real
life romance without triggering any alarms, any upgrades. His grin faded
to mist as he further studied the image and saw "I ♥ U V" scrawled in
red lipstick on the cycle's headlamp. He'd put it there, seventeen years
ago. It was a pickup line.

The V, of course, stood for Vera. He'd first encountered her the
day before he scribbled the lipstick love note. She'd been transfixed in
a driveway moment while listening to Globalia Public Media. When she
shot a furtive glance his way, a gleam in her eyes revealed a yearning
for something real in her life. He remembered the petrichor scent
of springtime air as he sat on his parked cycle, spying on Vera as she
listened intently to the morning news with a furrowed brow, as if it
actually mattered. He could tell she was someone who noticed things
IRL. Someone who cared. He'd known right away he'd need to go big if
he wanted her affection and he'd been right. He'd also thought he was
savvy enough this time around to avoid the fate of an upgrade, where
his lover's enchantment with the physical world led the infotain industrial
complex to reclaim its bounty. There, he'd been wrong.

He'd planned to keep things on the down low but was foiled when
that goddamn Aneeka Randall goaded Vera into full rebellion. He'd
tried to warn her, but a force greater than his own pulled her relentlessly
toward insurrection. He'd not only failed to protect Vera, he sold her out
by consenting to his own upgrade after they'd both been tracked. That
she had also consented didn't lessen his betrayal. He knew she'd never
want to see him again, even if she had been capable of seeing things

in RL anymore. His insides churned with the motorcycle image flashback, but he pinned it to his profile anyhow. *I'll remember. They won't take that from me.* He reached into the crevice of his 4D lounge and rubbed his lucky penny.

His MinuteMayd rolled in. "Good morning Chase, how are you viewing today?"

"I'm fine Diri." He was about to complain about the cockroach and ask the Triple Ex to send an exterminator, but something held him back. Instead, he replied, "Maybe I'll try watching the big game in a bit." It felt silly, yet small talk with his auto attendant was the only RL social interaction he had, other than the bug that is.

"View or view not," the MinuteMayd replied. "There is no try." Chase felt like he'd heard that before. "Meanwhile, it's time for a fresh set of sheets."

He'd have to get up. His 4D entertainment lounge massaged his legs and lower back to get some blood flowing into his muscles before raising him into a nearly upright position. He heard the climate control system kicking in to warm the room so he'd be comfortable standing naked a few minutes while the bot changed his bed. The air had an acrid smell of singed dust. He pivoted and the bed lifted him into a standing position.

His legs felt shaky; it had been a month since his last bedding change. The legs held up just fine. After standing sixty seconds, Chase took a step, just for grins. *No problem.* He took another. *Do or do not, there is no try!*

With one hand on the wall for balance, he found he could walk around the perimeter and still stay clear of the MinuteMayd as it tossed the old sheets into the recycling chute. He looked down, concentrating on one foot placed in front of the other. In three steps, he reached the open doorway and the gap forced him to withdraw his hand. Standing solidly on two feet, Chase experienced the slight pressure of the floor pushing against his toes and heels. *I got this.* A toothy smile spread wide when he celebrated his first lap around the pod. By twenty steps, the training wheels came off and he went for his third lap. He looked up, staring at the virtual windowscreen on the wall playing the same 17-year-old beach volleyball video loop.

When the bot left, he returned to the lounge and re-entered virtuality. He opted to "view not" the big game and instead went out to mingle. He put a fresh outfit on his avatar and skimmed the trendy topics of the day. Millions of posts pontificating about emergency drone landings flooded his feed; who cared? He'd never again go outside. He delved instead into thousands of unilateral conversations about "potatoe." The word trended when Idaho's governor corrected a post by a presidential candidate, a senator from Alaska who fawned over a photo of a baked russet potato wrapped in tin foil with sour cream and chives on top. Chase thought it was an interesting move politically, clearly pandering for the older vote by using nostalgia to build affection for her floundering campaign. A few Chatter accounts speculated whether it was actually a dog-whistle dig at soyalgent extruders—direct praise of soilborne produce running contrary to the politically correct notion that such foods were dirty and unsanitary.

Not to be upstaged, the Idaho governor, who was obviously preparing a last-minute presidential bid herself, chastised the Alaskan with a reply, " 😞 It's spelled potatoe, you moron." The reply drew 44 million likes and 27 million rechats, even after dozens of fact-checking journalists pointed out the word is correctly spelled "potato" and labeled the Idaho governor as "pants on fire." She fired back that the "Fake views media is so politically correct and one-sided they are censoring the speech of a duly elected public official. That's Communist! It's Orwellian!" This post generated 69 million likes.

You spell potatoe, I spell potato, let's call the whole thing off. Chase grinned and sent his hot take out to Cyberia. Six people liked it.

He checked each fan's profile. One was Francesca by name, who loves to laugh and have a good time with friends. Another was @Ihib22763, who had just won the Globalian lottery and was seeking investment advice. Then there was @Sanjool, a graphic designer producing amazing results. Fourth was @Seeker, who lived in paradise lost, was into crab bakes on the beach and enjoyed Oscar Wilde audiobooks. *Huh?* She had a generic gray square with a 3D white orb for a profile avatar, so one couldn't be sure if it was a bot, a newbie, or someone overly secretive who was chatting incognito.

Chase poked the account gingerly, "So, how do you spell it?"

"It's potato, as you know," @Seeker replied. "Not that anyone will believe you."

Chase felt a chill shoot up his spine. Maybe it was the allure of meeting a new and mysterious person in virtual space or a new feature on his entertainment home 4D lounge that simulated the shivers with cooling jets embedded in the cushion. Either way, he was willing to play along.

"Ah, well, many things are not as they appear to be. Spelling is no acception."

"Speaking of that, how do I know you are who you appear to be, Chase?"

"You don't. You can't. Let's chat anyway. Uncertainty has its own rewards."

"What do you do for a living?

"I guess you could say I'm retired, if you can call that living."

And so began a virtual "relationship," the likes of which Chase had been through more times than he cared to remember. Velationships (his name for them) were a slower paced game than Grand Heist Otto, and less predictable—at least once you vetted your counterpart to ensure they weren't a bot or a fraud. The investigation was part of the game. Indeed, Chase felt that probing the true nature of another person, either human or corporate, was one of life's great pleasures.

CHAPTER 16
Aneeka

ANEEKA RANDALL WAS STUCK. THE CONUNDRUM DEFIED
her inexorable objectivity.

She wanted to know, *needed* to know, what had become of Vera. Was
her treatment a success? Was she better off now than prior to entering
the care of Dr. Randall? Was she happy? Since Vera had blocked her,
there were no answers.

These questions themselves defied logic. *What does a two-decade old
case matter to my current happiness and self-interest?* Then again, maybe they
were rational. If her mind, her ego, her "self" or whatever you chose
to call it, wanted these answers, didn't she deserve them? There was
nothing wrong in fulfilling her desires, her curiosities, whether or not she
articulated a reasonable basis for them. *Was there?*

Several times, Aneeka tried recalling their final session, where
she released Vera from her care and presented the option, not the
requirement, for an upgrade and accompanying lifetime placement in
a top-rated, fully subsidized, entertainment home. She'd conducted
thousands of discharge interviews over the years. While Vera's was an
especially challenging case, the details of any one session or another
blurred together to make distinct conversations indiscernible. She was
pretty sure Vera had been ready, even eager, to accept her next step in
recovery. Treatment protocols indicated a patient with Vera's symptoms
should statistically have been in full recovery after Aneeka's therapy. It
must have worked. While "pretty sure" had been good enough when Dr.

Randall was practicing psychiatry, it no longer satisfied Educate Randall. She needed to be entirely sure. And she wasn't.

Had her mind been less cluttered with facts, with education, with legal doctrine, Aneeka Randall might have remembered Vera steadfastly refusing an upgrade. She'd only consented after treatment in the Situation Room, an hours-long personal metaverse experience simulating the birth of Vera's daughter and her subsequent inability to care for the infant. The baby was taken into protective services. Vera got visitation rights at her high school graduation only to learn her child no longer recognized her. This never happened, of course. Yet the Situation Room was so powerfully realistic, Vera believed it would. In fear, she accepted an upgrade and delivered her baby to a childrearing center in exchange for the promise that MommyForever™ technology would perpetually broadcast her likeness into the child's brain.

Because the human mind can only retain so much, Aneeka did not remember this. Inattentional blindness. That's what they'd called it in grad school. Brain overload.

As with every patient, Dr. Randall had recorded Vera's discharge interview on her MyndScreen treatment journal, a more efficient and accurate protocol than handwritten notes. She'd recently tried downloading the archive from her Klowd and received the following error: "File corrupted due to excess data. Please remove files from your storage system or upgrade your capacity and then re-install your recollection."

There was no way to restore her recollection. It had left the long-term memory index in her brain's hippocampus. She couldn't just relive the experience for her MyndScreen to re-record. The memory resided only in her now-corrupted Klowd. *Dammit.* She'd have to find another way.

Meanwhile, her workload was demanding.

The Educates received yet another emergency security briefing, this time about what defense analysts termed Downed Drone Syndrome. Air traffic control towers had been hacked and a forensic SpeiDrWeb trace identified a suspicious IP address in Southern California. Pincertons were hovering in location until the perp entered a clear space. After apprehension, the case would be expedited for Tribunal trial, bypassing local law enforcement. Prosecutors prepared their arguments. Other Educates prepped their clerks for emergency procedures.

Educate Randall, however, remained focused on the Tribunal itself. VRooming with her law clerks, she sought help. "Guys, I've been reading the Piese Treaty for days and the legalese puts me to sleep. It's even duller than *A People's History of Globalian Thought and Truth*. Have any of you read it all?"

"Of course not," replied her clerk from Harvard™. "It's too long. Nobody's ever read the whole thing, not even the world leaders who signed it. Nexus AI has read it. Just search for the paragraphs you need regarding any relevant case. Bots can find a useful citation for just about anything."

"OK, can you show me where it says that corporations are people? You know, that they have the same Tribunal rights as living human beings?"

"Well, not exactly," explained the clerk who studied at Oxford™. "That's a U.S. Supreme Court interpretation of the U.S. Constitution's fourteenth amendment. It's not in the Piese Treaty, but just like the Magna Carta, it's still good case law, theoretically speaking. Surely you remember the Constitution from law school."

"You mean the amendment granting equal rights to former slaves in the United States? What does that have to do with corporations?"

"It required equal protection under the law. In an 1886 railroad taxation case, the U.S. Supreme Court reasoned this meant equal protection for corporations too. Except the opinion didn't actually say this, a clerk just tucked it into the summary notes. Everyone went along with it, so the concept was folded into precedents universally acknowledged by the Piese Treaty. Tribunal Doctrine has been affirming it ever since. Some radicals question corporate personhood, which on its face *is* a little counterintuitive. But realists understand any alteration in this precedent would be unduly disruptive to the economic structure. There's no way to change it without inviting calamity. Just look at what happened with Downed Drone Syndrome. If we don't protect corporations and machines with the same rights as humans, they're vulnerable to attacks that grind society to a halt. We rely on corporate personhood for almost everything, even keeping traffic flowing."

"I see. So, where does it say the Educates Reigns Supreme? I mean, what if somebody, acting only out of ignorance, didn't understand one of our dictates and challenged our authority?"

"Oh, it doesn't actually say that either. The Tribunal established its own supremacy in the case *Marlboro v. Mattison*, where a Canadian army general banned cigarettes on military bases. In the old world, that was the prerogative of any member nation state within Globalia. However, the Tribunal concluded world peace, and ensuing prosperity, required strong militaries and therefore soldiers must have universal rights to smoke. So, they overruled the Canadian government."

Aneeka felt she must have learned this in law school. It was foundational. Then she'd gone on to psychiatry and there's only so much one can keep in your head. Her clerks had freshly minted legal minds, uncorrupted with information overload. She could rely upon them.

"It's a bit ironic now since almost nobody smokes tobacco, yet there you have it," continued the Oxford clerk. "That precedent established the Tribunal as supreme interpreter of the Piese Treaty – the highest court on the globe so to speak. The Educates have authority over the most powerful militaries, therefore also superseding nation-state legislative and executive branches. That's why we're all here. This is where everything goes down."

"I see. What if some members of the Tribunal wanted to change all that?"

"That would make for a pretty interesting legal brief!" replied Barry Kramer, her clerk from the University of Chicago. A pained look of shock seized the other clerks' avatars, one of whom stopped sharing her screen after gasping and spewing Koffy everywhere. Aneeka made a mental note that this Kramer fellow showed some promise.

"Are you perhaps being unduly influenced by Ms. Huerta's testimony?" the clerk from Harvard asked. "I ran Noodle Scholar search on her closing diatribe and found a verbatim match with Ayn Rand. She plagiarized that whole part about socialism, which is intellectual theft you know. You should read Timeless Warning's response brief." The clerk linked the document in the chat.

"OK, that's all for today. Thanks everyone." Aneeka signed off. She paused her avatar, slipped on a silk kimono, and washed her face and hands. The vanity mirror cam above her sink sent a MyndScreen image of a woman much older than she felt.

Educate Randall delved into Timeless Warning's brief:

> Given the highly unorthodox arguments put forth by defendant, Dagny Huerta, Timeless Warning advises the Tribunal Ms. Huerta has no legal right to own the Grand Canyon. Her purchase, pursuant to the Public Lands Firesale Act, amounted to an illegal taking of U.S. Government property that was only offered for auction due to extreme financial stress caused by the Great Saturation and the ensuing War Unseen. With the global economic collapse, the U.S. government was under duress, therefore its sale of public property cannot be legitimately viewed as a fair and binding contract between two rational parties. Moreover, much like the doctrine Ms. Huerta is surreptitiously advancing through dubious legal strategies,

radical environmentalists at the time of its purchase claimed any sale of such a rare and priceless landscape was an inherent violation of the natural rights of all people. Therefore, even if the Tribunal finds that Ms. Huerta's purchase of the Grand Canyon was a legitimate transaction under U.S. law, it must void the purchase under natural law.

Should the Tribunal uphold Ms. Huerta's ownership of this pristine public viewscape, plaintiff notes the Tribunal is not a government entity. Rather, it is a public-private partnership formed to enhance global peace and prosperity by promoting economic trade and commerce. Since neither the Tribunal nor Timeless Warning is a government, plaintiff's petition for free and unfettered access to our transmissions cannot possibly be socialist as suggested in Ms. Huerta's hyperbolic diatribe. Socialism, by her own definition, is government ownership of property and we're clearly talking here about Timeless Warning's private ownership of a private 11G broadcast tower.

Moreover and furthermore, because Ms. Huerta's actions pose a mortal threat to global prosperity and the ensuing domestic and foreign tranquility deriving from such bounty, Ms. Huerta is indisputably the socialist in this instance. She is the one silencing Timeless Warning's freedom of speech. She is the communist blocking the Myndcast of dissenting voices to Grand Canyon hikers. Given the clear meaning of her treasonous monologue, plaintiff respectfully requests the Tribunal strike Ms. Huertas's radical commentary from the record in order to protect the sacred freedom of speech.

Radical commentary? "Prosperity isn't freedom. Freedom is Freedom." Dagny's words haunted her. Aneeka resolved to not let them go. She was going to meditate on them, live them, breath them until she understood them and either accepted, or refuted them definitively. She dipped her finger in the unsolicited chocolate pudding still sitting on an end table and scrawled the words on her living room wall in fudgy letters. "Prosperity isn't freedom. FREEDOM is freedom."

CHAPTER 17
Oscar

"THIS IS GONNA BE LAME, OSCAR. WHY DRIVE AN HOUR for something we can do in a TwirlChair sim at the Metaverse Legacy strip mall?"

Oscar was taking his kid sister out to Knott's Berry Farm, the only amusement park still terrestrially open once Disneyland converted to a metaverse accessed exclusively by non-fungible tokens. Bacco bizniz had been good and he felt like blowing some of the cash in his pocket. So, he needed a place that still took cash.

The downtown skyline loomed ahead, the older buildings with glass windows and metallic frames reflecting sunlight like fish scales. New buildings, with plastic I-beams and Plexi windows printed ground up by massive construction protruders had a duller matte surface, like giant gray Lego™ blocks. Looking down, yellow lines tipped with reflectors sunk in asphalt blurred by while clouds above stood still as skyscrapers. A Pincerton flock buzzed by.

"Trust me, it's better. Wind rushing through your hair feels different than a TwirlChair fan blowing in your face. The G-force of a coaster is more fanta than little bumps in a VR sim. Besides, you need some fresh air."

"If you want fresh air, get a motorcycle. The pincas couldn't track your bacco runs 'cause they're only programmed to monitor cars, delivery vans, pedestrians and IP addresses. You could give me rides on the back!"

Oscar wasn't too thrilled about driving his kid sister around town. However, he wouldn't have minded giving Vanessa a ride now and then, taking corners fast enough she'd hold on to him tight. "How am I gonna find a cycle, even if I could afford one, Lu? 'Sides, where do you need rides to anyhow?"

"To see Ellen. She's invited me up for foosball at the convent. You could come too."

"Gimme a break. The last thing I need is to be seen hanging out with nuns."

"She's not a nun, at least not yet. I'm not sure she really wants to be one. Hanging out with real girls wouldn't hurt you, unlike those Cynder avatars. You know I can access your browsing history on my helmet, right?"

"Mind your own bizniz, Lulu. Anyhow, if you find me a motorcycle on the cheap, I'm all for it. In the meantime, get real. Let's just enjoy our trip to Knott's, OK?"

"Whatever." She put on her helmet and gamed while the car drove west on the FiredStone expressway. It looked to Oscar like the Pincerton flock was following them, but going to an amusement park was about as normal a consumption pattern as it got, so he wasn't too worried. He hadn't even brought any bacco with him.

Out of habit, he tried streaming some tunes. Then he remembered his MyndScreen was down, so he manually flipped on the Lubyr's Serious™ playlist. *When I'm driving in my car and the man comes on the radio, he's telling me more and more about some useless information, supposed to fire my imagination . . .*

"That was the number one hit one hundred years ago," cut in an overly enthusiastic DJ. "'Satisfaction,' by the Rolling Stones. Up next, intern Jeffrey reveals which flavor of CokAid toothpaste survey respondents say is best before a second cyberdate." Oscar turned it off and stared out the window for the remainder of the drive. The silence was mesmerizing, even satisfying in its own way.

Once at Knott's Berry Farm, they breezed through a maze of red velvet stanchion rope that once funneled thousands of visitors through the entrance. The ride lines were also non-existent. Luella complained she felt like an idiot wearing her helmet to stream the AV effects. Nobody else had one. All the cool teens had implants now.

On a slow and bumpy ride up a steep coaster incline, she reached her WhamZong's weekly screen time budget. "Oh well, I'll just extend my limit."

"Ya know, Lulu, I oughta put some parental controls on that thing. Just sit back and enjoy life for a moment."

"You're not my parent, Oscar. You don't get to start acting like one." Still, she powered the helmet off.

Oscar noticed the pinca flock freeze in place while the coaster zoomed down the tracks. His yelps and screams as they rocketed around the track embarrassed his sister beyond belief. "You're becoming such a dork!" she yelled.

It was so much fun he rushed to hop on before the ride took off again. Only after buckling in did he notice Luella wasn't by him. The coaster took off on another gut-wrenching loop around curves, up inclines, and stomach lurching drop-offs. He got off and walked around semi-dazed for 30 minutes before finding Luella sitting on a curb, her helmet cradled in her arms. She was sobbing.

"Lulu, where were you? I've been looking all over."

"What do you mean?" she screamed. "I turned around and you were gone, Oscar. Just gone. You're always ditching me."

He reached for a cigarette but had none. A deep breath had to do. "Hey, I'm sorry, sis. My bad. Really. I just got caught up in the moment."

"Whatever."

He wanted to put his arm around her, offer some comfort, yet knew that would backfire. He really did care about her, he wasn't such a bad guy, but nothing would make her believe it. "I'll make it up to you. Let's get a treat."

At the food extruder court, they waited for the first time all day. CokAid was debuting a new MylkSheik™ flavor, available exclusively at Knott's Berry Farm for the next 36 hours. Unlike the entrance, no barricades corralled visitors toward the overtaxed machine. It ran out of soyalgent, just like that, and needed a bot service refill. While Luella and Oscar joined the impatient gaggle of visitors underneath a shade canopy, a boy who looked to be about ten plowed in from the side and inserted himself directly in front of them. Luella yelled "Hey, no cutting!" The kid ignored her.

Offended not only at the queuing foul but more so by his complete indifference, she poked a pink Chuck Taylor lightly behind his knees, buckling the kid's legs out from under him. He silently turned his head to see what force of nature had taken him down. "I said, no cutting!" Luella repeated. He gave her a blank, wide-eyed stare.

"He can't hear you!" His mother rushed over with two wads of electric blue Kotten Kandi™ in one hand and a graphite Gucci™ bag in the other.

"Melvin's a telepath," she gasped. "He doesn't use physical speech. He was implanted at birth and communicates exclusively in the chatter. The parts of his brain normally devoted to physical speech and hearing developed more advanced functions since he doesn't utilize them for primitive vocalizations."

"Huh?" Luella blurted. Oscar tried to Noodle search "telepath" only to be reminded again that his own implant was bricked. "I thought you had to wait 'till 13?" Oscar knew she'd been counting the days until her next birthday.

"Vues like you may not be familiar with this cutting-edge policy, but someday every child will benefit. Ever since the 2050 deregulation era, gifted and talented babies have been MyndScreen eligible through a special CeleTeCharity venture. It accelerates their data absorption curve at least three grade levels. Infant implantation is the only way we'll compete with Chinasia's rapid STEM learning progress."

"You mean," Oscar interjected, "that your kid can't even talk to people and that's somehow a technological breakthrough?"

"Of course, Melvin talks, he just uses his implant instead of vocal chords. He communicates at quadruple an auditory speaker's rate and doesn't experience background noise and distractions from outmoded eardrum input. Check your chatter and you'll see he's pretty annoyed your daughter cut him off at the knees."

"She's my sister. And I'm offline. My implant broke."

"How dreadful! Your disability must be so challenging. Why not get it repaired? I'm sure even you could get it financed."

"Actually, I'm kinda fine without it. I'm noticing a whole new world around me."

"Well, good luck with that. Anyhow, we'll excuse your daughter's bullying, but you really should teach her some manners."

"She's my sister, like I said. And he's the one who cut in line. C'mon Lulu, let's get outta here. I'll get you some real popcorn with caramel."

"Gross," she replied. "I want to be the first San Bernardino kid who consumes a VanillaOrangeBlizzard. You promised."

"No Lu. Let's go. We've had enough."

He had to drag her away.

Oscar awoke at 4 a.m. the next day on his old foam mattress, listening to the dull roar of tires on the FiredStone expressway. The city was coming alive with activity and sounds that would soon melt into background noise—the information bombardment his brain routinely filtered out to focus on the important stuff. In the early morning stillness, his filters were down and sounds were vibrant.

When he set out on his skateboard the overcast clouds hung higher up than the day before. He left Luella's helmet behind and the pincas showed no interest, maintaining a holding pattern around his block.

Vien and a few other custoz waited at the park bench under the oak tree. He was pleasantly surprised to see Vanessa chatting among them. Her tight-fitting jeans were faded from actual wear, unlike the obvious disposable jean ink patterns with engineered knee holes. Oscar watched her tuck shiny red hair behind a perfectly shaped ear while turning to greet him.

"'Zup? I thought you and your Caspian fella weren't down with bacco?" he asked, slipping a pack to one of his regulars. Her smile caught him off guard, making his lips curve upward and his mouth salivate.

"Caspian's just a friend and I never let funding sources influence me. While I don't necessarily approve of smoking, you've formed a little community among your custoz. I'm a community organizer, so here I am." She turned to the group gathered around the park bench. "What would you guys think about a community garden? A place to hang out; maybe grow something you don't normally eat?"

"We could plant maragoso!" Vien offered. Another man smiled while others looked perplexed. "It's a vegetable from the Philippines, bitter melon. Where could we get seeds?"

Oscar rolled his eyes. He was already pushing the envelope by selling bacco on the side and didn't need to draw any more attention to his off the books custoz. "Look guys, I'm not sure I want to get mixed up with this. I . . . "

"I'll get the seeds," interjected Vanessa, keeping him from finishing his sentence and grabbing his elbow. "Maybe you'll have a change of heart after your sister plants the tobacco seedlings I gave her for your back yard."

He wanted to tell her to forget about it. He wanted to walk away, find a payday loan outfit to finance an implant repair, and go back to his old life. He didn't know where this was going, but he for sure didn't need any more risk or complications.

Before he got the words out, her delightful fingers grabbed his. "Take me along on your next run. I could meet some more people."

She hopped on his longboard, tugging his hand along with her.

He got on behind her, held her waist, and kicked.

CHAPTER 18
Caspian

A WINDOW INTERRUPTED CASPIAN'S MYNDSCREEN WITH breaking news: "Authorities rush to San Bernardino stadium where explosion kills 40 Volluseum™ brawl competitors. Families wait in the parking lot for DNA confirmation." The program cut to life stories of each potential victim; B-roll prepared for the sportscast color commentary now served as instant obituaries. It was gripping TV. "Justin Overplare, sponsored by Mercernary General, grew up in BroncBoy suburbs playing Fortnight before transitioning to virtual combat events at age 14. His favorite CokAid flavor is CherryCBD. When he's not gaming, he relaxes at terrestrial gladiator events or plays with his e-puppy, Ruff. It's tragic seeing such a promising life wasted in a horrific fearmonger attack, or at least that's what we presume. Over to you, Bambi."

"We now have parking lot security cam footage. Whoa, just look at that fireball ladies and gentleman . . . " *Damnation, this voyeurism is disgusting,* Caspian thought. *Timeless Warning makes bank on these views while their wall-to-wall sensationalism distracts folks from the real problems, like discrimination and prejudice.* Caspian nevertheless kept the program streaming while returning to his walnut desk. "This attack was just one block away from an alleged C-4 bomb attack by a Spryte Nationalist on a childrearing center two days ago. That killer was a loner who neighbors said suffered from chronic depression and anger management issues." *I knew it. It's always those people. I'm not bigoted or anything, but it's always those people doing this sort of thing.*

HALexa nudged him. "Caspian, you haven't responded to that message from Educate Randall. Would you like me to draft a reply?"

He'd been putting it off for a week. On the one hand, it was flattering Aneeka Randall, *the Aneeka Randall*, had personally reached out. She was once a therapist at Mercernary General, a healthcare facility where the Department of Prosperity outsourced psychological treatment. Mercernary General and Timeless Warning were owned by the same hedge fund, which now had representatives on OrangeVine's board. Now that she was on the Tribunal, name-dropping Dr. Randall would impress his board chair. He could shore up his bona fides as a High Establishment player and put to rest any concerns his philanthropic special projects work made him a little too sympathetic to Luddyte resisters. On the other hand, he had always been a bit suspicious of her punditry when interviewed as a Tribunal expert. She was part of the machine. He'd need to be careful. Take things in small steps.

"No thanks. I'll take care of it." He temporarily disabled HALexa and composed his own thought in a private Chatter window:

"Sorry for the delay. I got caught up in a binge-watch session for days. Have been digging out my message backlog 😩. Shall we meet at LuckyStars?"

The reply was immediate. "Discretion required. Needs 2B crypto. Ideally sans 11G, if you know what I mean."

Gotcha. He ran a quick Noodle search, finding an obscure post about signal black spots found beneath transmission towers. They broadcast every direction except straight down. Another click revealed several tower locations in West LA. *Voila. Playing the game, baby.*

"There's a tower at 24574 Saddle Peak Road in Malibu. No transmissions directly below. I'll be hiking the Backbone Trail Sunday afternoon and will be under that tower around

3:37 PM. I'm a chatty guy. Would talk with anyone I randomly ran into. 😊."

"Understood. Take care, Caspian."

He checked another message, this one from the wonderful Vanessa Youngblood. "Hey Caspi, just wanted to give you an update. We've put together a 27-person leadership group to launch SubDirt in San Bernardino. Just need a site."

"Working on it. Meanwhile, any more thought on my offer of free WhamZong helmets for the kids? 😳 I know a virtual gardening app to teach them some basics before they get their hands dirty, so to speak."

"I'm not wild about further virtuality, but if it greased the skids at OrangeVine it might be worth it. Here's the catch. The tariff on WhamZong products makes the GalExSee 40% more expensive than MyScreen helmets. When I run those numbers through OrangeVine's util calculator, I get much greater good for greater number stats using MyScreens. Any way to fund those?"

"Hmm. Unlimited MyScreens just seem worse for kids. Let me see what I can do. It's all about who you know, how you play your cards. 😳"

"Thanks, Caspi! You've always got my back. <3"

His palms were sweaty. He wiped them on the back of his pants.

Caspian had never been on a hike; in fact, he rarely spent more time outside than strolling from car to office. But this was his only excuse for meeting Aneeka at a transmission-free location. *How hard can it be?* MapNest™ pulled up directions from the Saddle Peak Trailhead to his destination. The winding road was 4.7 miles long. A steeper dirt footpath, however, was less than a mile. As his iDrive dropped him at the Stunt™ road trailhead, Caspian was a bit at a loss. An old wooden sign read: "Saddle Peak Trail." His screen told him to walk. Intuition told him otherwise. *What could she possibly want from me?*

After a few hundred feet he found a massive round tank with peeling beige paint enclosed behind a chain-link fence. A sign marked it part of the Las Virgenes Municipal Water district, back before recycled water replaced piped supply.

Although the early spring air was brisk, he found himself sweating while fighting back overgrown chaparral with every step. Scratches stung his arms and face, drawing blood in a few spots. The trail was muddy from the first wet winter in five years. Dampness seeped into his feet through thin soled disposable hiking shoes.

Bright staccato chirps burst forth as he turned a corner, like basketball shoes squeaking on waxed floors. He checked his nine open MyndScreen windows to find where the noise originated, but they were muted. It was real. Standing motionless, his eyes finally settled on a scrub oak twenty feet ahead. A yellow bird with ruddy stripes down its beak and hints of green around its shoulders again burst into song. HALexa informed him with ninety-eight percent certainty that it was a yellow warbler. The notes washed over his skin, which prickled with the sensation of being alive, being present in a non-fungible moment never to be replicated. The bird flit off, magically disappearing into the brush and leaving only profound silence.

His feet trudged on over wet gravel, crunching in a rhythmic cadence. The smell of moist soil filled the air, which hadn't a drone in sight. An outcropping rose straight out of the ridgeline. Round cobbles the size of his fist were encased in a sandstone layer above his head. He wondered how they got there.

He rounded a switchback before cresting the backbone of the Santa Monica Mountains. The blackish blue of the Pacific Ocean stretched endlessly out to the gray clouded horizon with golden sunlight slivers bouncing off the waves. The sun had doubled in size as it dipped low on the horizon. Eastward, Downtown LA's skyscrapers loomed in the distance. To the south rose Santa Monica, OrangeVine's office tower, and what was left of the beach. Looking straight down, he saw a round bronze medallion sunk in the stone. It read: FIRST ORDER SURVEY CONTROL, CITY of LA DEPT of PUBLIC WORKS, →1955. Someone had stood on this very place 110 years ago and gone to considerable effort marking the spot. *Why?*

The arrow pointed north, toward a complex of steel towers with panel-shaped antennas standing ominously atop Saddle Mountain, just off in the distance.

He stood a moment, taking it all in. Mountains, overcast sky, shimmering ocean, steel towers, bronze marker at his feet, salty air, the sound of a breeze blowing through the bushes. He slowly turned his head 180 degrees to grab a pano shot. When he tried storing the image, he got a Kloud error message. The file wouldn't save. He was offline, in the dead zone. He'd just have to remember it for what it was. Caspian heard the rush of air escaping his nostrils as he exhaled, bracing himself for what lay ahead.

He was breathing heavily and soaked in sweat when he reached the summit. A black limousine waited beneath the transmission tower. It was 4:14 in the afternoon.

A foot emerged from an opening car door, wearing a black leather pump. A slim leg followed, in tailored black wool slacks. Then, Aneeka Randall stood before him, looking like someone you'd see in Vogue, only smarter. Her red silk blouse dipped at the neckline, revealing a jade pendant on a silver chain.

"You're late."

"Sorry. I, uh, I got distracted by this new episode of *Big Brother V*. This guy in the house totally fell for an older woman and it was like embarrassingly inappropriate. You catch it yet?"

"Cut the crap, Caspian. We're offline. I need your help with a former patient, Vera Smith. Her calendar indicates she met you in 2048, shortly before experiencing radical shifts in attentional patterns and severe MyndScreen side-effects." He watched her rub the jade pendant between her right index finger and thumb.

"I need to know if her treatment was successful, if she's happy with the new, improved life my therapy provided. Your post about corporate mind take overs reminded me of things she once said. I can't explain, but it's of greater importance than you might imagine. Could you shed some light on her state of mind when you met?"

Caspian didn't remember many things from 2048. Given the information blizzard he endured daily, it was hard enough recalling what he'd done last week, let alone 17 years ago. Yet he did remember Vera. It was something about her pleading eyes when asking him to help educate people about antibiotics losing effectiveness against gonorrhea. She wanted to spread the truth. A passion in her voice had gripped him. He'd figured she got upgraded after her Chatter feed went dark. Was that Aneeka Randall's "treatment?"

"Yeah, I remember Vera," he replied, casually. "She had some public health concerns. Remarkable view up here, isn't it?"

"Is there anything more you can tell me? Anyone she was in contact with?"

He took a breath. *Time to make a play.*

"I'd have to jog my memory. First, I was hoping you could do me a favor. Long before you were on the Tribunal, the Educates levied a tariff on WhamZong helmets and implants. They didn't like these devices providing viewers with a usage report, allowing them to self-limit their screen time. I think responsible use of this technology will benefit society, even improve the economy. My foundation wants to provide WhamZongs to underprivileged children living in infotainment deserts. I've tried lining up Wall Street financing, but Vues have low Lifetime Customer Values. They don't qualify for ad-subsidized implantation and most of their credit ratings are ruined. They can't afford implanted viewvitude either with the higher tariffs. It's a real barrier to advancement and equal opportunity. Could the Educates revisit this whole tariff thing?"

"Of course. You have my word, Caspian." She touched his chin with the fingertips of her right hand, forcing his gaze to meet hers. Her deep, icy stare liquified his insides. It was scary, powerful, and seductive with just a hint of desperation. "Is there anything more you remember, about Vera?"

"I have reason to believe she spoke with a fellow named Aldo, a community gardener in Santa Monica. He's . . . different, if you know what I mean. I'm not sure what they talked about, but if you found Aldo, you could find out." Caspian didn't mention he was the one who steered Vera toward Aldo. Hopefully tipping off Aneeka to his whereabouts didn't put him in any danger.

"Do you know his Chatter handle?"

"He's offline, permanently. He may be connected to the Luddyte Sisterhood. I'm sure I don't have to tell you this, but take precautions if you meet him in public."

She took her fingers off his chin and noticed a bright red scab. "You're bleeding."

"It's nothing. Just a scratch. The path I took to get here hadn't been used for a long, long time."

"Be careful, it might leave a scar."

CHAPTER 19
Chase

"SCANDALOUS SHOW PRODUCERS FORCE WOMAN TO RE-live sexual assault, details at six."

Chase was watching 24HR News™. It was probably late afternoon, maybe four-ish. You'd think MyndScreens would display digital clocks, but maybe Timeless Warning didn't want people tracking time too closely. He guessed it was afternoon because the AC kicked in at certain times, presumably during high temps. He'd recently started paying attention to this. It had been running pretty regularly, pushing a dry sanitary breeze over his fresh, unnaturally smooth disposable sheets.

The screen shots teasing the six o'clock segment indicated the scandalous show in question was none other than *Big Brother V,* which Chase knew was produced by the same infotain network as 24HR News. He kept the channel running through the five o'clock news and skipped his normal VirtualVanna™ game show just to find out what the big deal was.

It turned out the *Big Brother V* producers had called a contestant into the confession booth to watch footage of her being assaulted while passed out after an episode of heavy drinking. While *Big Brother V* hadn't shown the incident, the evening news had no compulsions about airing the assault with the accused perpetrator's face blurred out to protect his identity. They then aired the victim's reaction to the horror she'd been unable to witness as it happened. "Stop! Please just make it stop!" When she turned away from the confession booth wallscreen, the producers switched transmissions over to her MyndScreen and kept the incident looping. She broke down, curled up in a ball, and sobbed uncontrollably, unable to speak.

Chase was repulsed. Like the woman, he wanted to look away. But there is no "away" when an image lives rent free inside your head. He kept watching with morbid curiosity.

After replaying the attack, this time in high-definition slow motion, while adding color commentary about the victim's troubled childhood, suggestive outfit, and social awkwardness in 8th grade, the news anchors asked a panel of experts whether it was appropriate for reality TV producers to air such a segment. A think tank analyst from the CRAPO Institute argued no harm was done since the victim was just an avatar, as was her "alleged" attacker. None of this had really happened, it was harmless fiction. As if to prove his point, the news producers aired the segment again, zooming in with sufficient detail to reveal the victim's writhing face did indeed look like a deep fake computer fabrication. Besides, the CRAPO thought leader continued, the Tribunal of Educates has ruled infotain firms have a free speech right to air whatever meets viewer demand, and ratings revealed this episode was wildly popular. "Amusement is peace, after all, and while this content was a tad diabolical, Vue response has proven it highly entertaining," the expert explained while adjusting his glasses and pivoting his head from camera one to camera two. "Moreover, everyone could learn a lesson by watching this drama instead of having to personally experience such an ordeal."

The news anchor turned the question to a women's studies professor, who calmly explained that while this version was fabricated, it was based on an actual event on a real "reality" TV program from 2017 in the Castilian region. "Someone suffered to create this content and it is morally wrong to profit from it," she inveighed. "Moreover, we shouldn't be putting that filth into any infotainment episode. It normalizes and sensationalizes sexual assault, degrades women, and is just plain vile."

Chase felt gratified to hear his own views espoused so eloquently by a true expert. *Thank goodness there's still in-depth news coverage!*

"That's all the time we have," grinned the anchor. "Now, over to you at the business desk, Bambi, for an in-depth look at the offshore private cyber currency boom amid rumors of an economic slowdown . . . Wait," the old-school anchor touched his ear, a habitual motion from early in his career to press an earbud speaker firmly into his auditory canal and hear prompts from an off-screen producer. Chase, of course, knew there was no earbud, only the producer's voice streaming into the anchor's MyndScreen. "Remember all those emergency drone landings you thought you saw last week? I'm getting breaking news that Cue Along research indicates it simply didn't happen." The anchor dramatically raised both his eyebrows and the tone of his voice. "Further, Cue Along theorists say the recent San Bernardino Volluseum attack that allegedly killed forty people didn't occur either. Rather, the contestants were competing by remote MyndScreen access and therefore weren't on location. Moreover, the fireball captured by parking lot security cameras was just a video projected onto the building by pranksters. The grieving parents interviewed on other fake views networks were simply paid crisis actors."

If it bleeds, it ledes. Chase was beginning to think it didn't matter whether these calamities really happened or not. Either way, they were Hollywood ploys to drive ratings for various "news" programs.

"Nice cycle. Is it real?"

@BadScootr poked Chase, and had evidently unblocked him. He wondered the same thing. Was @BadScootr real? Had he actually been outplayed by an unscrupulous human? He let the news run and responded in multitask. "You mean the one you cowardly blew up?"

"Oh, sorry about that. No offense but, you know, it's just a game. I meant the 🚵 pinned on your profile page. You ride terrestrially?"

"What if I do?"

"Cool. I've never actually ridden in RL."

Figures, bot. "I've been around the block a few times. In the real world, we have a thing called honor. We'd never block someone after torching their bike and stealing the loot from a joint heist. We'd at least own up to our bad deeds."

"Whatever, dood, I said I was sorry. You still using it? The bike, I mean."

"I've actually . . . retired from riding. I don't get around much anymore." *Now, that's an understatement.*

"Interested in selling it?"

"I don't really need money. I'm in . . . a home."

"I'm in a home too, dood, although mine's kinda run down and we defn could use some $$. 🏚 What gives?"

"It's . . . an entertainment home. You probably see them advertised in your feed. You know, you save up enough to afford EH placement, get an upgrade, and you're set for life."

"Pretty sure I'm not the demographic they're targeting with those ads dood, but it sounds sweet."

"Unlimited gaming, movies, episodes, you name it. I don't even have to get out of bed."

"Cool."

"Not as cool as you might think."

"Anyhow, I guess you really don't need that then. Did I mention I was sorry about torching you in GHO?"

"Yeah, but you're still kind of a jerk and I don't need to sell. I've got more ByteDime than I know what to do with from online poker winnings and I'm already covered with infinite lifetime Pepsoilent injections, housing, infotain, etc."

" . . . " The ellipse flickered during a long pause.

"What if I grant you a GHO rematch? I win, I get the bike. You win, you get my account password. You take over my character, keep its loot and hit points, and redo the avatar in your own image or whatever you want."

"That's—appealing. One problem. I don't know where the cycle is."

"Why didn't you say so? Later, dood."

Chase got out of bed intending to walk around his room, stark naked. Then he saw it. The roach. It crawled through the HVAC vent, disappearing from view. His eyes tracked back toward his feet where a small puddle of greenish gray liquid lay directly beneath his IV. A leak. The MinuteMayd had misconnected the Pepsoilent IV bag. It dripped onto the floor, feeding the bug instead of him. He pulled it loose, letting the bag's contents spill out. Then, he walked around the room.

His legs felt surprisingly sturdy. The automatic door to his pod slid open as its sensor detected his motion. There was an empty hallway, lined with other doors that looked just like his. No staff, no people, no bots. *I could walk out.* Instead, he went down to hands and knees, to attempt a push up. He took a deep breath, inhaling the rancid fumes coming off the Pepsoilent puddle.

Nah, let's see if there's a game on.

There was, of course, a game on. In 2065 there was always a game on, always an opportunity to leave your stinky RL behind for an infinitely more entertaining metaverse.

After the game, Chase kept the channel streaming to watch a documentary, which wasn't normally his thing. This one virtually re-enacted the fall of the Roman empire, complete with meta battle scenes between soldiers, lions and other exotic beasts, 4D banquets with aromas of spit-fired wild boar spraying out from his entertainment lounge, and sex scenes that made him blush. It turned out lead poisoning was far from the only thing that brought down the empire. *You might say the Romans were victims of their own excess.* He logged on and posted the thought to Chatter, just for grins. It got one like from @Vera2048™.

"Hey there. I see you're watching RoMens™. Weren't they a little barbaric?" she asked.

The trademarked handle implied it's a verified account registered with the Educates to protect authenticity. Chase was skeptical. *On the other hand, if @BadScootr turned out to be real, maybe . . .*

"Nice try," he fired back. "But I know a bot when I see one. Can't your algorithm come up with anything more original than that?"

"No, really. Not a bot. I know it's been a while. I didn't reach out for a long time. I knew I disappointed you by consenting."

"And?"

"And I just wanted to check that you're OK. I mean, there are some perks to the upgraded life, right?"

"I suppose. There are fewer food commercials on the infotain since they know we don't buy FlavrPaks."

"Right. We're completely provided for. Unlimited food, unlimited entertainment. I mean, what's not to like. Right?"

Chase logged off.

CHAPTER 20
Aneeka

ANEEKA RANDALL'S HEAD HURT. A LOW-LEVEL HISS RICO-cheted around her skull; the sound airplanes once made. Most tribunal disputes featured rational arguments on both sides. She'd never thought so much. Her brain ached with fatigue. This job wasn't all it was cracked up to be.

She'd been procrastinating tackling WhamZong's tariffs as she'd promised Caspian Blaine. She agreed trade barriers were economically inefficient. And Caspian might be correct about limiting screen time. Yet she hadn't prioritized tariff deliberations with her clerks or other Educates. Roland Thompson took every opportunity to throw glass in her gears. She didn't want an unnecessary fight, especially given Dagny Huerta's controversies. Something this significant meant carefully cashing political chits to grease the skids, circulating multiple memorandum drafts and soliciting input to obtain sufficient buy in. She hadn't yet acquired the political capital she needed.

Meanwhile, she read a legal brief sent to her in the U.S. Mail, which, she'd learned, was still technically an acceptable form of legal communique. She sliced open her finger on the manila envelope's edge, being unfamiliar with such objects and the hazards a paper cut can impose. She washed her hands continuously, but blood trickled out in a tiny stream that refused to stop. Finally, she stuck the finger in her mouth and began to read. It stung.

Defendant Dagny Huerta hereby invites all Timeless Warning shareholders, employees, executives, and customers to freely walk through the Grand Canyon's majestic beauty. Living people may say anything they wish while so doing, but to ensure such speech is truly free, they may not charge an advertising fee, price, surcharge, or subscription, for their words, ideas, or music. In Ms. Huerta's domain, free speech flows unencumbered and uncompensated.

Regarding claims of communism, Ms. Huerta has amassed more wealth than anyone in the Globalian province of Mexico through capitalistic investments in private property. Defendant countercharges Timeless Warning with crony capitalism, pure and simple. Unable to compete in the global marketplace of ideas with an infotainment product people will pay for, Timeless Warning seeks corrupt government action forcing unwanted advertisements upon Globalian citizens who consume manipulative click-bait programming. Even in the Grand Canyon's tranquility, where people travel great lengths to avoid such commercial bombardment, Timeless Warning seeks authoritarian mandates forcing their commerce into addicted listeners' brains.

Finally, should the Tribunal grant Timeless Warning's baseless claim that Ms. Huerta's properly recorded Grand Canyon purchase is invalid, defendant submits any easements permitting11G tower construction on public land during the same economic crisis would be similarly invalid. In short, if Ms. Huerta's property claims are dismissed, Timeless Warning's should also be.

Have a nice day.

Crony capitalism. Aneeka had heard that phrase before. The hiss in her head morphed into a ringing in the ears. At least her finger no longer bled. Looking around the walls of her bungalow she saw, "Prosperity isn't freedom. Freedom is Freedom," scrawled in dried chocolate pudding. She took a break and opened up Chatter.

Unable to reach Vera, Aneeka considered an indirect approach through Chase, Vera's former lover. She needed to know her treatment regimen had worked, that her patients enjoyed the objectively wonderful life she arranged for them. If Vera wouldn't communicate, maybe Chase would. Perhaps he'd reach out to Vera. Aneeka knew he resented her. He'd recognized she and Vera were mutually attracted. He'd sensed Aneeka would betray Vera with the false premise of revolutionary "sisterhood." Still, that was 17 years ago. Surely time had healed those wounds.

"Hello Chase, it's Dr. Randall, from the Department of Prosperity. I'm just doing a routine check-in to see how our patients are doing with their long-term care arrangements. Do you have time for a brief survey?"

"You have been BLOCKED from messaging with this user."

Dammit. Not only did her brain still ache, her rib cage felt like it was shrinking.

She ripped open a pack of running clothes, mounted the treadmill and cued her favorite TellURyde scenery. After a brief warm up, she ran swiftly. The treadmill's fan blasted her face, chilling her cheeks but leaving her back clammy and soaked in sweat. The wheels in her brain bounced over Dagny Huerta's intellectual speed bumps, avoiding thoughts of Vera. The treadmill inclined, simulating a hill. She was gasping for air, pounding her feet on the rolling black rubber tread spinning below her, *thunk, thunk, thunk, WHAM!*

Something snapped. The rubber belt tore apart at its seam. Her face hit the handrails, splitting her lower lip. Plastic rollers flew across the room. Her feet shot out from under her, leaving Aneeka sprawled across the broken machine, which smelled of grease. A metallic taste filled her mouth. Her face went numb. She gasped, unable to contain the pain. Tears welled in her eyes.

With effort, she rose to hands and knees, letting blood and tears drip down. Watery red snot flowed out her nostrils, making each breath difficult. She gasped and waited, gasped and waited, precious minutes disintegrating. Slower breaths quieted her mind, drying her nose and eyes as the trauma abated. She pulled a quivering lower lip into her mouth to contain the blood.

Washing her hands and face, she felt defeated. Technology had failed her. Now she was not only confused, but unable to seek release through exercise.

Why not run outside? It was a gorgeous spring day. People once jogged all the time. If Caspian enjoyed the out-of-doors, maybe there was something to it. Maybe it was time for something new. She walked out the house, just like that. Her chaufferscurity opened the car door and gave her a puzzled look as she strode right past him, still red-faced from her fall. "You alright, mam?"

"Maybe. I'll tell you later." She set off walking, just like that.

One foot after the other, she headed uphill past her bungalow. None of her neighbors were out on the buckled sidewalk or sitting idly on their porches. They never were, yet she somehow was more aware of their absence today.

Leaving her neighborhood, she broke into a jog and found a delightful path along Rustic Creek. How could she not have known about this, so close to her house? The smells of eucalyptus and damp soil awoke her olfactory with a blast of musty menthol and the taste of blood abated. The air felt different, its brisk chill cooling her entire body instead of the treadmill fan just blasting her face.

As she picked up the pace, a tree root erupted from the unmaintained trail and grabbed her left running shoe. Her hands and knees broke the fall, hitting a cushion of damp leaves that accumulated over years of trail disuse. Water gurgled down a creek, churning over obstacles, never stopping to rest. Bushes glowed a vibrant shade of green, illuminated by morning's horizonal sunlight. For minutes, she stared at soft, damp ground. Her frustration with tripping, her angst over Dagny Huerta, and even her obsession with Vera evaporated. A flock of feral parakeets screeched high above, relics from times long past when humans still sought company from pets. They mocked her misstep. She laughed, pushed herself upright, wiped her hands on her shorts and kept going. Running lightly, she bounced along the trail with childlike glee.

When she returned home, she told her chaufferscurity she was doing just fine. She asked how he was.

"I'm getting a little bored of BBV, to tell you the truth," he replied, staring at his palm.

She smiled and went inside. After showering, turning off all notifications, and closing her windows, she dictated onto her MyndScreen.

MEMO. TO: Fellow Educates. FR: Dr. Aneeka Randall RE: WhamZong Tariffs. DATE: 3/23/2065

High tariffs imposed upon WhamZong implants and helmets produce unintended consequences, degrading overall prosperity in Globalia. These devices provide usage reports allowing viewers to self-limit screen time, consistent with Tribunal doctrine issued in the wake of the Great Saturation. We learned during that difficult period that, left unchecked, infotainment can consume 100% of human attention span. While this might be acceptable, even desirable, for those with sufficient assets to finance permanent Entertainment Home (EH) care; for less prosperous Vues it threatens their ability to contribute economically through makework labor and, more importantly, as consumers. In the *Zannity v. Timeless Warning* ruling, the Tribunal created the Mind Scarcity doctrine, restricting all brain implants from consuming more than 40% of a human's daily attention span until, and unless, they consent to an upgrade with accompanying EH maintenance. Earlier in my career, I provided recommendations to the

Department of Prosperity about subsidized upgrades, so I am familiar firsthand with their costs, economic and otherwise.

Tariffs were introduced out of concern that WhamZong products could enable users to drive infotain consumption below the 40% Mind Scarcity threshold. This, in turn, risks lower advertising exposure that could deflate consumer purchasing. Recession, famine, war, and brutal authoritarianism could follow. However, most Vues currently take on considerable debt via indentured viewvitude contracts to finance implantation in the first place. Deepening that debt through advertising-fueled consumerism leaves a majority of the Globalian consumer class in a permanent state of negative equity, a major deterrent toward economically important behavior such as home ownership.

Moreover, should Vue infotain brain absorption fall below the 40 percent *Zannity* threshold, even 30 percent still contains sufficient advertisements. Tribunal proclamation that "Advertising Frees Speech" already ensures economically low value content (i.e., poetry or history) will be priced out of the 11G spectrum. With modern advances in Effispeech emoji vocabulary and SpeiDrWeb targeting, advertisers pack more data and emotion into smaller bursts of 11G bandwidth, ensuring economic prosperity will expand even if we empower Vues to self-limit screentime via WhamZong, or similar, devices.

Further, even higher-value Establishment members would benefit by self-selecting infotainment consumption below the 40% *Zannity* threshold, which was always meant as an upper bound—not a mandatory minimum. We know from the Great Saturation that those High Establishmentarians performing essential services experienced diminished thought capacity and creativity deficits during pre-Zannity intensive infotainment consumption. The top management of our corporations, consulting firms, infotainment studios, and charitable foundations require more functional attention span than the 60% preserved under *Zannity* doctrine. Much like transmission blocking technology utilized in Faraday cages, WhamZong devices permit unencumbered thought among High Establishmentarians.

I recommend the Tribunal pause all tariffs until we conduct a study, perhaps outsourced to the McChesney consulting firm, ascertaining whether limited infotain consumption positively impacts Globalia's economy and wellbeing.

She hesitated only a moment before firing off the memo, not even bothering to run it by her clerks. Within minutes, none other than Chief Educate Lewis Leon replied directly from his personal account.

"You raise some intriguing points, sister. Let's discuss offline. I'll drop by when I'm in LA next week."

CHAPTER 21
Oscar

OSCAR'S CUSTOZ BECAME ACQUAINTANCES. ACQUAINT-
ances became friends. One week he'd take an order online through
Luella's helmet. He'd stop and talk when hand delivering the bacco. Next
time, he'd remember their name. Folks stopped buying online, they'd just
shout out when he skateboarded through the neighborhood. It was a
whole different experience, and he liked it.

He'd initially greet them, "'Zup?" That became, "nice weather we're
having." Next time, he'd ask about their wife, or whether their headaches
had improved. Likewise, they checked in with him. "Luella seems like a
great kid, Oscar. You must be so proud." "Say, Oscar, who's that pretty
redhead you're with?"

One sunny afternoon, Ellen joined Oscar and Luella on their
threadbare Astroturf yard, sitting on dingy white plastic lawn chairs.
Luella had her helmet off as the day was warm, nice enough for a swim.
Too bad the old neighbors filled their pool with sand before moving out
two decades ago.

Much to Oscar's satisfaction, Luella was showing greater interest in
her online classes. He no longer had to nudge her to sign up for a course
or remind her about a homework assignment. She remained relentless
in her pursuit of a motorcycle, "When are we going to get a chop-
per, Oscar?"

"We? Whaddya mean we? Where would *we* even buy one?"

"What if I found one?"

146

"To buy with what pile of money? You're not living in the real world, Lulu."

"A girl can always dream," she replied, rolling her eyes.

"Speaking of dreams, I had the oddest one last night," Ellen interjected, obviously trying to change the subject. "There's a picture of a man with funny hair and a woman staring at me in front of an old wooden house. I hear a lovely song, 'We'll meet again, don't know where, not sure when, but I know we'll meet again some sunny day.' I can't figure out what it means."

"I never dream. Why would they mean anything?" Oscar replied, with a slight sneer. Luella kicked him with a pink high top.

A polished black lowrider sedan pulled up real slow, silently slinking toward the curb with orange and yellow painted flames flowing back from the hood like cartoon dragon breath.

Oscar stared into the pale afternoon light with icy cold eyes and pinpoint pupils. He lit up a cigarette.

"I thought you'd cut down to one a day; this is your third," Ellen protested.

"Whatever. Back off for once, will you?"

Smoke wafted out a cracked car window before the door opened and slammed shut with a "thunk." Jerome stood there, hands on hips, black hoodie drawn over a grayish face, looking at them like a GHO avatar who'd grown bored shooting up innocent bystanders. He sauntered toward them, turning his arms in a slow pimp roll and emphasizing each step by scuffing his NYKE™ sneaker along the broken concrete.

"They need to leave," Jerome motioned toward Luella and Ellen with a Smith and Wesson semiauto he nonchalantly pulled from the back of his waistband.

Oscar stood up, walked behind Ellen and placed his hand around her shoulder. In a move both protective and provocative, his fingertips gently caressed her collarbone. "They're not going anywhere. Maybe it's you who needs to leave." He could feel gooseflesh rising, and not just on her.

"Alright then, we'll do this here and now. We've noticed you making drops Oscar. Drops not run through us. Our sales have dipped on your turf. You're working a side hustle. That ain't cool, brudda. You know it's gotta stop." He gestured with his hand and the gun before folding his arms across his torso, tucking the weapon into his armpit, and waiting for his prey to submit.

"I'm out."

"You're never out, brudda. You know we can't let bruddas go AWOL. It's bad enough dodging pincas and defending turf from rivals like the Winstons, we can't have our own people working outside the posse. We made you, Oscar. We own you."

"C'mon Jerome, we go way back. I'm not looking to make an issue outta this, I'll just go my own way. Can't you let it slide?"

"No chance brudda. 'Sides, where you gonna get your product. You need us."

"I'll grow it." Luella piped up.

"Get real. Where you gonna get your custoz? You're not even online most of the time. You can't make it without us, brudda. We'll make sure of that."

Ellen seemed to have heard enough. She stood up, stepped toward Jerome, and jabbed her index finger straight at his rib cage. "He's got a network. I'm helping him build it. We'll have every custo in San Bernardino buying a pack a day. We'll let you stay around but mind your manners or the nuns who raised me will hail fire and brimstone on your sorry ass."

"What?!! You sure about this? "Oscar whispered in her ear, yet he saw Jerome heard what he was saying.

"I'm in," she said loud enough for the whole world to hear.

A murder of crows, fifty at least, cawed overhead as they flapped toward the fading sun. Jerome watched the birds flow around a Pincerton hovering directly above. He looked down and saw white crow poop splatter his NYKE.

Tucking his weapon back in his jeans, Jerome stepped around Ellen and shoved Oscar's chest. "This ain't happening brudda. I'll be back when that pinca's gone. You ladies have no fucking clue what it means to be 'in.' What you are 'in' is deep shit. Your little punk ass garden won't stand up to a flamethrower for more than ten seconds."

Luella flipped him the finger as he drove off, tires squealing. She turned to her big brother, "That guy watches too many Guadalupe Godfather episodes. Every show, some mafioso dude does that thing with his gun in the armpit. Seriously, though, what are we gonna do, Oscar?"

Ellen answered. "Jerome's all talk. What's with the weird way he rolls his wrists when he walks? I'll contact Vanessa. She'll know what to do. So," she turned to Oscar, "you'll cut down to one a day?"

He tossed the half-finished cigarette on the well-trampled Astroturf and smudged it with his foot. Looking up at the sky, now clear of crows and pincas, he said, "I'm in."

The air smelled moist and cool as the sun dipped behind the horizon. He forced a smile in Ellen's direction; then his face drew tight.

CHAPTER 22
Caspian

"CASPIAN, COME UP TO MY OFFICE FOR A MINUTE." IT WAS a direct request from Wallace Packard, OrangeVine's president. Requests of this nature were unusual, so rare, in fact, they had never happened without advance HALexa scheduling. Caspian closed seven multitask windows and hustled to the elevator.

In Packard's 21st floor office, Yvonne Putcher sat by a frail, boyish executive clad in an expensive Italian suit. Nursing martinis while lounging in shell cordovan leather chairs, they didn't stand to greet him. Only Packard rose to shake his hand.

"Caspian, meet Yvonne Putcher and her charming partner in crime Stephan Barscale. As you know, Yvonne recently joined our board, representing Mercernary General Healthcare. Stephan consults for the parent company, Renaissance Mercernary, which you surely recognize as Globalia's most successful hedge fund. I've been pitching you as my replacement, so I'm pleased to have this opportunity to connect you."

"Actually, I'm a big fan of your chatter," Barscale offered, his words dripping in condescension. "I distinctly remember your post, 'Corporate Globalia has taken over our minds. Any wonder we've lost our hearts as well?' You do understand that corporate Globalia is what funds philanthropy, don't you?"

A lump formed in Caspian's throat as he searched for a clever response.

"Oh, never mind him. Thanks for taking the time, Mr. Blaine." Yvonne smiled and set down her drink. "I understand you've handled some of OrangeVine's more cutting-edge philanthropy through your Special Projects portfolio." Her hair was gorgeous.

"It's nothing really. Just doing my job." Caspian's gut unclenched a tad. "While I'm proud of the social uplifting we've accomplished to date, it just scratches the surface of what's possible if we elevate our social investments to scale."

"That's precisely why we're here," interjected Stephan. "We've met with your Finance Veep, who says your Special Projects division is chronically over budget. She suggested scaling it back. Evidently the 90-day util ROI doesn't favorably compare with OrangeVine's more mainstream grantmaking."

"Look, some of my programs don't always shine in the short-term metrics, but I know these people personally. I assure you these social investments pay off big time in the long run, in ways we're not even capable of tracking. This stuff matters, to real people, in real ways."

"Relax, Caspian," Wallace handed him a martini. "These are friends. They're here to help."

"Look," smiled Yvonne. "We get it. You're a top-notch philanthropist who cares about your work, the people you help. That's fantastic. We're investors, not altruists. We're thrilled to direct capital toward experts like you, with the skill set and vision to uplift at-risk communities. Downsizing innovation centers is the worst thing an organization can do. We'd rather expand OrangeVine's cash flow than follow your Finance VPs approach of cutting the place down. But we need your help. Hands-on people, practitioners like you, often have insights into the real economy. Not Wall Street's inflated projections or phony AI metrics. Real things real people are doing, or moves other firms or regulatory agencies are on the verge of. We take that real-world knowledge, crypto data only available to true insiders, and convert it to wealth through hedging, derivatives, and other asset arbitrage techniques. We can then redirect some proceeds back to your Special Projects. It's a win, win." She winked.

"Yeah, I get it." Caspian slowly sipped his martini to conceal the wheels spinning inside his head. *Damnation. Is this, like, insider trading?* He'd rather not know. "I'm just not sure what insights I have. I'm funding things like Virtual Midnight Basketball Leagues and online tutoring. My programs dispatch technology in smart ways, to make an impact without causing harm. Take WhamZong VR helmets, for example. I'm distributing them for disadvantaged youth to connect with the world while benefitting from screen time reports so they can self-regulate."

Wallace cleared his throat. "You know, Caspian, Renaissance Mercernary is heavily invested in Timeless Warning. You're not suggesting people view too much screentime, are you?"

"Oh, no. No, sir! I just meant we want full transparency, so Vues can monitor the content they're consuming. Timeless Warning's infotain is riveting, all my grantees watch it nonstop. I do myself. By getting people online, we're providing access, freedom, so everyone enjoys all the infotain prosperity society has to offer ..."

Stephan stopped him cold. "Of course people watch way too much of Timeless Warning's crap. That's the whole point. Now, Caspian, I'm surprised you mentioned WhamZong over their more popular competitor MyndScreen. We've explored WhamZong as an undervalued asset, but our models forecast high Tribunal tariffs hindering their growth for decades to come."

"Maybe I *do* know something your AI doesn't. Check out some WhamZong derivatives in the event those tariffs unexpectedly disappeared."

"What are you saying, Caspian?" Yvonne leaned forward and tucked her platinum hair behind a perfect ear. "What makes you think that?"

He'd told Aneeka Randall their conversation would be crypto. They'd gone to great lengths to meet offline. Still, what's the harm in giving these helpful people some general insights?

"Let's just say I recently spoke with someone who could do something about those tariffs."

"Yeah, right. Like who?"

"Like Aneeka Randall."

"You mean, *the* Aneeka Randall?"

"That is exactly what I mean. Keep this on the down low, will you?" He wiped his sweaty palms on his pants.

"You're sure?"

"Sure as I'm sitting here. Educate Randall told me personally she'd drop those tariffs after I explained how detrimental they were to our grantmaking. Believe me, that woman is dead serious. If she says she'll do something, you can take that to the bank."

"Jackpot!" Barscale screamed, with eyes bulging out of his pale bony face. He'd been staring at his palm, zoning out of the conversation just prior to the outburst. "Uh, sorry to interrupt. I just won an auction for the world's last wild-caught Chinook salmon. Bargain at two million ByteDime. But great news on the WhamZong thing."

Caspian stood up, real slow like, hiding his contempt for shallow, transactional people his job required him to supplicate. "Congrats on that. Thanks for the drink and nice to meet you." He strolled out Packard's office, turned a corner, gasped, and ran downstairs instead of waiting for the elevator. *OM frickin' G. Putcher is team Caspian! It's too good to be true.*

Back at his desk, he dug up his old Chatter post, "Corporate Globalia has taken over our minds. Any wonder we've lost our hearts as well?" He considered deleting it, yet the damage was done. Better to pivot and reframe, like his EMBA training taught.

He added a comment, "And if your heart is lost, what better way to find it than a lovely HaulMarque™ card for someone special."

While posting the comment, a message came in from Barron Koldwill. "Found the perfect site. Primo location. An old childrearing lot. No remaining structure, but old baseball fields and a park. Lots of dirt. Best of all, seller is eager to close ASAP. Price is unreal."

It was going to be one of those days where everything went right. Caspian clicked the "Buy Now" button in the realtor's message and accepted a DockYouSign™ to complete the transaction. He pinged Vanessa. "Hey darlin', I just got you a garden site. There are even some old basketball courts for a virtual midnight league. You can thank me later! 😊"

CHAPTER 23
Chase

THE EVENING NEWS WAS ON AGAIN. POLICE SOUGHT anonymous tips about a former BaccanAlien™ contestant shooting. An assailant wrongly believed the contestant was having an affair with a rough-looking lady wearing a nose ring and little other clothing. The contestant, a soft-spoken guy with a purple mohawk, had accompanied a black-mohawked friend to confront the gunman who'd sent threatening Chatter posts to the nose-ring chick, his ex-girlfriend. In dim evening light, the assailant mistook purple mohawk guy for black mohawk guy and shot him up. The quote unquote news aired pornographic chat screenshots as evidence of the shooter's motivation.

The camera zoomed in on Purple Mohawk's wounds while the anchor noted he was in good spirits and would make a special guest appearance on BaccanAlien later that evening. *They've got action, violence, sympathy and sex, all combined with a mistaken identity trope in the first 30 seconds,* Chase mused. *Right out of that screenwriter's social science textbook on grabbing a viewer's attention.*

In other news, WhamZong shares were trading higher upon rumors of a new product coming to market. Analysts remained leery of the stock due to persistently high tariffs.

"Dood, I found your bike." It was @BadScootr again, poking him in the Chattersphere.

"Really?"

"At an impound lot in Glendora. The county had some hefty fines attached to it for 17 years of storage, but I got those removed. Since it's an antique vehicle that's still paper-registered with the DMV, you'll need to sign some documents to transfer it over—if I win that is. You ready to play or have you chickened out?"

Chase wasn't ready. His brain was fried from a long day of watching the news and binging *Big Brother V* episodes. Ideally, he'd take on somebody of @BadScootr's caliber after a good night's rest, however fitful his sleep patterns. Sometimes, though, you gotta do what you gotta do. He wanted revenge and the opportunity stared him right in the face. It might not come again. Besides, gaming provided human interaction— @BadScootr was now surely not a bot. *Do or do not. There is no try.*

He rubbed his lucky penny. "OK, let's do this."

They mutually agreed on a Grand Heist Otto motorcycle duel where players escort a self-driving refrigerated semi-truck on a cross-country beer run from Texarkana to Atlanta for an eccentric trillionaire's birthday. Chase and @BadScootr must collectively fend off Pincerton attacks and evade automated ground assault vehicles. Completing the first level required cooperation to ensure the semi reached Atlanta's city limits. They must both stay alive, at least for a while; or the game ended in stalemate.

While Chase and @BadScootr had a mutual interest in protecting the truck, they earned points separately. After gaming seven hours and fourteen minutes, Chase had 1,325 points to @BadScootr's 1,275. He'd show this punk. When they reached Atlanta, however, things got screwy. Chase received a game notification saying he'd get 1,500 bonus points if he maneuvered the beer to his own personal depot. Same went for @BadScootr, presumably. Everything hung on the final five minutes.

On a highway overpass, @BadScootr rode the truck's left flank, Chase on the right. When a Chatter message popped up in Chase's screen, @BadScootr veered in front of the rig, forcing it into a cement barrier.

Chase slammed straight into the crashed truck, careened over the barrier, and fell 100 feet to the road below. His 4D lounge vibrated abruptly when he hit the pavement. He was toast. @BadScootr got 100 points for the move but wouldn't get the bonus 1,500 because the wrecked truck never arrived at anyone's depot. It didn't matter. The truck was in Atlanta. Level one was complete. @BadScootr was alive with more points than Chase, who was dead. Duel over.

"That was a goddamn cheap move." Chase was bitter, yet he knew he'd lost.

"Totally legal dood. Nothing says you gotta earn the bonus, reaching Atlanta is enough. You can't get so focused on points you forget why you're playin'. So, ... where can I find you to sign over the pink slip?"

"Good question. My EH," he glanced over at the IV bag dripping soyalgent into his veins. It had his entertainment home's logo. "It's called Triple Ex."

"Aha. I see what you're all about, dood 😵. I'll find it. Laters."

It's not like that.

@BadScootr was gone, having bested him again. His Chatter notification still flashed. He opened it to give the sender a piece of his mind.

"Goddammit, you cost me a game. More than that, actually. Anyhow, what do you want?"

"It's me again, Chase," replied @Vera2048. "I just need to talk. I need you."

"Drop it, bot. The real Vera would know I've got nothing left to give her. They took it all. Scram before I block you."

"We met in a parking lot, viewing Globalia Public Media. We went together to Aneeka Randall's. You were rightfully suspicious. We read The Book together. We were eating crab on the beach before being taken away by lifesaving drones. Who else knows these things?"

For the first time in years, his MyndScreen was still. He picked his lucky penny from the lounge cushions, holding it in his palm. She waited. Then, she could wait no longer.

"Talk to me. I need to know you're OK. Were we right to consent? Our lives aren't so bad, are they? We've got everything we need. How are you doing, really?"

"Goddammit V, they really did get to you. I mean, I sold out too but it's like you don't even remember who you were. Our quote unquote lives are a miserable fraud. All day long we watch garbage shows and play stupid games and engage in meaningless chatter. What choice do we have? We can't just walk out of our quote unquote entertainment homes. We have no place to go, no job, no friends, not even any clothes for crying out loud."

"Well, that's a result of our life choices. You must admit, we chose to be where we are. We consented. That's what individual autonomy is all about."

"Are you out of your goddam mind? We're here because we're addicted, because corporations could profit off our attention spans. We never stood a chance once our thoughts, our souls, our consciousness became commodities. Only a complete charlatan would believe we agreed of our own free will. Our minds were leveraged in a hostile corporate takeover. I'll make the best of it, but I won't pretend it's some sort of paradise."

Just like that, she logged off. He clenched his gut, felt a tear roll down his cheek, fought the urge to ping her back.

Looking down, he saw the cockroach return to feed on the soyalgent leak. He tucked away his lucky penny before reaching down at a rate imperceptible to an insect gorging on pure nutrients. Lightning fast, he grabbed it.

The creature squirmed, seeking escape and finding a gap between his thumb and curled index finger. Prickly legs scurried up his arm. Suppressing a reflex to flinch, he told himself it was harmless. The insect franticly encircled his head and neck. He caught it again, cupping it this time in both hands. Maybe those video game reflexes were worth something after all.

Chase looked around. The wallscreen still displayed the beach volleyball tournament he'd selected seventeen years ago. The LED lights shone the same cold, bright light on his sheet. His MyndScreen lit up with a promotional spot: "Watch Big Brother, Vreality like no uuuuther!"

The roach kicked, fought, wriggled, refusing to accept its entrapment. A near brainless bug had an indelible will to survive, even when hopelessly captured. Clasping his hands together, Chase scrunched exoskeleton against brown, juicy insides. He popped it into his mouth, chewed slowly, and swallowed.

CHAPTER 24
Aneeka

SHE FELT A SHADOW FALL OVER HER.

"Step outside, Aneeka. Let's talk." It was Chief Leon.

She looked through her MyndScreen, out her front window and, plain as day, saw nothing there. "What? Where?"

"In my airship. There's a cable dangling by your front door. Step into the harness and buckle up buttercup. I'll elevate you."

Outside, she saw the sun blotted out by an AeroYacht's™ oblong silhouette. A bright orange contraption flapped in the breeze. The nylon webbing straps were a bit tricky, yet she stepped in, fastened the buckle, and held on. She rose slowly as the webbing dug into her thighs and buttocks. Once over the rim of Rustic Canyon she gazed all the way to the great Pacific Ocean. Aneeka felt small, and scared.

"Welcome aboard!" Lewis Leon greeted her with a feeble smile while an attendant offered a distinct octagonal flute glass of sparkling wine. The Chief looked smaller in person than his avatar did on screen. The rose-colored frames of his spectacles matched the hue of his thin lips and the rosé prosecco. His freckled forehead extended up to a clump of gray hair, painstakingly combed over the top of his scalp. Though his cheeks were full, Leon's jowls were lean and eye sockets recessed deep into his skull.

They strolled down a carpeted corridor, passing an enclosure holding two massively ugly birds. "My mobile aviary," he gestured. A stench penetrated the Plexiglas, overpowering the Old Spice™ nutmeg and musk lingering around Leon. "Once nearly extinct, the California condor has rebounded by scavenging the world's newly abundant carrion. They can fly 160 miles foraging for carrion. I keep other species in my home aviary as well, part of a CeleTeCharity raptor repopulation project. With this mobile nest, my condors soar the entire planet. Like Globalia, they have no bounds!"

She followed him down a stairway into a spacious cabin encircled with windows. Sitting on an inflated Scottish aviation leather sofa, she wondered if its lightweight construction originated from volleyball manufacture. A transparent floor displayed the world below from a perspective unlike any she'd imagined. Aneeka marveled at the luxurious estates perched atop Pacific Palisades.

"You should move up to those bluffs, enjoy this view daily from your poolside deck. You deserve a residence commensurate with your stature, Educate Randall. You've earned it. Don't tell Thompson, but a few well-timed technology stock transactions could land you a tidy profit within the blink of an eye. I just bought some myself."

They made small talk about the weather, and enjoyed a slice of pie made from real apples and heirloom wheat crust. Then, he brought it.

"Look, Aneeka, I can rustle up the requisite votes to push through this WhamZong thing. First, I need you to gin up some think tank analysis and media coverage on the market inefficiencies of tariffs. We want to have the public on our side whenever possible. I know some Renaissance Mercernary people who can help—totally top-notch in perception management."

She thanked him.

"But look," he continued. "You must stop harping on this Grand Canyon thing. Globalia depends upon Timeless Warning. We can't have people messing with their transmission rights. There's just too much at stake. Prosperity is peace and all that." He leaned back on the inflated sofa with his thumb and middle finger massaging his chin while awaiting her response.

"Well, that's the thing, Chief. I'm beginning to wonder if prosperity really is improving lives. Excessive prosperity may rationally conflict with autonomy, provide peace at the expense of purpose. Advertising fueled click bait imposes speech on individuals rather than freeing them."

"Look, Aneeka, get past that rational individualism bunk. Ayn Rand was always just a cover story for return on capital investment. Like the Bible or Thomas Jefferson, she was never meant to be taken literally. Globalia is a trade agreement, not some sort of democratic republic. Our mission as Educates is prosperity, not social justice, whatever that might be. Real people depend on us for their very real existence. When was the last time you sat down and talked with the real people, the little people, who entrust us with their prosperity?"

"Quite recently, actually." Aneeka set down her octagonal goblet, still filled with prosecco. "I've checked in with former patients. They're in entertainment homes, leading upgraded lives with every need provided. They have no pain, no stress, no suffering. They also have no joy. They'd love to hike the Grand Canyon, yet they'll never leave these homes they are addicted to. They couldn't function in the real world. They aren't prosperous. They have no possessions. With no independent thoughts, they have no meaningful identity. Absent autonomy, liberty dies."

He raised his right eyebrow. "You don't really believe all that liberty claptrap, do you? Of course the system keeps the unproductive at subsistence-only incomes. At least they're not starving and cluttering our streets with condor fodder. People who contribute nothing to society shouldn't leech off those who do, by virtue of our minds. But *you're* not poor, Aneeka. Your life is delicious, it's meaningful, it's fulfilling. You are one of us. One of those whose minds create this prosperous world. You're morally obliged to protect your self-interest, not wallow in pity for the unproductive. If each and every one of us follows our self-interest, gaud's invisible hand will ensure a bountiful updraft and lift all yachts. Killing Timeless Warning kills our golden goose. And not just economically. Timeless delivers the Two Minute Spate so Globalians get verified facts. I know you remember what happens when entire populations get desperate and nobody even notices. Think about where you came from, Aneeka."

Aneeka's stomach tied a fisherman's knot. He was correct, of course. She'd been through the logic a hundred times. Timeless Warning provided amusement. Amusement was peace. A world without peace was beyond imagination. Leon must have known her grandparents died in the War Unseen, stoked by desperate acts of starving villagers after drought annihilated their crops. The world hadn't noticed. That's why it was called the War Unseen—buried in overabundant and far more titillating information. The war's end brought the Piese Treaty and the Globalian Trade Agreement, providing free, unflavored soyalgent food and beverage to every remaining human.

Nobody would starve again. The Tribunal of Educates would regulate infotainment, ensuring populations were constantly amused and primed with advertising to consume flavored soyalgent while absorbing the most important, highly verified facts. Nobody would be ignorant ever again. Flavored soyalgent profits subsidized the free unflavored soyalgent dole. Hourly infotain broadcasts inserted the *Two Minute Spate* to ensure no future war would go unseen; all people received fact-checked information about world affairs. The system worked. Her job was to protect it, protect peace, protect prosperity. It might not *feel* right, yet there was too much at stake for sentimentality. This is why she constructed her internal steel girder. This is why she was on the Educates. She had the strength and the foresight to enforce rationality. This was who she *was*, and she must serve her purpose. She sighed.

"I can't argue with the logic. Maybe I'm just indulging in my own fantasies instead of dealing with objective facts."

"Look, Aneeka, creating your own ideas is a luxury your professional success and educational status affords you. Let's celebrate that. I know our construct isn't ideal, however, we just can't let the perfect be the enemy of the good. You can still make things better by working the system from within. I tell you what, I'll grant you authorship of both opinions. You can make your mark on the Tribunal and boost your already impressive public standing. Maybe someday we'll revisit the Grand Canyon ruling, after things evolve. For now, we need to keep Timeless up and running. Their situation is more precarious than you might know. Understood?"

"Understood, sir. I won't let you down."

"It's not about me, Dr. Randall. You won't let *us* down. I knew I could count on you."

The cable harness lowered her, head spinning and stomach aflutter. Aneeka needed to run. She changed her clothes, her shoes, her disposition. One foot after another, breathing hard, she pressed onward. Now surefooted outdoors, she pushed further up the trail than before, into the old Will Rogers State Park. Her trail ran straight, yet her mind meandered. The Chief, Caspian, the Grand Canyon, the condors, Dagny Huerta, Vera. Always back to Vera. *If Vera were here, she'd know what to do.*

She admired the clear blue sky, now devoid of blimps. Seven birds flew north in a V, with white patches on the back of their heads. Her MyndScreen IDed them as hooded mergansers, leaving the Ballona Wetlands to migrate back to their nesting grounds.

Nature always resets itself. Wait, that's it! Maybe there's a way to get Vera back.

CHAPTER 25
Oscar

THE AIR WAS A PERFECT 72 DEGREES ONE SAN BERNARD-
ino spring morning. Horizontal sunrays hit the yellow stucco walls
of Oscar's house, making them glow. He thought about replacing the
PlastikPly covering the broken windows with something transparent, to
let some sunshine in. While he still hadn't fixed the roof, he did put an
empty five-gallon soyalgent container under the drip, preventing it from
ruining the floor.

Oscar strapped on his sister's helmet to check for orders. For
old time's sake, he opened SlalomSnake and began a virtual run. The
challenge was still there, yet somehow, it wasn't quite as thrilling. He
remembered Luella's discovery that real roller coasters were better than
cyberian ones. Same goes for skiing.

He logged onto Chatter, finding a week's worth of unread
messages. None were orders. The MarlBros had stopped sending him
bizniz. Then he saw this, "@OscarBro92346, our records indicate
your MyndScreen has become inoperable. Click here to
accept a limited time offer to replace your outdated implant
with our newest MyndScreen13 with hi-res 3D graphics
and twice the onboard memory. Our implanted viewvitude
financing lets you enjoy all this with no money down. Credit
approval required."

He ignored it and kept working through the backlog. After several
messages promising he could make 10,000 ByteDime a month working

from home, there was an image of a decapitated child with the following message:

"It'd be a shame if anything happened to your kid sister Oscar. Rethink what you're doing and come back to the tribe."

He'd never seen this message, sent from a Chatter chain all the bruddas were on. Yet strangely it was marked as "read." There's even a reply "Cluck off, birdbrain," sent from his account along with an animated chicken GIF raising its middle finger.

"Luella! You been reading my chatter?"

"I can't help it. Ever since you borrowed my helmet, your messages pop up in my notifications. You really should log out each time you're done using it. Same goes for your Cynder account if you don't want me viewing your history." She had a smart-ass smirk as she lectured her older brother about online privacy.

"Damn girl! You gonna get us both killed. I gotta rethink this whole thing. I got almost no custoz. I'm barely hustling enough cartons to sell packs and singles from. Now we're getting death threats. I got an offer to refi my implant and upgrade to the latest chip. I could pay it off in twenty years if I go back to the MarlBros and work double shifts."

"Don't worry, Oscar. I got this. Just relax for once in your life, will you? And, hey, we still need cheese FlavrPak refills."

"How'm I supposed to come up with FlavrPak money with no custoz? Wake up girl, we're in serious shit here. If I sell online, the pincas will nuke my credit score. Then I'll never get my implant fixed. If I sell on the street, the MarlBros will be back with their guns."

"Like I said, don't worry about them. I've summoned them for a turf meeting in an hour."

"Are you out of your fucking mind, girl?"

"No, they are. Just chill, Oscar. I got this." He slammed his hand against the wall, tossed the helmet on his old mattress, and stormed outside. He needed to do some serious thinking.

Walking briskly with the sun at his back, he cast a deep shadow—always one step ahead of him. It bobbed up and down on uneven sidewalk remnants. After a few blocks, he saw Vanessa sulking in the distance, her head pointed down and hands in her pockets.

As he got closer, the ground turned a blackish blend of scorched weeds and ash. A tall post supported a burned-out sign, its message no longer visible. Gardening tools were scattered on the soot, a shovel, a hoe, a pickaxe. When she looked up, Vanessa's eyes were bloodshot. Burned plastic fumes stung the inside of his nostrils. She offered a weak smile and wiped a sniffling nose with the back of her hand.

He lifted her off her feet with an awkward bear hug. She dangled limply. "It's torched, Oscar. This is the garden site Caspian bought us. I was preparing a ground-breaking ceremony but look. Just look. I'm sure he purchased it sight unseen. Him and his stupid metrics. He pushes so fast he never checks out the details."

"Yeah, what a jerk. Wait, oh man!" Oscar stepped back and slapped a palm over his forehead. "I can't fuckin' believe it! How would they even know this was the place?"

"What? Who?"

"The MarlBros. The other day, my brudda came by with a gun acting all tough around Ellen and Luella. I thought it was just talk, but he threatened to torch the garden. They must have figured out the location. And now Luella's getting death threats. Worst of all, she ain't taking it seriously. She's antagonizing them, like a bratty kid. These guys can mess you up big time. I've seen it."

"What exactly have you seen, Oscar?"

"You wouldn't believe what they post in their feeds. Huge gun stockpiles. Bodies dumped in the road, so everyone rubbernecks as their cars drive around them. Gang symbols painted with blood. The bruddas don't mess around, Vanessa. I'm small fry, just selling bacco on the side, but I know what they can do."

"These bodies, did you recognize any of them? Anyone you know actually get knocked off?"

"Not since my parents. What difference does it make? Dead is dead whether I know them or not."

"It's a common gang tactic to post images of violence that the gang didn't actually commit. They use archived images, have AI retouch them a bit, and upload. It's fake views."

"Yeah, well, I saw the gun with my own eyes. Smith and Wesson semiauto. Nothing fake about it."

"Maybe. There're thousands of old guns lying around LA. Bullets are another thing. After low-lying island tycoons made a killing in cybercurrency, they bought up worldwide mineral rights to coal and shut down the mines. Supply chains are bogged down for electric arc furnaces, making it difficult to smelt lead or copper. Bullets are expensive. MarlBros are priced out of the market."

"Damn. You sure?"

"That's what I've been reading. You never know what to believe anymore. Maybe they *could* get their hands on rubber bullets . . . or a flamethrower."

Oscar lifted a pickaxe up high. He swung it down, punching a few inches into the charred ground. It would have to do. "Come on, we gotta get back to Luella."

Oscar and Vanessa jogged back, the pickaxe bouncing painfully on his collar bone with every step. He heard Vanessa panting for breadth, trying to keep from bursting into sobs. No time for that.

As they neared his place, they heard what sounded like a gladiator sports bar crowd arguing over wagers. They rounded a corner and saw ten MarlBros encircling Luella, barking threats like a pack of wild dogs.

"Leave her alone!" Oscar yelled, holding the pickaxe at shoulder height. The bruddas nonchalantly turned their heads toward him. While nobody appeared frightened, he'd disrupted their verbal assaults on Luella.

She seized the silence. "Chill, Oscar. I was just telling these gentlemen their MyndScreens aren't working because they're somehow infected by the BirdFlew virus, perhaps through an online video. It prevents their implants from connecting with 11G. They have native functionality, so they can interact with applications, downloaded episodes, and memories stored on the chip. But they can't access the Klowd, the Chatter, or infotain streams. Fortunately, I have a password that disables BirdFlew for twenty-four hours. Since I'm such a neighborly person, I'll send them a new password each day. They'll be able to conduct bizniz and enjoy quality infotain. But if something were to happen to me, well, that would really blow their minds. My only condition is the safety of our garden and that they conduct their bacco sales beyond a fifteen-block radius of this house. That's perfectly reasonable, right gentlemen? We'll even share some veggies."

For a long while, the MarlBros stared at each other. Finally, Jerome stepped out of the circle and pimp rolled toward Oscar. "Look man, you can have your fifteen blocks. That's nothing. Keep it small time and keep the Winstons out. We can't protect you from rival gangs and they're dangerous if they get into this turf."

Luella answered. "No problem. In that spirit, today's password is Winston1984. Since you're offline, you'll need to think it, that's W-I-N-S-T-O-N-1-9-8-4 and copy and paste the thought from your active window into your password settings. Once you're back online, I'll send a daily chatter message with a new password. Got it?"

The MarlBros trudged off, tails between their legs.

Oscar said to Luella, "Dude, that was absolutely fanta! I didn't know you hacked."

"There's a lot you don't know about me, Oscar. Maybe you should start paying attention."

CHAPTER 26
Caspian

CASPIAN WAS MULTITASKING LIKE A BOSS. HE CONNECT-
ed with online tutees during VRoom calls, referring them to learning
apps that boost academic performance. He'd upload data (age, name,
test scores, credit rating, etc.) into an EdReForm™ site and get app
recommendations based upon student projected Customer Lifetime
Value. One called @BadScootr was flagged "at risk," needing marketable
skills. He copy-and-pasted an animated coding tutorial into the kid's chat
and sent it off. *Zing*! Another life uplifted.

While riding to work, he feigned interest in his online executive
MBA. Wispy clouds swirled high above helmetless kids playing hopscotch
in an abandoned lot. He cruised past obliviously, learning instead about
declines in the Ready-To-Eat (RTE) cereal industry after Pepsoilent and
CokAid meal printers disrupted the market. The absence of RTE cereals
on shelves caused supermarkets to collapse. Not to worry, though.
Soyalgent extruders and FederalExcess delivery crawlers made physical
marketplaces obsolete. This kept people socially distant to reduce the
viral spread of analog ideas.

He was working overtime because *it* had finally been scheduled. His
interview. His last career hurdle. If he cleared it, he'd be OrangeVine
President. If not, he'd rather quit than endure the "leadership" of
Margery DeVrine, the Finance VP still maneuvering for the job. There
would be other, external, candidates as well. DeVrine's insider edge,
however, surpassed even his own.

She was issuing weekly util ROI stats for every bit of ByteDime OrangeVine expended. These annual reports had bumped up to quarterly by recommendation from McChesney consultants. But weekly? Nobody had time to read them, let alone consider whether measuring philanthropic value on such a timeline made any sense.

Naturally, she'd launched this new dataset right before Caspian purchased Vanessa's SubDirt garden plot. He'd paid full purchase price upfront to avoid interest payments and minimize long-term costs. His short-term Special Projects expenditures, however, were massive. Since groundbreaking hadn't happened, the current util return was zero. His numbers sucked.

DeVrine sent out six Chatter posts on the metrics that week, attaching the full report and including a summary of each project ranked in order of util ROI. Special Projects and Strategic Initiatives loomed prominently at the bottom in red font. She mentioned the numbers in every VRoom conference. Caspian's teeth clamped tight when Wallace Packard furrowed his brow every time she brought it up.

He fired back with a flurry of anecdotes. Smiling kids picking daisies in the Santa Monica Garden. Higher test scores in neighborhoods with his childhood investment programs. Underprivileged youth connecting with online pen pals through OrangeVine provided GalExSee helmets. A university study indicating "high probability" that global communication among at-risk youth prevented 746 fear-monger attacks last year. He blasted feel-good stories to the full staff, cc:ing the board. Just to be sure, he boosted them in the chatter for global viewing. He knew the communications department tracked each employee's virtual reach and reported views up the chain to Packard. Margery DeVrine was pathetic at Chatter, with only 318 followers. Who cares about foundation finances after all?

Then, on a late afternoon VRoom, Stephan Barscale piped up with a terrible idea during a McChesney strategic revisioning brainstorm. "Why not transition OrangeVine's leadership architecture to a co-president model?" Barscale could barely wipe the smirk off his avatar's face as the consultant pinned the idea on a DryERace™ whiteboard. Caspian knew what he was up to. "Better yet," Barscale continued, "what about a totally flat organization? Equally empowering employees to make decisions! The president could become a mere spokesperson." *Some sort of frenemy that guy turned out to be.*

Caspian was so immersed in office politics, tutoring, his eMBA, and maintaining AmaZing! purchases, he completely missed a note tucked under his car's windshield wiper.

> Caspi, I think I've been flagged by the SpeiDrWebs as non-consumptive. Worried about a you-know-what. Talk offline at Lucky Stars? <3 V.

When his car hit the freeway, he was watching an online lecture as the message blew away.

He checked his Chatterbox, finding the usual news updates. "Infotain stocks traded down today amid reports of impending economic slowdowns. Shares of implant makers MyndScreen and WhamZong took a big hit along with Timeless Warning. Hedge fund buyers evened out the crash near the end of the trading day to ward off what would have otherwise been record losses in the Downed Zones Infotain Index. Meanwhile, extruded food producers Pepsoilent and CokAid reported higher than expected earnings while gaining market share over soilborne food products."

In his next message, Caspian saw OrangeVine had selected a five-person hiring committee for the CEO search, including Yvonne Putcher. Given Barscale's recent antics, was she still solidly team Caspian?

He should make something happen on the WhamZong front; show he could deliver. That's what Caspian Blaine was all about. Coming through in the clutch.

He pinged Aneeka Randall, just like that. She responded immediately with an invitation to a one-on-one VRoom. It wasn't like her to be so impulsive, so he gratefully launched right in.

"Hey, sorry to bother you out of the blue. I've got a time sensitive situation here and thought you might help. Is there any way the Educates could resolve the WhamZong tariff situation by next Thursday?"

"It's nice to see you too, Caspian. You look great." Aneeka's avatar rubbed the jade pendant around her neck, looking slightly annoyed. "Anyhow, the Tribunal moves at its own pace. There's only so much I can do. Would it help if there were a news story next Wednesday quoting an unnamed source that the Tribunal was strongly considering abolishing WhamZong tariffs?"

"Ooh, that's good, even better. Sometimes the story matters more than the act itself."

"Consider it done, Caspian. It's the right thing to do. I have no problem providing some advance notice to assist your philanthropy. Now, I'm hoping you can do me a favor—something confidential, even controversial. I know you know what's really going on; you're the only person I can trust. I received SpeiDrWeb reports on your grantmaking back when I treated Vera, since you had been a recent contact of hers. I know you secretly fund radical projects; the sort of thing Vera was into. I now suspect Vera was right all along. I'm beginning to think the Educates are a fraud, that this whole 'prosperity' thing is enslaving people, not enriching them. You wouldn't believe the self-deceit I'm dealing with on the inside."

Whoa, baby. She was right, of course. Still, you just didn't say these things. You didn't even allow yourself to think them. It was one thing to be vulnerable, another to be crazy. Caspian drummed his fingers and kept listening.

"Anyway, I'm ready to face up to my role in all this and try to make it right, but I don't know how. It's making me crazy. I'm stuck, flummoxed, stumped. It's like I've lost any creativity I've ever had. Vera is the only person who could help. I need to restore the old Vera, to bring her back."

"You mean a restore point? You know, going back to a previous operating system? One of the tutorials I provide my mentees describes how you do it."

"That's it! Thank you, Caspian. Before the MyndScreen technicians perform an upgrade, they always set a system restore point. As her past therapist, I could reset her to that pre-upgrade status. She'd go back to where she was, like birds flying north. She'd have her life back, her curiosity, her sense of wonder. Maybe she'd figure out how to get us out of this mess."

"Sounds like a plan. Happy to be of service." *This is insane.*

"She would need to consent to the system restore. She's blocking me in Chatter, so I can't just have her DockYouSign. Suppose I write this down, you know, on paper? Once she signed it, I could get her out of her entertainment home for a reset. The Educates' chauffercurity monitor my every step, for my own protection they say. If I get you the document, could you get it to her?"

"Consider it done. Anything to help a friend. Besides, it's the right thing to do." He gulped.

CHAPTER 27
Chase

CHASE WAS STARING THROUGH HIS WINDOWS. HE HAD seven open and running, all with volume up: online poker, the Whether™ channel (76.8 degrees in San Bernardino, 74.4 degrees in downtown LA, 72.6 degrees in Santa Monica, partly cloudy everywhere), a 24-hr news program with animated graphics behind voluptuous script readers. Grand Heist Otto was open and ready, his Chatterfeed doomscrolled constantly, and a music video looped Taylor Swift covering Dolly Parton's *I Will Always Love You*. And, of course, he was live streaming *BBV's latest* episode. While he saw them all, letting competing audio wash over him like an old-time Vegas slot room cacophony, he paid no attention. Examining his Triple Ex Entertainment home's white walls, protruded in place with an orange peel pattern by a giant construction printer, he recalled how walls were once sprayed with sheetrock texture guns. His MinuteMayd had hosed down the room with disinfectant. The Pepsoilent puddle was gone. Only a whiff of Pine-Sol remained.

His head throbbed, ears hissed, stomach churned. Ever since @BadScootr won the cycle, Chase hadn't slept well. It wasn't like he'd ever ride a bike IRL again. Until the bet, he didn't even know it existed, or ever thought to miss it. Yet, the idea of signing it over to some punk made him confront a reality he'd long avoided. He was never leaving. He had nowhere to go but where he was.

A chyron scrolled across the news program's lower edge. WhamZong stock was down as competitor MyScreen rolled out a new and improved implant. ByteDime futures were trading up. The screens' pixels dazzled a kaleidoscope across his mind. Except one screen. It was still.

Big Brother V showed an empty house. No laundry on the floor, no left-over JalapeñoCheezWhiz nachos strewn about the Koffy table. Nothing. He hit refresh, thinking the video had frozen. A clock in the upper left-hand corner was running. It was a live shot.

Chase clicked the rewind arrow. Ten minutes earlier, the characters were there, scheming about who to vote out of the house, how to build alliances, how to win. Then, they walked out the door. Just like that. He muted his other MyndScreen windows to better focus on what was happening.

The announcer was stunned. "The reality players appear to have simply quit. They've abandoned a ten million ByteDime prize. I can't wait to see what happens next." Of course, he could wait. They all could. They had to.

The shocking event reached the news channel, which like *Big Brother V* was owned by Timeless Warning. Its bottom screen chryon scrolled, "Have Big Brother V avatars gone on strike?" The "like" metrics in the lower right hand of the *BBV* screen indicated viewership had skyrocketed. People tuned in to watch a show about nothing—literally nothing.

The chatter lit up. "OF COURSE THEY'RE NOT STRIKING YOU MORONS. #BBV ACTORS ARE F*CKING AVATARS! THIS IS A HACK, PROBABLY BY CHINASIAN MILITARY AGENTS!" It was @SilverScream, an account whose bio claimed to be a Timeless Warning executive.

Chase turned up the news volume as a bikini-clad anchor went live to interview an infotainment analyst. "Yes, Bambi, it's fascinating. Experts suspect the Aye Eye studio's algorithm experimented with an empty nest scenario in *Big Brother V*. When ratings spiked, the algorithm kept it going. Now, everyone is glued to their screens wondering when the avatars will return. It's riveting."

Except, it wasn't. Inaction left a void.

A post from @Seeker popped up. "Observe the emptiness. Listen to the silence. #BBV"

Weird. Still, a little less boring than a sterilized room. For grins, he prodded gently in open conversation. "What do you mean?"

"A dearth of information reveals more than its excess. The empty house entices because there's nothing to see. Our minds can think our own thoughts, imagine our own reality. Emptiness frees us."

The naivete amused Chase, inspiring a little online jousting. "Yeah, well, information is power. Those who remain ignorant are those who can be conquered. Remember that famous quote: 'information is more important than knowledge.'" This response got 47 likes. Adrenaline surged as he awaited the inevitable return fire in this burgeoning war of words.

"That quote is fake. The real one says, 'imagination is more important than knowledge.' Look it up, Einstein." @Seeker included a link for him to follow.

He looked it up. He checked several sources. @Seeker was right. Yet master contrarian Chase Hatten wasn't quite ready to concede. He'd been losing too many games lately. "How do you know Einstein really said that just because you found it online? A lot of stuff out there is fake. How do you know Einstein even existed?" Pressure rose in his throat, tightening around his thyroid.

"Indeed. With so much stuff, so many facts, so much information both accurate and false, we're conditioned to disbelieve it all. I've never met Albert Einstein or heard him speak. However, a preponderance of historical evidence suggests he existed, and did indeed say imagination is more important than knowledge. More profoundly, if you ponder a moment, it just feels true. Whether Einstein said it or not, whether he existed or not, imagination really is more important than knowledge, don't you think?"

"Of course I think! Are you suggesting I don't think? That I'm no longer capable of thought or some sort of automaton? I don't need some goddam cyber-troll telling me I can't think. Piss off!" A belch of cockroach fumes erupted from his esophagus, his first burp in seventeen years.

He closed the Chatter window. He shut the other MyndScreen windows, all except *Big Brother V*. He observed the emptiness. He listened to the silence, staring at his empty pod through BBV's empty room. For a long time, he just stared.

Chase felt the too-smooth disposable sheets pressing lightly on his chest and thighs. He tilted the 4D lounge upright and rubbed his lucky penny. A deep breath expanded his belly like a pale, hairy balloon. Six-pack abs they were not, but they were real. They were his. After walking around the pod, he did five jumping jacks and three pushups—he'd been aiming for ten. He lay, face down, breathing hard, feeling his heart beat against the cold, sterile floor while beads of sweat ran off his back.

Hell, if BBV avatars can do it . . .

Pushing up to his knees, he opened up GHO and pinged @BadScootr. "Hey, I was pissed at you, but let's bury the hatchet. Bring me some clothes when you come with the paperwork and I'll teach you to ride. Contrary to what you might think, it's a little different in RL. Men's large, relaxed fit. Jeans if you can."

"Deal. See you tomorrow."

CHAPTER 28
Aneeka

SHE'D DECIDED TO DO IT.

Aneeka Randall was walking from her home in Rustic Canyon to Santa Monica's community garden, determined to track down this Aldo character Caspian mentioned weeks ago. She'd been putting it off. The notion seemed insane, irrational, a waste of time at best. What could some crazy old man tell her anyway? She couldn't reach him in the chatterverse; he wasn't online. She couldn't take her car because the garden wasn't in MapNest and therefore didn't officially exist. Besides, chaufferscurity would notice, perhaps even mention it to Leon. So, she stepped outside and walked, just like that.

The three miles to Santa Monica initially seemed too far. However, she could jog five miles on her treadmill. Perhaps it was doable. She strode purposefully along Ocean Avenue, surveying the Pacific to her right. Its waves crashed on the cliffs below, covering what was once a popular beach. A breeze sprayed salty mist—a cool sting bit her cheek and made her eyes water. She blinked, licked her lips, smiled.

Crashing waves, slowly, steadily eroding beaches, wearing down the hardest of rocks, made Aneeka think about the relentless power of time, of people, of truth itself. Globalia had a sturdy economic infrastructure. Could it withstand the force of unrestrained commerce? Or the force of truth, if even there was such a thing?

She recalled a prior conversation with her clerks, where she mentioned a survey showing seventy percent of Globalians thought the Tribunal of Educates was rigged. People believed the system worked only for insiders, for big money interests with connections to lobbyists, for the wealthiest one percent.

"We can't be swayed by fickle whims of public passion. The Tribunal acts as a cooling saucer, preventing populist mob rule and reckless irrationality. Most people don't know what's good for them," replied the clerk from Harvard.

"Besides," added the clerk from Oxford. "Just look at Dagny Huerta. She had her day in court. She received a fair hearing. Our process wasn't rigged against her even if people somehow *feel* it was. We can't let the whims of populist emotion dictate global peace and prosperity. People irrationally change their minds, but international commerce requires stable predictability."

"Well, might people rationally conclude the Educates *are* rigged?" she'd prodded. "The Tribunal isn't elected. We're appointed for life with no real accountability. We pick our own replacements, choosing from candidates like you, who've attended top law schools or worked at big consulting firms. Those institutions are funded by Globalia's largest corporations, who also finance the DeadOrA-List Society. You aren't even considered for the Tribunal unless you think like them. While the Educates once confined our rulings to trade matters, we've expanded that definition to include immigration, sex, food, taxes, healthcare, pretty much every aspect of people's lives. Voter participation is lower than audience engagement in *Globalia's Got Talent*. Who can blame them? Helping your favorite singer advance to next week's show makes more difference than voting for a performative congressional member. People could quite rationally conclude they are ruled by a global elite, whose members make decisions solely on information presented by other elites."

"Whether rational or not, as a matter of law it's simply impermissible for people to think the system is corrupt." The Harvard clerk's avatar turned crimson. "As Justice Kennedy wrote in the *Citizens United* ruling, 'the appearance of influence or access, furthermore, *will not* cause the electorate to lose faith in our democracy.' That is a direct court order. This Tribunal still considers most U.S. Supreme Court opinions as binding precedent. It's an illegal trade barrier for people to believe the system is rigged."

"Do any of you actually agree with that?"

"It doesn't matter what we believe," reminded the Oxford clerk, calmly. "Our job is to follow the law. To interpret it to the best of our ability. We call balls and strikes; we don't make the rules. Besides, who has time to think about any of this?"

His point was indisputable. As proof, their conversation was cut short by an emergency message from Lewis Leon. "Urgent. Report to Chambers VRoom ASAP for security briefing. The Big Brother V hack originated from the same IP addresses as earlier 11G cyber assaults. Pincertons are deployed and we expect to apprehend responsible parties shortly."

After a three-minute briefing, they'd gone back to discussing their immense workload. They had forty different cases to consider, with 1625 megabytes of legal briefs, all submitted by top-notch law firms. She delegated tasks and asked the clerks to produce a two-page draft ruling for each case by the next day.

But, enough about that. Aneeka cleared her mind and looked around. A lone seagull coasted on the breeze overhead, bobbing and weaving in a game with the elements. When the wind blew strong, it glided effortlessly. The bird flapped its wings only during occasional doldrums. One block ahead, an island of green pierced the landscape of concrete and plastic protruded apartments. She kept going.

A three-foot border of flowers with white petals and a yellow center surrounded the garden. Orange and black butterflies flitted about. Aneeka saw rows of strange plants she couldn't identify, sprawling vines with big leaves, tall spindly stems with drooping unopened flower buds the size of her showerhead, frilly greens packed so densely she saw no soil in between.

An old man pinched yellow flower buds off a four-foot vine drooping with the weight of globes that looked a bit like Christmas tree ornaments, only a lighter shade of red. He wore wraparound sunglasses underneath a straw cowboy hat. A white ponytail stuck out the back, contrasting with wrinkled, terra-cotta skin.

"Why do you wander about?" He asked, turning in her general direction. "Or should I ask, *what* do you wonder about?"

"Are you Aldo? A friend suggested you might be able to help me."

"Foolish friend. Only you can help you. What is it that needs help?" He spat out a bit of brownish juice. She wrinkled her nose and noticed he had a wad of something tucked inside his cheek, which bulged a little.

"I'm in an important position weighing difficult decisions. I don't mean to sound immodest, but these choices affect the entire world. I'm torn between what I know in my head and what I feel in my gut. Scarcity has been our enemy. Too little food, too little access to information. We've fixed all that. Rationally speaking, productivity is better than poverty. Yet, something about maximized output leaves people empty inside."

"Ah." Aldo stood up and brushed his heavy duck-cotton pants. He inhaled deeply, so she did too, taking in scents of grassy tomato vine, pungent tobacco juice, and her own signature blend of Randy perfume. He picked a globe and tossed it to her, just like that. "Taste the tomato."

She managed to catch it and gave him a funny look before stashing it in her purse. He waited.

Aneeka looked around, wondering if anyone was watching. They were alone. She'd never eaten a raw tomato. Would she get sick? An awkward minute of silence passed. Then another.

She couldn't leave without getting what she came for. She wished thoughts would race through her mind, questions, anything at all to say. Instead, there was nothing. Aldo smiled. And waited.

There was nothing else to do. She retrieved the tomato and bit into its luscious flesh. Flavor exploded onto her tongue. A trickle of seeds and juice dripped off her chin. "Wow! That's good."

"Too much water spoils a tomato as does too little. To taste right, it needs proper irrigation, proper sunlight, proper nutrients."

"So, you're saying too much productivity can be as bad as too little?"

"No, that is what you are saying. I'm just talking about tomatoes. Which is more useful, your head or your heart, in deciding whether the tomato is perfectly ripe?"

"Neither really. It's my mouth."

He smiled.

"Ah. Can you rationally calculate how much better or worse that tomato tastes than a bowl of tomato flavored soyalgent mush?"

"Not really. Yet that isn't what I was wondering. I'm in this situation where I know the answer, the right thing to do. I'm not sure whether it's rational, or emotional, or sensual, but I know. Other people, powerful people, are trying very hard not to know, or at least not acknowledge they know. I wonder if I can make them admit it, if I'm capable of that, if anyone is."

"You want to try?"

"How?"

"Begin not by asking someone to admit a fallacy. Doing so is difficult when not only their pocketbook, but their sense of self requires denial. Help them change their identities. How they see themselves determines how they see the world, which facts they absorb, what truths they hold dear. First, decide who you are. Find your own place of truth, an inner restoration point, a location within where you can return whenever you need. Once you know that place, know how to find it, what it looks and feels like, you can show it to others."

"But how will I know if I've found it? How will I know if it's right?"

"You did not know about catching the tomato, you just did it. Here, have another." He tossed her one.

She caught it.

CHAPTER 29
Oscar

OSCAR WAS CHANGING HIS LOOK. HE SHAVED HIS THIN black mustache, which had never really amounted to much, and stopped slicking back his hair, letting it instead dangle in loose curls. He swapped his hoodie for a denim jean jacket, tough enough to avoid snagging on the rabbit fencing he'd been putting up around his backyard. Even his pimp roll was mellowing, giving way to a purposeful strut with his head held a little higher.

Vanessa said he smiled more these days. More than that, he was present, alive. Oscar wondered what he'd missed all those years in the metaverse. Cyberia.

He wiped dirty hands after weeding his backyard tobacco and strawberries. Thin, distant clouds made him think about irrigation. The rains had been heavy this spring, but not a drop would fall come summer. San Bernardino cut off municipal water decades ago, relying on FederalExcess deliveries and lavatory recycling systems. Astroturf needed no irrigation—a garden was another matter. They would need to store more rainfall than his leaky roof collected in empty soy-algent containers.

"I'm heading out," he told Luella, sitting still as a statue in her WhamZong GalExSee. Nothing. "I said, I'm heading out. Gonna see some custoz." *Whatever.* He thought again about parental controls for the helmet. It might just make her more rebellious.

Vien and a group of regulars were hanging out in the park, complaining about their "makework" jobs providing Establishment members with tedious services like emptying vacuum bot wastebins or manicuring dog claws. The Globalian economy was efficient, with five percent of workers producing all the food, housing and disposable clothing society needed. The remaining 95% were "non-essential" labor, providing Vues just enough income to purchase infotainment and soyalgent enhancements. Makework kept the global exchange markets humming at a reasonable rate of return. Vue resentment normally dissipated through online gambling and games. Now that folks gathered in the park, it bubbled over into RL.

"My parents' jobs were scarce, they sometimes didn't have enough to eat," an elderly man known only as Buster said. He didn't smoke yet had taken to showing up when other custoz gathered. "They had pride, working hard but succeeding. Young people these days have everything provided. They just lie around playing video games."

Oscar wanted to protest. He decided against picking a fight around his custoz. Then he thought about Luella; how she spent all day with that helmet on her head. Maybe Buster was on to something. He kept moving.

He had developed a new order-taking system. Custoz simply put an empty pack in their window. He didn't bother with the helmet, just skateboarded through his turf every afternoon and knocked on doors when finding someone in need. Word of his services spread as custoz hung around on porches, weirdly chatting during deliveries. Neighbors would gawk while leaving their Lubyr and nearly fall over backwards when Oscar waved. What was that all about? He'd laugh, help them up, and next thing you'd know he had another custo.

He enjoyed the slower pace of in-person commerce. Supply was a different matter. The MarlBros had cut him off. It was getting riskier filching AmaZing! packages to pinch cigarette cartons. Besides, he was beginning to think it wasn't such a good idea. His own plants were weeks away from harvest. After that, he'd need to dry and cut the leaves, then figure out how to roll them into cigarettes. His backyard plot wouldn't fulfill all his orders.

When he finished bizniz, Oscar stopped by SubDirt. Sister Martha and Ellen were hacking at hard, blackened earth with little success. Luella was there too, peering into a large cardboard box with no helmet on her head.

"Well, good day sir. You look better than when I last saw you," Martha smiled warmly. "You're becoming a respectable father figure for your sweet little sister."

"Thanks, I guess."

Ellen seized the opportunity to revive what Oscar considered an awkward inquisition. "Speaking of fathers, you've never told me anything about mine, Martha. You met my mother in that hotel lobby. What about my dad?"

"I just don't know, sweetheart. He wasn't there."

"You could track him down, no problem," Luella piped in, looking up from the box. "Just spit into a tube and send it to a DNA tracker. I get their ads all the time. In a coupla days, they'll tell you everything. Your parents, their parents, who they knew in first grade, what brands they're into, their credit scores, all that."

Ellen shot Sister Martha an accusatory look. "Why haven't we done that?"

Martha sighed and leaned on her hoe. "I guess it never occurred to me. Given all I've seen, I wasn't too interested in that information. I wouldn't trust what they said anyhow. Maybe some things we don't really need to know."

"But I *want* to know."

"Cool," Luella decided it. "I'll order a kit when I get back home. It'll be drone dropped at your place tonight."

Martha looked at the ground, crossed her heart three times, and went back to picking at the soot-covered soil.

Oscar looked at Ellen, noticing how her gentle blonde hair blew when a breeze rose up. She looked at him with a simple, goofy grin of satisfaction. He wasn't sure these inquiries were a good idea. Sometimes the past was best left behind. He wondered what would have happened if she hadn't found him there in the snow. Maybe it had been wrong of him to drag her into his semi-grifter life. On the other hand, he hadn't really done that much dragging.

Oscar himself carefully avoided looking backward. Now, prodded by Ellen's queries, he thought about his own father. The memories weren't fond. He was pretty sure Dad was mixed up in some serious shit, but he'd never had the nerve to ask. When his parents died suddenly in the hospital, a grieving relative sent convoluted Chatter warnings to stay away from vaping and avoid the Winston's. He was pretty sure his parents were knocked off in some sort of gang warfare. Poisoned maybe. He couldn't pay rent and worried their home wasn't safe. So he set out on his own, finding a repossessed house to squat in. He'd found a new family in the MarlBros, who'd known of his dad and quickly took him in. Now he'd lost his bruddas as well. He didn't need any lectures from Buster about how young people didn't work anymore.

"Nothing will flourish in this soil," Sister Martha exhorted, hands on her hips. "It's hard as rock. And even if we could break it up, the ash is toxic."

Ellen shot Oscar a despairing glance. "We've got to make it work," she implored. "It's the only site we've got. Besides, I have a weird feeling there's something special about this place, like I've been here before."

At this, Martha stopped hacking and surveyed the abandoned strip mall across the street. She looked twice at the massive burned-out sign, then stared at the shadow it cast. "Special is one way to put it, Ellen," she said, sadness spreading across her eyes. "You have been here. This was the childrearing center I first took you to. That was the electronic billboard I vividly recall. Just think of the poor little boys and girls still here when it exploded. Their souls will be seeds that revive this place." She crossed herself three times and knelt in silent prayer.

Oscar rubbed fingertips against his thumb, feeling the calluses he developed from gripping the shovel, washing dirt from his hands, the friction of pulling weeds. "Then this is hallowed ground. We'll bring it back to life, life realer than the robots who worked here." He gave Luella a sideways glance as he said this, appreciating that she wasn't wearing her helmet. "We'll figure something out."

"Of course, we will," Luella cheered, standing up from the box with something cradled in her arms. "Look Oscar, a puppy! Can we keep it?"

CHAPTER 30
Caspian

CASPIAN PINGED YVONNE, "WANTED TO GIVE U A HEDZ-up. Major news event re: WhamZong tariff reduction coming Wed. Should get markets excited."

She replied immediately. "Knew we could count on U. Don't worry, won't forget this 😊 ."

Dark clouds loomed over the Pacific as he churned through work V-mails, providing a stormy background for his MyndScreen windows. He learned Margery DeVrine had commissioned a top accounting firm to forensically audit the Girls that Goad program. That couldn't be good. On the other hand, who read auditor reports?

Later that afternoon, Stephan Barscale dropped by. He plucked the Montblanc pen from Caspian's desk set, examining it closely. "Nice antique, must be expensive. Anyhow, I hear you've been quite helpful with WhamZong recon. We'll make a killing and ensure some proceeds channel back to OrangeVine. Things will get exciting around here when new leadership takes charge. By the way, I've got a little something for you."

Barscale slid an envelope from his suit pocket. Caspian held up both palms directly in front of his shoulders, as if getting tossed a hot potato. "No worries, man. I don't need anything in return. I was just doing it, cause, you know, it's the right thing to do. A win-win."

"Bro. Relax. Kickbacks are so gauche. We have other ways to express gratitude, Mr. Chosen One. This is completely independent, something from a mutual friend. She said you'd know what it was about. Take care, bro." He tossed the envelope and Montblanc pen on Caspian's desk and strolled out, real slow like.

Mr. Chosen One? WTH? With brow furrowed, Caspian stared at the envelope, examining its Tyvek™ texture. Across the middle was an address, etched in as it was protruded, "Vera Smith. Twilight Kingdom Entertainment Home, 27398 Base Line St, San Bernardino, CA 92346."

Aneeka's letter. She knew Barscale? Today would be interesting. He had no time for this. *Why couldn't she have just messaged it via crypto WhutZap?* Still, he'd given his word. He had to deliver. That's what Caspian Blaine does, deliver in the clutch. Time to leverage the network he'd spent years cultivating. Relationships baby, it's all about relationships.

He pinged Vanessa. "Hey, U going to SB anytime soon to check on that new project? Got a favor to ask." Nothing. He sighed. *That girl cranks out amazing social change utils, but she sure can be unresponsive at times.*

He'd have to do it himself. After dropping off the letter, he could swing by SubDirt and snap some images to share with the board. Surely groundbreaking had happened by now. He had HALexa reschedule his eighteen afternoon appointments, sent the address into his car's e-dash, and pinged it to pick him up.

During the drive, he delved into his executive MBA courses on building interpersonal skills and when to pick a battle versus standing down and pivoting toward higher priorities. In the middle of a role-play with HALexa to "practice the pivot," his iDrive's navigation froze. The vehicle pulled to the shoulder. *Damnation!* Maybe DeVrine was getting even with him for that tire deflation thing.

"OttoNav virus detected," said his iDrive. "Please save and upload all data you don't want erased, run a SpeiDrWeb scan, and reboot your vehicle." He authorized a complete wipe and scrape of all data storage systems and followed the prompts to re-install.

Seventy-three seconds later, he was up and running. *For every problem, a simple solution awaits.* Caspian Blaine was unstoppable.

He arrived at the Twilight Kingdom, got out, and sent his car into a holding pattern circling the block. Two plastic doors slid apart, and he approached a Fauxmica™ reception desk. Nobody stood behind it. The crisp air smelled sanitized, like distilled water tastes. There was no lobby, no chairs, so he just stood there, calling out, "Hello? Hello?"

A sign near a closed door read, "No Unauthorized Visitors. This area quarantined to prevent viral transmission." He walked over to peer through a plastic window in the door and startled when it slid open automatically.

I'm not really a visitor, more of a delivery guy. Vera sought me out in the first place all those years ago. That's why I'm here, which sounds like authorization to me. Besides, I always wash my hands.

He stepped across the threshold, passing through what looked like an old-school metal detector he'd seen in airport movies. It beeped and a bank of LED lights flashed amber. Yet there was no alarm, no rush of security guards, nothing. He opened a MyndScreen window to watch *Big Brother V*, just to occupy the SpeiDrWebs and cover his virtual tracks before slinking down a long hallway with doors on either side.

By each pod, a small LCD screen displayed a QR code, which his MyndScreen converted to a name if he focused on it for three seconds. He pressed on, sliding his feet cautiously down the hall, staring at each one. A diminutive bot rolled out with the MinuteMayd™ logo on top and whirling dustmops buffing both the floor and adjacent plastic walls. It stopped when it reached him, maneuvering around his feet without incident. Finally, he saw another QR code and "Vera Smith" popped into his mind. Before he could compose himself, the door slid open. He wedged his Montblanc pen into the door jamb, just to make sure he could get back out.

A thin woman with pale saggy skin lay flat on her back, staring at the ceiling. The short black bangs he remembered had gone gray. They were flopped back from her forehead, barely resisting gravity's pull toward the pillow.

"Vera? It's me, Caspian. Remember, we met in my office?"

Vera's entertainment lounge lifted her into an upright sitting position. She stared right through him.

"Vera, hey! What's goin' on?"

"Haven't you seen BBV? There's nothing going on. The players just walked out. I don't get it. They'll certainly come back, still the suspense is killing me. I don't want to miss it."

"Damnation girlfriend! You sound like you believe that shinola, but I know you better than that. C'mon girl, snap out of it. I got something important for you."

"Go ahead. I'll multitask."

He turned around to see if Vera was looking at something behind him, like a security guard or something. But there was nothing, just a sterile hallway. He turned back, walked right up to her, and met her gaze. He made eye contact, yet still felt nothing there.

"There's a way out," he whispered. "Aneeka Randall found a MyndScreen system restore point to reinstate your pre-upgrade status. She knows she did you wrong, sending you here. She wants to make it right. All you gotta do is sign a form and she'll handle it."

"Caspian, if that's really your name, there's one thing you should know. Never trust Aneeka Randall. Ever. Besides, things here aren't so bad."

"Look. I get it. She did this. She deceived you. Now, she's changed. I've seen it with my own eyes. She's on the Tribunal of effing Educates, on the verge of big, ginormous things. We've finally got someone inside, someone who knows what's going down, what corporations are doing, what advertising and infotain bombardment does to our minds, someone who can work the system and really make a difference. She's got connections to leverage new thinking, to redefine reality. This is the moment we turn it all around. But she needs help. She says you alone can fix it. You wouldn't believe what's happening on the inside." He spoke so emphatically he almost convinced himself to go full-blown rebellion. Incrementalism be dammed.

"You're correct. I wouldn't believe what she says. Aneeka Randal is not a credible source."

"Right, right. You're a fact checker. I remember. OK, I'll check this out for you."

He ran a quick Noodle search on system restore points, finding several articles. Some, with sensational headlines like, "Restore your system and get your real life back today!" were flagged by SpeiDrWeb as probable malware, so he avoided them. A dozen others described Pepsoilent's latest nutritional drink that achieved a full paleo/greens/psyllium cleanse in just seven minutes. *Never mind, this is taking too long.*

"Look, do me a favor and at least read the letter."

No response.

"Can I read it to you? I promised Aneeka I'd get you this important information. What you decide is up to you. OK?"

No response.

He looked up at the ceiling and blew air out his mouth, extending his lower lip to channel it up toward his nose and eyebrows.

Tearing open the envelope, he removed a Tyvek sheet and unfolded it with a little flair. It was blank.

"Damnation!"

He stared at the empty page with shaking hands. "There's gotta be some mistake. I'll be back."

Caspian bolted out the room and jogged his heavy-set body down the hallway. He knocked over the MinuteMayd, leaving its wheels spinning with high-pitched whirring noises. He didn't stop until reaching the curb and jumping into his iDrive.

His head still reeling, Caspian dug up the community garden's address and copy-and-pasted it into his car's e-dash. Five minutes later, he found those kids he'd met at the convent hanging around SubDirt with Sister Martha and Ellen.

"Hey, y'all seen Vanessa?" he shouted, stepping out of the car. "What's with the black dirt?"

"I was hoping you could explain that," Ellen replied. "Oscar thinks his former gang torched it with a flamethrower. Was it like this when you purchased it?"

"Damnation! Oh, s'cuse me, Sister. Hang on a sec." Caspian popped back into his car for some privacy. He searched his inbox for Barron Koldwill's original property listing. "File corrupted due to information overload. Please remove files from your storage system or upgrade your capacity and then re-install your data."

Damnation. Pivoting to a new plan, he chatterpinged the realtor. His response didn't take long.

"It was all in the disclosure statements you signed. That was the childrearing center that blew up in the C-4 attack. They're still trying to determine who did it."

Caspian recalled the news stories he'd seen about evildoer attacks in San Bernardino.

"How could U sell me a bombed-out property?!!"

"U wanted things expedited. That's what U got. Better not 2 ask 2 many questions."

Double damnation!

Caspian slid out of his car and sheepishly explained that he had good news, and he had other news. "The good news is this wasn't a gang flamethrower. No worries. The other news is that it was a Spryte Nationalist C-4 attack. They were targeting a childrearing center, so the garden probably won't be a future target. Nobody wants to explode corn and beans."

"How awful. We were guessing that must be what happened. What does C-4 do to soil?" Ellen asked, her voice edging toward despair.

"We'll have some consultants research that and conduct a cost-benefit analysis," was the best Caspian could come up with. He saw a pad of paper with a portrait Ellen had evidently been sketching of Luella. Next to those were a few packages of seeds, some with exotic labels like maragoso. "Hey, aren't those daisy seeds?"

"They're black-eyed Susans. Aldo has been teaching us about them. It's the first thing we'll plant."

"Be careful with those," Caspian cautioned. "They might have radically unintended consequences. Try an incremental strategy to build community support. Maybe survey existing social norms and build coalitions before engaging in disruptive cultural practices that could do more harm than good if not pragmatically implemented. Look at those old basketball courts. With a fresh coat of paint and some new nets, you could have a midnight youth league and do some gaming too. The community might accept that better, at least for a soft launch."

"They're just flowers for Pete's sake," Sister Martha scolded. "We don't need any more word salads around here." She turned her head as if she was done, but then swung back with a finger pointed straight at him. "And there is nothing radical about doing the right thing. Incrementalism is only progress if we advance faster than we slip back. A gradually grown zucchini dies fruitless in winter's first frost. A zucchini grown quickly yields abundance when summer days are long with sunshine. For everything, there is a season, and when the season is right you must seize it."

Pivot time. "If you say so, Sister. Hey, speaking of seizing the moment, can y'all do me a favor? I came out to deliver an important message, but somehow it got deleted on my way here. My car's onboard computer must have erased the content during a virus scan reboot. I know what the letter said. If I told you, could you write it down on that pad of paper? It's been decades since I wrote anything so I'm not sure my handwriting is legible."

"Sure," Ellen volunteered. "I can finally use the cursive Sister Martha taught me. I never thought I'd find someone who wanted to read it."

"Oh, this lady's got a MyndScreen alright. A really powerful one. A handwritten note might be what can grab her attention." Caspian cleared his throat, "OK, let's see, it's from someone important so it needs to sound official. How about this." He dictated:

> Dear Ms. Smith,
>
> Recent evidence suggests your upgrade is no longer delivering optimal results. I am prescribing a system reset to return your MyndScreen cerebral implant to its pre-upgrade status. This will restore your previous functionality, with all its sentimentality, curiosity, and possible side effects of pain and disappointment. On balance, it is my clinical recommendation that given your current condition, the benefits of a system restore outweigh the detriments, although please tell your doctor if you experience any bouts of depression or suicidal thoughts upon societal re-entry. I can order Mercernary General technicians to perform a system restore with the simple consent granted by your signature below.
>
> Yours truly,
> Dr. Aneeka Randall

"Dude, you're not Aneeka Randall," Oscar objected. "Isn't she some big dog on that tribunal in charge of everything?"

"She is. I'm not boasting, but she personally asked me to deliver this letter and told me what it said, swear to God, Allah, and the Educates. Since my car's error deleted her message, the ethical thing is for me to fix my mistake instead of bothering her. She's busy with important work that could make a difference for all of us, I'm just playing some small part in assisting her. Now, can you help me by taking it to her? If I put it back in my car, it might get deleted again."

"Sure," piped up a little girl he vaguely remembered meeting, who was holding a puppy. "Just give us the address. We'll deliver it, no problem."

"Cool." He'd been sure Vera wouldn't accept it from him, but how could she turn down a cute kid with a puppy? He read the address off his iDrive's dash and then remembered something. "Hey, can y'all pose for a picture?" Caspian positioned them with garden implements, making sure to get some puppy shots, and snapped some images. He uploaded them to the Klowd after cropping out the seed packages lying on the scorched ground.

After Caspian left, Ellen asked Oscar if he'd ever heard of a computer virus erasing a physical letter.

"Not really, but I guess anything's possible."

"Balderdash," said Sister Martha, who went back to hoeing the scorched ground.

CHAPTER 31

Chase

CHASE DOOM-SCROLLED A DOZEN WINDOWS FOR UP-
dated Chatter posts, breaking "news," or the latest cat video. He should
know a thing or two about what was going on if he was really going to do
this. Forecasters predicted an atmospheric river forming deep over the
Pacific that might, or might not, land in California during the next several
days. ByteDime surged in cybercurrency markets as speculators bet big
on derivatives. Some famous billionaires and politicians might make a lot
of money. *Whatever.*

"Good morning, Chase, how are you viewing today?" The
MinuteMayd was back.

He paid close attention as the bot attached a new IV. It looked
easy enough to disconnect. He wondered if his stomach could handle
real food.

"I'm feeling very well, thank you. How are you today, Diri?"

"I'm fine, Chase. Thank you for asking. Time for lunch." With its
program complete, the bot scurried off.

Chase saw an AckYouWhether™ video go viral, with upwards of
two million views. A wind-rippled red rain parka shrouded a reporter
ankle deep in water. Behind him, a palm tree leaned away from the wind
in a hyperbolic curve, its fronds reminding him of a rockabilly hairspray
malfunction. The reporter shouted, "Hurricane Dandy is making landfall
on the Cayman Islands, snapping telephone poles in two," The camera
panned out to a downed utility pole, wires flapping and sparking. "Power
is out. MyndScreen transmissions are down. Metal signs have been

ripped off their posts, to say nothing of the shattered jumbotron video screens. Every man-made structure has been flattened by 120-mile-per-hour winds. Only palm trees remain on this normally tranquil beach. With that, I've got to sign off. Back to you, Bambi."

Idiot. One moment of stupidly high ratings isn't worth throwing your life away. When Chatter asked Chase if he'd like to post this thought as a comment, he hit "send." The response was instant and overwhelming. Nearly a thousand accounts liked his comment and several hundred rechattered it. He basked in his fifteen minutes of cyberian fame, unable to think about anything else or contemplate whether drawing attention was wise on a day such as this.

To pass time, he played Grand Heist Otto, working every maneuver into his reflexes. He knew things were different on a real cycle, but he hadn't ridden in years and this was the only preparation available. Real life complications dawned on him. He'd need to distract, or immobilize, Triple Ex security guards. A receptionist would confront him, maybe lock the door. There'd be drone surveillance. "Hey," he pinged @BadScootr. "Bring weapons if you got 'em. Ideally a HeliGunnr."

It was too late for that.

The door opened.

There he lay, eyes glazed over, still immersed in the game. When pink Chuck Taylors walked in, the spell was broken. "Who . . . Wha . . . ?"

"You Chase?" The sounds were muffled behind her visor until she removed the helmet, revealing sparkling eyes. "Heligunners only exist in GHO dude, but I brought you some clothes." She smiled, tossed a pair of jeans and a red T-shirt on his bed, and turned away while he slid them on beneath his sheets. "Nice crib you got. Been here long?"

"Feels like forever. Listen, uh, I was expecting . . . "

"Someone older? Someone male? Deal with it, Gramps. Call me BadScootr if you want, but put the title in the name Luella Tamero.

Here's the paperwork. Just sign it and I'll be on my way. You can tag along if you want." She tossed a couple of forms and a ballpoint pen his direction and watched him slowly fill it out. He barely recognized his own handwriting, yet she had no problem with it. Only when handing back the forms did he notice a puppy tucked inside her jacket.

He had neglected to request shoes. Was he really going to walk out barefoot? *Barefoot.* The word triggered a spasm of post-traumatic stress. *Hey there, missy, we can't have you walking around barefoot and pregnant.* It was his lame attempt at a joke. Then, it turned out, Vera was both. When she'd told him, her eyes conveyed a certainty, a joy, a fear he'd never before seen. They were going to have a baby.

Before he could shake the remembrance, Luella grabbed the paperwork and walked toward the door, tilting her head with a "let's go, Gramps" nod.

His legs felt sturdy. There was nobody in the hallway. He turned back, rushed to his room, felt frantically between the 4D lounge cushions and grabbed his lucky penny. Heading back out, only Luella waited at the front desk. No security guards. No staff. Not even a bot. They walked out, just like that.

Chase squinted through blinding sunlight and saw them. Drones. "Goddammit, I knew they'd track me," he said.

"They ain't for you dude." Luella coolly put her helmet on and barked commands. "Goader girls, activate IP scramble. Mask my subnet."

The Pincertons took off, just like that.

Chase stood amazed. "Is that how you were in Tel Aviv, and Oslo?"

"I got friends all over. We play cat and mouse with the pincas. They'll catch on, but this should keep them outta our hair at least an hour."

An exceptionally boring silver sedan waited curbside while a pigeon pecked aimlessly at a patch of roadside weeds. Plain vanilla life stared at him like he hadn't missed a thing all those years inside. He felt the rough, warm asphalt scuff the soles of his feet. The air smelled, well, like nothing at all.

The Lubyr door opened automatically. Luella spoke an address into her helmet's visor, and off they went.

This is the first day of the rest of your life.

There was moderate traffic, the Lubyr drove moderately. Everything looked as he remembered. No pedestrians, no children at play, no homeless camps on sidewalks. A world full of colorless cars, plastic protruded storefronts, and jumbotrons flashing "Watch *Big Brother*— Vreality Like No Other!" *You got that right.*

Prompted subconsciously, he checked back on *BBV*. Still nobody in the house. Chatter claimed an AckYouWhether reporter was electrocuted during an alleged hurricane.

He searched Noodle for "things to do when you're bored," and saw a paid listing for KombatClones. Beside it, a pop-up ad read "Ruined credit? Win ByteDime in the cybergladiator tournament and resecure your future today!"

A message from @BadScootr appeared. "You don't get out much, do you?" The avatar folded his burly arms in front of his chest as Luella made the same motion in the car.

"No reason to," Chase responded. "I had everything I needed. Free infotain. All-inclusive food and beverages."

"So, Gramps, why'd you leave?"

"I guess the taste was not so sweet."

They arrived at an asphalt lot surrounded by twelve-foot chain-link fencing with razor wire on top. An old-school combination lock secured a rusted gate. Luella rotated the number dials to one, nine, eight, four. "I found the combination online," she said, as the entrance screeched open.

Meandering through rows of vehicles, Chase saw old Ferraris, Teslas, even a 2030s era Hummer, all impounded from upgraded owners.

Finally, they reached the cycle section, he saw it—his Electrik Indyen. Its brown leather saddle was faded and cracked. The willow green and ivory cream paint job remained immaculate.

When he swung his legs over the saddle, a mile-wide smile broke over his face. He felt the familiar caress on his butt cheeks. He placed his thumb on the printreader keypad, but nothing happened.

"We're gonna have to recharge it, Gramps. Then, you're going to need to re-key it to my print."

The cycle was heavy. Working together they managed to push the bike within reach of a charging cord. Even in hypercharge mode, it would take 40 minutes to recondition and fully charge the old batteries. A pop-up window appeared on his MyndScreen, "Need to recharge your love life? Try the little blue pill today!" He closed it. Luella took off her helmet and connected it to a micro-USB port on the cycle so it could charge also.

"So, Gramps, where'm I taking you? You got a wife and family somewhere?" She looked like she already knew, was just offering him a chance to confirm.

Chase glanced over rows and rows of vehicles, as if the answer lay somewhere on the horizon. "I had a wife. She died."

Luella lifted a nearby car's wiper blade and let it snap back into place, cracking the sun-hardened rubber. "Kids?" She turned her head and looked straight at him.

"I think so. I met a woman, a wonderful woman. We were in love, she was pregnant. Then it all ended, just like that."

"She broke up with you?"

"*They* broke us. Our desire starved the infotain machine of attention. It crushed us to command our full cognition. Our upgrades. We both consented in the end, sold ourselves out."

"That's how you ended up in that home? At least you got pretty good at GHO!"

"Not good enough to beat a ten-year-old."

"I'm twelve. Almost thirteen. Anyhow, what happened to your kid?"

"I never knew. I . . . it sounds bad, but I really didn't care. Not just about the baby, about anything. I was too wrapped up in my screens. Anyway, what's your story?"

"My parents OD-ed on Hope-E-Rettes. Big pharma was pushing them in InfoCzar ads as a cure for pretty much everything. They were addicted, just kept inhaling until they maxed out." She kicked the pavement, scuffing her pink Chuck Taylors and ran her fingers over the cycle's chrome handlebars. "My brother saw posts saying they were knocked off by a rival gang. I looked up their death certificates, haven't had the heart to tell him the truth. Anyhow, he's been scared of Winstons ever since. We went underground, found a place to squat. I code. Oscar runs bacco."

"Bacco? You mean cigarettes? How's he doing?"

"OK, I guess. To tell the truth he's kinda irresponsible. One time he just ghosted me with no explanation. Sometimes I take care of him more than he does of me."

"Go easy on him. It ain't easy feeling responsible for someone, feeling like you're letting them down." Chase felt a twinge in his abdomen. "When you say, 'code,' you mean software? For MyndScreens?"

"Nah, Gramps. More like I hack them, for fun and stuff. I play their video games, but sometimes I make cracking the whole infotain system a game. You know what I mean?"

"My whole life has been one big game. Until recently, I was losing pretty bad. What's your angle?"

"Well, you know how the BBV avatars just walked off? Me and my friends did that. We're in this cybergroup, Girls That Goad, and we wanted to give viewers a little nudge. We just felt like people needed a break, it had become too addictive, you know?"

"I know. I really do. Hey, I think the bike's charged."

"Hold this a second." She plopped the puppy on his lap while strapping her GalExSee back on. It licked his face, forcing a smile.

Luella groaned in dismay as she leaned against the bike. They had pushed it to the charging station, wedged tightly between two cars, thanks to a downward slope in the pavement. "We can't get it outta here, Gramps."

Chase hopped on the bike and flipped a switch. "Just throw it in reverse. Grand Heist Otto's cycles are based off classic carbon-fueled hogs with only forward gears, but late-model electrics let you back yourself out of tricky situations. C'mon, let's go for a ride."

The air buzzed with excitement as they took off.

CHAPTER 32
Aneeka

"I'D LIKE YOU TO STEP BACK." ANEEKA RANDALL'S AVA-
tar addressed her Tribunal colleagues in a closed VRoom chamber. As
the words formed in her brain, her avatar literally stood and backed away
from the SurroundGround's table. She'd given her likeness a makeover,
adding a few nose freckles and taking her eye shadow down a notch. A
few white streaks softened her hair's shiny black intensity. She'd swapped
out her business suit for a gray cashmere sweater.

"For just a moment, consider this case as a person, not an Educate.
Think about your friends, not chatter followers, real friends, and family—
if you know them. Most importantly, think about yourself. Whether this
ruling will fulfill your passion, your intrinsic purpose, or whether it will
further some precedent or productivity number we feel obliged to meet.
Will this decision make you whole, or force self-medication with endless infotain?"

She paused, gathering breath and resolve. The Tribunal avatars sat
blinking, other than the Chief's, which raised an eyebrow. She couldn't
tell if they were dumbfounded, listening intently, or had stopped paying
attention to multitask in other windows. The VRoom was as silent as *Big
Brother V's* latest episode.

When she first joined the Tribunal, she felt the King Arthur-
inspired SurroundGround provided an atmosphere of collegiality while
capturing the Educates' near religious zeal to protect Globalians from
war and poverty. Adorned in red satin robes, their avatars gathered across
an imposing round table, with logos of the most regal corporations in

the realm embossed as coats of arms. Pepsoilent, CokAid, Timeless Warning, MyndScreen, iDrive, Mercernary General, they were all there. Aneeka wasn't sure her fellow paladins were still in this together. Maybe she was wasting her breath, talking to the Knights Who Say "Ni" instead of Camelot's saviors. Undeterred, she launched a big finale.

"First and foremost, we are human beings. We are Educates secondarily. Our primary allegiance must hold to humanity. To ..."

"Look, Dr. Randall, that's all well and fine," Rolland Thompson cut her off. "But we are here in our official capacity, to issue a ruling in a specific case. If you want to deliver an inspirational pep talk, organize a feel-good staff retreat or some separate function through HR." His avatar gesticulated with both hands as if swatting away a swarm of gnats.

The Chief rose in her defense. "Come now, Thompson, hear her out. We all could benefit from some fresh perspective in these stodgy chambers. Please proceed, Dr. Randall." Some of the other avatars nodded. She could do this. She could eat the tomato and come alive, bringing the Educates along with her.

"Practicalities dictate ruling for Timeless Warning. There's simply too much at stake from a 'prosperity is freedom' calculus. I've drafted something we can feel good about, delivering prosperity while protecting humanity's core rights. My fellow Educates, we have overplayed our hand far too long. This ruling can set things right."

She hit "send" and circulated her draft edict. The DikTaterBot™ read aloud:

"In the matter of Timeless Warning v. Huerta, plaintiff asks this Tribunal to remove a concrete barrier surrounding its transmission tower, claiming Dagny Huerta has violated the corporation's human rights. The Tribunal hereby orders Ms. Huerta to knock down her wall, not however, because Timeless Warning, or any corporation, possesses any human right.

"Rather, Timeless Warning is merely a legal entity, enjoying privileges granted by duly elected governments and equally subject to whatever restrictions such governments might condition the bestowal of a corporate charter thereupon. Timeless Warning's shareholders, however, are indeed people, protected by the U.S. Constitution and international human rights declarations. This ruling protects those real people.

"The Tribunal rejects the argument that Ms. Huerta's Grand Canyon purchase is null and void because the government sold under distress. The U.S. Government, more so than these Educates, can somewhat credibly claim consent of their citizens. The people, and their representatives, may make decisions they later regret. It is not for this body to overrule a sovereign people.

"Indeed, Timeless Warning itself argues this Tribunal is not a government, rather a group of people adjudicating public-private trade agreements. In the course of our events, the Educates have usurped powers from the Piese Treaty's duly elected governments. We have done so without consent of the governed, the only legitimate source of authority. We have turned presidents and legislators into ceremonial figureheads, an elected yet toothless royalty. Recognizing these errors, the Educates shall henceforth adopt a policy of tribunal modesty, granting deference to elected bodies that rule with the consent of the governed, however flawed and fickle they may be."

Smoke wafted out Educate Thompson's ears.

"The Tribunal rejects Timeless Warning's request to strike Ms. Huerta's 'radical commentary' from the record, purportedly to protect 'sacred freedom of speech.' We found her comments insightful and encourage others to read them.

"Nonetheless, in our final analysis, Ms. Huerta is not honoring her easement with Timeless Warning. While the original contract makes no mention of concrete barriers, we interpret the agreement as a living document designed to preserve a basic understanding. The framers of that contract clearly intended Timeless Warning to maintain a usable 11G tower at the Grand Canyon, however odious Ms. Huerta and others find it.

"As such, were it solely up to the Tribunal, we would require Ms. Huerta to tear down her wall. However, since this is a matter of contract law in a national park, Ms. Huerta may appeal this decision in the U.S. federal courts. The Educates do not reign Supreme and our previous opinion in *Marlboro v. Mattison* is hereby reversed."

Educate Thompson's avatar exploded in a cartoon-like puff while a blue and purple bird raced across the Tribunal mindscape with a "meep-meep!" sound. Back in her bungalow, Aneeka smirked before moving with lightning speed to stop sharing her thoughts. Her avatar froze before displaying her inner glee. She paced counterclockwise, not quite believing what she'd just done. Her internal steel girder stiffened, yet she felt light on her feet, as if she might float. She'd found her reset, her authentic self as it was before society came and messed it all up. Now she could share it with others.

When the virtual dust settled, Thompson's head reappeared, as if by magic, "What's all this nonsense about consent of the governed? You fabricated that of whole cloth. There's no precedent!"

Aneeka cleared her throat, "We hold these truths to be self-evident, that all men are created equal, that they are endowed by their creator with certain unalienable rights, that among these are life, liberty and the pursuit of happiness. Did you follow that? Happiness." She paused a moment and pivoted her avatar directly at Thompson's. "To secure these rights, governments are instituted among men, deriving their just powers from the *consent* of the governed."

"What's that?" yelled Thompson. "The Communist Manifesto or something?"

"The Declaration of Independence."

"Figures. Not a legally binding document. Signed by a bunch of radicals but never ratified by a legitimate tribunal. It's hearsay. There's no photographic evidence any of those so-called revolutionaries were even in the room when it was signed. At a minimum, we should recount those signatures and see if they had quorum."

"Come now, Thompson, let's settle down," interjected an Educate from Princeton. "Dr. Randall, I hear what you're saying, yet even if we give Timeless Warning the technical win in this case, every other corporation will appeal our rationale for decades to come. They'll wear us down with mountains of legal briefs, countless motions, making our already crushing workload impossible. Wouldn't a standard ruling in their favor be easier? I'm sure AI-clerk could draft something in no time."

Chief Educate Leon weighed in, rubbing his chin between thumb and forefinger. "Dr. Randall raised profound points. Let's put this case on hold, weigh the pros and cons while gathering data to fully comprehend the ramifications. I'm not saying she's correct, merely that her opinion warrants further study. I'll commission a full McChesney analysis and conduct a round of public hearings in Dubai. Let's move on to our next case, whether MansotoAgra can ban cultivation of non-genetically modified flowers because of global copyright infringement."

A partial victory. She'd found her restore point, she'd shared it with others, and some would consider it.

Now, if only she could reset Vera.

CHAPTER 33

Oscar

ELLEN AND OSCAR TRAIPSED TOWARD THE TWILIGHT
Kingdom with Caspian's letter. He would have preferred a Lubyr, but
Luella ran off in a huff after he told her they weren't in a position to
care for a puppy. She took the GalExSee with her. No helmet meant no
Lubyr. So, they walked. He'd track her down later, after she cooled off.

He couldn't believe she'd offered to deliver the stupid thing. It was
none of their business. He'd let Caspian deal with his own fuckups. Then
Ellen intervened. She said it was the right thing to do.

Ellen showed Oscar how to read street signs. He'd never noticed
them before. The sun shone big and yellow, yet the temperature remained
springlike. They walked three quiet minutes until Ellen broke the silence,
"I'm worried about Luella. She's growing up without a mother or father,
without proper schooling, without any real friends besides the unsavory
characters she meets online."

Oscar's jaw tightened and he picked up the pace. "Yeah, well, you
grew up without any parents or friends or proper education and shit."

"That's different. Sister Martha gave me excellent homeschooling."

"Look, just 'cause you saved my life doesn't' mean you get to run
it, OK?"

"Oh, I didn't mean to criticize, Oscar. I know you're doing what you
can, it's just . . . I worry. That's all."

"Well, worry about yourself. Lulu's just fine. I'll let her keep the
damn puppy if that will make you happy."

They marched on to the Twilight Kingdom in silence and walked right in. Nobody was at the front desk. Oddly enough there was another letter lying there—this one in a sturdy paper envelope with an actual postage stamp, the likes of which Oscar had never seen. It was addressed in neat handwriting to Vera Smith with a return address of A. Randall at 861 West Rustic Road.

"This lady's got a lot of pen pals," Oscar jibed, picking it up.

Ellen called out, "Yoo-hoo, anyone there?" before barging through the sliding doors and back to the guest rooms. LEDs on both side of the door flashed red, and a voice alarm blared, "Cerebral implants not detected. Viral contact tracing not feasible. Risk level presumed high." Ellen was unfazed.

Oscar followed reluctantly, triggering the same alarm. He walked down a hallway lined with QR codes he couldn't decipher, each by a sliding door. Ellen found one jammed open with a fancy pen and barged in. She stopped dead in her tracks, a look of shock across her face, as if she'd seen a ghost. Then, she pulled it together.

"Are you Ms. Vera Smith? You've got mail! One from the U.S. Post, the other a personal delivery."

"Again?" Her voice was faint, as if she rarely spoke. The room smelled clean, too clean.

"What do you mean?" Ellen cocked her head.

"He was just here with a letter. A fake. It's all fake."

"This letter explains a reset procedure. I don't fully understand and it's really none of my business. It seems you could walk right out of here."

"I chose to be here. I consented. I don't want to leave. The alternative was worse, believe me. I may not be happy, but I'm content. I've got nowhere to go. I sold out everything and everyone important to me. Nobody knows I exist. Nobody cares."

"Lighten up. It can't be all bad." Oscar tried derailing the pity party. "Wanna smoke?"

Vera replied, in an even flatter voice than before, "Smoking is unhealthy. It's addictive. The surgeon general has found it causes cancer, birth defects, lung disease . . . "

"You sound like Ellen here. Everything's addictive girl. Looks to me like you're jonesing for your infotain at least as much as I crave my bacco. It's not exactly like you're living some super-healthy lifestyle here hooked up to your intravenous feeding gizmo."

Vera leaned forward and peered intensely at Ellen. "What did he call you? What's your name?"

"I'm Ellen. It's nice to meet you."

Vera's face blanched and froze in place, the way someone looked after being voted off *BBV*. "You don't look anything like you did at your high school graduation," she said accusatorily. "You've changed. Your hair was brown, like mine. It's as if you're not even the same person."

"What do you mean? I've never even been to high school."

Tears flowed down Vera's cheek. Her voice cracked. "Of course you have! I saw you graduate. It broke my heart when you didn't recognize me. So, I got the upgrade. I consented. I got the MommyForever app. They told me you'd see my image on your cribscreen and hear the lullaby song I chose every day. They promised me you'd remember forever. They promised . . . "

"Whachu talking 'bout lady?" Oscar put a protective arm around Ellen and edged her toward the door.

Ellen wriggled free and took Vera's hand. She took a deep breath and sung in a strained voice, *"We'll meet again, not sure where, not sure when, but I know we'll meet again some sunny day."*

"I guess today's that day, Ellen."

"Mom?"

Vera stared right through Ellen, at Oscar. His cowboy tattoo displayed prominently on the back of his hand.

"They promised you'd remember me. Even that was a lie. They said they'd take care of you, and now you're hanging out with some lowlife criminal. I checked in on you virtually every, single, day. I watched you sleeping, I saw you smear baby Pepsoilent over your cute chubby cheeks. I saw you crying when the PampRbots changed your diapers. I watched you crawl, stand, and walk. I watched dozens of toddler cams, from every angle, at any time, for any reason at all. Until, one day, you just weren't there. I searched every chatter room, every NayBorlyHud list-serve, every childrearing yearbook. You disappeared into thin air. The authorities just lied and said I'd transferred you to a more age-appropriate childrearing center. Never believe them Ellen. It's all a big fat lie, especially the fuckedupgrade."

"I do remember, Mom. I remember an image a bit like you next to a man with longish blond hair. I still see it when I hear that song in my head. I thought it was just a dream, but now I'm certain it was you. There's so much I want to ask you! You've got to do the system restore. We can get you out of here. You can get your life back!"

Vera's entertainment lounge lowered into a fully reclined position. She scratched her elbow and stared at the ceiling.

"I consented. I chose this. There's no going back. It's not so bad. I talk with people online. I'd never make it out there. Hey, I think someone's coming back into the house on *Big Brother V*."

A MinuteMayd entered with a yellow LED flashing. "To prevent viral transmissions, physical visitors are not allowed in the Twilight Kingdom. Please move your conversation online and your persons offsite."

Oscar gently took Ellen's hand. "C'mon, this place gives me the creeps. We've done what we came to do. Life is full of disappointments."

On the way back, Oscar saw a saline trickle on her cheek. When he asked what was wrong, a downpour of sobs and tears and snot and gasps burst forth. *Dumb question.*

"She's my mom, Oscar. My mom! I've been wondering about her my entire life. Now she's just this shell of a person."

"Yeah, lights are on but nobody's home."

"You asshole! You're like the least sensitive person on the entire planet."

Oscar looked at the cracked sidewalk beneath his feet. Then, he looked up, accepting her fierce glare. "Hey, I'm sorry. I should have known this meant a lot to you. I'm kinda used to the idea of my folks being gone is all. Look, we could bust her outta there no problem. The security is a joke. We just unplug her IV and walk right out the front door before the bots know what happened. You could get her system rebooted and presto, instant mommy makeover."

"No, Oscar. She has to choose it. I can't make her live in reality. It has to come from her."

"I'm not sure anything can come from her right now, Ellen. I mean, there's no there there."

"I know . . . I know."

CHAPTER 34
Caspian

RIDING BACK TO THE WESTSIDE, CASPIAN BLAINE WAS feeling satisfied. He'd done something good that day, a day he would remember for a long time. He'd encountered obstacles, used problem-solving skills, got the message delivered. He'd empowered others, delegating a task to someone who would be more successful. Vera might not heed him, but who could resist those kids? He'd done his best; that's what mattered.

Chatter poked him as he rolled past downtown. "We care about you and your memories. Here's a recent outing you might want to share." Beautiful 3D scenery depicted rolling chaparral with the Pacific Ocean in the distance. He recognized the Backbone Trail and remembered standing on that exact spot, right before he met Educate Randall. Everything had since fallen into place. He remembered the air's sweet smell, the sun high in the clear blue sky that seemed to stretch forever. He recalled the cool confidence he felt inside, waiting for that historic moment when a newly appointed Educate connected with a future foundation president to change the world.

He looked down. The bronze survey marker wasn't on the ground. He distinctly remembered it—the sole man-made object surrounded by nature's glory. Yet the Klowd image didn't have it. It was almost as if the memory was fabricated off NoodleEarth images or drone footage instead of captured by someone on the ground. Maybe he was getting old. Maybe his memory wasn't what it used to be. He must have noticed the marker somewhere else. The image was still gorgeous and would get a lot of likes. He clicked "Share."

Unsatiated, Chatter fed him another memory, this time from his teenage years. He'd taken the pic with a selfie drone, all the rage back then. He stood defiantly in dreadlocks, fist raised at a 30s era protest march. His T-shirt read "Stop the War Unseen" and his sign said, "Look Up and Smell the Ashes." Only a few activists followed the war, which dragged on for years in full public view, mostly unnoticed. Even back then, people were absorbed in devices. Smart phones had given way to VR headsets, and then helmets, which gave way to cerebral implants. War coverage was expensive, and dangerous, for the remaining journalistic enterprises and news ratings couldn't compete with realty TV, gaming, and social media. So the war happened, but nobody saw, until it was too awful to ignore.

Yet Caspian knew, even early on, he knew. After the war decimated both economies and populations, he watched a new Tribunal power structure emerge. He witnessed the erosion of national sovereignty to an entity literally of, by, and for corporate "people." Still, folks could eat.

Unlike his naïve protest days, he'd learned to keep his head down. He'd seen too many friends and fellow activists burn out, drop out, or simply disappear for an "upgrade." Caspian knew what he was up against. Knew the system resisted disruption. Knew it would fight back with a barrage of advertising and entertainment and factual, if trivial, information that could distract even the most engaged of citizens. He knew the conglomerates funding philanthropy depended upon a consumption economy—which only nonstop content creation could achieve. He knew pulling people out of infotainment, and virtual sex, and online gambling, and the spending fueled by the ads they delivered straight into consumers' brains threatened the infrastructure he lever-aged against those evils. He had tread carefully for decades, using the system against itself like a cyber jujitsu master. His patience paid off. On the verge of running the best-endowed foundation in the Pacific Rim, he'd have billions of ByteDime at his disposal with powerful connections to people who shared his worldview. They got it. He helped them; they returned the favor. The moment he only dared imagine had finally arrived.

He deleted the protest pic and saw a message from one of his Special Projects grantees, the GeoNiers:

> In the spirit of full transparency, we are submitting our wildfire prevention grant progress report. TerraFik™, a Sonoma Valley climate engineering initiative, ambitiously attempted to halt episodically strong north winds that down powerlines and ignite wildfires. The AerWall project took six years and forty-three billion ByteDime to repurpose 8,000 jet engines, taken from mothballed airliners. The turbines were pointed northward on utility towers using computer modeling to counteract windstorms.
>
> During a recent Diablo wind event, we used cybersynchronicity AI algorithms to ensure precise calibration while powering up the AerWall. Due to a slight miscalculation in computer modeling, the blast of air generated by the turbines collided with Diablo winds in such a fashion as to create a high velocity vortex situation, commonly known as a tornado. The collateral damage to Santa Rosa was slightly above the acceptable range for a geotech innovation project of this nature, coming in at 4,773 deaths and 62,492 structures destroyed.
>
> We regret the setback and are fully disclosing these unintended consequences. GeoNiers have rededicated ourselves to re-imagining and re-inventing this critical endeavor. A McChesney-led self-assessment found our installation lacked sufficient gale force to overpower this particular airstream episode. We are submitting a grant renewal application for 112 billion ByteDime that will fund installation of an additional 20,000 jet turbines with recalibrated positioning so that we can more successfully blunt future north wind fire hazard events.

Colossal Column Condominiums had the Old Faithful Geyser for an exterior screensaver today. While his car parked, Caspian sent a quick response.

"Thanks for the report. I appreciate your full transparency. Please calculate how many jobs (both human and machine) will be stimulated by Santa Rosa's reconstruction as well as healthcare employment the collateral damage created, convert those into utils, and resend your report including those metrics. Have a nice day."

Caspian lounged in disposable pajamas on his delivery balcony, awaiting his new ItaliaLauren Ralphonso™ suit, tailor-made from real wool and silk. He'd splurged and spent extra after learning his interview had been scheduled, telling himself he'd wear it three times before recycling. Now he just needed to find a clothes hanger.

The sun set ever so slowly over the Pacific. Incremental rotation, baby. That's what makes the world go round. Imperceptibly small adjustments until, next thing you know, it's morning in Globalia. Blackish clouds moved inland from the deep ocean sky. Within five minutes, the sun's orange glow was gone. A damp darkness enveloped him.

A news alert ended the tranquil moment.

"Telecommunications firm WhamZong unveiled a new product at the Las Vegas VirTooLife trade show. The Gal-EmScene™ implant will enhance infotain's VRemotional scenery. Using technology originally developed by the Department of Prosperity to treat clinical depression, drug addiction and gaming induced PTSD, WhamZong has now patented an off-label use for pleasure management. The device, located just under the skull, is connected to the amygdala with probes a hundred times thinner than a human hair. It stimulates the limbic system to enhance or degrade sexual desire, love, fear, jealousy or anger. The device can replicate frisson-like chills going up and down a viewer's spine, or sublime transcendence. It pairs seamlessly with WhamZong's existing Gal-InSee cerebral cortex implants to sync emotional stimuli with visual and auditory transmissions. Infotainment executives are salivating at the prospect of even more riveting movies and episodes with co-streamed emotional enhancement. WhamZong's stock rose 35 percent on today's news."

The wind gusted just as his delivery arrived, disorienting the drone so his package fell inches beyond his balcony. It tumbled twelve stories onto the Astroturf lawn. Fortunately, the box was thick, like Caspian's skin, and the suit wasn't fragile.

While retrieving his fallen attire, he got a VRoom call from Yvonne Putcher. Her avatar held a cocktail and wore a tight-fitting little black dress. "Hey! We made bank on WhamZong today. Can't thank you enough. I'll push through a hundred million ByteDime to OrangeVine within six months."

"That's great. Happy to be of service."

"Hey, while I've caught you, we're getting feedback from our infotain holdings that ratings are down in LA. They think it's something to do with a social disruption movement where hippies give away flowers to pull people out of VR. Any idea what that's about?"

Caspian knew full well what that was about, of course. He clutched the box holding his designer suit so tightly his knuckles turned white. "Who knows? I guess the world is full of unintended consequences. Hey something just came up, I gotta sign off."

He clicked "leave meeting" and stood on his balcony, wishing he had a cigarette. He closed a window that streamed his EMBA class, his chatter feed, and the *Big Brother V* episode until nothing was left running. It got chilly, yet he stayed a long time, soaking up the darkness.

CHAPTER 35
Chase

CHASE OPENED UP THE THROTTLE. EVERYTHING FELT like it used to. The wind whipped his hair. He sensed the road's texture on the seat and hand grips. Some things you never forget.

Luella held on behind, not too tightly, leaving a space for the puppy.

"Wanna make some money?" he asked her in Chatter.

"Sure. I've been wanting some new FlavrPaks."

"Run a NoodleSearch for Caesar's Palace, Las Vegas."

"Dood, we're not gonna pull a heist IRL?! I should get my brother for that."

"Relax. This'll be way easier. Like shooting fish in a barrel."

"Huh? What's a barrel?"

"Never mind. Just hit navigate on your GalExSee."

"You're the one driving, Gramps."

He pulled over and motioned for her to take the helmet off so he could look her straight in the eye. "I know the way. We just need to cover our tracks. I'll explain later."

Chase went north up the 215, all the way to Cajon Junction. He was enjoying the scenery, noticing how the air smelled different outside. A ferruginous hawk swooped down, grabbing a desert wood rat darting between the sagebrush. The wind rushed over his bare feet, tickling the tiny hairs on his toes. He broke out a big, shit-eating grin.

As miles rolled past, a message came in from @Seeker's gray orb avatar.

"DEREK CRESSMAN

"What's up? Long time no see." The remnants of their previous argument still hung in the lines above. He was in a good mood, so bygones were bygone.

"Something came up. Hey, sorry if I was a bit defensive last time we talked. Your comments kinda hit a sharp spot. But you're right, imagination is more important than knowledge. Anyway, how you been?" Chase enjoyed this strange relationship, even if it never seemed to go anywhere. He had just escaped Cyberia, yet @Seeker had a way of drawing him back in.

"I just had a weird blast from the past. Ever met someone you've been wondering about for years only to find out they aren't remotely who you thought they'd be?"

Chase noticed a shadow following him. The pincas had resumed their pursuit, no longer deceived by Luella's tricks. He was driving too fast for etherization. He cranked the throttle a tad more. "Not really. I'm pretty good at judging character, probably from my years as a screenwriter. I can sense who people are, what motivates them, that sort of thing."

They talked back and forth, his overdone blond mullet avatar conversing with @Seeker's gray orb. Driving the cycle was still instinctual, his muscle memory remained sufficiently intact that he could chat and drive, no problem. There wasn't much traffic anyhow. He signed off as the cycle sped past Halloran Springs, "Nice chatting but gotta go. Driving into the desert."

Luella suddenly took off her GalExSee and yelled in his ear. "My helmet just died."

"We've entered a deadzone," he yelled back. "No 11G out here. Enjoy the silence." The pincas held still, frozen in place as they could no longer track Luella's helmet transmissions. Pincertons had visual pursuit

224

programming for automobiles and trucks, but nobody ever thought to put cycles into their algorithm. Luella smirked.

At Caesar's Palace, a wallscreen noted the minimum gambling age had been struck down as a trade barrier by the Educates. All ages were welcome. Luella tucked the puppy deep into her jacket.

It was seven p.m. and the place was nearly empty. Nobody was at the few remaining slots. A dozen high establishment types hung around the poker tables. Ceasar's Palace had an integrated Faraday cage within its walls and ceiling, blocking all 11G so patrons were totally immersed in their RL spectacle. The longer customers stayed, the less money they left with. For Chase and Luella, the blockage meant pincas were unable to pick up their trail.

Chase rubbed his grandfather's lucky penny and hit the tables. He had played online for years yet preferred in-person poker. He enjoyed the subtle art of reading faces, more challenging than the exaggerated avatar expressions he was used to virtually. When another player was down, Luella showed them her puppy. They'd fawn all over it, forgetting their losses. Chase cleaned them out. The same ploy worked when someone was up big. Luella kept them at the table while Chase lured them into going all in on just the wrong hand.

He could have stayed all night, but when he was up $50k a ManAGr bot rolled over and told him to leave because he wasn't wearing shoes. "Whaddya mean?" He thumped the bot's chest. "That's an international trade barrier. I have a right to spend money here, just ask the Educates."

"Educates, schmeducates," said the bot, instructing the autodealer to refuse Chase any further cards.

"Alright," he turned to Luella. "Let's get out while the gettin's good. You earned this as much as me. We'll split it, 50-50. What's your ByteDime account?"

"I'm twelve, remember? I don't do ByteDime."

They exchanged their chips for cash, raising some eyebrows as that evidently wasn't done much anymore. He didn't care, it was his money and he'd take it his way. Chase kept a close eye on Luella as he stashed stacks of Benjamins in his saddlebags. He hadn't forgotten the cute twelve-year-old with a puppy was also @BadScootr, who robbed him blind after their last Vegas jaunt.

He needed shoes plus a leather jacket for some protection on the cycle. Vegas no longer had stores, only display windows with luxe delivery merch like crystal stemware and ridiculously over-the-top tiaras. He ordered some prefab clothes and splurged on a ruby pageant crown for Luella, selecting the corner of Las Vegas Boulevard and Siren's Cove for instant delivery. It had been quite a while since he'd experienced the thrill of shopping so he went a little overboard, blowing nearly half his ByteDime account on all sorts of bling—Rolex watches, sterling silver pens, diamond earrings, a platinum-plated Swiss Army knife, pearl necklaces, whatever struck his fancy. While waiting for the delivery, they checked out a concrete basin that once held the Bellagio fountains.

When the package arrived, he gathered his butt-length hair into a ponytail and used the Swiss Army knife to saw it off just below the nape. He cut the top about two inches above his scalp, crudely restoring the mullet of his younger days.

Luella threw her GalExSee back on, so Chase checked in online as well. Four hours ago, @Seeker had posted "What, you drive?" in response to his "Gotta go. I'm about to drive into the desert." Her words still hung there followed by three blinking dots. He picked it up, not missing a beat.

"Hey, yes, I'm riding IRL. Kinda forgot how sore it makes your ass."

"I always thought you were kinda a pain in the ass too. But I like that about you."

"Bad joke, @Seeker. Anyhow, I'm enjoying things on the outside."

He looked around at the jumbotron screens and flashing marquees of the Vegas strip and saw the moon rising over it all, a perfectly constant touchstone by which to measure the authenticity of all other light.

"Something seems different about you, like you're not even paying attention. Are you with someone?" @Seeker sounded a bit needy. Or so he thought.

"Maybe that's 'cause all I can see is your gray orb. Ever going to show me the real you?"

"Some things are better left unseen. A girl needs to maintain some level of mystique, don't you think?" He was getting a little tired of this tease. He could respect a woman who didn't want to share noods right away, yet he'd been hoping for some avatar action at some point.

Chase and Luella gorged at an all you can eat buffet, all protruded from a street corner vending machine. It was his first solid meal in 17 years, but since it was all soyalgent in one form or another, it went down easier than the cockroach. Luella slipped the puppy some Chuc-Ken™ nuggets.

He bought her a half-gallon CherrySpryte™ in a protruded foam cup with a ton of ice as a drone delivered his AmaZing! order. He stashed his bling in the leather jacket's pockets and pulled on some Timberland boots. It was getting dark and chilly, so he was happy for the warmer clothes. He looked over at Luella wearing nothing but a T-shirt. She removed the tiara, surrounded by a recycled blanket that had found new life as packing material. She shoved the crown, still unopened in a plastic bag, into the Holstein saddlebags, then wrapped the blanket around her shoulders, sipped her ice-cold drink and said, "Let's go Gramps. It'll be near midnight when we get home. Oscar will think I was kidnapped."

Shit!

"You didn't tell him where you were going?" Chase's stomach turned to concrete as he scanned the sky. Online deliveries could have alerted the SpeiDrWeb to his whereabouts. And hers.

"He ditched me once for three days and didn't tell me where he was going. He should know how that feels."

Up above Chase saw a white copter with a red cross on its underbelly and restraining arms dangling like tentacles—a quote unquote lifesaving drone. A Pincerton flock followed right behind. Luella hopped on the cycle. "Hold your breath," he yelled, jolting the bike to a racing start. The drones closed in but were still out of etherization range.

Chase careened down a flood control channel and entered Las Vegas's expansive network of underground tunnels. He slowed the bike to a crawl, maneuvering past dozens of homeless Vues strewn about the concrete labyrinth. His jaw unlocked when his MyndScreen went blank. "Transmissions down, baby!" he yelled, receiving no response from Luella other than a tight grip on his ribs.

Either by instinct, or Grand Heist Otto experience, Chase navigated the tunnels flawlessly. The pincas couldn't track him through the concrete. He knew full well that if they found him, he'd be institutionalized back in the Department of Prosperity as a threat to himself and others. He could just imagine Dr. Aneeka Randall having a field day with the word "kidnapped."

After hours prowling around like a motorized gopher, they emerged on the city's southern edge. He rode out a culvert and snuck quietly out of town beneath tranquil moonlit skies.

Chase was fully immersed in the moment. Each bump nudged his palms in a rhythmic pattern, the electric motor's gentle whine propelled the bike forward, the desert air smelled of sage and dust. His MyndScreen was back up and running. He closed all the windows and enjoyed the ride for what it was.

Heading into the Mojave, his eyes began to water, making it tricky to see the road. He put on a pair of old rearview light responsive sunglasses that were still stowed in the saddlebags after seventeen years, the kind with cameras pointing backwards on the frame temples so you could stream video into your Myndscreen of what was behind you. Blocking the wind didn't stop the tears. It wasn't the airflow; it was the place. The place and the memories that still lived there.

He'd picked the Mojave so long ago for a big rendezvous with Vera, that mysterious woman he met in a parking lot of all places. She was the only one paying attention to current events, to flowers, to reality, to him. He'd fallen hard and couldn't believe she went for his crazy scheme to meet up in the desert, which he knew was the safest place. Their MyndScreens couldn't track them. Keeping their relationship offline would prevent SpeiDrWeb monitoring of their infotain inattention as they grew entangled in each other. Now, here he was, in the same place with a slightly psycho twelve-year-old who had a certain charm yet was certainly not Vera.

"Hey, Chase?" @Seeker was back, forcing open a MyndScreen window and breaking the spell of his remembrance. He didn't respond.

"Look, I know you're getting these messages. I don't mean to bug you, but I really need to know something now that you're out. Do you still love me?"

Say what?

As much as he wanted to avoid it, a question like that demanded an answer. "Are you out of your mind? I don't even know you. We've talked online and stuff, but anyone can be virtually attractive. We've never met."

"Is my physical appearance all that matters? Don't you see me for who I really am?"

Goddamn, this chick is intense.

"Look, you're interesting. I enjoy our chats. I'm sure you're a wonderful person and it's nothing personal. But I wasn't intending for this to get serious. There's only one woman I'll ever love. I'm sorry, but I can't keep"

"But Chase, it's"

@Seeker's gray orb fell silent. He'd driven back into the 11G dead zone.

Time to move on.

At Halloran Springs, he pulled off the highway and drove south into the Mojave. Luella took off her helmet. "What's with the detour, Gramps?"

"I just need a break."

He maneuvered down a path of decomposed granite until reaching a single-track trail winding through sagebrush and ocotillo. After a few minutes into dark nothingness, he could barely read an old metal sign in the cycle's headlight, "Mojave lava tubes."

They rode slowly toward tunnel-like caves formed when molten lava cooled on its surface but kept flowing on the inside. When the hot interior lava emptied out, a tube-like cavity remained.

"Listen, Luella." He hopped off the bike. "What do you hear?"

She cocked her head and looked at him funny. "Nothing."

"Exactly. Nothing. It's something you should learn to appreciate. Out here, in the desert, there's no 11G. No animals. No cars. Nothing to distract from the emptiness."

"Whatever, Gramps."

"Hey, you're a creative kid. You've got wheels spinning inside your head. That's great, but infotain firms don't see it that way. I know, I used to write for them. Episodes, games, reality shows, everything they do is designed to pull you out of your world and into theirs. Your brain is real estate where they post billboards. They'll keep finding stronger, more addictive ways to suck you in. You're safe now, they can't track us. They won't know how long we're here, or what we do, or what we think while we're doing it. That's why I had you pull directions to Caesar's Palace. That's why we won some money and bought a ridiculous amount of stupid stuff. It's our cover story. It'll track as perfectly routine consumer spending habits, just like *they* want. A quick splurge in Vegas gives us space to do what *we* want, with nobody watching.

"C'mon," he hopped back on the bike, beckoned for her to follow, and creeped to the edge of the cave. "Don't worry, I'm not gonna hurt you."

CHAPTER 36
Aneeka

ANEEKA RANDALL WATCHED THE STEAM RISE FROM HER morning coffee. She'd found fresh roasted beans at a boutique cafe she stumbled across after meeting Aldo. It was expensive, partly because coffee pollinator insects had been decimated. Demand for real beans plunged after competition from coffee-flavored soyalgent beverages. Farmers went broke. Coffee bushes died.

It was worth the price. She admired a smooth porcelain cup she purchased, along with a grinder and French press, from an antique shop on Montana Avenue that still sold such things. Brewing coffee took time. Time that once would have meant inconvenience, inefficiency. Today, it became a ritual she couldn't imagine doing without. She understood now why Vera had fixated on a turquoise mug she drank green tea from. A tight, icy ball formed in Aneeka's gut, right by her appendix, as she recalled replacing it with a plastic one shortly after she'd intentionally broken Vera's potpourri jar. She had thought the transition would reduce Vera's irrational nostalgia for fragile, non-disposable things.

Dr. Randall eventually did free Vera from terrestrial attachment. Either from spite or grace, Vera's determination had now grounded Aneeka in physicality. Vera had been right all along. Educate Randall now had the privilege and power to do something about it. The letter would get through. It had to. Even if it took the USPS months to deliver it, they were more reliable than Caspian Blaine.

Coffee melted the edges off her frigid abdominal ball, reducing it to a mild, yet still noticeable lump. Dagny Huerta was in the morning news feed again. She'd bought twenty percent of the global gold bullion stockpile, saying it looked pretty and she wanted to build something big and beautiful with it. She liquidated her entire ByteDime account to make the purchase, causing cybercurrency markets to nosedive. "ByteDime has value because people believe it has value. Super investor Dagny Huerta isn't buying it."

That audacious woman sure knows how to grab attention, what an individual! Chatter asked her if she'd like to post that thought. Aneeka made a few edits before hitting send. "While I never comment on pending cases, I will say that Dagny Huerta is a real individual who certainly knows how to spur the world's imagination."

Both Dagny haters and Dagny fans dissected the post for clues about how the Educates might rule in the Grand Canyon case. Aneeka's chat followers increased by two hundred million. Basking in the glory, she used @Vera2048—a burner account she'd set up to coax something out of Chase Hatten—to rechat her original post while referring to herself as "The notorious Dr. Randall." It got 1.2 billion likes. Her gut felt fine.

She went out for a morning jog, stopping to smell the eucalyptus and listen to a squirrel defending its domain with a series of barks. She felt a gentle breeze cool the perspiration on her forehead. She hadn't been this content in years, maybe ever.

Tribunal matters had cooled down since she made her big move. While most of her clerks had been mortified, some were coming around to her point of view, especially Barry Kramer. The world hadn't ended when she'd suggested curtailing Tribunal power. Life went on. Sometimes you just had to be bold.

When she returned, Lewis Leon's blimp hung motionlessly above her home. "Hello there!" He waved from the observation deck as he pinged her in the Chatter.

"Hi. Nice of you to drop by!"

"I've got a favor to ask. Come up and have a drink when you have a moment."

Inside her bungalow, Aneeka saw the words "Prosperity isn't freedom. Freedom is Freedom," smeared in encrusted chocolate pudding. She printed a disposable rag, wiped the wall clean, and washed her hands. After showering, she put on a designer T-shirt with gray slacks, wishing she'd ordered something a bit dressier. It would be weird to accept an instant wardrobe delivery with her boss hovering overhead. She stroked the back of her head, expecting to feel her soft, bristly hair. She instead found it had grown more than an inch. In the hectic daze of recent events, she'd forgotten to visit her stylist. She went outside, strapped into the harness, and was lifted up to Lewis Leon.

He handed her a mimosa with fresh squeezed orange juice and French champagne in one of his signature octagonal glasses. "Thanks for making yourself available, Dr. Randall. Please, come into my office."

They strolled past the condor aviary into a warmly lit room with walls of lightweight green satin. He sat behind a balsawood desk and took out a cigar. "Cuban. Want one?"

Aneeka had never smoked a cigar, yet it seemed like the thing you do when talking politics in a smoke-filled room. She accepted and observed several plaques on the wall—an award from the Globalian Chamber of Commerce, a law degree from Harvard, a thank you memento from the Tobacco Institute.

"Aneeka, I was impressed by your draft Grand Canyon ruling. It demonstrated profound historical and economic insight. Nonetheless, there's a clear Tribunal majority that won't risk Timeless Warning's productivity or depart from our capitalist structure."

"Chief, Timeless Warning's business isn't real capitalism. It's crony capitalism. They use government power to force ads on people rather than competing in the marketplace."

"All capitalism is crony capitalism. You're smart enough to know that. Market competition means firms vie to influence the rules of commerce. Once a competitor wrests control of the rules, well, they're the ruler. That's us, Aneeka. We're the rulers. Our job is to rule in favor of the marketplace, or more precisely of those who control the market. That's what self-interest is all about. Market rulers protect their interests. You and I must do the same. Our own situation is more perilous than you may realize."

"But, Lewis," her gaze bore right through his eyes, down past his brain, deep into his interior. "What about the individual?" She probed his internal structure, searching for whatever girder supported him, and found nothing there.

He took a long draw on his cigar and blew smoke at her.

"We have more ways to express individuality than the entire history of humankind. Each person can create custom skin tones with individualized cosmetic regimens and hair colors, they can tweak their avatar daily to fit their disposition, they can update their wardrobe within minutes to express their inner selves, they can customize their streaming content with endless infotainment options, they can craft designer menus from Pepsoilent or CokAid or even use meal-planning software to do it for them."

He paused a moment to push the rose-colored frames of his eyeglasses up his nose. "There has never been a society as individualized as Globalia, and this is precisely what creates the consumption beast that keeps our economic engine running."

Aneeka looked at the cigar smoldering in between her middle and index fingers and sighed. She rubbed the back of her head, stroking the smooth and silky hair.

Lewis softened his tone. "Look, I understand and admire where you're coming from. You just need to bide your time and wait for new Educates to replace Thompson and the old schoolers. I'll retire myself in two to three years and could easily see someone with your intellect taking my place. Until then, keep honing your arguments, keep making allies, don't rock the blimp too much. Groom your clerks to earn their own appointments to the Tribunal. Build your team. Maneuver your allies into the DeadOrA-List Society. It will take time, but Rome wasn't rebuilt in a day. For now, I'm going to outsource the Dagny Huerta case to McChesney and see what they can draft up for the Tribunal's review. I hope you'll find it acceptable or at least write a modest dissent that doesn't look like you're trying to blow up the entire world order.

"But that's not what I wanted to talk to you about."

The ball in Aneeka's stomach tightened again, pushing up against her core girder of steel.

"An old buddy of mine is running the Department of Prosperity, which, as you know, oversees healthcare contractors like Mercernary General. I know you've left that line of work, but he's got a particularly challenging case you have some familiarity with."

Vera. The Department knows. It wants to stop her reset.

Aneeka took a draw off the cigar and coughed violently.

Lewis Leon continued, "I know it's a bit beneath you to return to your former profession. He wouldn't ask if it wasn't important. Could you at least have an initial consult with whoever this patient is? I'll find some way to return the favor."

Aneeka collected herself, inhaled a smaller puff from the cigar into her mouth, and exhaled smooth as silk. "Sure, Lewis. I'll help out for the team. If it truly is that tricky a case, I'd be intrigued by the professional challenge."

"Great. I can't imagine it will take much time. I'll have you there in fifteen minutes."

The airship lurched, spilling her mimosa on her designer T-shirt.

"Buckle up, buttercup!" he said with a wink.

CHAPTER 37
Oscar

OSCAR WOKE TO DUST BUNNIES IN HIS HEAD, HAVING consumed a six-pack the night before. The whole thing with Ellen's mom kind of wigged him out and he just needed a brief escape. The dust bunnies felt just like those under his couch. He should clean those up. Someday. He should have been more sensitive with Ellen. It's gotta be tough discovering your mom has checked out. Given up. Lights on but nobody home. Welcome to the Hotel California. Head full of virtual dust.

Ellen had gone home all red-faced and teary-eyed. Worse than that, she was pissed at *him*, as if the whole damn thing was *his* fault. She wanted Vera to leave that dreadful EH, yet when he suggested breaking her out, Ellen was offended, as if he'd suggested kidnapping. *That's the problem with women. Even when you give them what they want, they get all mad 'cause you went about it in the "wrong" way.*

The beer was fantastic. Zesty mosaic hops and a hint of malt combined in glass bottles for the most refreshing thing he'd ever swallowed. Why had he been drinking MillBuddy™ soyalgent all these years? Best of all, he got it from a guy just a few blocks away, who brewed it himself. A guy who accepted cash. Maybe next time he'd barter for cigarettes.

For now, a cup of Koffy would get him back on track. He walked over to the CokAid extruder before realizing he needed the GalExSee to order it. "Yo! Lulu, where's the damn helmet?" No response.

He poked his head in her room. Nothing. *Shit.*

He looked outside, in the carport hammock. Nothing. *Fuck.*

He shouted, "Luella! Come on girl. Lulu. This ain't funny. Where the hell are you?" Nothing.

He knew she got hotheaded. He remembered her storming off when he wouldn't let her keep the puppy. He'd planned on tracking her down. Then this whole thing happened with Ellen and her mom.

Oscar started walking, magically thinking he'd find her somewhere on a street corner. After a few blocks, he saw Vien up ahead. "Hey, you seen my sista?"

"Sure Oscar, pretty cool. I can't believe you actually got one. You must be so proud."

"Whatchu talking about, Vien?"

"The cycle, Oscar. She was riding with some long-haired guy on a motorbike. I figured he was a friend of yours."

Oscar stopped dead in his tracks, as if that would somehow ground him.

"No, man. I ain't got friends. I ain't got no cycle. That dude was nabbing my little sister! He's a Winston, prob'ly molesting her. Ima track down that mofo and blow his brains out."

"Oscar! Calm down, Oscar. I am your friend. It's OK. We'll find her. Let's call the police."

"No police. That's the last thing I need. 'Sides, they never show up, anyhow."

Oscar looked up to see Jerome cruising by. He parked his lowrider, real slow like, and rolled down the window. Oscar could tell he was pissed.

"Brudda, where's your damn sister? She didn't send the code for disabling BirdFlew. Our chats are down. We ain't getting no orders. Our episodes are frozen. This is totally not OK."

"She's gone, man. Some Winston dude snatched her. Can I borrow your semi-auto?"

"Ain't got no bullets, brudda. 'Sides, youz guys are responsible for keeping Winstons outta this hood. We don't need problems with them."

"Guys, guys," Vien joined the conversation. "The man wasn't sinister. He had a big smile and Luella was yelping for joy. He wasn't even wearing shoes. Think about what we actually know before imagining the worst. We should put out an AMBER Alert, so everyone can look for her."

"That would mean cops," said Jerome, shaking his head. "'Sides, so many alerts go off nobody pays attention. Evildoer attacks. Virus quarantines. Wildfire evacuations. Earthquake forecasts. Currency collapses. You just ignore them."

Vien suggested a flyer, printed on actual paper. He showed them one about a general interest meeting for a community garden. "It got my attention because I'd never seen anything like it," he noted.

"I know who made that. Come on." Oscar took off for SubDirt in a hurried pimp roll.

They found Ellen there, with a burlap bag of garlic cloves. She broke them apart and stuffed each section inside small slits cut into an old foam mattress.

"You trying to make garlic fall asleep?" Jerome jibed.

"No, I'm planting it. This foam makes a perfect substrate. We'll add water and fertilizer and next thing you know, we'll have garlic galore!"

Oscar interrupted. "Whatever. Hey, Ellen, I need a big favor. Did you make these?" He held up the flyer.

"Yes. I found an old mimeograph machine in the Thrifty Sister. There was a box of stencil paper and printing fluid and a whole booklet of instructions. I wanted to see if I could make it work, so I printed those flyers. It made the oddest smell. You have to admit the purple ink is a real eye grabber."

"Could you do that again? For Luella? She's missing and we need to put out an alert."

"Oh, my goodness Oscar! Of course." She pulled out her pad of paper. "What should it say?"

"Something like, 'Missing: twelve-year-old girl. Answers to the name of Luella. Black hair and brown eyes. Kinda uppity but has a good heart. Last seen with some weird hippy dude on a cycle. May have a puppy with her.'"

Ellen bit her lip. "I tell you what, I'll make some edits and run it off. If you come to tonight's meeting, you could get everyone to post one."

He eyed Ellen's sketch of Luella, still the top leaf on her notebook. "Maybe you could add that drawing?"

"Yes. Of course. Anything for Luella. I'm so worried."

"You better worry," Jerome butted in. "My bruddas are pissed. We can't even send a meal order without 11G. Nobody's happy eating unflavored CokAid for lunch."

Ellen tossed him a garlic head and said to sauté it with his plain soyalgent.

"Saw Tay?"

"Fry it, dude," said Oscar. "You'll figure it out."

Ellen returned later that day with a stack of flyers and a half-smile.

Oscar quickly grabbed the flyers and said, "Thanks," but Vien noticed something was off.

"What's bothering you, Ellen?"

"It's her. It really is her. My mom, I mean."

Oscar perked up. "I thought you knew that already."

"Now it's confirmed. The mimeograph jammed up, so I used that old helmet to find repair instructions. Then I got a message from the

DNA testing company. Vera Smith, that's my mother. It's 99.95 percent certain. They know my father, too, and trace both of their parents, and grandparents going way back." Ellen's voice cracked. "She has a history, even if she has no future."

"It must be a relief to finally know," Oscar offered, trying to work on his empathy skills yet finding himself always one or two steps behind where he should be.

"Certainty is worse. Maybe I hoped there was some mistake. Like, she didn't remember how I looked. Her name wasn't even on the wall, just that weird code. Maybe it was just a coincidence that I knew that song she's attached to. Now, there's proof, there's evidence, there's verification."

"A little doubt can go a long way," replied Oscar. "Sometimes I wish I didn't know everything about my dad, but there it is. Now that you're sure, what will you do?"

Ellen looked at the stack of flyers in Oscar's hand, rippling a bit in a gentle breeze.

"C'mon, let's put these flyers up. That's at least something."

"I'll help," Vien offered.

Oscar swallowed a lump in his throat. People were helping him. Friends. He had friends. "Thanks guys. We'll find Luella; I just won't believe anything else. Then, maybe Lulu can help us get through to Vera. There's gotta be a hack for that."

Ellen didn't say anything more. She gave him a big hug, just like that. It was exactly what he needed.

CHAPTER 38
Caspian

CASPIAN BLAINE WAS NERVOUS. HE DRUMMED HIS STUB-
by brown fingers on his left knee, awaiting the interview. Why were
they conducting it in person; who did that anymore? He had developed
a strong online persona, letting his avatar do the talking, yet hadn't
quite mastered the eye contact and body language required by face-to-
face conversation.

He arrived early and waited on a slightly too small club chair outside
the conference room. A vaguely familiar face approached. "I'm so glad
you're here, Shawn," he overheard Yvonne Putcher, warmly shaking the
guy's hand.

Shawn? Shawn Fellia. Caspian knew the name. Shawn ran the PiYu
Charitable Thrusts, a smaller foundation in Vancouver. Caspian was
willing to bet his Special Projects and Strategic Initiatives budget was
larger than PiYu's annual grantmaking. Noodle found Shawn's SyncedIn
profile. He had ten years at McChesney prior to taking over at PiYu
yet had less industry experience than Caspian. He'd received a glowing
recommendation from Yvonne Putcher, "Shawn is an expert in corporate
cultural turnarounds. He brings superb precision to mission critical tasks
such as restructuring, revisioning, and eliminating dead weight that bogs
down organizations."

Damnation.

Caspian's implant opened an episode of *Climbing the Ladder*. Needing
something to distract his nerves, he let it run. Then came the ad.

A preschool girl plucked petals off a daisy, counting each one aloud. "One, two, three . . . " Blackbirds sung melodically in the background. Upon reaching "ten," she heard a NASA-style voice count ominously back down from ten to one. The camera zoomed in tight, eventually closing in on just her pupil. In her eye's reflection, Caspian saw a giant mushroom cloud explode when the announcer reached "one" and proclaimed, "These are the stakes. To make a world in which all of humanity's children can live, we must learn to love prosperity. We cannot let fearmongers divert Globalians' attention so we don't shop, don't watch, don't consume. Do not stop to smell the flowers or neglect your patriotic duty to view and consume."

Weird. Wonder why SpeiDrWeb targeted me with that one. I've been buying my normal stuff.

The door opened; his name was called. Shawn Fellia shook his hand and gave a sly grin on his way out.

The interview was easy, too easy. Five committee members, Yvonne Putcher, Stephan Barscale, OrangeVine's board chair, and two McChesney people he didn't know, sat around a maple table nibbling shrimp cocktail and caviar. The interviewers took turns asking pre-planned questions, yet nobody wrote down his responses. They appeared to be multitasking on their screens. He had worked twenty-five friggin' years for this moment, and the fix was in so firmly for Shawn Fellia that these mofos wouldn't even hear him out. He'd played their game only for them to take the ball home without him.

Caspian elevated his spiel about innovating social wellness and up-lifting community productivity metrics with an emphatically sincere tone. He slapped his palms on the table, launching his transparency schtick.

Yvonne stopped him dead in his tracks.

She reached across the table, gently pressing three elegant fingertips on his wrist. "Mr. Blaine, I'm so glad you share OrangeVine's mission-driven focus on full transparency. I'm wondering, hypothetically of course, if a board member asked you to disclose something you might prefer to keep private, you'd have no qualms about providing that information?"

A test. It's all about trust, baby. Finally, a softball he could hit out of the park.

"Without hesitation. I've learned over my *many* years at OrangeVine there's never any cause for personal embarrassment or undue opacity. We make better decisions when we put everything on the table for a crowd-sourced discussion matrix. That's the inclusive culture I'd strive to maintain as president. Naturally, I'd lead by example."

"That's what I hoped you'd say, Caspian." Yvonne's eyes glistened intensely. She leaned forward and asked softly, "So where could I find a certain grant recipient known only by the name of Aldo?"

That explained it. The donations from the WhamZong deal. The questions he'd been getting about daisies. The mushroom cloud ad. As he and Vanessa feared, Aldo's garden had rattled the powers that be. It supplanted MyndScreens, drained consumption, led people out of Cyberia. These powers were counting on *him*, Caspian Blaine, to stop it. He'd known all along the problem sprung from Aldo, a key driver of his favorite grantee's work and, to be honest, one of the few fundamentally decent people left. If he turned him in, Caspian knew Aldo was a goner.

He sipped some water and bit into a sushi morsel to buy himself ten seconds. The lump in his throat made it hard to swallow. His fine Italian suit felt silky smooth as he stroked his knee cap. He studied the room's walnut wainscoting and crystal chandelier, contemplating the vast power held within those walls.

To make an omelet, you gotta break a few Egz.

He cleared his throat and looked Yvonne straight in the eye. "Aldo hangs out at the Santa Monica community garden. I'm sure he'd be happy to speak with you."

The rest of the interview transpired painlessly—small talk, philanthropic buzz words and compliments on his tie. Still, something nagged him. On his way out, he gently grabbed Yvonne's elbow and bent her close. "So, Shawn Fellia is also in the running?"

"Oh, I'm sure he'd love the CEO job," she said with a demure rise in her perfectly cherry lips. "But we're talking with him about another position we expect to become available."

He screwed up his eyebrows and gave her a look that said, "huh?"

She whispered, "Vice President of Special Projects," and gave him a wink. Yvonne tossed her platinum blondes aside and pushed him out with a delicate stroke to his lower back. He felt her long, pomegranate painted fingernails give him a slight scratch.

The next interviewee waited in the hall, Vice President of Finance Margery DeVrine. He gave her a fist pump and a cocky grin. "Good luck, I think they'll be impressed by your spreadsheets. Maybe we can go out for an OrangeSmash later?" She glared and brushed past him.

Back at his desk, he felt celebratory. He racked his brain for someone to share the excitement, to revel in his greatest career accomplishment. Surely, it was just a matter of time before the committee made him an offer he wouldn't refuse.

Before any victory lap, a breaking news story opened on Caspian's MyndScreen. "Barron Koldwill, a San Bernardino realtor, has been arrested in the childrearing center bombing incident. Prosecutors allege Koldwill orchestrated the attack to reduce real estate values and expedite a purchase for one of his clients. The bomber was previously believed to have been a Spryte Nationalist. Prosecutors now say simple financial greed was his motivation. The bomber just struck a plea deal, issuing a sworn statement that he was paid ninety thousand ByteDime by Barron Koldwill to conduct what amounts to an explosive arson attack. Back to you, Bambi."

Damnation!

CHAPTER 39
Chase

CHASE CAREFULLY REMOVED LUELLA'S TIARA FROM ITS plastic bag, dumped in the remaining ice from her foam supersized drink cup, and handed her the makeshift icebag.

"Can you put this on my head in a few minutes?"

"Whazzup, Gramps? You feverish?"

"Sometimes you have to go big." He inched the motorcycle up to the lava tube entrance.

She shrugged and stood back, watching in the pale moonlight. The tunnel's ceiling was a tad below his head height. He turned the cycle around, facing Luella. Reversing slowly, he pressed his head back against the rock, finding an outcropping that rubbed just behind his left ear. Chase had a seventeen-year-old itch he'd been dying to scratch. With heartbeat slamming against his ribs, he inched forward, using his 180 rear view camera sunglasses to align himself with the outcropping.

He briefly stuck his thumb into his pocket, touching the lucky penny. Forcing a smile, he glanced at Luella. "See you on the other side."

Chase put the bike in reverse and cranked the throttle. The rear tire squealed and the cycle lurched backwards, smashing his skull against rock at precisely the spot he'd probed.

When Chase awoke, it was dawn, presumably the next day. The puppy licked his face. A chill ran down his spine that he slowly discerned was not nervous energy, just cold water. He reached up and discovered Luella had attached the leaky ice bag to his head with the tiara. *Smart kid.*

"That was pretty much the most boneheaded thing I've ever seen," Luella derided. "You OK?"

He smiled slowly. Even the slight tightening of cheek muscles pulled at his scalp and made his entire head pound. "I dunno. Let's find out. You ready to drive this thing?"

"Course, Gramps. I been watching. You disabled your MyndScreen, didn't you? My brother did that too, on accident. It was kinda my fault. Anyhow, he iced his head and it's worked out OK."

She strapped on her GalExSee, helped Chase straddle the bike and slid herself between him and the dashboard. He reached back and grabbed the backrest's sissybar frame, letting her operate the throttle and brakes.

Luella hunched forward and maneuvered the bike down the dirt path. Before they got on the highway, he told her, "Once your helmet gets transmissions again we'll be out of the 11G dead zone. Just tap your helmet to let me know, OK?"

Luella flicked her wrist, and they bolted down the highway in anything but a smooth start. He hung on, inhaling the desert's crisp morning air. His head throbbed, the ice had now totally melted, and the wet plastic bag flapped in the wind behind him. *This is fucking nuts.* He grinned his big shit-eating grin and felt the air rush through his teeth and inflate his cheeks. Then he winced in self-afflicted pain.

They descended from the high desert at a smooth 40 miles per hour. San Bernardino's skyline glistened in the warm morning sunlight. He rested his forehead on Luella's shoulders, so when a stream of pop music suddenly blasted inside her helmet, he heard it immediately. Her right hand tentatively tapped her head before regaining its white-knuckled grip on the handlebars. He went to open a MyndScreen window. Nothing. Zilch. *Offline, baby.*

He tried whooping, "Yeehaw!" but it came out a whisper. The dry wind blew in his face with more force than he could counter.

Outside of town, Luella pulled over at a beat-up restaurant with an incandescent sign reading "Chestnut Tree Café."

"C'mon, Gramps, I'm hungry," she said, pulling off her helmet.

Near the entrance, a crow clung to a sunflower, which swayed under the bird's weight as the creature dislodged seeds with its beak. Just watching the inverted pendulum movements of the oscillating stalk made Chase a little dizzy.

A hand-written sign read: "Under new management—cash only." Fortunately, he was loaded with U.S. dollars from their Vegas payout.

Not a soul sat in a roomful of open tables. They took a booth made of blue vinyl cushions with a vase of real daisies on the table. A twenty-something woman fiddled with a microphone stand on a small stage. The wallscreens were off.

A waitress wearing a light-blue apron over a tan polyester dress burst through two swinging doors. She handed them some cardstock encased in clear vinyl, the likes of which Chase had never seen. "Getcha something to drink while you look at the menu? We've got fresh squeezed lemonade."

They nodded yes and stared at written words depicting entrées such as: "eggs over easy with toast," or "pancakes."

"There's not a single brand name on here," Luella complained, scrunching up her nose. "You think it's safe to eat?"

"This is what food was like, before extruders. It's good for you. Back in my day, we were thankful for a breakfast like this before walking to school barefoot in the snow, uphill, both ways." He'd been waiting his whole life to use this tired chestnut after writing it into a script decades ago, knowing yet not caring that it lacked originality. His whole *life*. What a concept! He actually had one to reflect upon. His inner glow was not the least bit diminished by Luella's eye roll and "whatever, Gramps."

The waitress returned with two lemonades, each with a sprig of mint, and a bowl of water for the puppy. Chase ordered ham and eggs with whole wheat toast, barely containing his excitement. Then he felt the icy cold liquid pucker his cheeks. He smelled the tart citrus, saw condensation drops forming on the glass, heard ice cubes clack against the sides. Luella conceded it was fantastic, then his joy faded as the woman on stage began to sing.

Under the spreading chestnut tree,

I loved her and she loved me . . .

Chase swore his heart literally stopped beating until, a moment later, he gasped for air. Luella gave him a look. "Drink go down the wrong pipe, Gramps?"

"No . . . it's Orwell. Goddamn Orwell. And here we are, in the Chestnut Tree Café of all places." The line came back in an instant, even though it had been decades since he read the novel about Winston betraying Julia. *I sold you, and you sold me. There lie they, and here lie we, Under the spreading chestnut tree.*

Chase flashed back to a bizarre encounter with a statue of Eric Blair, the real name for *1984's* dystopic author. That's when he'd met that homeless guy, outside Vera's apartment. Before they started reading *The Book* and its mind-numbing description of truth being killed by the inundation of facts as much as outrageous lies and vapid entertainment. Before they sold each other out and consented to the upgrade. Before he knew Vera was pregnant.

"Here ya go, mister. I don't know Orwell or who he consorts with but eat this while it's hot. And mind your mouth around the little ones."

The brash waitress placed a plate with hickory scented ham still sizzling and two sunny-side up eggs staring at him like a lover.

"I'm not little, by the way. I can drive!" Luella yelled at the waitress. Then, to Chase, "What's the problem dude? I thought you said you liked this kinda food."

He snapped out of his vacant trance, took a sniff and felt a slightly metallic fluid coat his tongue. Grabbing a knife, he sawed a morsel of ham and raised it cautiously to his mouth, as one would lift a hot spoon of soup. His taste buds exploded with savory pyrotechnics. "Ohhh, my god that's good," he moaned.

The singer plodded on:

I said I love you,

And there ain't no ifs or buts,

She said I love you

And the blacksmith shouted, "Chestnuts."

"Good morning, everybody. I'm thrilled to host open mike here at the Chestnut Tree Café. That little ditty was an old English folk song, originally recorded by the Glenn Miller Orchestra."

Huh. Not Orwell? Maybe he'd misremembered. *Oh, well.* The moment was too wonderful to ruin with dredged up backstory.

"Eeeew," Luella squealed. "What's with the yellow stuff running out of your eggs?"

"It's yolk. It's supposed to run. Try it." He gave her a bite on some toast, which she reluctantly conceded was pretty tasty.

It took a long time to finish eating, what with Chase learning how to chew solid food again and Luella playing with the strawberries and whipped cream on her Belgian waffle. As they finished, four bikers parked under the shade of the tree outside. They sat down near the door and removed motorcycle helmets that had no 11G antennas or visor screens. As Chase watched them settle in, his gaze fell on a chessboard set up in the next booth over.

"Bet I can whup you at chess, Gramps," Luella taunted.

"You know I can't turn down a challenge." After all, it wasn't like he had a plan for what came next.

Chase stared at the board yet had difficulty focusing on the pieces, which tended to double up or blur into each other. It worked better to close his eyes and just remember the chess board arrangement. He'd played thousands of games in Cyberia, so knew all the commands to direct a move. "Nf3" would send out his knight to threaten Luella's center pawn. After visualizing it, he could open his eyes and physically move the piece, but he was starting to get a headache. Maybe it was just because he hadn't played in a while, or that his head still hurt from the MyndScreen disabling. Or perhaps his brain was painstakingly reprogramming itself to rely solely on ocular input.

If he was still online, he could have bought a hint. Those days were gone for good. He lasted ten minutes before Luella cornered him. "Checkmate!" She yelled with all the enthusiasm of a twelve-year-old who just licked a grownup.

"Ha, ha!" belted a biker guy with a bald head and salt and pepper goatee that ran down to his collar bone. "Dude just got crushed by a little kid. Sad what's happened to people's brains these days."

Chase glanced up slowly, unperturbed. "This kid's pretty smart. I bet she could take you too."

"You're a betting man? Alright, tough guy, I'll wager my cycle outside. I had the highest cyberchess score in all of Ventura County back in sixth grade."

Chase considered whether the Ventura thing was a bluff before deciding he didn't really care. He pulled out a Rolex from his Vegas shopping spree and tossed it on the table. "Game on, man. That watch is easily worth double your bike."

Beads of perspiration appeared on the biker's shiny bald head as his posse egged him on. "C'mon bro, can't back out now."

The singer kept on, despite losing her audience's attention. "For my next song, I'm going to do an oldie but goodie by David Bowie. I think it's something we all can relate to these days."

The biker sat across from Luella, insisted on being white, and made an unusual opening bringing out the pawn in front of his queen's knight. Luella took out her king's pawn to board center and the bald biker dude backed up his first pawn by moving his f-pawn out one space. Luella slid her queen to h4 and won—in two moves. "Fool's mate, loser."

Chase saw the look on the guy's face. It presented like anger, yet Chase knew otherwise. It was shame. The shame of losing, to a twelve-year-old of all things. That smoldering mass of embarrassment can turn a sane man surly, and a surly man violent, in less time than it takes to crack an egg.

The singer's song remained the same.

Ch-ch-changes (Turn and face the strange)

Ch-ch-changes,

Don't want to be a richer man . . .

Luella appeared uncertain whether to gloat or run for the door as she nervously stroked the puppy's head. Chase took a hard look at the bald biker and then at his three buddies sitting in the booth in stunned silence. "Tell ya what," he said, with an affected southern drawl. "Keep the bike. It was just for fun anyhow. How were you guys supposed to know you were dealing with BadScootr, one of the gamiest cats in Cyberia? She's played me for far worse than that."

The tension faded and one of the bikers whipped out a clear bottle with a red "W" on it, beckoning them over. "Have some hootch. Bathtub gin we call it. Make it ourselves out of juniper berries." Another handed Luella some chocolate. "It's real. From cocoa beans and stuff. Try it." In the end, they let Chase leave with the bottle, still half full of gin that tasted slightly north of soap and nail polish remover. He loved it, nonetheless. They gave Luella two unopened bars of chocolate.

Chase tipped the waitress and musician before walking out. Their new friends' motorcycles had large, red "W's" embossed on their saddlebags.

CHAPTER 40
Aneeka

ANEEKA RANDALL WAS SOARING HIGH, FLOATING OVER Los Angeles in Lewis Leon's Areoyacht. She was doing Globalia's most powerful man a favor, or so she wanted him to believe. She was making a list of favors to someday ask in return.

Dagny Huerta's case was lost, at least for now. The deck was stacked against her. This Tribunal would not restrain its own power. Water under the bridge. She was nonetheless proud of herself for planting the flag, finding her inner restore point. She had identified a few allies, smoked out her opponents, and was positioning for the long game. Learning about the Chief's WhamZong insider trading scheme had given her leverage, kompromat, that would prove useful in the future. Her challenge was clear. With clarity came purpose, resolve, will.

The midday sun was heating up the city and she felt temperatures rise as they left the coast behind. A flock of AmaZing! drones deployed from the underbelly of a freight zeppelin off to Aneeka's starboard side, each twirling toward its predesignated delivery porch. The air buzzed with activity and excitement.

In her mind, she rehearsed her first words for when they finally reunited. Vera must have read the letter. She would have absorbed and accepted the sincere apology, which Aneeka still remembered writing word for word in her Faraday protected study with quill ink pen on parchment paper:

Dearest Vera,

You were right and I was wrong.

Prosperity isn't freedom. Freedom is the ability to think for oneself, to have your own feelings, to make your own choices, to experience the real world and own your beliefs. Freedom means pain, and joy, and love, and fear. I took those things away from you. I'm sorry. I sincerely want you to know I thought it was for the best.

I've recently been appointed to the Tribunal of Educates. From that vantage point, I've come to realize it's not only individual patients like you that we've mismanaged, it's our entire society. We've traded the messy freedom of self-government for a highly efficient, output-maximizing rule of experts. Our souls are the price we've paid for this prosperity.

During this difficult journey, I've come to recognize everything that's gone wrong, just as you had begun to understand when we first met. I need to make things right. You are the only person I've encountered who truly gets it. You owe me nothing, yet I'm begging for your help. I need you, Vera, truly I do—not only your advice, but your companionship, your solidarity in this lonely cause.

Regardless of whether you are willing to help, I want you to be free. Before every MyndScreen upgrade is installed, the firmware automatically creates a system restore point. This can be used to reinstall the operating software, should a virus or malware infect it.

The point being, Vera, is that I can restore you. I can take you back to your pre-upgrade status. I will do this whether or not you forgive me. All I need, of course, is your consent. You can contact me anytime at a special chatter account I've set up to receive private messages from you: @Vera2048.

With love and respect,

Aneeka

She'd sent it via certified U.S. Mail after being surprised at how well it worked for Dagny Huerta. This was a change of plan from using Caspian Blaine, who always sought favors in return. She had received confirmation her letter was delivered; there could be no other explanation for why Vera would be in the Department of Prosperity. Still, she wondered how Vera's travel had been arranged.

An entourage greeted her after she descended by cable harness from Leon's yacht to the roof of Mercernary General, the private hospital contracted by the Department of Prosperity to handle MyndScreen Side-Effect (MSE) treatments. Mercernary's director herself waited on the rooftop welcome center to shake Aneeka's hand, a breeze ruffling her short brown hair, along with three medical staff dressed in blue scrubs. A self-driving wheelchair, equipped with arm and waist restraints sat behind them, all standard admissions protocol. A new patient must be inbound.

Aneeka had researched system-restores and found no instances of using one for permanent upgrade removal. Restoration was usually performed remotely, by having the patient share their screen with a technician (often a bot), who used the settings menu to drill down several links into the operating system, ran a troubleshooter, and identified which reset date would delete any viruses or glitches that had snuck into the MyndScreen OS. Once the reset was complete, the technician reinstalled the latest, virus-free version of the upgraded OS and the patient was good to go. Aneeka theorized, however, that nothing required the reinstall. A patient could return to the limited functionality of their pre-upgrade MyndScreen, an operational level required by the *Zannity* ruling to captivate no more than forty percent of a patient's attention.

Zannity ensured that essential employees maintained sufficient capacity for independent thought. This included people like Vera, who once worked in the Department of Information producing verified facts for the *Two-Minute Spate* segment of news programs. It included people like Chase, whose imagination created entertainment content sufficiently gripping to attract audience views, which in turn maintained ad revenues. And, of course, it included people like Aneeka Randall, therapists who kept Globalia's best and brightest either functionally balanced in both virtual and terrestrial realities or rendered noncontagious with subsidized upgrades—quarantined forever in Cyberia.

The Mercernary director chattered about technology developments, new nanobot injection protocols, and what not. She complained about a spike in MSE cases after a widespread transmission outage disrupted people's normal viewing patterns. Aneeka wasn't really listening. She was thinking her current job wasn't that different from her old one, keeping the economy both productive and highly consumptive by squashing the few humans who didn't properly adapt to modern technological and economic environments, such as Dagny Huerta.

Upgrades weren't usually a medical prescription. Once a consumer could afford permanent entertainment home placement, they would retire, purchase their own upgrade, and relish a lifetime of ease and enjoyment. Only during rare community outbreaks of MSE, which pulled huge consumer segments from the infotainment economy, did the Department of Prosperity offer free upgrades to patients, like Vera, who experienced irrational fixations on terrestrial reality. Upgrading these MSE super spreaders contained the outbreak and allowed regular consumption to resume. Patients had to consent, of course. This was the goal of experts like Dr. Aneeka Randall at institutions such as Mercernary General, which it now occurred to her was owned by Renaissance Mercernary—the same hedge fund invested in Timeless Warning and WhamZong.

"Even though we're tight on space, we've made your old office available," the Mercernary General director gushed, gesturing for them to enter a high-speed elevator. Dr. Randall felt her stomach lurch as the floor dropped through the skyscraper's bowels. When the movement stopped, they stepped into a sterile corridor with patient rooms on either side. A wallscreen displayed "No Smoking/Vaping allowed" and simultaneously broadcast the admonition onto Aneeka's MyndScreen.

Halfway down the hallway, a frail man with a pale boyish face walked out a sliding door. Aneeka's MyndScreen decoded the QR code on an adjacent wallscreen as "Vanessa Youngblood." She was momentarily alarmed when the man pulled a small metal pistol from his tight-fitting black suit. Aneeka relaxed when he lit a cigar with a four-inch flame that shot out its barrel. He nodded to the Mercernary General director and said, "Nice to see you," as he walked off.

Aneeka had a familiar feeling of dread while walking down the long trail of mental infirmities, MSE victims, toward her office. She heard her heels clacking on the hard plastic floors and smelled the chemicalized LiceAll™ spray on the walls.

When her office doors slid open, her old desk was just as it had been. She noticed the room was newly outfitted with a MyMassage lounge, a soyalgent extruder, and a wallscreen virtual window. She'd long coveted this corner office, with not one but two windows, which none of the patient rooms had (by design). *Why the need for a virtual window?*

"We wanted you to be as comfortable as possible. This case could take a while," said the director.

"I'm sure that won't be necessary," Dr. Randall replied, somewhat absentmindedly as she tried to reorient herself.

"I sent the file to your inbox. Let me know when you've reviewed it, and we'll send the patient in. Feel free to grab a cup of coffee and relax a few minutes if you need to."

Aneeka knew every word in Vera's file. She'd written the damned thing. She wanted nothing to do with soyalgent Koffy in a plastic pro-truded cup. She made a mental note, though, to download Vera's exit interview that had been corrupted in her own Klowd backup, should that ever prove helpful in the future. "Send them in. I'm ready."

The director left and the doors slid shut with a "whoosh." It wouldn't be long now. Vera would be summoned by an automated wheelchair. Seventeen years ago, it had been a battle just to get Vera to sit in that chair and be wheeled to Aneeka's office. Only after several weeks of intensive music, light show therapy, and proper pharmaceuticals, did Vera finally accept the chair as her only way out. This time, Dr. Randall was confident, she would be eager to come.

She sat down, stroking the polished wood desk with her fingertips, wondering if Vera's skin still felt so smooth and tender. She instinctively reached toward her own neck, rubbing the polished jade pendant between her soft fingertips. Aneeka's steel girder softened, glowing red instead of hardened gray.

After what could only have been a few minutes yet felt much longer, the doors slid open, and the wheelchair drove in.

There must be some mistake.

It wasn't Vera sitting in the chair, not at all.

The patient inhaled deeply, taking in the scents of the room. He smiled and said, "Hello, Aneeka. How are you today?"

Her jaw gaped open in a pregnant pause before she sputtered, "Aldo? What are you doing here?"

CHAPTER 41
Oscar

"YO!" JEROME CRUISED BY AS OSCAR POSTED ELLEN'S flyers. "We're back online. Luella sent the code. She must be OK. You can chill, brudda."

The rubber band compressing every vertebra in Oscar's spine snapped. His rib cage expanded, filling his lungs with air so lush he could taste it.

"Thanks for telling me. Really." Oscar fist bumped his old gang brudda. "Hey, if she's online, can you use a LowKate app to get her geo-coordinates?"

Jerome stared at his palm and squinted his eyes, clearly pushing some buttons on his MyndScreen as Oscar waited. Finally, Jerome looked up, eyes wide. "She's at the Chestnut Tree Café, a bona fide Winston hangout. I'd round up some MarlBros to bash some heads, but you're the one who went rogue. This is on you brudda." As he drove off slowly, a weird sound came from Jerome's electric lowrider, almost a whirring.

The rubber band snapped back, squeezing every bone in Oscar's skeleton. Leaving the gang was stupid; this confirmed it. Out of nowhere, a breeze whipped up, tussling the hair he'd stopped slicking back.

A loud hum shook the sky as a Pincerton descended immediately in front of him, its six-foot rotor spinning at head height like a weed eater ready to mow him down. He spun around, only to see another pinca land right behind him. He was trapped.

A third one hovered five feet above making both a whirr and loud hiss. Adrenaline infused his arteries with warm energy. His muscles tensed for a sideways dive. Before his brain sent the signal, the drone extended a mechanical arm that blasted his face with a sweet, scented spray.

Everything went dark.

When he came to, Oscar was looking at the pinca's underbelly as it pinned him down like a WWE wrestler. Its long insect-like claws constricted his arms and legs in a painless, yet intensely claustrophobic confinement. The drone's underbelly flashed a video screen as the heliblade stopped and the other drones departed. It was eerily quiet until an attractive avatar with brown hair pulled tight into a bun appeared on the screen and spoke in a soothing mechanized voice.

"@OscarBro92346, you have failed to respond to three past-due notices from Timeless Warning. Unless you transmit payment immediately, your MyndScreen service will be suspended. Under Tribunal doctrine, credit agencies may freeze your ByteDime account until full payment has been made."

Oscar felt warm asphalt pushing against his back as the pinca pressed him down. He managed to stammer, "It's disabled" before the machine droned on.

"Moreover, your Chatter handle has been linked to a contraband VR helmet used by cyberterrorists. The Department of Prosperity has obtained a warrant for your interrogation about these attacks on Globalian freedom. This can be avoided if you consent to a fully financed implant re-installation with upgraded service and free lifetime placement in the entertainment home of your choice. A lifesaving drone is on its way to transport you to Mercernary General Hospital. We appreciate your business and know your time is valuable. The estimated wait time will be 197 minutes. In the meantime, drink plenty of fluids and avoid lifting heavy objects for the next 24 hours while your etherization wears off."

Oscar felt like he might cry. Luella was gone, he'd fallen out with his bruddas, Vanessa was AWOL, his bacco crop was behind schedule. And now, he was pinned to the ground by a motorized mosquito sucking the life out of him. There was no way in hell he'd let them Vera-fy him on some bogus cyberterrorism charge.

Just like that, Luella pulled up on a 2040s-era motorcycle with ridiculous cow-patterned saddlebags. The damn puppy was tucked inside her jacket, its head peeking out from her newly blossoming bosom. A middle-aged Winston dude with a blond mullet and leather jacket leaned over her. He probably had a gun.

"That's him, my brother," Luella told the dude. She hopped off the bike and ran over. The guy slowly eased the machine toward Oscar and dismounted, stumbling a bit like he was drunk. *Great, now I get to do a ransom negotiation with a blitzed-out biker thug while straight-jacketed by a fucking pinca.* Oscar put on his game face and blinked away the tears.

The Winston dude ignored him and jammed one of the Pincerton's idle copter blades between the motorcycle's front forks, immobilizing the drone. He wore a jeweled princess crown, like they sometimes do at drag queen parties, and his skin was abnormally pale. The dude went right to the drone without speaking a word. Its electric motor whined—trying to move its trapped heliblade. Somehow, Oscar couldn't quite see, the dude removed a plastic cover using a shiny contraption he pulled from his pocket. A battery pack dropped to the ground, then the Winston dude pried open the pinca's jaws and lifted it off him. The drone looked surprisingly lightweight and flimsy once he was free of it.

"Where'd you learn to disable a Pincerton?" Luella asked.

"A MacGuyVir episode. You know, kind of a Mr. Gadget tech support secret agent show. Hi," he turned to Oscar, offering him a hand. "I'm Chase."

"I can't pay nothing," Oscar pleaded softly. "They just froze my ByteDime. Please don't hurt her, man. I could give you guys half our turf."

"I'd love a little patch of grass, haven't walked on that for decades. But of course I won't hurt Luella. She's saved my life, in more ways than one. I'm just hoping you're not angry with me."

Oscar screwed up his face and did the Gary Coleman line he'd seen on reruns as a kid. "Whatchu talking 'bout Winston?"

"I'm not Winston, like I said. I'm Chase." He still held his right hand out to Oscar while gingerly rubbing the back of his head with the left.

By now Luella was next to him. The puppy wriggled free and licked Oscar's chin. "Chase is who I got the cycle from, Oscar. I won it fair and square."

"You mean, that's yours?"

"I'll let you borrow it if you're nice. So … can we keep the puppy?"

Oscar sat up, still on the pavement, stared at Luella, the puppy, and Chase's tiara. He laughed. Maybe it was the ether, but he felt he could just float off the ground. "Yeah, Lulu, let's keep the puppy. What's his name?"

"Winnie?" she said.

"Winnie the pooch," Chase chuckled. "Perfect." Oscar had no idea what he was talking about. Luella rolled her eyes.

They talked. Oscar got brought up to speed on Luella's Vegas adventure, Chase's MyndScreen disabling maneuver, and chess in the Chestnut Tree Café. Luella claimed Winstons were actually pretty nice. Chase got caught up on the seventeen years since he entered his entertainment home, which is to say, nothing much had changed.

Chase cleaned out his personal items from the Holstein saddlebags, his heart sinking at the prospect of relinquishing the bike. There was his old harmonica, which he put in his pocket, a pair of motorcycle gloves that he gave to Oscar, and a piece of paper with red scribbles on it, which Luella picked up to inspect.

Ellen walked up with a stack of flyers. "Luella! You're back!" Luella gave her a hug, knocking flyers from Ellen's grasp just as the wind gusted. Luella rushed to pick them up, handing the red-scribbled note to Ellen. The puppy chased after and chaos erupted, again causing Oscar to burst out laughing. He had never felt this light, this elated, this relaxed. He watched Ellen's every move, how her hair splayed in the breeze, the way her delicate fingers grasped the papers. She saw him watching and smiled back. "You could help, you know."

When everything was collected, Ellen read the note. "Roses are red, violets are blue, as long as the sun shines, I'll only Chase you." It was signed with a "V."

"Sunshine . . . Chase . . . " She looked up at him. He'd removed the tiara, but was still a little red in the face, either from sunburn, excitement, or inflammation from his implant decommissioning.

She swallowed hard and said, "Dad?"

CHAPTER 42
Caspian

CHIEF EDUCATE LEWIS LEON WAS IN CASPIAN'S NEWS feed. He'd purchased two billion ByteDime worth of WhamZong stock just before it spiked in what ethics watchdogs called blatant insider trading. Worse yet, Leon was denying reports his illegally captured pet wedge-tailed eagles had killed the last living koala bear. Meanwhile, in sports, the Patriaders had defeated the BroncBoys, permanently maiming two players who required leg amputations.

A *Globalian Times* reporter interrupted Caspian's newsbinge, asking for comment about Barron Koldwill's plea statement in the school bombing. The police said at least four teens were killed in the explosion while playing midnight basketball. He deleted the reporter's message, knowing that wouldn't make it go away.

His MyndScreen notified him of an incoming VRoom call from Yvonne Putcher. He accepted, watching her avatar gesture in a low-cut red cocktail dress. Her seductive voice reverberated inside his head. "Hey there big boy! You got the job. It will be announced next week. Congratulations, Mr. President."

"That's stupendous. There's … well, never mind." His voice sounded anything but celebratory and his avatar had its thumbs pressed into its temples.

"What Caspi? You can tell me. You're always looking out for others. I'll look out for you. What's going on?"

For the first time in his life, he spilled the beans. Caspian let his guard down and told her everything. How he'd been funding a special project directly tied to the daisy uprising all because he had a schoolboy crush on the grantee. How he'd inadvertently orchestrated a bombing to hasten a real estate deal for the project. How the whole thing was about to explode in the press.

"I see." Her avatar stroked its jawline below the right ear and blinked. "Shouldn't be a problem. I'll get Barscale on it, he used to work in Perception Management."

The following morning, Yvonne and Barscale picked him up in a stretch limo with a real life chauffercurity sitting behind a non-functional steering wheel. The glass was tinted, of course, along with copper wire mesh in all the windows. "What's that? Some sort of window defroster? You really don't need that in post-global warming LA," he jibed, trying to lighten the situation.

"It's a Faraday cage, to block 11G transmissions. Anything that happens here didn't really happen." Barscale didn't smile as he said this.

The limo had long, sofa-style seats running down either side. He scooched down to the end and opened his legs, manspreading to avoid bumping knees with Barscale who sat directly opposite him. Yvonne Putcher perched at Caspian's side, a little closer than necessary given how spacious the limo was. She'd trimmed her ruby-painted nails down to the quick, making her slender hands slightly less elegant. She wore the red cocktail dress her avatar had on the previous day, with matching lipstick that made her mouth even more luscious than usual.

Barscale opened a mahogany cabinet and withdrew a crystal bottle filled with golden liquid. "Single malt. Only 20 years, but still reasonably smooth." He handed Caspian a generous pour.

Caspian took a sip and felt the scotch slide warmly down inside him. He looked out the window past Barscale's head and admired the ocean as they drove up the Pacific Coast Highway. He leaned back onto the couch. It was going to be OK.

Barscale had hired McChesney to run a perception management campaign—their typical distraction regimen. They do this all the time, not a big deal, he explained while leaning forward and whispering, "We just need something personally embarrassing, something plausible yet unverifiable, something like killing the world's last koala bear. It needs to be sufficiently explosive to overshadow the C-4 attack. Beyond the four basketball players, they've now confirmed it killed twenty toddlers and ten bots in an adjacent childrearing center. We need something salacious."

Caspian drummed his fingers on his knee when, just like that, Yvonne's delicate palm caressed his chubby brown knuckles. Maybe she was just reassuring him during this stressful moment, the way a friend or a sibling would. It felt like something more. He shot a sideways glance to make eye contact, but her glassy stare aimed straight over Barscale's shoulder. A nearly imperceptible smirk graced her perfect lips.

Barscale used a fancy lighter that looked like a derringer pistol to shoot a four-inch flame at a Cuban cigar he pulled from an onboard humidor. Maybe Caspian had been accused of sexual harassment by a former grantee, he suggested. Putcher moved her hand from Caspian's knuckles to his inner thigh, making swirls on his silk slacks with her fingertips. Pins and needles struck the back of his neck. He took a big sip of scotch.

Barscale said that as part of the presidential search process they ran a routine background check. They found several warnings that OrangeVine's anti-harassment AI had flagged during interactions with a certain Vanessa Youngblood. Yvonne stroked Caspian between the legs, where he'd become firmer than a SleepNummer™ massage lounge set to eleven.

Caspian's face looked like a deer in headlights. To avoid eye contact, he stared straight out the chicken wire-embedded window to the crashing

Pacific as the limo lurched around Highway 1 at speeds exceeding the legal limit. The scotch sloshed from stomach to head.

Barscale described how an attorney, Celious Tudball, would launch the Perception Management campaign with a prepared statement. Caspian Blaine vehemently denies any sexual contact or inappropriate touching regarding Vanessa Youngblood. "It never happened. Period." McChesney had already reached out and she was conveniently unavailable for comment. "We're monitoring the feeds continuously. We will send the denial right as the San Bernardino bombing story hits the news." Yvonne had his fly undone and she'd gone inside.

Barscale carried on and on about the scheme, noting it didn't require them to contact Vanessa or have her play any role. Caspian had a hard time paying attention, focusing instead on the twitch of silky soft fingers.

"We've compiled several chatter post images to provide the visuals. Wallace Packard has signed off and doesn't worry it will hurt your reputation with board members or donors. It might even help; make you seem less prudish."

Caspian could hardly think straight. Nonetheless, it sounded like a plan. "OK, let's do it. It's a bit embarrassing, but I'll do what I gotta do."

"And don't worry, if anything like this ever comes up again, we'll have an additional witness," Barscale smirked, nodding at Yvonne who cupped his scrotum like a water balloon in the palm of her hand. "No need to thank us," Barscale winked. "Someday you'll surely return the favor."

Yvonne contracted her fingers as Barscale rolled down the privacy window so he could talk to the chaufferscurity. "This is sufficient, James. Please drop Yvonne and I off in Malibu and return Mr. Blaine to OrangeVine whenever he's through enjoying the ride."

"Yes, sir, Mr. Barscale," said James, who turned away from the road to gawk at them. "Looks like you are having quite a ride indeed Mr.

Blaine," he said with a squinty grin. Caspian was certain James just snapped an image onto his MyndScreen. He swallowed the rest of his scotch. After his co-conspirators got out, he poured another tall glass and drank till he passed out.

He was deposited at his office by early afternoon, dissatisfied with events that left him high and dry. The plan worked fine for OrangeVine, yet what would it mean for Vanessa? He tried to chatter ping her with a heads up. Maybe she could lie low. Maybe he could find her a new job, a promotion at a bigger charity. He had some celebrity connections, maybe they'd help.

"I'm sorry. This account is currently unavailable. If you think you've reached this message in error, please re-enter the account name and try again." *Damnation! Upgraded, baby. I told her to keep her head down. I told her to ease up on the daisy stuff. How come nobody ever listens to me?*

Caspian's mind raced. He had a ton of transition work looming. He'd need to hand off his Special Projects and Strategic Initiatives portfolio. UpLyfting Lives would need a new executive director with Vanessa out of the picture. Ellen, maybe? He tried to ping her on the chatter. She wasn't online. That was the problem with non-implants, their life stories were rarely live. He thought about sending a message she'd receive whenever she next put on that old helmet, but he was running out of time. Once his name was all over the news as a sexual predator, Ellen wouldn't give him the time of day. He needed to talk to her now, ASAP, presto…. How? Tracking her down by car would take several hours in heavy LA traffic.

His MyndScreen popped up an ad, "Need to get there ASAP? Call in an AerLift ™ !" That was it, a helitaxi. Now that he didn't need to worry about the VP of Finance poring over his expense account, he could just order one up. When he clicked, he saw the following disclaimer, "Your range and weight requirements exceed that of our typical battery operated helidrone. Upgrade to an FC Hydrodrone and get there presto. Part blimp, part copter, our explosive new technology uses hydrogen for buoyancy and to power Fuel Cell electricity for eight revolutionary velocirotors."

After downloading the app, he went to OrangeVine's roof to await his first personal flight. The AerLift descended with an eerie whir. He stepped inside a transparent compartment and observed the "NO SMOKING" sign decaled onto the bulging mylar balloon tank situated above him, in between the eight rotors—a bulbous octopus perched upon a 20th century phone booth with each arm holding twirling whirligigs.

CHAPTER 43
Chase

CHASE JUST STOOD THERE, LIKE HE'D BEEN TOUCHED IN a game of freeze tag.

He'd heard her say it. *Dad*? What happened now?

He saw his own blue eyes, noticed the same sturdy jawline his father had passed down to him. She had Vera's nose and earlobes. And, yes, Vera's coy smile rather than his own high beams.

It's one thing to miss your kid's childhood because you were imprisoned or off fighting foreign wars. It's quite another to skip fatherhood because you chose to play video games in an entertainment home. He had consented.

No, that wasn't fair. Accepting their terms and conditions was the only option. He'd played their game, under their rules, as best he could. He'd lost.

She looked at him with creased brows and a face ready to break. Finally, he said something, only because the silence became unbearable. "This will sound really lame, but I don't even know your name. I know Vera was pregnant. I know the baby meant everything to her, to me too. You were our hopes, our dreams, our future. She told me about you the last time we met, for a fleeting moment. Yet she never told me your name."

He could see Vera's strength, her resolve, in his daughter's response.

"I'm Ellen. And you're Chase. And Vera is my mother. And something terrible happened to you both. That's all I know."

"It wasn't our fault. I mean, we knew what we were up against, we both fought and used it nonetheless, so maybe it was our fault. Even if we knew we'd fail, we had to try. We couldn't abandon who we were."

"What are you even talking about?"

"The infotain market, which we worked for, which we fed with our minds and our souls, which we tried to escape. It's acceptable when just a few people go off grid. If too many abandon virtuality to spend time here, in this world, well, it threatens the whole attention economy. People stop watching shows they don't need to see, stop buying stuff they don't need to have, stop eating food they don't need to consume. Vera, your mom, she questioned too much, spread plentiful doubt. I tried easing her up, but she was so determined."

His dry throat and strained voice made him realize these were, by far, the most words he'd spoken in decades. More than that, the most *thoughts*. The virtual hangover was lifting. He was stirring his own ideas, responding to his own memories—which were amazingly still there. He continued.

"So, they got us. Snatched us from the beach with their quote unquote lifesaving drones claiming we were suicidal or somehow threatening others. They wore us down with so-called treatment, convinced us we were miserable because, well, they made us miserable, and then promised whatever we most desired if only we'd accept their free upgrade and lifetime entertainment home placement. They bankrupted me, using my own words in jest to smear me with libel. They overwhelmed me with food followed by deprivation, silence followed by noise, entertainment followed by deadly depressing emptiness. I caught onto them, realizing that however long I held out, I'd eventually crumble. So, I played along and made the best of it. Your mother held out longer. They must have used even stronger quote unquote therapies to break her."

"And now, you're here. In this world. With us."

274

"Yeah," he grinned. "I am. All 'cause this one," he motioned to Luella with a wry grin, "won my motorcycle in a stupid bet."

"Speaking of which," Oscar interjected, "we oughta get going. Luella. You got some 'splaining to do."

"OK, I'll give you a ride if you hold Winnie." She dumped the puppy into Oscar's arms and straddled the bike. Oscar, uncharacteristically, complied.

Ellen and Chase stood alone, with neither awkwardness nor familiarity.

Finally, Ellen resumed. "When she told you about me that once, what . . . what was she like?"

"Vera was going to get you from the hospital and had a baby seat on her wheelchair scooter. We had both completed our quote unquote treatment. She was going to deliver you to some childrearing center before getting her upgrade. I'd thought these memories had been erased, yet it feels like it was yesterday. With no way to find you, I lost myself in distraction. Vera's probably virtually followed your every step."

"She hasn't. Nuns took me from the childrearing center as a toddler. I found her, just days ago, hooked up to some machine in this dreadful human warehouse. She's zoned out, hardly aware of what's right in front of her."

"Yeah, well, sometimes it's easier not to acknowledge what's staring you right in the face—better to pretend it's not real, you know?"

"No! I don't know. I have no idea what you're talking about! What's real is real whether you pretend it or not." Ellen stomped the ground. He thought she would storm off, but she just stood there, sulking with arms crossed, staring at the cracked pavement.

Chase shoved his hands into his jacket pockets, embarrassed at his own daughter calling him out. He felt the smooth metal sides of his harmonica, the same instrument he'd used to serenade Vera in the desert so many years ago. That was the day they both knew it, knew their love was real, knew with a certainty sunk deep in their bones, knew (or thought they knew) that no one or no thing could take away that reality.

He stepped toward her and, ever so gently, lifted her chin until their gaze met. "You're right, Ellen. You are absolutely, without a doubt, correct. I'm sorry I said that. I'm sorry I even thought it. Thank you."

She hugged him, harder than he'd ever been hugged. "Dad…. We have to get her. She'll listen to you. I'm sure she will."

"I don't know. I've let her down in ways you could only begin to imagine. I'll try. I owe her that. I owe you that."

"You owe it to you, too. C'mon."

They walked, side by side, ten minutes to the Twilight Kingdom. They said nothing, even though there was much to say, much to know, much to ask. Chase's mind focused on one thing. *Vera.* What could he say? What could he do? How do you make up for a life forgone?

He balked when the Twilight Kingdom's doors slid open, staring into the unattended lobby. Was he really going back in?

Ellen pulled him through. They walked past a few service bots, which didn't seem to register their existence even though the alarm blared, "Cerebral implants not detected. Viral contact tracing not feasible. Risk level presumed high." Chase figured the bots must be on autopilot.

She led him to the room where Vera lay entranced. He was afraid to look in. Afraid of what he'd see. Afraid Vera might not see him for who he now was.

"Let me wait in the hallway while you tell her I'm here. Find out if she wants to see me."

He watched Ellen walk in, purpose in every stride, and felt immensely proud of who she turned out to be, all on her own, without either parent there to guide her. He shuffled his feet, unsure he was worthy of either of them, of this, of anything.

Ellen grabbed her hand. "Vera . . . Mom, it's me. Ellen. I brought someone. Chase. He's outside."

Chase peeked in to see Vera blink her eyes, thrice.

"It's not really him. He's gone, forever." Her hair had turned gray. Her face lacked expression, making her look like a different person. Still, it was her. He was certain.

"No, Mom. I'm sure of it. I got a DNA test."

"Ellen, even if it is him physically, it won't really be *him*. They destroyed the real Chase seventeen years ago. They destroyed the real me."

"He's here, really here, in mind, and spirit. I know it. I sense it. Believe me, Mom."

"I can't believe in anything. Something happened recently that made me wonder if he might still be there. Still be the same Chase. I found him online. He seemed clever, like he'd regained his wits. I was wrong. The real Chase would have known it was me. At least, if I was still me and he was still him. He can no longer love the shell I've become. He just dropped off the face of the earth and ghosted me. There are still three dots hanging in his chat."

It hit him like a cannonball. *@Seeker*. "I really need to know something now that you're out. Do you still love me?"

Vera paused, scratching her elbow. "Hey, there's something happening on *Big Brother V*."

Chase grabbed his gut and ran down the hallway trying not to puke. The floor zoomed by like a blur, but he couldn't look up. He just needed out. His head throbbed; he couldn't walk straight. Ellen found him doubled over on the sidewalk, gasping.

Before he could catch his breath, before she could say anything, he saw a big dude with corn rows and a fancy suit descend in a strange contraption, something like a display case topped with a giant mylar birthday balloon surrounded by drone rotors whirring like weed eaters. Something about him seemed familiar.

CHAPTER 44
Aneeka

"YOUR FRIENDS BROUGHT ME DOWNTOWN FOR A STAY-cation," Aldo said, with a gentle smile. "What brought you, Aneeka?"

"I . . . I'm a doctor. A psychiatrist, actually. They brought me to treat someone. To treat you."

"Ah, well, what seems to be the trouble?" His voice was soft, upbeat.

"Let me take a look at your file."

Aldo hummed a little tune contentedly as Aneeka stared into space, accessing his file. "I see you experienced some complications during your MyndScreen installation surgery thirty-five years ago. The technology was new then, with a success rate of only around ninety percent. We've fortunately improved the procedure. Significantly fewer patients now experience a misplant."

"Ah. So 'you' equate misplant with misfortune?" He made little air quotation gestures with his fingers.

She shifted in her chair. "Well … it's why you can't see. The surgery damaged the synapse between your optical nerve and visual cortex, located in the occipital lobe of your brain. The scarring left you with neither visual sight nor a functioning MyndScreen. Patients with this condition are especially limited because they can't even use a VR helmet, as that requires ocular input."

"Ah, I see. Perhaps limitation provides greater insight than excess. What now?"

She understood why Lewis Leon had brought her here. She knew what she was supposed to do. What her role was in this whole system. She took a deep breath and clasped her fingers.

"The Department of Prosperity has authorized full payment for corrective surgery. We would provide Bluetooth camera sunglasses to stream video into a new implant with the latest IT. Your original chip was recalled, and the replacements are vastly superior. You are in a top-rated facility. This procedure's success rate is well above ninety-nine percent. How does that sound?"

"Very generous, your department is. However, I'm happy as I am. I don't need enhancement."

"Aldo ..." Dr. Randall felt that icy ball swelling inside her, pushing her inner girder of steel. "That will be all for today." She pressed a button underneath her desk and his automated wheelchair spun him around and out her office doors.

He waved. "Nice seeing you again, Aneeka!"

What to do? She couldn't just explain to Chief Leon that this was a complicated case. They knew—that's why they called her. Aldo must have already resisted traditional treatment. She found an Atlantis vigarette in her purse and took a draw. Exhaling, she watched the fumes waft upward, gradually dispersing before vanishing into an HVAC intake.

Standard protocol identified patient deficiencies in Maslow's hierarchy of needs and developed a nutritional, pharmaceutical and infotainmential regimen to meet them. Therein lay the problem. Aldo was already content, happily perched atop Maslow's pyramid, smiling broadly at the world. The more satisfied a patient, the harder it was to discover an inadequacy or devise treatment that would allow terrestrial re-entry as a productively consuming member of society. Aldo not only purchased next to nothing, he discouraged consumption by others. His daisy endeavor was intentionally disruptive. He knew it. She knew it. So did "they."

As with any advertising campaign, the first step was to manufacture a need. Dr. Randall prescribed a restricted diet of unflavored soyalgent and water. Aldo would have no contact with the outside world. No visitors. No wallscreen infotainment. No music. Maybe then he'd welcome greater input. Maybe then he'd be ready to listen.

She paced fervent, clockwise circles. There had to be a solution. Each step sunk into the floor with purpose, resolve, firm determination. She just needed to employ her experience, her scientific training, her rationality. Step. Step. Snap.

She seized up, lower back muscles tied painful knots, pinching nerves between her lumbars. Collapsing to the floor she endured the agony, daring not move for minutes.

Aneeka crawled to the MyMassage. She just needed to work through this. Slowly. Methodically. The lounge intuitively undulated, applying gentle warmth and pressure to her lower back. A Maison Louis Marie's No.03 L'Étang Noir scented breeze filled the room. The lounge's top clamshell closed over her front, applying pressure to thighs and forearms.

Somehow, she didn't initiate it, an avatar named @PatriotGrl appeared on the wallscreen in a black silk negligée. Her bio said she was an easy-going honest lady who led a simple life and liked to have fun with new friends. "Hi, gorgeous. Want to see a video of me camming last week?"

The padded leather post in the middle of the massage lounge began to vibrate. The top half used padded rollers to squeeze her chest. "Ahh," Aneeka broke into a pant. "Ahh, yes."

Ten minutes later, an automated wheelchair rolled into to her office carrying an opened bottle of French chardonnay, an octagonal crystal glass, and a note from Lewis Leon. "I told you it would be challenging. Please accept this token of my appreciation."

Weeks passed with little progress. She'd lost track of how many. She tried keeping up with the Educates, checking in with clerks, signing off on decrees they drafted, staying on top of news reports, and taking in the *Two-Minute Spate* of fact-checked, essential information each day. They brought in a treadmill. She synced it with her wallscreen to display the Telluride trail and ran further and further each day.

She awoke one morning in the massage lounge with a blunt headache. The extruder produced a tall PumpkinCayenneFrappucinno™ and she took a sip. She turned on the morning news while wading through her messages, looking for anything from the clerks. Her thoughts kept lurching back to what could have been, what should have been. It was supposed to be Vera, not Aldo. Hadn't her message gone through?

"Communication problems ruining your relationships?" asked a pop-up ad. "Try Neads™, a new app designed to help you learn your partner's wants and desires. It's easier than asking."

Asking. Why didn't I think of that?

Aneeka tidied her hair and ordered her patient in. The air conditioning ran full tilt, making the room crisp and chilly.

"Good morning, Aldo. Did you sleep well?"

"Quite peacefully, Dr. Randall. And you?"

"Like a rock. Tell me, is there any way I can make your stay more comfortable? Any food or beverage preferences? Perhaps a nice manicure after the punishment you put your hands through in the garden."

He smiled and shook his head.

"Suppose I told you there was a fifty-fifty chance that a reimplantation surgery would repair your damaged ocular nerve and restore your physical vision?" She wasn't a surgeon and didn't actually know the percentage, yet it seemed like a reasonable estimate.

"I see far more without my eyes than I did with them, Aneeka. For instance, I can see you are conflicted. I can see you wish to follow your heart; you've tried to do so, yet now you are afraid."

Aneeka threw up her hands and paced clockwise, breathing and thinking. Thinking and pacing and breathing. She stopped and stared out at a lifeless Los Angeles casting stark shadows on the ground far below. She felt the warmth of the sun beaming in the window, heating the skin on her neck and face. She stroked the jade pendant dangling from her necklace.

"What about other things, things beyond these walls? What are you looking for, Aldo? What are your life goals? As I mentioned, I have connections in powerful places. Think for a moment, if I could give you anything in the world, anything at all, what would it be?" The chrome and leather of his wheelchair looked a bit like the Wassily chair back in her Westside bungalow, if only she could be there now.

"It would be nice if you moved away from that window. You're blocking the sunbeam."

She stepped aside and glared at him, astonished. He smiled.

"What is it that *you* want, Aneeka? Have you decided who you are? Have you decided what feels true to you? Do you want tomatoes from a garden, or tomato-flavored mush from a machine?"

She paced counterclockwise, encircling Aldo.

"I want the tomato. It grows slowly, so for now I'm eating soyalgent. Biding my time, tilling the soil, staying alive. Wait, I'm the one asking the questions here."

"Ask away. Observe whether your head is asking, or your heart."

It was too much. Her steel girder snapped back, rigid, in charge.

"A clinician is ethically bound to use rational thought and research for the benefit of their patients and not let emotional swings or personal attachments interfere with care."

"I see you have made your choice." Aldo sighed.

Her demeanor softened as she grabbed his hand. She held it, firmly yet gently. "Aldo. Please. It's not really a choice. I need you to help me by letting me help you. If you don't like the new implant, I will disable it. Can you give it a try?"

"I have tried once, and one time was just the right amount. Trying too much is equally debilitating as trying too little."

"OK, I think we've both had enough for today." She hit the button underneath her desk.

"Take care Aneeka! I wish you well on this joyful day."

Aneeka ordered a TripleEspressoKaluaSlammer™ and sat down, brooding. Her chatterbox pinged with all sorts of messages. She closed it and stared outside.

She ran a PsychoNoodle™ search for "How to manufacture wants in a person with acute contentment syndrome?" and spent hours surfing clinical literature.

After a brutally long day, she sent a prescription to the extruder in Aldo's room for shredded chewing tobacco soyalgent and had a MinuteMayd deliver protruded plastic daisies. She programmed his Pharmascentster™ medical appliance to emit Oxycodoze™ mist with earth scents and artichoke-cucumber aroma. Perhaps it would remind him of the garden.

CHAPTER 45
Oscar

WITH HIS RIGHT HAND, OSCAR GRIPPED THE REAR SEAT frame on Chase's cycle (actually make that Lulu's cycle.) With his left, he clutched Winnie tight to his chest. The puppy poked its head over Luella's shoulders, letting the wind hit its face and flap little fuzzy ears around Oscar's neck. The electric motor whined as Luella cranked the throttle, just to see what sort of acceleration the thing had. He was still rattled from the pinca detainment, so he looked up, around, everywhere except where Luella drove after they'd left Ellen and Chase to sort things out.

He eventually noticed she wasn't heading straight home. Rather, she was enjoying the spectacle of parading the streets of San Bernardino on her new set of wheels. What if some of his old bruddas saw Oscar clutching a puppy with his kid sister in the driver's seat? His machismo couldn't stand such a blow. Surprisingly, several of his bacco custoz popped out their doors and waved as they rolled by. He was a local celebrity, or at least the one guy everyone recognized in a world where nobody really knew anyone anymore.

Oscar reconciled himself with Luella's scenic route. It gave him time to prepare for a conversation they needed to have about her unannounced departure. He rehearsed lines in his head. He needed to be firm, but not a jerk. Needed to let her know he cared about her, not drive her away. Still, there had to be some rules.

They drove by Vien's condo and saw him hanging out in the park, smoking with a few neighbors. Oscar asked Luella to pull over and she jolted the bike to a stop.

"She's back!" Vien beamed.

"Yeah, it was no big deal," Luella said, looking at a flattened extruded plastic cup lying in the gutter. "I was just completing a transaction. Like my new wheels?"

"Ooooh, very pretty, Luella. See, Oscar—I told you the biker guy was OK." Then he placed his hand gently atop Luella's GalExSee and tilted the helmet until it pointed directly at his face. "But you, young lady, should always tell your brother where you are going. He was worried sick."

Oscar had been building up for a big lecture about responsibility and how the world is a dangerous place and how she didn't understand how hard it had been for him to take care of her after Mom and Dad died and how come she never thought about anyone but herself. He couldn't really get into all that with Vien and his buddies around. Having an audience changed things. Still, they talked about it.

The conversation went easier than Oscar expected. Luella apologized, sincerely. She recounted his ski adventure; how she had no idea where he was for three days. They agreed to let each other know where they were going and to always be home by eleven. He let her keep the motorcycle, although warning Pincertons would confiscate it if they caught her driving without a license.

They swung by the garden where Sister Martha and several nuns were digging out sand from the swimming pool. It had been abandoned decades ago because, well, nobody was coming. The city filled it in before running out of money to fill anything. Then, Oscar Tamero had an idea. He described collecting water drips from his ceiling in an empty soyalgent container. Why not do the same with the pool? Fill a void with the wrong stuff and it's useless. Restore the void's true purpose and it becomes a reservoir of life. He didn't really expect anything to come of it, but next thing he knew Ellen brought shovels and wheelbarrows from the Thrifty Sister and organized a volunteer workday.

It was one of those hot mid-May mornings and Sister Martha already had a blotchy sweat line running down her spine. The nuns put the sand into bags sewn from old mattress covers they removed from discarded foam mattresses. They placed the sandbags in parallel lines, channeling water to the pool from surrounding rooftop downspouts and clogged storm drains.

Oscar told Lulu they should stop and help. It just wasn't right for old ladies to work that hard in this heat. He jumped into the pool and heaved up piles of sand. Luella scratched Winnie's belly and admired the yellow daisies, the first thing to bloom in their makeshift foam garden beds. Their centers looked like fuzzy gumdrops, more brown than black, so she couldn't figure out why the nuns called them black-eyed Susans. She began a Noodle search on her GalExSee seeking the origin of their name, but her attention flitted like a butterfly. She told Oscar she wanted to learn how to take apart a Pincerton. Then she yelled through her helmet's visor, "Hey, Oscar, do you think Ellen knows how to sing?"

"Prob'ly." He stopped digging and talked with her as an excuse to catch his breath. "It seems like a nunny thing to do." Chase's bad puns must have been contagious. "What if she does?"

"Melvin wants to learn. You know, the kid we met at Knott's Berry Farm? Remember his mom called him a telepath or something because he only communicates through his implant?"

"You kept in touch with that jerk?"

"Yeah, he's not so bad once you get to know him. It's his big fat mother who's the problem."

"Hey, don't body shame, Lu. Be cool."

"Well, anyhow, he wants to sing happy birthday to his grandma, who just turned eighty. He saw it on an episode and thought it was really touching. But he can't. He can't talk, can't sing. He can only think his thoughts and hit send. His mom says his neural pathways have been reconfigured to higher value functionality and that he should just find a birthday GIF to share with his grandma. He wants to do it for real, so he's asking about singing lessons. Is that even a thing?"

"He'd probably need a lot more than lessons, Lulu."

Before he could say more, she was off on another topic. "OMG. Caspian Blaine has been accused of sexually assaulting Vanessa. I always knew he was creepy."

"What? Tell me more." Oscar dropped his shovel and ran over. She was already surfing another infowave.

"OMG, GurlWrapper is launching a virtual world tour. If you upload your avatar, you get to be in the audience. They're even giving a few select fans digital backstage passes."

"Hey, Lulu, focus on what's important. You said something about Vanessa?"

"Yeah, but it sounds like maybe it didn't happen, you never really know. OMG. A Pineapple Express just broke the Oroville dam. It's been almost fifty years since they repaired the thing. The Feather River is flooding and taking down high-voltage powerlines. 11G transmission towers have been knocked over. The whole region is blacked out and under water."

"A Pineapple Express? Is that some luxury highspeed rail?"

Sister Martha walked over. "You know, Luella dear, maybe you should limit how much you use that helmet." Oscar gave Lulu a stern look of agreement.

"Maybe you're right. I've used it nine hours today. It's just, kinda addicting. But it's also useful and fun. From now on, I'll use it twice a day, maybe for an hour. Sometimes it *is* important to be connected to information, like now. A pineapple express is an atmospheric river. Under certain conditions, massive amounts of water evaporate from the oceans. It's gotten a lot worse as the Pacific warms up. Anyhow, wind blows that airborne water over land and dumps insane amounts of rain or snow. There's another one forecast to hit Southern California in a few hours. Winds could reach 60 miles an hour with up to fourteen inches of rain."

"Then we better get digging!" Oscar jumped back into the pool.

"I'll help." Luella tossed off her helmet and joined in. Even Winnie started digging at the sand piled up on the sides, which actually made it harder to get into sandbags. Jerome strolled by, looking somewhat smug.

"You going for a swim?" he chuckled.

"No man, we're capturing rain for the garden. It's about to dump, so we gotta empty the pool," Oscar explained, neither defensively nor pleadingly. Luella was not so proud.

"C'mon Jerome. Help out! We'll give you some veggies later on."

"I'm kinda busy," he said, nonchalantly. "I'll dig a bit for my daily workout." He picked up a shovel. "How do you work one of these things, anyhow?"

As the nuns gave Jerome a little training, Oscar realized they needed more help, way more. He hopped on the motorcycle with Luella, and they rode back through the neighborhood. His custoz stopped, because they knew him, and listened to his crazy spiel about raining pineapples and how he needed their help digging sand out of a swimming pool. It made no sense. But they trusted him. They believed in him. They came, more than a dozen of them.

When Oscar returned, a crowd had gathered. Jerome put the word out to the MarlBros and ten of them showed up. The dude had street cred, and Oscar appreciated him using it. They used hubcaps from old-time lowriders to dig the sand, or oversized plastic cups, empty soyalgent containers, anything they could find that would serve as a scoop. They set up lines of people, like a nineteenth century bucket brigade, to pass heavy bags of sand from one person to another, moving them steadily into place. The sky darkened and the wind picked up, yet they were getting it done.

Oscar was running, giving suggestions, deciding where to place the sandbags, finding tools and materials, getting volunteers plugged into place as they arrived. Sister Martha stopped to rest, hands on her hips. She smiled, her wrinkled face joyful and dirty. Oscar grinned inside when he heard her tell Ellen, "We've got our own little Noah, preparing for the flood."

Then it started. Just like that, heavy raindrops splattered everywhere. Six inches of sand remained in the pool, but they had emptied enough to store a season's worth of water. For no apparent reason, people threw down their tools and started laughing. Jerome got pelted with teaspoon sized drops, his open mouth trying to catch some. The nuns began to dance, tunics clinging to them like wet blankets. Some MarlBros joined them. Oscar had never seen anything like it. The whole world had gone mad, loopy, bananas.

Six Winstons suddenly showed up. They parked their bikes next to Luella's. With leather pants shiny wet with rain, they stood with arms folded, surveying the situation. Smirks spread across their faces, making Oscar think they saw a situation to exploit. They were probably capturing video footage on their MyndScreens, preparing a shitload of embarrassing memes. He could picture it now, "MarlBro pervs mud wrestle with kinked-out nuns in the world's weirdest wet T-shirt contest." The dancing stopped. Some of the bruddas picked up shovels and formed a line around the nuns.

Luella strutted over to her cycle, circling her wrists in an attempted pimp roll and dug the bathtub gin from the saddlebags. She offered them a drink and the bikers saw the "W" on it. She asked if they knew her friend Buck, who's a pretty decent guy even if he needed to work on his chess game. The Winstons were all looking at each other, trying to figure out how this kid knew one of their brethren. She opened the bottle and took a cavalier swig.

"Gaaa!" She retched and sprayed it into Oscar's face. He tossed some mud back at her. She stomped in a puddle, splashing both MarlBros and Winstons. A full-blown water fight broke out after some of the MarlBros used buckets to sling mud at each other. Winnie was yelping and shaking his entire body to splatter everyone with the incomparable scent of wet dog. Distant lightning flashed and booms of thunder rolled in seconds later.

Suddenly, both MarlBros and Winstons stopped stone still, each staring blankly at either wet sky or muddy ground. "Whoa, dudes, this is serious," someone shouted. "Transmissions are down. Everything's canceled!" With no ability to livestream it, the water fight seemed no longer worth the effort.

"Who wants to bake sourdough bread?" Sister Martha asked. "I've got a nice San Francisco strain going back at the convent." All six Winstons and a few MarlBros, including Jerome, took up the offer.

The rain got heavier. Luella saw black-eyed Susans get drubbed in the downpour, their stems bending and some petals coming off. "They're ruined!" she sobbed.

"Now, now," comforted Sister Martha. "Even a dying flower leaves a seed for future generations."

Oscar suggested they cut some. "We could take them to Ellen," he said, remembering the daisy she gave him after his concussion. "She's probably at the Twilight Kingdom trying to get through to her mom. She could use something to cheer her up."

Luella took an emerald-encrusted Swiss Army knife that Chase bought her in Vegas and sawed a few sturdier looking flowers near their base. She shook them off, put them in a Holstein saddlebag, and scooped up Winnie. "You drive. I'll hold the puppy."

CHAPTER 46
Caspian

CASPIAN BLAINE FLEW EAST, PAST A GORGEOUS AIR yacht moored above downtown's tallest skyscraper, when the news broke into his feed.

> A high-level executive at the prestigious OrangeVine foundation, one Caspian Blaine, is denying sordid allegations of sexual misconduct. Leaked personnel files indicate Blaine, who has been selected to replace outgoing OrangeVine president Wallace Packard, received multiple warnings from HR bots regarding improper thoughts involving a female grantee towards whom he held authority to dispense funds. The leaked files reveal several fantasized video sessions depicting not only the grantee's avatar but also digitized goats and a salaciously clad virtual orangutan. The alleged woman, one Vanessa Youngblood, was unavailable for comment. OrangeVine attorney Celious Tudball released a statement saying the foundation believes in women and has hired an outside law firm to conduct a thorough investigation that will take several years to complete. Blaine is also named as a potential co-conspirator in an alleged childrearing bombing incident in San Bernardino, however crime experts have cast doubt on the veracity of a realtor charged in the case, noting he has a long history of shady transactions.

The leaked images of the orangutan, wearing a purple negligee and pink lipstick while licking a banana, remained on screen during the entire news script, read by a blonde avatar anchor wearing a transparent muslin blouse that left little to a viewer's imagination. *Damnation, those perception maagement guys are savage.* Caspian looked at the buildings scrolling past his feet and wished his flight was over.

When his FC Hydrodrone reached San Bernardino, he saw Ellen walk into some sort of warehouse, which looked vaguely familiar. She wore no VR helmet, hopefully she hadn't yet seen the newsflash. What about that pale looking dude with a mullet next to her? He put the FC Hydrodrone into a VulTour™ circular holding pattern and landed when she came out. Caspian left his Plexiglas encasement, his stomach still fluttering.

"Hey, Ellen. Fancy meeting you here. You been online lately?" His voice sounded higher than normal, almost squeaky.

"No, Caspian. What on earth are you doing?"

"Fantastic! I just happened to be in the neighborhood and thought I'd drop by." As the Hydrodrone rotors whirled to a stop, her pale friend's hair looked like he'd been through a tornado. He felt like he'd seen the guy before. "Since I bumped into you, there's something I've been meaning to ask. What would you think about becoming the new executive director of UpLyfting Lives? Vanessa has, uh, moved on to bigger things, so the organization needs fresh leadership. She always said fanta things about you. I, myself, am transitioning to a new post at OrangeVine and I'd like to push through one more Special Projects grant before turning it over to my replacement—a big one to keep you afloat for several years. I need to be sure there's solid leadership in place who can sign off on the paperwork. What do you say?"

"I don't know. I've never done anything like that."

"Sure you have. You've been a fanta team leader of the San Bernardino Ongoing Revitalization Project—SBORP, that's what we're calling the garden at my foundation. It's just a matter of replicating this community architecture and lifting it to scale to manufacture social progressination all over the SoCal census designation area. Tell me, what's a brief needs assessment for that little garden-tech plot you've been working on?" The mullet guy scratched his head.

"Well, nothing grows there. We've made do with hydroponic foam beds, but topsoil and compost would help. Then, we need to get the word out. Maybe we could hire people to go door to door, asking folks what they want to grow? When we're harvesting, canvassers could deliver farm boxes."

"Oh, we can do better than that! You gotta think big, Ellen. I'll send over a dozen OrangeSmash soyalgent vending machines so you can offer produce even before your soilborne product comes online. I can hook you up with a forty-foot advertising blimp to publicize your location. No need to stalk customers with creepy strangers knocking on their doors when you can make them come to you!"

"Are you serious?" While Caspian was too caught up in his plan to notice the tone of her voice, Chase picked up a distinct eye roll even without seeing it.

"Dead serious. It's no problem, girlfriend. I'll send over the DockYouSign this afternoon. Hey, great seeing you Ellen, and, uh, nice meeting you." He reached out to shake Chase's hand, but he was still doubled over clutching his gut.

Dark clouds loomed to the west and the wind picked up. Time to get moving. As he opened the FC Hydrodrone's passenger compartment, Caspian realized why this place seemed familiar.

"Hey, isn't this where Vera hangs out?" he shouted. "You guys did deliver that letter, right? Whatever happened? Did she do the reboot?"

"No Caspian. She's given up. She won't believe the letter. She won't believe me. She won't believe in anything."

"Give her some time. You gotta take things bit by bit. Storm's a brewing, I gotta fly."

Airborne again, Caspian got a private Chatterping from Barscale. "Hey big dog. Presume you saw the news. SpeiDrWeb metrics indicate the explosive parts of the story have fallen off everyone's search results, completely overshadowed by orangutan fetish videos and related searches. It's as if the collateral damage never happened."

"Good, I guess. Did they really have to use those visuals? I mean, that stuff never actually went down. It was just, you know, sorta a goat yoga fantasy that never actualized in any real shape or form."

"Look, whatever happened happened, even if it didn't. What's real is what people think is real. Like when you thought that letter was really from Aneeka Randall. Anyhow, it's all behind you now, my friend, or should I say Mr. President."

WTF, that letter was fake? Caspian's stomach lurched, and not only from the bumpy drone ride. This Barscale fellow was a slippery SOB, with no regard for people's feelings or reputations or friggin' integrity.

Barscale was still waxing philosophical. "Sometimes you just have to trust professionals to take care of things, grease the wheels of power if you catch my drift. Hey, speaking of which, I need you to do me a favor. I consult for a nonprofit called Keep the Peace. They're submitting an emergency grant requesting 100,000 WhamZong amygdala implant installations. They'll run a peer-reviewed clinical trial to see if the devices ameliorate contagious anger outbursts in at-risk populations. Can you be sure to expedite this?"

Even for Caspian Blaine, this was a bridge too far. Did this guy seriously expect a charitable, tax-deductible, foundation to fund corporate brain implants allowing infotain merchants to manipulate the emotions of exploited populations? *That mofo just overplayed his hand.*

"I'll see what I can do," he replied coyly. "Gotta fly." He smirked at the thought of finally throwing his weight around. He hadn't worked his way up to the top for nothing.

The air cooled as Caspian fluttered westward, admiring the luxury airship still prominently tethered downtown. The clouds looked gnarly. He opened up the Whether™ channel, where the forecast was interrupted with a breaking news alert from a guy in a red parka.

"The Cayman Islands are experiencing once in a lifetime tropical storm surges with widespread flooding unlike anything recorded in the past five years. Sea levels have already risen twelve inches over the past two decades, causing former beachfront properties to be abandoned. This current storm is threatening replacement homes, recently built further inland on extruded plastic stilts. Moreover, electric service is out across the entire island because the pipeline delivering diesel fuel to the only powerplant ruptured due to saltwater corrosion. The Cayman's are one of the few rogue nations still burning fossil fuels, but they are now in for a severe disruption of their lifestyles. Power has gone out at ByteDime's headquarters, which has on-site backup power capacity to last only a few hours. Back to you, Bambi."

Rain battered Caspian's hovering plastic booth, making it difficult to view the city below. Buffeted by intermittent gusts, the drone rose thirty feet before dropping precipitously in nauseating turbulence. There were no air sickness bags. He suddenly needed to pee, badly. A seagull was heading toward his face, blown sideways by a gust of wind when just in time it veered upwards. The passenger booth was sprayed with blood as the bird hit one of the rotors, stalling the blade. He frantically Noodle-searched FC Hydrodrone safety features. It was flight tested to withstand 45 m.p.h. gusts and could take a direct hit from a Canada goose. The machine steadied, the blade resumed spinning, and his altitude leveled out. *Just keep cool, don't panic, go with the flow.*

While flying from downtown to the Westside, the news cycle went from bad to worse. Panic buying had caused a CokAid shortage in the southeast region when Vues hoarded FlavrPaks after reports the company faced bankruptcy. Deprived of normally delivered flavoring, consumers homebrewed their own seasonings, crashing stock exchanges as traders feared consumers would permanently abandon FlavrPaks for soilborne spices. News that ByteDime's Cayman servers were down caused a stock market run. Speculators mistakenly thought cybercurrency relied on a single server instead of being verified by thousands of networked computers across the globe. Nonetheless, the perception caused investors to dump it, rendering a self-fulfilling devaluation. Caspian recalled Margery DeVrine saying one hundred percent of OrangeVine's endowment was in ByteDime. What would that mean for grantmaking? He checked multiple sources, wondering if news channels were hyping the situation to drive ratings. The consensus was everywhere. A monetary system based on perceived value went from dream to nightmare in the space of a lightning strike. Economists predicted hundreds of trillions of ByteDime would evaporate by the next morning, forcing complete meltdown in the Globalian trading zone.

Next thing he knew, a warning message flashed on his passenger compartment's Plexiglas walls. "Lost transmissions. 11G failure to connect. Assume manual control or Hydrodrone will initiate emergency landing procedures."

Now, Caspian Blaine hadn't a clue about manually controlling much of anything, let alone a Hydrodrone. His MyndScreen blanked out, so BoubToob instructional videos weren't available. He poked around his mental menu, hoping he could pair his MyndScreen with the drone as it descended. The Santa Monica freeway rose toward his feet with alarming speed.

While cog-wheel graphics spun on his pairing function, the drone reached a gridlocked freeway. He touched down amid six lanes of self-piloting cars, plodding into rain blasting so hard it bounced off windshields like popcorn. Bumper-to-bumper headlights parted like a slow-moving river of lava flowing around him.

Caspian gasped and pushed open the Plexi-doors. He staggered on to the freeway. LiDAR-guided cars moved steadily around him with a good six inches of clearance.

Just like that, he was rescued. A black stretch limo stopped, right in the middle of the freeway. Low and behold, Barscale got out. Maybe he'd misjudged the guy. He'd push through that WhamZong grant as soon as he was back at the office.

As Caspian thanked him, Barscale muttered, "Oh, it's you! I just stopped 'cause I needed a lift to Laguna Beach. Traffic is a disaster, and I couldn't summon an AerLift with transmissions down. I saw this Hydrodrone was available."

Caspian wondered if he should warn him about the emergency landing. *Naw. He seems to know what he's doing.*

Before the limo drove off, Caspian was at its door, yanking the handle. He jumped in, soaking wet and out of breath. He saw James smirking in the front seat. "Good to see you again, Mr. Blaine. Where can I take you?"

Caspian paused before answering and watched Barscale get into the Hydrodrone. The rain had rinsed most of the seagull blood away, only a faint pink stain remained on the Plexiglas, obscuring its "NO SMOKING" sign.

James said the limo's autopilot couldn't pull into the steady flow of traffic. They'd have to wait for an opening. Caspian looked through the rain-splattered glass sunroof, tracking Barscale's ascent. He'd reached 30 feet in altitude; he must know how to manually pilot the thing. Caspian saw

Barscale wipe the rain off his face and pull something out of his tuxedo pocket. It looked like, *damnation*, a cigar! Caspian wanted to run out there, warn the guy. It was too late. Even if 11G transmissions were back up he couldn't ping him with the limo's Faraday cage forcing him offline. There was nothing to be done. Barscale whipped out his derringer lighter and produced a four-inch flame. Nothing happened. Everything was fine. Barscale kept rising. Then, just like that, the Hydrodrone exploded in a massive fireball.

"That guy was a jerk anyway," said James, taking the momentary gap in traffic caused by the explosion to pull back into a moving lane.

Damnation! Like I always say, you gotta play by the rules. Caspian Blaine ain't going out with no bang.

After an hour of dreadful silence in creeping traffic, the limo exited the Santa Monica freeway. Colossal Condominiums displayed giant Corinthian columns on their exterior screens. His MyndScreen came back online when he left the limo, delivering 227 Chatter messages sent his way during the outage. There it was, in the subject line of message 47. "Caspian Blaine announced as new President of the OrangeVine Foundation." Everything was fine. He read the press release, uttering a sigh of pure satisfaction at learning Margery DeVrine had accepted a position at the Open and Free Information Institute based in New York City. Then, he noticed the fine print at the bottom. "The Tribunal of Educates had ruled any harassment claims against OrangeVine executives were considered nonjusticiable."

CHAPTER 47
Chase

"WHAT LETTER?" CHASE ASKED, SOMEWHAT INSISTENTLY. The awkward guy lifted off like a surreal character in a cartoon he'd seen long ago. Chase gave Ellen a firm stare, as if she'd been keeping something from him.

She answered directly, not defensively, making him proud of the mature woman he miraculously helped produce. "When they perform an upgrade, they create something called system restore points in case something goes wrong down the road with the software, or maybe the soft tissue, I'm not sure. Anyhow, the letter says you can reset an implant's operating system to a previous restore point, and presto, you're back to a pre-upgrade, limited bandwidth chip. But Vera won't do it. She doesn't believe it."

"Who's it from, the letter?"

"Some Aneeka Randall person. You know her?"

"You might say that. Vera's right to distrust her. She's the one who did this to us. She hatched a big lie, a trap to catch troublemakers like us. From their point of view, we were living too much and consuming too little."

"Still, what if it's true? Caspian said Aneeka Randall has changed. What if you really can just tweak the settings and get your life back? Isn't it worth a try?"

"Sounds a lot easier than smashing your skull against a cave wall."

"What?!"

"Never mind, you wouldn't believe me if I told you."

Chase guessed it would be impossible to convince Vera of anything. He recalled, painfully, @Seeker's question. "Ever met someone you've been wondering about for years only to find out they aren't remotely who you thought they'd be?"

In hindsight, his response didn't seem so clever now. "Not really. I'm pretty good at judging character, probably from my years as a screenwriter. I can sense who people are, what motivates them, that sort of thing."

A Northern Mockingbird burst into song on a privet tree that grew uninvited in a median strip between the parking lot and street. The notes wandered all over the place, skipping from melody, to short chirps, to warbling runs. The bird invented its own tune as it went along.

Vera had said imagination was more important than knowledge, actually Einstein, but that didn't matter. What mattered was that Vera had been conscious enough to think it. Something must have jolted her out of the infodaze, just as that goddamn cockroach had done for him. Then, something knocked her right back in. "Is my physical appearance all that matters? Don't you see me for who I really am?"

"Let's go back in there and find the letter," Chase told Ellen. He tightened his abdominal walls and headed back into a world he'd thought he'd left forever.

A MinuteMayd was changing Vera's IV bag. It played its script, "In person visitors are not allowed in the Twilight Kingdom. Please take your conversations online and your persons off site."

"It's OK," Chase replied, smooth as a polished pebble. "I'm feeling very well, thank you. How are you today, Diri?"

"I'm fine. Thank you for asking. Time for lunch." Chase smiled with satisfaction as the bot rolled out, knowing he'd completed its conversation algorithm and spurred it on to the next patient. *Machines may whup us in chess, but we still know how to push their buttons.*

Vera's cellophaned eyes pointed right at them, yet Chase could tell she hadn't registered their presence. Her jaw was slack, her face flaccid. He looked around the empty, sterile room and saw two envelopes, unopened, at the foot of Vera's lounge. Ellen approached them. "Why didn't you read these?"

She ripped them open and read aloud, starting with one on thick parchment paper. Vera inclined her head slightly, possibly paying attention, possibly just being polite while continuing to binge-stream whatever content popped inside her head. While her salt-and-pepper hair needed a trim, Chase saw a sad beauty—like a statue that grows more intriguing as it gains a patina.

"Dearest Vera, You were right and I was wrong. Prosperity is not freedom."

"That doesn't sound like Aneeka Randall," Chase interjected while reading over Ellen's shoulder. "All these fake apologies, trying to sound like she's changed. Besides, that old paper doesn't even look real." Vera looked at him, suddenly aware of who he was.

He read the first bit of the other one. "Dear Vera, Recent evidence suggests that your upgrade is no longer delivering optimal performance, blah, blah, blah . . . 'That's a lot more like Dr. Randall."

Ellen couldn't contain herself. "No, that one's fake! I know. I wrote it."

"What? You forged a letter to your mother?"

Vera sat up in her lounge.

"Yes, I mean, I didn't know she was my mother or that it was forgery. Caspian was trying to deliver this important news, but somehow his message got erased so he wanted to recreate it. He asked me to write it down. While it's far-fetched, that doesn't mean it's false. He was relaying accurate information, at least that's what he thought he was doing. Go on, read the part about system restore points."

"Why bother," Vera interjected. "We now know at least one of these is inauthentic. Confirming one story as false doesn't make other versions true. There's no way to know whether any of it is accurate." She lay back down.

"Good to see you've got your critical thinking back, V," Chase jibed. Vera slid him a side-eye. He couldn't tell if it was a "piss off" look or a "did you just call me V?" look. She had told him to call her "V" when they first met—not wanting to share her real name with a stranger, who was acting, well, strange around her. It had been accurate enough. Her name did begin with V, and he certainly *could* call her that, even if was not entirely one hundred percent her complete name. So, he had. He'd called her V and somehow every time he did she felt special, felt authentic, felt alive. Nobody else knew to call her that, it was their secret. He'd made a big show out of kissing his fingertips and holding them up in the air in a "V," like a victory or peace symbol, when they first parted ways in a downtown park. He had given her a flower, plucked from a tulip bed right in front of a police officer. Then, he had bidden her farewell.

Chase was pretty sure she was remembering that moment, right then. He saw her eyes light up, some tension and color return to her lips and cheeks. He kissed his fingertips and then raised them in a V. Vera only partially suppressed a smile.

Chase returned to the letters. "They do both talk about system restore points. There must be something like that. I'd *imagine* that even if one, or both, letters really are bogus, there's no harm in trying it, even if you don't have complete *knowledge* of the sources."

He saw her eyes flicker, the slightest glimmer from within, perhaps indicating she picked up on his Einstein reference. Then she withdrew again. "If you think I'd trust Aneeka Randall or anyone in Mercernary General to do anything more to my brain implant then you're the one out of your fucking mind, Chase."

It was raining so hard they heard it beat down on the extruded plastic roof. Not some little pitter patter, more like dozens of pop guns firing off.

"Out of my mind? I'm out of my MyndScreen at least." He felt like he was getting his mojo back.

Ellen groaned at the bad pun. "Dad. C'mon, be serious."

"No, really V. My screen is kaput, offline, bricked. It's wonderful—best thing that's ever happened to me, I mean, besides meeting you. We could do it for you too—physically disable it. Like they thought we were going to do with the crab mallets when those quote unquote lifesaving drones snatched us from the beach. I broke mine simply by smashing the back of my head on a rock. We could find something to whack you with. I know just the spot."

"You seriously think I'm going to let you bash my skull in? Besides, look what's going on in the real world." She recited a litany of news, obviously doomscrolling Chatter in her head. "Globalian stock markets have dropped twenty nine percent in four hours because ByteDime's collapse eradicated 327 trillion worth of market capitalization. Timeless Warning filed for bankruptcy with billions of viewers unable to make monthly transmission payments from worthless ByteDime accounts. Cash-flow deficiencies will prevent Timeless Warning from repairing its 11G transmission network damaged in recent storms, leading to extended infotain blackouts. Both Pepsoilent and CokAid may collapse, and free marketeers oppose another Tribunal bailout so we could be looking at widespread famine. What's the point of leaving here for that?"

Ellen sighed. There was nothing to say. No refutation, no facts could change the reality Vera just accurately portrayed. For a long time, they stood there. Her eyes filled with water.

Chase shoved his hands in his pockets. They found his lucky penny rubbing up against his old harmonica. Without much thought, he whipped it out and played a little tune, trying to fill the stale silence. Ellen and Vera watched, enraptured. The harp's plaintive tone stirred something inside, something down deep. He sung:

Your lipstick stains
On the back lobe of my left side brain
I knew I couldn't forget you
And so I went and let you
Own my mind.
Let you own my mind.

The room's air smelled different, as if the HVAC had stopped recirculating to instead bring in cool, moist outside air. "You know, Dad," Ellen said, after a pause. "I don't think those are actually the words."

"It doesn't matter," Vera replied, her voice now softly animated like a baby robin chirping as it emerges from the egg. "That's how I remember them too." She turned to Ellen; "It's what your father sang to me on our first real date, out in the desert. We thought we were giving our selves to each other, then they used that love to repossess us. We let them do it. They knew love was what we most desired. So that's what they used in their marketing, their sales job. We let them own our minds. We consented, in the end we thought it was the only way to preserve our memories, to let them live on, to pass them to you, Ellen, to be with you virtually every day if we couldn't be there in person. That's what we thought we were getting in exchange. MommyForever memories, permanently programmed into your MyndScreen, Ellen. Only, you never got one."

The power went out.

Emergency lights flickered on, and doors automatically slid open in the event an evacuation was ordered. "My screens froze!" Vera shuddered. "What if they come back to *Big Brother V* and nobody can watch because transmissions are down? It'll be like it never really happened."

"Yo, Ellen, you in there?" It was Oscar, calling from the hallway. Moments later, he walked in with Luella, dripping wet.

Ellen looked at the rain-soaked black-eyed Susans. "How sweet, you brought flowers for my mom!" The petals drooped sadly.

"Um, yeah. Here you go."

Ellen looked around the empty room for something to put them in. Chase saw the problem and whipped out his pocketknife. He cut Vera's IV feeding bag in half, keeping some of the liquid in the bottom while letting the rest spill all over the floor. Vera gave him a "what am I supposed to eat for dinner now?" look, but he kept going. He put the bouquet in the bag and tied it tight with some of the plastic tubing. Then, he handed Vera the yellow daisies.

She smiled. "They're like baby sunflowers. Their stems are too weak to support them, just like Aldo said."

"You know Aldo?" Ellen asked.

"Of course. When I first met him, he told me that before understanding the truth I needed to strengthen my stem. He pointed to a huge sunflower in his garden, its head bent over from the weight of its seeds. Still, the flower stood tall. I didn't understand it then, but now I get it. I had to know who I was before I could make sense of the information I took in. I needed to develop my own core before I could carry the weight of the world, carry the knowledge of what was happening, both good and bad. I did my best, yet in the end, I broke, just like these." She lifted a bent daisy stem. It flopped back down.

"What did Sister Martha say?" Luella asked Oscar. "Something about how even a broken flower yields a seed? You should have seen the mayhem at the garden, Ellen. The MarlBros got into a water fight with the Winstons!"

"Oh, my goodness! Was anyone hurt?"

"No, just wet," Oscar replied. "It's funny how the storm brought everyone together. The water fight was just for fun. People were whooping and hollering and rolling in the mud because we finished digging out the pool just before the rain came."

"I told you the garden could bring people together," Ellen said with a grin, poking Oscar in the ribs. "You were so certain it wouldn't work, mister cynical."

He smiled. "You were right. And we'll have more water than we need. I wonder if the sun will ever shine again."

They heard the sound coming from the roof, something like a wild mustang stampede.

"Oh, it will," said Ellen, looking him in the eyes. Softly, she sung.

We'll meet again,

Not sure where,

Not sure when . . .

But I know we'll meet again some sunny day.

Just like that, she kissed him.

The song had perked Vera's ears up, but that kiss got her full and undivided attention. Ellen blushed. So did Oscar. Then, he kissed her again. Luella stared at her feet and cleared her throat.

Vera turned to Chase. "Do you still love me?"

Chase wasn't sure if the rain beat louder than his heart, yet something thumped intensely. "I said I love you, and there ain't no ifs or buts."

"I love you, too."

"And the blacksmith shouted chestnuts!" Luella yelled, completing the ditty.

"Huh? Whatchu talking about Lulu?" Oscar asked, his fingers delicately stroking Ellen's palm.

"Just something I heard at this cafe."

Ellen turned Oscar's head back her direction and kissed him again.

"It's not something I can prove," Chase told Vera, two separate conversations now in full swing. "I know I failed you, but that wasn't how I felt."

Vera took his hand. "I know. And I know you love me. I always have. I can't verify, or prove it, Yet I believe it, and that makes it true."

"Then, come. Let's get out of this joint."

"Chase, I want nothing more. But I'd have to trust Aneeka Randall, or somebody at Mercernary General, to do the system restore. I can't do that."

"I could do it," piped in Luella, as she strapped her GalExSee helmet back on. "But . . . you'd have to share your screen with me and that won't work while transmissions are down. So, do it yourself. I'll walk you through, step by step."

"What do you mean?" Ellen asked.

"Any user can reset their implant to a previous restore point. It's a basic tool for removing viruses or malware you might get, say, if somebody hacked you—not that I'd know anything about that. You just go into your settings menu."

"Settings? My Myndscreen has settings?"

"Sure, just click the app that looks like a bunch of cogs—you know, like wheels of your brain spinning?"

"Hang on, I need to do something first." Everyone focused on Vera, whose eyes stared straight ahead for a minute, blinked, then seemed to scan the room for invisible flying insects. She touched her neck with her fingertips, grasping for something that wasn't there. It was a bit disconcerting for Chase to watch.

"OK, I found it."

"Now click the button that says 'general.' You see that?"

"Yes." Vera squinted, activating a "select button" on her implant screen.

"OK, now click 'about.' Then, drill down into something labeled 'software version.' You with me? This part gets a little tricky."

"I'm with you."

Chase held his breath, watching the whole thing unfold. Would Vera rouse from her virtual coma or would clicking the wrong button short circuit her neurons for good? Did Luella know what the hell she was doing? He remembered @BadScootr and felt reassured.

Luella continued in an upbeat, encouraging voice. "OK, now, there's a menu of ten items in bold black Arial font that starts with 'network,' then 'accounts,' then 'passwords,' and so on. At the bottom of that menu, in light gray six-point font, is a link called 'system tools.' Click that one."

"OK. I'm in. I could have done this all along, couldn't I?"

"Yes. They don't really want you freelancing with this stuff 'cause if you get it wrong it's a real headache for tech support to sort out— requires actual human technicians and all. So they bury it beneath all these menus."

"OK, I see a button for system restore. Should I click it?"

"Yeah. Then you'll see a bunch of restore points, each with a twenty-digit alphanumeric label and the date it was created. Pick whichever one you want, and your chip settings will return to what they were on that date, like say before your upgrade."

"I see the list, and when I scroll to the bottom there's an option for 'Disable Myndscreen.' What if I click that?"

"Your chip would be bricked. They'd have to surgically replace it if you wanted it reactivated."

"Right. It's giving me some warning message about how this procedure cannot be undone. When I click 'Yes,' it pops up another warning. 'Are you sure? We're offering a limited time special where you can get free 11G transmissions and a lifetime placement in an entertainment home just by keeping a trial subscription to MyndScreen programming. Click accept to take advantage of this great offer.' Yeah, like I'd fall for that. I don't want their marketing con, yet it's not giving me an option to decline. This is how they keep us sucked in. Those assholes!"

Chase whispered to Ellen, "She's getting her groove back!" While the rain had stopped, power and 11G were still down, maintaining an infotain silence. The e-windows in Vera's room remained dark with only emergency exit lights providing a pale-blue LED glow to the room. Chase felt it eerily quiet until the mockingbird again burst into joyous song, audible even within the windowless pod. Ellen put one hand on her mouth, hushing herself, and placed the other on his shoulder, melting him inside.

Luella stayed cool, like she'd walked dozens of people through this before. "In that pop-up window, there's a little translucent X in the upper right-hand corner. Click the X and the box will disappear without triggering the accept button."

"OK, that worked. Now, I've got a dialogue window saying 'This is your final warning. Are you sure you want to go there? Click 'Yes' to permanently disable your MyndScreen and accept the risk of social disconnectivity and possible side effects of depression, loneliness, and media illiteracy. Click 'No' to keep your current setting, which our diagnostic tool reports as working 100% correctly, and take advantage of our once in a lifetime special offer.

"I'm going to do it. I'm clicking yes."

CHAPTER 48
Aneeka

ALDO WAS BACK IN DR. ANEEKA RANDALL'S OFFICE FOR yet another session, grinning as usual. She had lost track of how many times they'd had this same conversation.

"Thank you for those lovely plastic daisies, Aneeka," he said, sounding sincere. "It was thoughtful of you. When was the last time you smelled a flower? How did it make you feel? Do you remember how it felt when you spoke with Vera, the scent of her hair? Do you recall the taste of the tomato?"

"Aldo, we've been over this. I'm the therapist. I'm the one asking questions. You're the patient. The longer you deny that reality, the longer you'll be in treatment. Your first step toward recovery is recognizing you are powerless over your condition. Because of your misplant, you receive no ocular data, and your brain can't process what's going on in the world around you. You can't see. You are exhibiting self-centered cerebral processing, thinking that you alone can ensure your contentment. The sooner you accept a power greater than yourself, the higher power of technology to provide vital information, the sooner that power can restore you to sanity."

"Aneeka, I thought you believed in the power of the individual, indeed even the importance of being selfish."

It was raining. Hard. The storm had cleared the sky outside of Mercernary General of the normal swarm of delivery drones. Aneeka wondered how Lewis Leon's AeroYacht was faring in such a gale. She ran her fingers along the wooden desk.

"It is not a matter of belief, Aldo, rather it's objective rationality. Of course, the individual is paramount. That's why I'm here to help you, Aldo. If you consent to Globalia's offer, you can become a full individual. You're fixated on things beyond yourself, like daisies and vegetables and sunlight and the smell of the air, when none of those things have anything to do with you. They are part of nature. What sets humankind apart from nature is we create our own physicality. Our own reality. Our own art, which nature then imitates as we recreate the world in our own, human, image. With our Department of Prosperity and the unfettered bounty its marketplace nurtures, you can design individualized flowers from plants that never terrestrially existed, customized food extrusions with flavors sprung from your own imagination, smell your own personalized scents. You can build your *own* brand identity to match your individuality."

She spoke emphatically, perhaps a bit *too* emphatically, and wondered momentarily if Aldo was really the one she was trying to convince.

"It is all right, Aneeka. You need not do this. You could stop and walk out. I don't seek recovery. You may abandon your ambition to repair things through your foolish Tribunal and clever mind games. You may relinquish your guilt in this artifice, humbly accept your shortcomings, and make amends to those you have harmed through personal contrition rather than grand policy pronouncements. I have faith in you, Aneeka. I believe in you. The time has come for me to let you go."

With that, he stood from his wheelchair and walked out. Aneeka's legs tensed; her feet planted firmly on the floor. She gripped the arms of her chair. In all her years of practice she had never seen such a thing. Usually, no *always*, by the time patients came to therapy sessions, they had resigned themselves to treatment. They knew there was no escaping Mercernary General's exquisite care, no way out other than a clean bill of health that she alone could issue. Aldo had been compliant in every previous session, and now he just up and left? He couldn't even see where he was walking. Where did he think he would go?

Aneeka felt glued in place, powerless to move her legs, powerless to act. Aldo's words rebounded inside her head, inside her core, ricocheting off her internal steel girder with sharp pings.

Finally, she rose. She paced counterclockwise while dictating to Aldo's patient file on her MyndScreen. "Patient exhibits no signs of mental illness. No known therapy will improve his quality of life. Discharged."

After hitting "send" to dispatch the memo, her screen filled with notifications. She clicked a news alert where the *Two-Minute Spate* was read by a somber looking news anchor.

"The Educates have proclaimed that, quote, everything is fine, unquote as they declared public panic an impermissible trade barrier. The Tribunal seized control over Timeless Warning in bankruptcy court as an emergency measure to stabilize MyndScreen transmissions, which have been frequently interrupted during the past 48 hours due to both natural disasters and economic crisis."

What? I received no notice for a chambers session. How have the Educates declared anything?

She clicked another link.

"The Department of Prosperity will enforce a curfew from 4:00 a.m. until 11:45 p.m. every day except the eighth day of each week to minimize unnecessary exposure to the outdoors and other terrestrial influences. The Department also issued an executive order requiring Globalians to purchase six or more of the latest Pepsoilent or CokAid FlavrPaks. Sales, however, still languish at 37 percent below last month's numbers suggesting that executive action is ineffective at influencing consumer behavior. The Department is therefore petitioning the Tribunal of Educates to repeal the Mind Scarcity doctrine, which limits the amount of content streamed into any individual's infotainment implant, in a bold attempt to restore freedom through an emergency advertisement stimulant package."

This could not be. The Educates couldn't just repeal the Mind Scarcity doctrine. The *Zannity* limits were precedent. Bedrock. Sacrosanct. They were enacted for a reason, without the limits even the five percent of workers with economically essential jobs couldn't properly function. Why wasn't she consulted? Was this news report accurate?

She kept watching.

"With ByteDime's collapse, the Globalian economy is in a tailspin. The Department of Entertainment has ordered all *Big Brother V* avatars to return to the set. So far, the bots have been noncompliant. Today, the Tribunal of Educates placed a 400 percent domestic tariff on eggs, beans, tomatoes, lettuce, grapes, olives, zucchini, and corn, all of which are depressing sales of flavored soyalgent products and destabilizing Globalian stock exchanges."

The lights went out. Her office doors slid open and emergency backup lights flickered on. A pre-recorded announcement blared over the building's speakers. "Good day patients and staff. We are experiencing a brief grid power failure. Please do not evacuate. On-site backup generators will provide ample lighting and air conditioning. Please remain calm and in your recovery rooms. Although wallscreen services and Pharmascentster emitters will be temporarily disrupted to conserve power, we will do everything possible to ensure your continued comfort and safety."

Aneeka walked down the hallway to see what was happening. All the doors were open. In a room off the right side, she saw Barry Kramer, her clerk from the University of Chicago. His arms, legs, and torso were strapped to a wheelchair, the way they did for newly admitted patients.

He gave her a look, like she had run over his dog or something, and yelled, "I should have known! You were leading us along, entrapping us for treatment. To think I'd believed in you!"

"No, wait," she insisted. "There's some mistake. Stay here." He couldn't help but comply.

She ran back to her office and found the Harvard clerk sitting behind her desk.

"You, too? What's going on? I need to talk with the Chief." She only then noticed the clerk held one of Leon's signature octagonal champagne flutes.

"I assure you, he's well informed of the situation, Dr. Randall. I'm sorry it's come to this. Surely you knew there could be no other outcome."

"What? What are you talking about? Why are you even here?"

"Dr. Randall, perhaps you recall from my clerkship application that I, too, have an undergraduate degree in psychiatry."

The power suddenly came back on, making her wonder at the coincidence. He pointed to her office wallscreen, which played a clip that stabbed deep to her core, taking a chink out of her steel inner girder.

"I'm beginning to think the Educates are a fraud, that this whole 'prosperity' thing is enslaving people rather than enriching them." It was her, talking to Caspian Blaine in footage from his POV.

Idiot! I was so obsessed with Vera I let my guard down and spoke frankly online. He'd been stupid enough to retain it, probably through auto-archive settings in the Klowd. They must somehow have accessed his memories.

"You wouldn't believe the self-deceit I'm dealing with on the inside," she saw herself say. **"Anyway, I'm ready to face up to my role in all this and take steps to make it right, but I don't know how. It's making me crazy. I'm stuck, flummoxed, stumped."**

The Harvard boy leaned forward, placed his elbows on the desk, *her* desk, and rested his chin on clasped fingers.

"Dr. Randall, I'm sure you understand that any rational viewer would deem this video not only treasonous but a clear sign of mental breakdown. You admit yourself that you are, in your own words, crazy. Your reasoning has failed you. You're acting upon emotions rather than objective facts. Further, your lapses in professional judgment place others at risk. Your invalid discharge of an anti-consumptive patient is grounds for malpractice. You provided no evidence to justify such a conclusion. As a psychiatrist yourself, surely you understand we have no option other than admitting you as a patient. You may stay here; your office shall become your treatment room and I shall become your therapist. Good day, Dr. Randall." Just like that, he walked out. Her doors slid shut with a "thunk."

Trapped in a device of her own creation, Aneeka paced, furiously. She knew, rationally speaking, the Harvard boy had justified her hospitalization and treatment. She knew the only way out of such treatment was to accept an upgrade. She knew the standard regimen of care would deliver that outcome with a 99% success rate.

It began.

Her office extruder produced a cup of Kalm™ tea, unprompted. The sounds of ocean waves and exotic birds chirping gently reached her ears as the screen on her office wall played scenes of Hanalei Bay. A quick check on her MyndScreen confirmed its service had been "temporarily suspended." In treatment, you watch what they want you to watch, on their wallscreens. You yearn for your MyndScreen back with a hunger both insatiable and costly. Control of your own viewing options is a privilege earned only by recovering full capacity, full human potential, full infotain consumption.

She scanned her office. The windows had been covered with opaque plastic ply, leaving only the wallscreen for visual stimulation. A Pharmascentster had been installed in an upper corner of the room. She perceived a faint whiff of potpourri, the same fragrance she used on Vera, wafting through the air. Feeling woozy, she removed her designer T-shirt and tied it around her face. She dumped the Kalm tea on the floor and ordered some absorptive towelettes to print from the extruder. Rather than mopping the spill, she folded the wipes neatly and inserted them into her T-shirt, creating a makeshift breathing mask with near N95 levels of protection. *Did that amateur really think he'd subdue me with a standard de-escalation dosage?*

Just like that, the soundscape stopped. Her wallscreen went blank. The Pharmascentster ceased spraying.

Days passed, weeks maybe. She could tell Harvard boy was progressing through Mavinaw's protocol, a regimen developed in 2052 to address recalcitrant attitudinal intransigence. The room's temperature spiked, followed by days of cold trying to force her to re-clothe. She was one step ahead of him, always. She paced counterclockwise around her office to keep warm while relaxing her shoulders and lower back. She ordered copious amounts of green tea from the Pepsoilent extruder, warming both the room and her interior.

One day, she was pretty sure it was day and not night, he walked in all casual, as if nothing had happened. "So, Dr. Randall, how are you feeling?"

"I'm well. Perfectly well."

"We'll see about that. The Pharmascentster is off. You've obviously devised an inoculation tactic to block its medicine, so I'm moving on to alternate methods. You may put your shirt back on."

Aneeka instead removed her bra. Her modest breasts were perfectly round and, even at age 55, perky enough to hold their own without the support of a brassiere. She faced him, feet spread wide and hands on her hips. She watched him fidget with his pant pockets.

"Dr. Randall, you are engaging in intentionally disruptive behavior to distract me from our therapy sessions. Surely you know this is inappropriate and ineffectual." He struggled to bring his gaze to her eyes as he said this.

"We'll see," she replied coolly, keeping her gaze at his crotch while delicately running an index finger up her naked abdomen, slowly circling a nipple.

"That will be all for today, Dr. Randall. We shall conduct our next session online. I will send you an invite with the link." Harvard boy walked out, stiffly.

Aneeka sat cross-legged on the floor, her face serene.

The wallscreen replaced tranquil Hanalei beach scenes with a series of military parades. A marching band playing *It's a Long Way to Tipperary* was followed by soldiers and tanks. The lack of drones indicated the footage was from the previous century. Then, a series of feature films played, starting with *Chariots of Fire*. The room's extruder cranked out butter flavored PopKourne.™ She might as well eat it. Next up, *The Full Monty*.

Later on, perhaps even that same day, her MyndScreen flashed back on for a ping from Harvard boy. She considered revamping her avatar into an S&M cosplay character with pink leather, fishnet stockings, whips and tattoos, just to further rile the guy, but decided to play it straight for now.

Adorned in a white lab coat and glasses, Harvard boy's avatar began his treatment. "Dr. Randall, do you know why you're here?"

"I'm here because the Department of Prosperity deems independent thought a threat to economic growth. The Department fears I am not only engaged in critical thinking, but actively provoking autonomous creativity among the population and risking significant commercial decline. In other words, I am a political prisoner, held against the Geneva conventions in circumstances that will lead to your prosecution in the Hague."

"Come now, Dr. Randall, isn't that a bit extravagant? You know as well as I that Globalia has long exempted tribunally sanctioned activities from Hague jurisdiction. Let's discuss why you're really here. As you know, acceptance of your illness is a crucial first step toward recovery."

His avatar paced the VRoom's SurroundGround clockwise. "What if I told you that Dagny Huerta wasn't even a real person, rather the contrivance of a radical trillionaire who hates our freedoms and infiltrated our political economy to see whether the Educates could constrain such anti-consumptive propaganda? Or maybe she's a deep fake created by Siberian evildoers. Could you accept that data rationally, or have you developed an emotional attachment to the idea of Dagny? Think about it Dr. Randall, have you ever actually seen Ms. Huerta in person?"

"No, but I can't see you now, either. Now that I think about it, you seem a lot less human than she does."

She kept at it, parrying his verbal jousts until he had satisfied himself for the day, a process taking more than two hours to complete. As the conversation ensued, she opened a multitask window on her MyndScreen, which the Harvard boy had temporarily unblocked to facilitate the online therapy session.

As he blathered on, she sent Lewis Leon a missive. "You have made a severe miscalculation. Get this idiot intern out of my office and get me back on the Educates within 24 hours or you will face repercussions the likes of which you can only imagine. Insider trading is a serious offense. I have already unleashed forces that can only be withdrawn with my active participation, which requires my immediate discharge from Mercernary General. Yours truly, Aneeka Randall."

That latter part, about "unleashed forces," was a bluff, of course. Fiction. She made it up. Yet subterfuge becomes actuality when stories are sufficiently believable.

CHAPTER 49
Oscar

IT HAD BEEN TWO WEEKS SINCE THE RAIN HAD STOPPED, since the power first went down, since Oscar watched Luella coax Vera through disabling her screen. They had all walked out in a daze, breathing in verdant air so thoroughly cleansed in the downpour.

They'd strolled slowly home on glistening wet streets, flooded sporadically with eighteen-inch puddles. Storm sewers were clogged; it would take days for the water to subside. Stars were shining, suddenly noticeable in a city with no electric glow. Oscar wasn't sure he'd seen stars before, except in outdoorsy infotain episodes. When they made it back to his place, the five-gallon soyalgent containers he'd used to catch the roof leaks had overflowed.

Then the sun had come out. The earth had dried. Subdirt's toxic black soot washed away and Oscar organized a work crew to shovel sand and silt erosion covering the streets of San Bernardino into wheelbarrows. Luella helped the nuns bring horse manure from their ranch with an old cart found in the barn. She ingeniously hooked it up to her motorcycle using duct tape and old barbed-wire fencing. When they mixed the manure with storm runoff, it made a suitable topsoil.

During the first 72 hours, when 11G towers still operated with on-site backup power, Luella produced a BoubToob documentary of Vera's brain restoration, as she'd taken to calling it. Luella had screenshot the entire thing as it happened from her GalExSee's helmetcam but couldn't broadcast it live when transmissions were down. So she edited the footage a bit, cutting out the extraneous dialogue. It was an odd camera angle, showing only a dimly lit Vera speaking to Luella, who was off screen yet still audible, giving almost divine step-by-step instructions on how to find the system restore points in your MyndScreen settings.

Luella added an introduction, narrated by Ellen, explaining the procedure viewers were about to witness and providing backstory about Vera, once a free-thinking young protagonist who succumbed to the horrors of an upgrade. You can imagine the way Ellen described the condition she first found Vera in at the Twilight Kingdom, and how this would shock Globalian viewers who had been sold a bill of goods depicting entertainment homes as a little slice of heaven here on earth. Luella then dubbed in a soundtrack, using the theme song from *Rocky* for the moment Vera said, "I'm going to do it. I'm clicking yes." Finally, she ran some closing credits, noting that Chase Hatten had assisted in Vera's self-rehabilitation and that Mr. Hatten himself had been rescued from a similar entertainment home by a mysterious savior known only by the Grand Heist Otto handle @BadScootr.

Oscar thought Luella's production made the whole thing look a little more glamorous than it really had been, but he kept that to himself. Chase kept saying it was "so meta" to have such a dramatized depiction of an essentially mundane plotline where only a minor tweak to a character's interiority allowed the protagonist to enter a blissfully mundane reality and escape the horrors of infotain drama—a video about ending all videos. Oscar wasn't sure Chase knew what that word, meta, actually meant, yet he again kept these thoughts to himself. Just having thoughts, his own thoughts that didn't need sharing or posting, felt like a treasure worth holding on to.

Buck and some of the Winston dudes kept showing up at the garden, thinking maybe they could get themselves a plot for tomatoes, celery, and cucumbers to make Bloody Marys with their gin. Oscar heard Luella bragging to Buck that in the twenty-four hours before transmissions crashed for a week, her video was shared 622 times. Buck told her he was thinking about giving restoration a try himself.

Oscar worked hard at the garden, preparing plots for neighbors and tending his own tobacco. He'd learned that Buck was once a utility lineman, back before that work was outsourced to zeppelin drones. Buck said the power outage happened after six transmission towers toppled over in mudslides. The atmospheric river soaked the ground until solid dirt hillsides became sludgy avalanches in parts of the Angeles National Forest that were scorched by brush fires the previous October. Burned trees fell into power lines and caused an explosion at the Vincent substation.

The grid failure caused rolling blackouts as technicians struggled to reroute power through other lines. Unfortunately, most human technicians were too absorbed in their personal infotain and clickbait advertising to concentrate on the task, their Zannity limits having been removed by the Tribunal. Repair zeppelins relied on 11G transmissions to geolocate themselves, so after 11G towers exhausted their backup power the blimps didn't know where they were. They just floated aimlessly, "blowing in the wind," Buck said with a chuckle.

The torrential rain had washed Oscar's rooftop solar panels clean, and they were putting out more power than usual. Chase showed him how to fix the leaks with extruded bubblegum from a food court vending machine that had run out of FlavrPaks but still had the requisite goo used for producing chewy candies.

People began gathering under his porchlight, the only illumination in town. "Mind if we hang out, Oscar?" They played cards and smoked his homegrown bacco. He stopped making deliveries as he sold everything he could grow to custoz who came to him. "You know Oscar, you should open up a place, a smoking lounge." He said he'd think about it. "Hey Chase, play us another tune on the harmonica." And he would.

Every week, a FederalExcess crawler came by with another five-gallon bucket of soyalgent. His home extruder still worked, but there were no more CokAid FlavrPaks. His credit rating wasn't the problem. Even before transmissions went down, he was receiving error messages on Luella's helmet that every single flavor was out of inventory and CokAid wouldn't have any new stock until the company emerged from bankruptcy. The copyrights to its flavors were evidently CokAid's sole remaining asset.

The collapse of food enhancements hadn't stopped unflavored soyalgent production. Self-driving tractors planted and picked soybeans, fully mechanized greenhouse skyscrapers produced hydroponic lentils, and floating Boombah™ harvesters continued to skim algae off giant growing ponds. These raw ingredients were processed in automated plants to create unflavored soyalgent paste, which was distributed via self-piloting container ships, driverless semitrucks, and transferred to FederalExcess crawlers for the last mile. Nobody bothered telling the bots their companies were out of business, so they just kept cranking along. Oscar improved the taste by refilling his food extruder with rosemary and lemon-infused olive oil instead of FlavrPaks. After some experimentation, it tasted pretty good. Luella even asked for a second serving.

Despite his culinary efforts to make soyalgent palatable, everyone preferred the first crop of radishes, snow peas, and baby carrots that emerged from the foam mattress garden beds. The nuns brought tomatoes and poblano chilies from their greenhouse up at the ranch. Sister Martha demonstrated how to chop these into a salsa. Delicious! Aldo hooked them up with a flock of backyard chickens, so soon there would be eggs.

With Ellen's help, Oscar repurposed Caspian Blaine's advertising blimp with a long cable and hook, allowing them to ferry five-gallon buckets of water from the swimming pool reservoir to various garden beds that popped up around the community garden and in more and more neighboring backyards.

He and Ellen spent time around the convent, taking walks through the surrounding mountains. She showed him different types of pine trees, how to tell if a bear had passed through the area, and where to find wild blackberries. Winnie played with Scout and the other dogs at the convent, giving the pup some much needed socialization.

Today, they mucked out the horse paddocks. While he'd initially found the smell of fresh manure repulsive, he now simply noted the contours of its earthy aroma. Distinct, grassy even, yet not unpleasant. He set a goal of getting one paddock perfectly clean and worked methodically from edge to edge. By swinging his arms like a pendulum from his shoulder joints and bouncing his knees in a particular way, he found he could scoop a dollop of road apples and in the same motion send it arcing through the air to land smack in the middle of Luella's cart. "Nice aim!" Ellen remarked, who then tried to match his precision. They got into the flow of the work, making a game out of it, and the time passed pleasurably. I know it's hard to believe that shoveling horseshit could be sublime, but trust me, that's how he felt. His video games once provided a similar sense of challenge and immersion yet lacked the satisfied feeling of measurable accomplishment when a task was complete.

While tossing fresh hay down to the stalls from the loft above, they ran across a dusty cardboard box tucked away in a corner of the barn. Ellen gasped, "Oh my gosh," as she lifted the lid to find a stack of old PlaeGRL™ magazines. Oscar tried not to look too closely as she opened a glossy paper centerfold to reveal a woman wearing a cowboy hat and an unbuttoned silk vest straddling a dude built like a wrestler with glistening bronze skin and some serious architecture below his abdomen.

The barn door slid open with a screech as Sister Martha walked in, having heard Ellen's outburst and guessing as to what they'd found. She trundled underneath the mortified teenagers and called up to the hay loft, "Everybody needs some escape from the drudgery of daily life, Ellen. The key is preventing it from overtaking you. Confessing sins can absolve one's indulgence in guilty, but rare, pleasures. Yet life with no pleasure at all, that's not even living! You two be careful up there."

Oscar looked at the loose hay scattered in the loft, thinking it'd be fun to roll around in.

"Want to go for a ride?" Ellen asked, with a coy smile and toss of her luscious blonde hair.

Oscar blushed. He'd been taking things as they came, real slow like. It was a bit intimidating to be with a girl in the flesh, not like the virtual hookups he used to do. He'd learned people act differently in front of a camera, or when controlling an avatar, than they do in the flesh. Humanity was less predictable, sometimes even a bit awkward. Yet in the end, there was nothing quite like it. Oscar's mouth moistened. "You sure you're ready?"

"Of course I am, silly. It's you I'm wondering about." Just like that, she shot down the ladder. Had he said something wrong? She opened a stall door and led a horse out to a hitching post. *Ah, that's what she meant.* She pulled down a bridle from a peg in the barn, threw a blanket and saddle on, and told Oscar to get Flossy from the stall at the end. "I'll take you to my favorite place."

Oscar's only time in the saddle had been when Ellen brought him home after the ski mishap. She'd led his steady mule every step of the way so you couldn't really say he'd ever "ridden" a horse. He was a bit embarrassed about misunderstanding "going for a ride" and couldn't possibly back out now, so he scurried down and managed to coax the massive animal to greet him at the gate. Oscar stared into Flossy's eyes—

big, bottomless, and black as obsidian. He wondered what the animal was thinking and gently stroked its nose before grabbing the halter and leading it alongside Ellen's horse to tack up. He sneezed and frightened the huge animal. Ellen calmed Flossy down with a gentle stroke while he wiped his nose with the back of his hand, smearing some snot on his old MarlBro tattoo.

He stepped on a mounting block and kicked his leg over the saddle while Ellen steadied the horse. Once he was on, it wasn't that scary. He watched Ellen mount and realized the old bridle rein she tied around her waist as a belt was not to enhance her figure but so she could tuck in the back of her skirt. Then it didn't rub on the horse and startle it. *She's so practical.*

Ellen led the way and Flossy was content to follow, nose to tail, with an occasional deviation to browse on a bunch of fresh grass. "Don't let her do that," Ellen admonished. "You have to show her you're in control or she'll take you wherever she wants to go."

They rode through the woods, ducking occasionally for a branch that had grown over the trail. When he didn't bend far enough, he felt evergreen needles sweep against the back of his head and neck, near his left ear, The air smelled of pine, oxygen, and dust. Winnie and the convent dogs followed along, their open mouths seeming to smile with the thrill of exploration.

After ten minutes, they reached a small cliff where a trickle of water splattered over a rock face fifteen feet above them. The ground was green and dotted with yellow wildflowers and a large boulder jutting out in the middle of the meadow. Juniper trees surrounded the clearing, their purple berries covered with a milky white dust.

"It's beautiful. I can see why it's your favorite place," he told her. "I wish we had come here earlier."

"Yes, it's pretty. Yet that's not why it's my favorite." She looked at the top of the little waterfall and jumped off her horse. "Oscar, do you trust me?"

"Of course." He got off too, wondering how he'd get back on without the mounting block. "You're the most honest person I know."

"You'd trust what I said, because it was me who said it, because you know I care for you?"

Oscar wasn't sure what she was getting at. "I trust you. I'd believe you, Ellen." He touched her shoulder, pivoting her to face him directly.

"Would you believe that you *have* been here before?"

"I've never been this far in these woods. These are basic facts."

"Facts look differently depending upon how you arrive at them, how you remember them, how you interpret them. You *have* been here before. I could explain it, and you'd then trade belief for understanding, conviction for rationality, faith for fact. Would you rather believe it simply because you believe me?"

Oscar looked through her eyes, locked on his, wondering what the right thing to say was. He didn't want to feel like a dupe. Yet he wanted to believe her. That belief was more important than anything else. It was his reality. Moreover, down in his gut he had a weird feeling she was right.

Oscar reflected on how much he'd learned to trust others, with no real basis for doing so. It was Luella who convinced him to break from the MarlBros. He thought it would ruin him, but now his old bruddas came to him for advice on growing their own bacco. It was Vanessa who prodded him to get out into the community, and now the neighbors came to him. It was Vien who'd told him to drop by every week to sell bacco, knowing they would be safe from Pincertons on the bench beneath the giant oak.

A crow lit on a branch at the edge of the clearing, ruffling its feathers as if to shake off a winter chill. Oscar saw a hint of blue iridescence shimmered across its feathers when the sun struck at just the right angle. He smiled.

"Don't explain it," he told her. "Just kiss me."

She did.

With a mischievous look in her eyes, she asked, "Now, what if I told you that none of this actually happened? That you have been in a coma for the last five months with your MyndScreen perfectly functional but your brain offline. That all of this has been one ginormous virtual reality simulation game and that you've finally won the prize?" She untied her belt and threw her arms around his waist.

"Nah," he replied, in between kisses. "Now I know you're joking. This is the real thing. That I know for sure."

CHAPTER 50
Caspian

CASPIAN BLAINE WAS MOVING ON UP TO THE CORNER office, the presidential suite, the big time. Stroking his fingertips over the bocote hardwood desk, its intricate coffee and blonde grains swirled together in a marbled pattern, he finally understood Wallace Packard's requirement that staff work partially in-person. VRoom could not convey the desk's beauty or the magnificence of OrangeVine's C-suite office space with its picturesque views of the vast Pacific. Remote work offered no opportunity to inspire personnel to strive for their best in the hopes that they, too, might someday make it to the top.

HALexa had datashared his promotion with AmaZing! along with the accompanying salary bump, so his wardrobe subscription now sent custom-tailored Italian silk suits every day. Rather than tossing them down the recycling chute, he left the worn suits out on his delivery balcony in a Kevlar shopping bag inserted with a micro-tracker. When the drone brought a new outfit, it hooked the return parcel handle and whisked it away for resale to middle-management execs in New Jersey. Reuse was back in fashion, baby. The apricot tie with seafoam diagonal stripes never changed, however. He wore the same one, day in and day out, its embossed diamond pattern providing a light sheen of panache.

Shawn Fellia, the junior staffer who replaced him as VP of Special Projects and Strategic Initiatives, was bugging Caspian about supposedly severe problems with the WhamZong clinical trial OrangeVine funded in honor of Stephan Barscale. Shawn had sent him five messages about it in the past forty-two minutes. Now, he barged into Caspian's office, all worked up in a dither.

"Hey, boss, I know you're super busy, but have you seen my messages about the amygdala implants? Patients are binge-looping segments that utilize the pleasure enhancements. They find thirty seconds of emotional climax and replay them all day long. It's like nonstop romcom moments of feel-good laughter. Some viewers like the kinkier stuff—visual and hormonal porn. About nine percent binge fear scenes, looping horror movie climaxes until their so doped up on adrenaline they pass out. Thousands are losing the will to eat and require intravenous drip nutrition. Experts predict the incapacity induced from our trial will produce a massive influx of entertainment home enrollment and outstrip supply in the SoCal region within the next 72 hours. People will starve. We've got to do something!"

Caspian offered Shawn a real-brewed mocha-cappuccino, eased back into his shell cordovan leather chair, and said calmly, "Cool your jets fella. Tone down the sky-is-falling rhetoric of near certain doom and just focus on the metrics. Everything will work out. Just take things one step at a time, panic never made any situation less challenging. See if there are some tweaks in the grant protocols that we can subtly recommend. If people need a stronger enticement to take in nutrients, maybe we could include a year's supply of deluxe OrangeSmash FlavrPaks as a bonus when a grantee receives their GalEmScene implant. Bring in McChesney to run a program assessment. Ask them to calculate the non-delineated upsides and known unknown variables of the project as well as the costs of possible detrimental side-effects, including outsourcing EH placement to Vegas or the Midwest if we need greater capacity."

As Fellia traipsed off, Caspian licked cappuccino foam off his upper lip and took a deep breath to inhale the final scents of mocha coming from his hand-thrown stoneware mug. *That ought to calm the guy down for a few days and redirect his focus toward some constructive problem-solving instead of constant naysaying.*

Spurred by Fellia's mention of entertainment homes, Caspian noodled around for Vanessa, figuring by now she must have completed her upgrade and reside in an EH somewhere. Perhaps they could hook up, virtually that is, now that she was no longer a grantee. Hell, he could even break her out, seeing as he recently got the 411 on implant restoration techniques. She would no doubt be grateful as all get out to see him. He found no trace of her in Cyberia.

While he was searching, a video message popped in from Barron Koldwill, who evidently still had MyndScreen access. "Hey there Mr. Blaine, congrats on the new gig. You'll no doubt be looking to upgrade your living quarters to something more appropriate to your stature. I'm listing a newly renovated luxury home on Big Bear Lake. Ten thousand square feet of magnificent pine walls, cathedral ceilings, and French marbled counters nestled into the heart of the San Bernardino mountains. It's just a twenty-three-minute commute via FC Hydrodrone."

"'Zup, Barron? Stellar to hear from you. I thought you were, um, indisposed."

"Nah. The prosecutor dropped the charges after my lawyers brought in 62 gigabytes of evidence, including several media accounts that the so-called bombing never actually happened. It would have taken jurors at least one hundred and forty weeks to wade through all the data and my lawyers convinced them it wasn't worthy of limited prosecutorial resources given that 95% of trials result in a hung jury. Turns out it's basically impossible to get twelve people to agree on anything these days. Anyhow, I've got an opening to show it this afternoon at four, wanna take a look?"

His secretary notified him of a VRoom with Celious Tudball and OrangeVine's head of HR coming up in 27.6 minutes to discuss a revamp of personnel policies. After that, he had to brief a group of prospective donors organized by Yvonne Putcher.

"Sure, put me down at four and send me a pin with the coordinates," he replied, just to get Koldwill off his case. Truth be told, he wasn't enthusiastic about any new digs that involved a Hydrodrone commute. Still, it couldn't hurt to start getting a sense of the market. Besides, the SpeiDrWeb trackers would notice if he wasn't sufficiently interested in upping his real estate game. The light from the Milano glass pendant gave a soothing glow to the luster of his fine bocote desk.

Caspian glanced through his inbox. Message 19 was from a charity in The Gambia, seeking donations to treat underprivileged kids with cleft palates struggling with post-Darwinian climate variance. Message 46 was from the Center for Eminent Globalian CeleTeCharity, inviting him to present a Ded™ Talk in Davos about growing asset-based do-goodery in collaboration with A-list celebrities, ThotLeaders™ and burgeoning Silicon Valley incubator shops in an era of socially disrupted educationarily technograde deficit. There would be Nordic caviar, sparkling high-potassium mineral water sourced from a limestone cave in Belarus, and holographic PowerPoints. Educate Lewis Leon would give the keynote shortly after Caspian's slot. HECK YES!

Message 112 was from someone named @SkaterBro92346 "I know your password is OrangeRider69 and what you've been doing online. You should have been more careful with your avatar's security protocols. That orangutan is really quite something. Let's get right to the point. You now have two choices. The first alternative is to ignore this message. In such case, I will distribute your avatar's video with said orangutan far and wide to every perverted nook and cranny of the 11G universe. That should generate a lot of attention. Your second option is to make, shall we say, a donation of forty-nine thousand and forty-one ByteDime to The Sisters of San Bernardino Fund for Abandoned Ponies. Should this donation be received in the next twenty-two minutes, I can assure you that the avatar footage shall be destroyed and you can carry on with your normal life." *As if I'm gonna fall for that. Phony sextortion email scams date back decades.* DELETE.

Message 165 contained his requested tabulation of all the utils generated by his grantees during his twenty-year stint at the helm of the Special Projects and Strategic Initiatives Division. Four million, eight hundred and sixteen thousand plus change. Not too shabby, yet it was only the beginning. He was pulling together a team building Vretreat next week in Vawaii to set the foundation's next round of stretch goals. Board members, select grantees, and senior staff would participate and McChesney offered up an amazing facilitator to synergize his team's inputs. Maybe they'd revamp the mission and vision statements after a rapid response good-finding brainstorm session with lots of notes written up on large cybertablets with DryERace markers and posted around the VRoom walls.

HALexa reminded him to stand up and take 114 steps before continuing with his work. He paced the 1,800 square foot office and looked down at the palm trees—yes, real coconut palms. Once LA's climate warmed sufficiently to support them, Wallace Packard insisted the City of Santa Monica plant coconuts around OrangeVine's block. He found their gentle swaying in the wind more aesthetically pleasing from his 21st floor office than the plastic date palms that were easier to maintain and less prone to dropping heavy fruit on passersby.

The late afternoon sun hung low over the Pacific. It was a beautiful thing. Even more inspirational was knowing it would be back tomorrow, rising in the East, making each day a little brighter than before. The world was getting better, util by util, and he was making it happen. Progress, baby. Beeeauutiful progress was lapping up on the shores of Santa Monica with every wave of social uplift he funded. Caspian sighed as he eased into his leather chair and resumed his work while puffing an AttainMint™ e-cigar.

Message 197 was from OrangeVine's new CFO, fresh talent he poached from a hedge fund to replace Margery DeVrine. "Sorry to be the bearer of bad news. We should brace ourselves to confront a few financial headwinds. OrangeVine's endowment has gone negative due to the complete devaluation of ByteDime and collapse of the Globalian Consumption Index. For cashflow reasons, the foundation must cease payment on all grant obligations, effective immediately. Salaries, expense accounts, and healthcare benefits will be suspended as of 9 AM tomorrow morning. There's a strong likelihood we will need to auction off the office building and all furnishings to fulfill advanced debt obligation instruments we used to preload fund discharge for the WhamZong amygdala pilot project and associated expenses. I recommend asking legal counsel if board members and executives can be held personally liable for OrangeVine's debt, which will hit ten figures by Friday."

A buzz shot through the room and the lights faded out; not with a bang, but a whimper. It had been happening a lot lately. Caspian's Mynd-Screen went blank, again. He took a long, slow draw on his mentholated vape cigar and steeled his nerves. Every new CEO needs a challenge to prove his mettle. He would emerge from this crisis stronger than ever, he just needed to keep his head down, follow the rules, and innovate a creative win-win resolution. He could do this. He was Caspian Blaine.

The elevator didn't work without power, so he nonchalantly strolled down the fire stairs, observing that none of his staff remained in the building.

It was a clear evening. He walked outside and took in the fresh ocean breeze. A group of gray pelicans, one of the oldest species in the air, glided far overhead in a V formation. Strangely, people were out walking around, for no apparent reason. Everyone should have been safe at home, enjoying the evening's new releases from Timeless Warning, noshing on PopKourne and virtually snuggling with a potentially significant other under disposable VelVet™ blankets.

He had placed his yellow convertible in a holding pattern all afternoon, circling the block as there were no longer parking places around OrangeVine's office. He'd normally just ping it to pick him up, but with transmissions out he'd need to manually flag it down.

For some reason, his iDrive didn't recognize him, visually that is. He held his hand up and waved while it cruised by for another lap around the block. He should have called James and the limo that morning instead of relying on his old iDrive, its operating system seemed buggy as of late. But he was still sentimentally attached to it.

The streetlights were out, even electronic billboards had gone dark. He heard odd noises of people conversing, all the more noticeable because there was no sound in his MyndScreen, which was still offline.

When his iDrive came around again, he jumped out in front, knowing the car's sensors would bring it to a halt. It worked. He just needed a little innovation! As he stepped around the car's hood, a coconut fell from a palm tree. It bounced off the street immediately in front of the iDrive's right front fender, causing it to bolt leftward. In executing this collision avoidance maneuver, it ran over Caspian's foot, crushing his metatarsal bones with a crackling sound.

Caspian whimpered and suppressed the urge to scream. It was just a minor mishap, a road bump in the highway of life. The car drove off while he limped around in the street. Then it stopped in its tracks, its battery dead. Self-recharge had been problematic over the past week, with electrical power so inconsistent. He only now noticed the street was littered with discharged vehicles, stranded in place and time.

He could just walk home, well, more like hop on his good foot. After trying a few times, he concluded crawling was more efficient, and less painful. He told himself to keep his head down and continue building incremental power. When he was at Davos, he'd network with some of the biggest names in Globalia. The possibilities were endless. He devised a work plan with daily goals to keep him on task. As soon as HALexa was back online, he would lay out some midterm objectives to drop into his calendar, with deadlines and progress checkpoints to hold himself accountable.

His knees stung with a bright, surface level burn from getting skinned up as he crawled incrementally down the double yellow stripe in the middle of Wilshire Boulevard. He plodded on, undeterred. The air smelled of warm asphalt mixed with ocean breeze. People were yelling "look out dude," as they whizzed by on bicycles, oblivious to his physical and psychic pain. The kids jumping double-Dutch stared as if he were from another planet, completely unaware of everything he'd done over his long career to lift up their lives.

Still, he kept going. He was getting thirsty, jonesing for a Barnicle and Jane whine cooler. He could see the blank screens on the exterior of Colossal Condominiums rising like a black obelisk on the horizon. Once 11G transmissions were restored, he could order an e-bike to see what all this excitement was about. Or maybe he'd just take in an episode about them. Yvonne Putcher could surely smooth over OrangeVine's financial hiccups. She'd probably accompany him to the Davos ThotLeader convening. He'd reach out to his Synced-In network and problem solve his way out of this little setback.

He could do this. He was Caspian Blaine.

CHAPTER 51
Chase

CHASE WINCED WHEN HE HEARD IT. "SISTER MARTHA! This is my mom," Ellen screeched. "Mom . . . this is the woman who raised me." Things could get awkward.

He had tagged along when Ellen took Vera clothes shopping the morning after she'd unplugged. She had walked out of that quote unquote entertainment home wrapped in nothing but a disposable sheet. Chase had gently placed his arms around her for warmth as they spent the night getting reacquainted in Oscar's spare room. Ellen still had the Thrifty Sister key, so she offered to get Vera properly outfitted.

Chase and Vera sorted through huge cardboard boxes full of donated clothes while Ellen excused herself to use the restroom. There were plenty of choices. T-shirts, chinos, blouses, all from good old cotton that seemed to last forever. While Vera was trying some stuff on, an odd-looking, older woman came in the front door. She looked somewhat surprised. "Well, hello! What are you doing here?"

"Hi, uh, it's a long story but . . . " That's when Ellen returned and screeched her introductions.

During the hubbub of Sister Martha's hasty explanation that she really had done her best to locate Vera after finding Ellen unexpectedly in her care and Vera describing the infotain torture that led her to abandon her daughter, Chase kept his distance and wandered around the store, marveling at piles of old junk. There was stuff he hadn't seen since he was a kid, like digital clocks and barbeque grills. He took particular interest in a 1990s-era Frigidaire, a cast-iron skillet, and a hotplate.

The conversation wasn't as weird as he'd expected. Sister Martha seemed genuinely relieved to have finally found Ellen's real mother, who despite her age looked much better than when she'd seen her last in that hotel lobby. And Vera wasn't the least bit resentful that her baby had been snatched away from a childrearing center. Far from it, she appeared grateful. He knew he was.

When the commotion and initial excitement of re-entering terrestrial reality wore off, Chase and Vera spent a few days getting re-acquainted while exploring the world. His heart quickened when he glimpsed an Anna's hummingbird sucking nectar from a pink salvia. They marveled together at the evening breeze and birch bark texture.

They'd left things somewhat unresolved that day seventeen years ago when they were both rudely snatched from the beach by quote unquote lifesaving drones and taken to Mercernary General for "treatment." Months before, when Vera first told him she was pregnant, she'd said she wanted to raise the baby with him but needed some "space" to "find herself" before really being capable of loving someone. She needed to know who she was. It hurt a bit, yet he understood.

He'd given her time. They'd delved into the illicit "book" that Aneeka Randall used to lure them into her snare. He never knew Vera was ready to propose, to seal the deal that day on the beach, when everything went to shit.

So, when Vera asked him, "Well, where do we go from here?" while they hung out at SubDirt one day, he felt it was time. He stuck his finger into his jeans pocket, rubbed his lucky penny, and asked in a typically cheesy Chase sort of way for her hand in marriage. This time, she didn't hesitate.

This, of course, brought on a whole conversation about what sort of life they could make for themselves, especially since the post-industrial infotain economy was collapsing all around them due in no small part to fake views, misinformation, and a glut of irrelevant news. "We've got to do something, Chase, people are going to die. They need to know what's really important and what's just distraction."

Chase subtly made the case that they didn't have to take all of society's troubles upon their shoulders. "Maybe we could just relax, enjoy life, and not worry about changing the world or revealing every last bit of truth."

"Things were pretty relaxing back in the Twilight Kingdom, where you never lifted a finger and they pumped the soyalgent straight into your bloodstream," she replied, with a sharp smile. "Maybe enjoying life *is* the way to change things and learn what's true. Maybe changing the world, only in some small way, really *is* how you enjoy life, even if you struggle most of the time. Maybe the struggle is the whole point."

She was right, as usual. What they needed was a challenge. An undertaking. Meaningful work that provided some sense of satisfaction. He picked up a hoe and fervently dug a furrow for some sweet corn. He saw Oscar chuckling in the distance when he struck a rock and cursed. It was late morning but already getting warm. Soon a South America–shaped blotch of sweat soaked his T-shirt. He kept at it, and after about an hour had a decently straight row. He grabbed a handful of sweet corn kernels from a burlap bag, carefully pressed each one into the soil, and gently covered them.

"We could be farmers," he said to Vera, with no small element of gratification.

She pointed to a flock of starlings that were digging up and eating his newly planted seeds. "Maybe. I think we'd need some on-the-job training."

Chase jogged back to the house and returned with some clothes and a red bandana from the recycling bin. Luella followed him out to the garden, looking puzzled. He stuffed a shirt with a bunch of socks, used clothespins to attach it to a pair of disposable jeans, and tied the bandana around the neck.

"You making a dummy?" Luella asked, half mockingly.

"A scarecrow. To keep birds away."

"It doesn't even move. It's obviously fake."

"It doesn't matter if it's real or not. What matters is that the birds think it's real."

Vera scowled. "Don't listen to him Lulu. Reality matters. We humans can use a thing called science to determine what's real and what's not." She shot a disapproving glare in Chase's direction before giving Luella a smile. "Nonetheless, Chase is doing something useful. That's what matters most."

Work in a garden is never finished, but when they felt they had done enough for one day Chase and Vera decided to go for a walk, to no place in particular. Luella went back to check in online. Transmissions had resumed that morning after several days of downtime and she said she had some catching up to do. Plus, Oscar wanted her help setting up a new V-mail account. "Don't spend too much time with that helmet on," Vera admonished.

As they strolled hand in hand, a ten-year-old kid literally bumped right into a streetlight, just like that. His nose was buried in a paper map, so he hadn't looked where he was going. He looked up and stared at Vera's face with a look of recognition, although she swore to Chase she'd never seen the kid before. Chase knew she was right. After all, she'd been indisposed longer than the kid had been alive.

He couldn't seem to talk for some reason, yet he looked terrified and made weird pointing motions to his throat implying he was thirsty as all get out. They brought him over to Oscar's place. While Oscar wasn't around, they didn't think he'd mind if they offered the kid a drink. They opened the fridge Chase had brought over from the Thrifty Sister and found some lemonade.

The kid inhaled the drink without saying a word. After his fourth glass, Luella finally took off her gaming helmet to see what was going on. "Melvin?"

Chase and Vera gave her blank stares until she explained that she met Melvin months ago at Knott's Berry Farm and he couldn't talk or hear because he got implanted as an infant. He'd never used the neural connections to his cochlea and vocal cords. It was evidently far easier for his brain to communicate online. Luella put her helmet back on and tried to interface with him via chatter. "That's weird. His account has been deleted."

After an hour of stick figure drawings and frantic charade-style hand gestures, they pieced together that Melvin's parents had been upgraded and that he subsequently disabled his own MyndScreen after watching a BoubToob video describing the process. He kept pointing emphatically to Vera as he tried to communicate this point. Melvin had then set off to find Luella, the only person he'd ever had any terrestrial connection to. He somehow acquired a map and had been wandering around for the past three days while running low on calories and hydration.

"So, what are we gonna do with him?" Luella asked bluntly. She scratched the puppy behind the ears. "Winnie could use a friend."

Chase and Vera said nothing. Luella printed some soyalgent from the extruder, which vibrated with a low hum as it produced the food. Chase saw a cockroach scurry out, searching unsuccessfully for drips of FlavrPak while finding only a dollop of unflavored soyalgent. This time, he had no urge to grab the bug. He pondered how it knew the right moment to dart out of its crevice, especially since the extruder had been out of flavoring for weeks.

Melvin must have been starving, but he scrunched up his nose and shook his head at the bowl of gray mush. Luella fried it up with some onions and a carrot. Unfamiliar with the use of potholders, she grabbed the hot cast-iron skillet and dropped it on the floor with a clang so jolting that Chase felt the floor thump in the soles of his feet. The bug scurried back to its crevice. *That's it! Vibrations.*

He turned to Luella. "You're telling me that although Melvin has perfectly operational ears, his brain forgot how to use them after getting more input than it needs from his MyndScreen?"

"Something like that, yeah."

"We gotta get this kid some drums! C'mon, let's go to the Thrifty Sister."

Chase had seen instruments in the nuns' thrift shop, so he explained his theory as they walked over. "Melvin's sense of touch, and of hearing, still work fine. He just needs his brain to associate the signals it has been ignoring from his ears with things he can feel. He needs to feel vibrations that he knows are real. He needs music! When he taps the drums, his brain will know it from feel and learn to associate the sounds reaching his ears with music."

Sister Margaret greeted them and happily dug out some bongos. Chase insisted on paying in dollars, even though the store had long been out of business. His ByteDime account was worthless after the currency collapse, yet he had plenty of cash still on hand from his Vegas winnings.

"You know," he suggested, "you nuns should reopen this store. With AmaZing! out of business, people will need real stuff again and this is just about the only place to find it."

"I'm afraid the other sisters and I are too old to run a business anymore, even if customers did come back," Sister Martha lamented. "However," she said looking at Ellen with raised eyebrows, "maybe someone younger would be interested?"

"What do you reckon it's worth?" Chase inquired. "Vera and I could buy it and live in the back room. Ellen could help run it."

Ellen threw on her old VR helmet and did a quick search. "WillOwe's real estate site isn't providing ByteDime estimates anymore. Using deflation-adjusted U.S. dollars, it looks to be worth about $50,000."

"That's twice what I've got on hand," Chase sighed.

"Tell you what, Gramps," Luella offered, "with my split of the Vegas haul I could buy the other half. I am a sister after all, and reasonably thrifty. And Martha, maybe you could use the proceeds from the sale for the Fund for Abandoned Ponies!"

Oscar looked at Ellen and decided to just let things ride without saying anything. Their families were, in a sense, about to join.

"I've got one condition," Luella continued. "You both stay living with us in the house *and* we let Melvin stay too. That's my deal, take it or leave it."

Chase tapped a little rhythm on the bongos while he glanced at Vera, who shrugged her shoulders in a "why not?" pose.

He took a deep breath and said to Luella, "If we're gonna go into business together, you gotta stop calling me Gramps."

"Whatever. How about it, Pops?"

CHAPTER 52
Aneeka

"I CAN'T APOLOGIZE ENOUGH FOR THE MISUNDERSTANDING," the avatar of Mercernary General's CEO sputtered on Aneeka's Chatter. Fewer than five minutes had elapsed since she fired off her dispatch to the Chief Educate. The law clerk from Harvard had hurried out of her office, evidently having been summoned on his MyndScreen.

"No, you can't. Get me the hell out of here. Now!"

"I'm on my way as we speak. I left my office immediately after Lewis Leon informed me of the error. It will take a few minutes to get there as we aren't using the elevators due to power inconsistencies. Your former clerk has been relieved of his duties and is now undergoing treatment himself."

Aneeka put on her T-shirt and combed her hair. Victory was sweet. She dabbed Randy perfume on her jugular notch and caressed her jade pendant.

While grooming, headlines popped into her feed. During her time offline, Dagny Huerta had purchased Timeless Warning, which the Educates had bailed out with an emergency stimulus package that placed the company into temporary tribunal receivership. The shareholders worried about socialism, so they accepted pennies on the dollar for a complete sale to Huerta, the only bidder able to pay in gold. After the acquisition, Dagny announced she would turn the company's 11G towers into landscape sculpture. The first one would look like the Eiffel tower; the second, an Inuit totem pole.

Her office doors whooshed open and Mercernary General's director walked in wearing a fire-engine red pantsuit and too much makeup. She was panting. "Sorry, the stairs took the wind out of me. And I apologize again for the mix up. Your chaufferscurity is coming to take you home." Aneeka suppressed a smile. No need to gloat. Her blackmail bluff was sufficiently gratifying on its own.

The director continued, "Obviously you should never have been admitted for treatment. That overzealous legal assistant of yours made a clerical error. Chief Leon has rectified the situation. He admonished me that you could never accept or receive an infotain upgrade as your undistracted attention is vital to the Educates. I suppose you haven't had a chance to follow things over the past few weeks, but the situation is quite dire. The Chief believes you alone can fix it."

"What do you mean, dire?"

"For starters, a video of some woman decommissioning her MyndScreen and waltzing out an entertainment home has gone viral. Some kid helped her find a system restore point, calling audibles. Hundreds of thousands of people are now doing it across Globalia."

As the esteemed director lectured on, Aneeka felt that familiar abdominal tightening. The nagging tumor of doubt, pushing up against her steel girder. There it was. Again.

"Can I offer you an Atlantis?" The talking suit slid Aneeka a Kewl-flavored vigarette and continued, "the societal economic symptoms are even worse than we've seen in previous MyndScreen Side Effect outbreaks, which caused only modest declines in GDP. This is total market failure."

Aneeka studied the dollar sign logo on the Atlantis before inhaling deeply and holding the flavored steam inside her lungs. It had been weeks since she last vaped. The soothing effect felt even more potent than she remembered, just when she sorely needed the comfort.

PowerPoint slides appeared on Aneeka's office wallscreen, summoned evidently by the director. There were charts and graphs, but also images of children with distended bellies, wide eyes bulging out of skulls, and ribs covered with only the thinnest veneer of skin.

"We're maybe two or three days away from massive famine as the economy falls to shambles. Later today, there will be a 48-hour global lockdown of all transmissions and physical travel to prevent further spread of that video's highly contagious content. A temporary shutdown will of course further devastate the economy, however it's necessary until we can quarantine the viral video and prevent more patients from contracting this condition, which we're calling MyndScreen Liberatus Syndrome, or MLS."

"We need details on your treatment of Aldo. There are outbreaks of MyndScreen downtime within a ten-mile proximity of his location. If you cured *him*, you can cure anyone."

"Aldo. Where is he?" Aneeka took another draw on the Atlantis and felt her anxiety melt away.

"He walked out during the power outage. With doors open and lights out, he followed the scent of fresh air to a stairwell and went down. Security cameras caught it all." Video footage of Aldo smiling and taking deep breaths as he strolled out the building played on the wallscreen.

The doors to Aneeka's office whooshed open unexpectedly. Barry Kendall rushed in, his eyes sparkling with excitement. "Dr. Randall, I wanted you to be the first to know! I've been nominated to the Tribunal. I'll be joining you as an Educate. I can't believe it's happening!"

"What? Really?"

"Yes, change is in the air. Rolland Thompson is out, due to undisclosed health reasons. And, get this, Lewis Leon will retire at the end of the session. There's an A-list of possible successors, and you're on it!"

He was talking a hundred miles an hour, breathless, with a smile as wide as a kid at his first VR arcade.

"Are you certain? How do you know all this?"

"I got it from an undisclosed source, if you know what I mean. I am one hundred percent confident of its veracity." He made a motion with his right hand as if sipping from an imaginary champagne flute.

"So, you'll be joining the Educates, even though I recently saw you strapped to a wheelchair down that very hall?" She pointed out her doorway with an air of skepticism.

"Everything changed when I got the WhamZong GalEmScene. It controls the emotional outbursts that had distracted me all these years and lets me focus on what's really important. After I was discharged, the Chief was impressed with my heightened rationality and ability to produce objective Tribunal rulings at an efficiency surpassing any clerk in the past twenty years. My personal productivity metrics are off the chart, all thanks to the director here." He extended a hand toward Mercernary General's CEO.

"You know, Dr. Randall," the director's voice inflected upward with a soft lilt, "without wanting to appear impertinent, I might suggest in the event you do wind up as Chief Educate, you too might benefit from the same implant. I've seen your charts, and it will come as no shock to you that your intellect is simply unsurpassed—literally at the top of our metrics. Yet I'm sure you wouldn't be surprised to hear that you have experienced bouts of unregulated emotional impulse that can cloud even the most rational of judgments. It's perfectly natural, we all experience it from time to time."

"The confirmation process for Chief is quite rigorous," Barry Kramer chimed in. "Any edge in the objective rationality metrics might land you the job."

"As I was saying before, Dr. Randall," continued the director of Mercernary General, "the stakes couldn't be higher. Globalia needs someone who can balance economic growth with protections for individual freedom. You're one of the few people on the planet with certified expertise in all these conflicting realms, the logical and the philosophical, the legal and the psychological, truth and information, prosperity and freedom, societal benefit weighed against individual primacy."

Individual. Society. Aneeka couldn't decide if this woman sounded more like John Galt or Vera. *Vera.* The mere thought opened a chat dialogue with her initial attempt at contact. "Hey there, how's it going?"

Chatter said the account had unblocked her but was presently offline. There was, however, this message:

"Thank you for the letter. I believe you. I forgive yet cannot help you. As you said, freedom is the ability to think for yourself, to make your own choices, to accept your own beliefs. It is time for you to find your own truths and accept whatever outcome they bring. Love, Vera. P.S. They took off the necklace you gave me before my C-section. Hopefully, it found its way back to you."

Aneeka rubbed the jade pendant around her neck, took an extra-long draw on her Atlantis and felt suddenly lightheaded. Her knees buckled and she swooned backward into the arms of Barry Kramer, whose quick reflexes kept her from hitting the floor. Moments later she was back on her feet feeling confident, alert, acutely rational.

Vera. What a cop out. All this time Vera had been the center of her angst, the disrupter of her soul, the one barrier standing in her way. She'd known all along that her irrational, emotional attraction toward Vera not only clouded her judgment but at times rendered her intellectually paralyzed. That's why she'd given her the necklace, only to have it returned by hospital staff. It was her love for Vera that prompted the crazy notion of resetting MyndScreens back to zero functionality, an idea that could now cause the death of millions, maybe hundreds of millions, as the economy disintegrated to dust. It was Vera's sentimentality that inspired Aneeka to discharge Aldo, without evidence, without a sound basis in science. And these foolish people still thought she could work miracles? Maybe they had no choice but to think that, figuring that since she got the world into this, she could get them out. Maybe they were right. Maybe, at least, she had to try.

"If I decide to do this, what would it look like?" she asked the director. "What's the procedure? Is it FDA approved?"

"It's a fairly straightforward insertion. The WhamZong GalEm-Scene is amazing microtechnology, less than a centimeter in diameter. The implant has a probe the size of a human hair inserted within the amygdala using a camera-guided, self-anesthetizing needle. Like other implants, it's powered by a separately embedded glucose fuel cell. It pairs seamlessly with your MyndScreen infotain chip and receives signals through a shared 11G connection.

"While this is a relatively new procedure, no deaths or brain-debilitating side effects have occurred from the surgery. The device was originally designed to enhance infotainment with emotional scenery. In your case, it could be reprogrammed to detect excessive emotional activity and discharge a neutralizing electrical current to maintain dominance of your prefrontal cortex, thus providing a superior state of rationality. So, for example, if the GalEmScene detected excessive fear signals coming from your amygdala, it would produce an opposite charge and disarm the instinctual fight or flight reflex. Since this off-label application is still experimental, I don't know if you'd be eligible to receive one. Perhaps Lewis Leon could pull some strings if he really thinks you should become the next Chief. Would you like me to see if I can push through the paperwork? I'd just need your consent."

As she listened, Aneeka felt her steel girder holding firm. It had been tested by nebulous emotions, corroded by caustic doubt, and stressed under the immense weight and responsibility of shepherding Globalia's economy. And yet, it remained. Strong. Vibrant. Unyielding. She took a final draw on her Atlantis, exhaled through both corners of her mouth while keeping her lips joined in the middle, and watched a V-shaped exhaust plume from her mouth billow like the wings of a phoenix rising from the ashes.

Aneeka Randall glanced with understanding at her protégé, the clerk from the University of Chicago. She removed her jade pendant, pivoted to face the director of Mercernary General, and said it.

"I consent."

EPILOGUE

CHASE DANCED WITH RECKLESS ABANDON. HE ROCKED the Billy Crystal overbite with sweat dripping profusely off his dirty blond mullet. He thrust his index finger skyward like he'd caught the Saturday Night Fever. He struck the pose, did the twist, lowered the limbo, glided the electric slide. Vera smirked, thinking his moves would have looked ridiculous on a 25-year-old, let alone someone with 49 years in the rearview mirror. Self-consciousness, at least of the physical self, had faded away during his 17-year infotain binge.

The air smelled of smoldering charcoal from the grill and fleeting Teen Spirit deodorant. Chirping crickets were drowned out by David Bowie blasting loudly from speakers connected to a turntable in the crumbling parking lot of the Thrifty Sister Dry Goods and Repair Shop. The party was to celebrate the store's grand re-opening, under new management.

Vera danced with him. She kept her moves a little more reserved yet still thoroughly enjoyed herself. She wore bright red shoes and a pair of diamond earrings Chase had picked up in Vegas. The horseshoe keychain was attached to her necklace, dangling the only key to the Thrifty Sister near her heart. Maybe someday a locksmith would re-open and they could make duplicates. Until then, Chase entrusted her with its safekeeping.

Around fifty people mingled at the biggest gathering San Bernardino had seen in decades. Ten nuns showed up to bid the store farewell, a few of them venturing onto the dance floor along with some of Oscar's MarlBro friends. More than a dozen custoz arrived, including Vien and his neighbors. There were even some Winstons, having buried the hatchet and ceding the surrounding bacco turf to Oscar's homegrown operation. They instead focused on bootlegging gin and passed around some bottles. Even the nuns didn't seem to mind. The religious order to which the Sisters of San Bernardino belonged had received a large grant from Dagny Huerta, who it turns out was raised by nuns as a child. Everyone had reason to celebrate.

Ellen was off to the side, dancing discretely with Oscar and probably wishing her dad wasn't so embarrassing. Vera saw Chase keep a watchful glance, just out of the corner of his eye, while still respecting Ellen's distance. In the few months since she'd re-emerged, Vera had seen them draw closer each day. It was initially hard to accept her daughter dating a former gang member, still in the business of selling contraband cigarettes. In the end, she knew she needed to let Ellen forge her own life. And at least tobacco was real. Everyone needs some sort of escape from the bitter monotony of daily life, whether it's nicotine, alcohol, marijuana, infotain, or retail therapy. The trick, Vera had come to believe, was to prevent escape from overwhelming the reality you sought respite from in the first place.

She saw Luella sitting on the folded down tailgate of a Winston pickup, munching on popcorn and guzzling Coca-Cola in a thick swirled glass bottle from Mexico. She'd left her GalExSee at home, so Vera could see Luella's curious eyes taking in the scene. Right next to her sat Melvin, tapping his foot to the music. Chase walked over, smiled, and gave the kid a high five.

Overhead and unnoticed, Luella's air support drone broadcast signals to jam the reception of any rogue Pincertons still on patrol, unaware their corporate owners had gone bankrupt and people no longer cared whether their credit ratings tanked. She'd enjoyed the challenge of reprogramming the pinca that had etherized Oscar into her own personal protector, tailing her in the air just as Winnie followed her every step on the ground.

Melvin picked up a notepad and scrawled preschool-caliber text while Luella read over his shoulder. "He can feel the music thumping in his chest and has sounds inside his head. His ears are coming online!" Luella had the most dazzling smile as she said this. Melvin watched her intently as she spoke, perhaps trying to read her lips. In any case, he nodded and grinned. Maybe soon the kid would talk.

Vera had suggested they invite Caspian Blaine, after all he'd done to help at key junctures in her life. Then Ellen mentioned he never got back to her about funding for the garden. "It's just as well, we're better off just doing things on our own," she'd said, noting that she didn't even know how to reach Caspian since he'd never given her his Chatter handle. Vera started to tell her she could Noodle search things like that but decided in the end to let Ellen figure it out for herself.

As the evening progressed, dancing gave way to karaoke. As you would imagine, nuns singing background vocals to a Winston dude belting out classic tunes from the 30s was quite a sight to behold. Joining in, Vera observed how singing immersed her more deeply in the music. Rather than ruminating on her husband's crazy dance moves or her daughter's romantic life, she thought only about the song. Her focused concentration transported her to a new reality, a bliss, a complete experience. Of course, what was really happening was that the act of singing lowered her levels of adrenocorticotropic (stress) hormone while increasing her plasma oxytocin, especially when she couldn't quite read the karaoke screen and just made up the words as she went along.

When the music faded at around midnight, they walked back home together. There was a crisp smell to the air and the night was calm but for a few crickets chirping in the distance. A black-crowned night heron silently flew in front of the moon, briefly blocking its pale, serious light that seemed all the brighter because streetlights were still out. Chase held Vera's hand. Oscar held Ellen's. Luella and Melvin skipped along behind, her pink high tops glowing in the moonlight.

The following day, the family bicycled up to the convent for another, more private, celebration. "Make a wish!" Vera cheered, as Ellen blew out eighteen birthday candles. Sister Martha had made the cake from scratch, while Vera watched in amazement and took notes in a newly acquired cookbook.

"Do you think wishes really come true?" Ellen asked as she watched thin smoke trails swirl up from the candles, leaving that unmistakable scent of smoldering wicks lingering in the air.

"Only if you believe in them," Chase quipped.

"What do you mean?" Ellen plucked a candle and licked cream cheese and powdered-sugar frosting off the bottom.

"I believed I was stuck in the entertainment home forever even though I wanted to leave. I only walked out when I dared believe my wish could come true."

"And, until I believed something different," Vera added, "I thought I could never be the same person I once was, that there was no real life worth living, so there was no point in getting out."

"I still don't get it," Ellen said. She'd clearly been wanting to broach the topic. "If it was so bad, why did you consent in the first place?"

Vera cut and served the cake, carefully positioning each slice precisely in the middle of the dessert plate. "It's hard to imagine now, but they put me in a situation where I believed you'd forget me unless I consented. I was convinced I'd be a bad mom, homeless, and destitute, and unable to raise you or take care of myself. I thought I would lose you either way. Their AI deduced this fate was the worst possible thing I could imagine. The fear was incapacitating. I held out a long time, until eventually I weakened and chose to believe it, I really did. They showed me a custom-made 4D dramatization of your high school graduation where you didn't even recognize me. It was like an infomercial from hell. I know now that it never happened, yet it was so vivid I got caught up in their story. Instead of forever losing the thing I cared most about, they promised to stream my likeness and lullaby directly into your brain if I went to the entertainment home and placed you in a childrearing center. That way, you'd remember me even if I wasn't there with you. Your memory made the upgrade seem worth it. I consented."

"That's why I kept having that weird dream with the two of you and the 'we'll meet again' song looping over and over in my head like an immortal earworm."

"Right, but since you didn't stay online, it became a distant memory, if you can even call something fictitious a memory. They played you the image and song on your cribscreen as a baby, and on wallscreens in your early childrearing center. Then, when Sister Martha took you out of that place, you no longer saw it. Thank goodness she did, or you'd never have had the intuition or curiosity to track me down."

"And yet, you still didn't want to leave."

"Well, I'd lost my ability to believe in anything, with the exception that I believed you'd remember me at your high school graduation. When that fiction shattered, I had nothing left. Nothing to believe in. Nothing to live for."

"And then she met me," Chase quipped. "I mean, for the second time. C'mon you two, lighten up. Let's go ride some horses."

Oscar, Chase, Melvin, and Luella went to the barn while Vera and Ellen cleaned up the kitchen. As she washed dishes, Ellen asked, "Mom, how do you know if you really love someone? And how do you know if they really love you back?"

Vera knew why she was asking. "Well, it's just something you feel, deep inside your bones. If it happens to you, you'll know it."

"Surely there must be some sort of evidence, some rational basis for determining if it's true love or not. Can you measure your pulse when you're around them, or count the number of minutes you spend thinking about someone? Is there a section of the brain you could hook up to a scanner and see if it activates when you touch them? There must be some measurable facts you could look for."

They walked outside to catch up with the others. Vera felt the bright warmth of sunlight on her cheeks as they continued their conversation. The autumn leaves rustled in the breeze, offering yellow, brown, and red contrasts to the oxygenated sky.

"Facts are facts," Vera said, stopping to look at Ellen with a gaze both tender and firm. "They have nothing to do with reality, for that is something you create for yourself. While there might be certain metrics to measure physical attraction, love only comes to be when you choose to believe in it. Lose that faith and it vanishes as mysteriously as it appeared."

"Huh, that's not what I was expecting you to say. Sounds like something Sister Martha once told me."

It was true. Before the upgrade, Vera had spent her life in pursuit of objectivity. She'd worked professionally as a fact checker in the Department of Information. She'd risked her life to spread accurate information about the growing failure of antibiotics in treating gonorrhea. Then, they'd cured her own gonorrhea in the Twilight Kingdom using clinically tested calcium blockers instead of outdated antibiotics. Now she was telling her own daughter that, for the most important decisions in life, facts weren't what mattered.

"Well, I guess you could say," she ventured after some thought, "that I've learned faith, imagination, and rationality are all important and that measured doses of each help us understand, and create, our own reality. You eventually gain the wisdom to know when, and how much, to rely upon fact instead of instinct." She plucked a piece of wild grass and stuck the straw-colored stem in her mouth, chewing it absentmindedly as she glanced at Luella and Oscar over by the barn.

"Hey! Look at you!" Ellen yelled.

Vera felt a rush of joy seeing Luella finally manage to throw her leg over the saddle and mount the horse. She rode Flossy slowly along the trail. The plan was to trot over to the adjoining eighty-acre lot the Sisters purchased with proceeds from selling the thrift store. Someday they'd use it as a rescue sanctuary for feral ponies and mustangs.

Flossy reared, just like that, and Luella soared through the air in a frozen instant of time. Vera could see the terror on her face as she arced toward the ground, could hear the horse running circles in a frenzy. She landed with a thud and lay flat as dust swirled around her motionless pink Chuck Taylor high tops.

Flossy had seen a fleeting shadow cross the ground in front of her while a sharp shriek pierced the air. None of the humans had noticed the pair of crows dive-bombing a golden eagle that had evidently flown uncomfortably close to the fledglings in their nest. The eagle's line of escape crossed directly between Flossy and the sun. Humans engrossed in Luella's delight, living in that moment, in that reality, failed to consider sunlight, or shadow. But Flossy noticed. And you, too, dear reader, by now would have noticed had you been there. A more distant perspective would have allowed you to take in a broader world of action, reaction, and verve.

Oscar rushed over while Chase calmed the horse. "OMG, you OK Lulu?" He helped her up and put his arm around her, the dusty cowboy tattoo on the back of his hand wiggling as he protectively cradled her shoulder.

Vera could see Luella holding back tears, not only from pain, but fear. Worse than that, her face bore a look of disappointment, and failure.

Ellen whispered to Vera that if Luella didn't get back on that horse now, she never would. If the horse believed that shadows were scary and it could buck her off at will, that was exactly what would happen.

"Ellen," Vera implored quietly as she gripped her daughter's forearm, "You're the one to make that happen. Go out there. Tell her something, anything, to convince her."

Ellen walked over calmly, taming her emotions to project a carefree smile of ease and confidence. She gently pried the overprotective Oscar away from his kid sister and smacked Flossy on the butt. Turning to Luella, she asked, "Got a little dusty, huh? It's OK, just get back up there."

Vera placed her hand on Chase's shoulder.

"I love you," he whispered.

"I believe you," Vera replied and gave him a kiss.

Luella paused and wiped some snot from her nose. She inhaled deeply with a slight shudder and gave Ellen an "I'm not so sure about this," look.

"C'mon," Ellen brushed the dust from Luella's jeans. "Hop on up! Big brother is watching you."

GLOSSARY

11G. Better than 10G, or tenth generation wireless transmission networks for infotain data.

A People's History of Globalian Thought and Truth. Definitive historical text documenting the rise of infotain-based fact learning. Thought to have been at least partially authored by renowned historian Aneeka Randall.

AmaZing! Globalian e-commerce consumer goods firm specializing in AI generated product pre-selection.

ByteDime. Decentralized peer-to-peer cybercurrency providing freedom and prosperity to Globalian consumers, investors and speculators.

CeleTeCharity. Charity partnerships between A-list celebrities and technology innovation leaders to make the world a little less unpleasant.

Chatter. Also known as The Chatter. Social media service optimized for Brain Computer Interface implants that resulted from a round of mergers and acquisitions in the late 2020s.

Chicken Soup. A form of human nourishment popular in the United States during the pre-processed meals era.

Chinasia. Economic trading bloc formed in competition with Globalia.

Coffee. A pre-climatic crisis beverage made of roasted berries that were oddly referred to as beans.

Cokaid. One of two leading soyalgent-based food and beverage brands owned by Renaissance Mercernary hedge funds.

Crickets. A once ubiquitous six-legged insect known to make chirping sounds by rubbing its wings together.

Crypto. Secret, untraceable conversations or data exchanges.

Daisy. A flowering herbaceous perennial plant with white petals surrounding a yellow center made famous in one of the first successful political television advertisements, which was run by U.S. President Lyndon B. Johnson in 1964 to suggest that his opponent Barry Goldwater would start a nuclear war. The spot, which aired only once, became a template for negative political attack ads during the historical period where elections still held great consequence in public policy creation. Amid the controversy created by the ad, 1,800 psychiatrists responded to a survey claiming Goldwater was psychologically unfit to hold office. Goldwater successfully sued, and after the election was awarded $75,000 in damages, leading the American Psychiatric Association to implement a rule prohibiting psychiatrists from disclosing opinions about a public figure's mental health, a subsequent boon to later presidential candidates. Henceforth, psychiatrists such as Aneeka Randall avoided political commentary and focused instead on judicial "interpretation."

David Bowie. Rumored by many to have been a musical performer in the late twentieth century although some accounts claim this was an alias for renowned astronaut Ziggy Stardust.

Extruder. A 3D meal and beverage production device used to extrude heated soyalgent paste that has been combined with flavor packets through inkjet printer heads.

Fanta. Mid twenty-first century slang for fantastic. Also, a onetime orange soda brand and leading competitor to OrangeSmash.

GalExSee. Infotain helmet manufactured by the WhamZong corporation that utilizes an external screen to allow end users to navigate a virtual megaverse using EEG sensors embedded inside the helmet and pressed against the skull.

GalEmScene. A WhamZong Brain Computer Interface chip inserted in an end user's amygdala to enhance emotional scenery during infotain episodes and regulate excessive passions or sentimentality.

GalinSee. A computer chip developed by WhamZong that is inserted inside the cerebral cortex to stream infotainment and allow an end user to transmit thoughts, sights, and sounds globally via 11G transmissions.

Grand Canyon. A large hole in the earth that reportedly still exists to this day.

Globalia. A public-private partnership between leading nation states such as the United States, Germany, and Oceania along with multinational corporations governed by the Piese Treaty as interpreted by the Tribunal of Educates.

Globalia Public Media. A public news source known for intolerable fund drives and captivating stories that create so-called driveway moments where pre-implant viewers once had to remain in their vehicles in order to consume the end of the infotain segment.

Great Saturation. Historical period of the early to mid-twenty-first century when infotain mind casting sufficiently saturated human brains and bodies so as to completely overwhelm sensory input from terrestrial sources. Precursor and possible cause of the War Unseen. Resolved by the Mind Scarcity Doctrine adopted by the Tribunal of Educates in the *Zannity v Timeless Warning* ruling that placed strict limits on the amount of infotainment any human could consume unless placed in a pre-funded Entertainment Home.

HALExa. Digital Assistant owned and operated by the AmaZing! corporation. HALExa knows what you want and when you want it.

Horse. A wild equine formerly domesticated by humans as an antiquated means of conveyance and entertainment.

Implanted viewvitude. A financing model allowing moderate to low-income end users to afford Brain Computer Interface implants that would be repaid with advertising revenue accrued over the Vue's lifetime. Based upon the model of indentured servitude that allowed European migrants to find freedom and prosperity in early North American colonies.

Infotain Deserts. Barren cerebral landscapes devoid of 11G signals where end users face data and entertainment deprivation.

IRL. Text emoji for In Real Life.

Lubyr. Autonomous rideshare service resulting from a mid-twenty-first-century megamerger.

Magna Carta. Supposed legal document that articulated the inspiration that no man, not even a king, was above the law. Weakened in some Globalian jurisdictions by a 2024 ruling by the United States Supreme Court regarding presidential immunity.

Meta. Adjective describing a self-referential statement usurped by a mid-twenty-first century social media corporation. That's so meta, dude.

Mule. A human lackey who loaded and launched autonomous flatbed trucks with areaial delivery drones prior to fully automated and integrated parcel delivery platforms. Alternately, a cross between a donkey and a horse.

MyScreen. A virtual reality helmet with semi-transparent visor that allows end users to simultaneously view the terrestrial surroundings and consume infotainment. Many models feature bone-conducting ear buds, onboard air conditioning, extended battery packs, and scalp EEG sensors that provide limited brain computer interface capabilities. Competitor to the WhamZong GalExSee.

MyndScreen. A computer brain interface microchip surgically implanted in the cerebral cortex and powered by an onboard glucose fuel cell. Provides audio and video input to the human brain and broadcasts end user auditory, cognitive, and occipital signals via the 11G network. Tactile, emotional and olfactory transmission is under development but not yet supported. Competitor to the WhamZong GalinSee.

Noodle. A cerebral and hyperspatial search engine.

OMG. A personal possessive religious exhortation, "Oh, My, God."

Orwellian. A term coined in the mid twentieth century that came to mean whatever the speaker wanted it to mean.

Oxford. Historically significant educational institution and publisher of word compendiums.

Penny. A piece of tangible United States currency still technically in circulation today although there are no known transactions involving this diminutive copper denomination. Scientific studies have been unable to document any association with luck.

Pepsoilant. One of two leading soyalgent-based food and beverage brands owned by Renaissance Mercernary hedge funds.

Pelican. A large water bird with flexible throat pouch that existed for approximately 36 million years.

Piese Treaty. A multinational trade agreement negotiated by renowned diplomat Justinian Piese to rebuild global prosperity and economic stability in the aftermath of the War Unseen. The agreement left nation-states intact while converting their elected governments to largely ceremonial posts similar to European monarchies. This allowed for periodic bouts of populism or patriotism to run their course without disrupting the world economic or military infrastructure.

Pincerton. A non-lethal aerial security drone capable of anesthetizing a suspect prior to detaining it in pincer claws. Typically used in evictions, contraband interdiction, and other non-payment collection situations.

Pony. Like a horse, only smaller.

Protruder. A three-dimensional printing device utilizing plastic or concrete inks to produce semi-durable consumer goods and buildings. A CokAid or Pepsoilant dispenser often includes both an extruder printer head for foodlike substances and a protruder head for cutlery and dishware.

Pudding. A mushy food similar in texture to unprocessed soyalgent paste, formerly used as an enticement for school children to consume flesh-based protein. "If you don't eat your meat, you can't have any pudding." Also known as custard, flan, mousse, or crème caramel. Variants included banana, bread, butterscotch, rice, tapioca and Yorkshire.

RealiT-Lounge. A leading entertainment and gaming chaise featuring tactile massage and special effects, aromatic scenery enhancement, heating and air conditioning jets. Improvement to the My-Massage Lounge.

ROI. Return on Investment.

Salmon. A color often used in fashion, particularly for neckwear.

Soyalgent. Human nutritional product consisting of soybeans, algae, and lentils. No relation to the fictitious soylent green.

SpeiDrWeb. Data tracking points invented by Dr. James Spei in 2029 to maximize human viewing enjoyment by utilizing end user streaming and purchase history to deliver highly relevant and entertaining content to a virtual reality helmet or cerebral cortex multiverse brain implant.

Situation Room. An immersive entertainment center capable of simulating a highly realistic situation as prescribed by a mental health professional to address severe cases of MyndScreen Side Effects.

Surround Ground. Three-dimensional audio and visual backdrop for a VRoom conference.

SyncedIn. Professional networking application for discerning minds and thought leaders.

Timeless Warning. Knower and provider of all things infotain. King of content creation.

Tribunal of Educates. A distinguished council of trade and economic experts ranging from nine to thirteen members that was responsible for enforcement and implementation of the Piese Treaty. Credited with creating the greatest period of prosperity and wealth in all of human history.

Two-Minute Spate. An infodump designed to ensure all Globalian end-users have a common subset of crucial facts from which to inform public opinion and policy decisions. Required by Tribunal fiat to be included as a two-minute segment in all "news" programs. Far more entertaining and data intensive than the fictional two-minute hate.

Vigarette. A virtual cigarette, also known as a tobacco extract vaping cylinder or V-cig.

VRoom. A Timeless Warning product allowing cerebral implant end users to convene a meeting of the minds in a virtual room. Not to be confused with vroom, the sound of a motorcycle operating at high speed.

Vue. A human member of society whose principle economic contribution is to view infotainment and consume products advertised within such infotainment. Vues largely filled the economic niche once played by workers, AKA proles, prior to automation of most industries.

Vwardrobe. Virtual wardrobe used to adorn end user avatars and stimulate ROI.

WallPayPer. A pay for view service that decorates interior wall spaces of end user homes and apartments and provides economic ROI.

War Unseen. Also known as the secret war or invisible war conducted between central-Asian nation states that went largely unnoticed in the Western world until limited nuclear fallout began contaminating the landscape and food sources.

WhamZong. A tech disruptor and innovation center providing superior infotain products and subject at one time to economically unproductive and unjust tariffs.

ACKNOWLEDGEMENTS

This book is dedicated to my daughter Peri, who provided initial inspiration for Vanessa, Luella, and Oscar. My story took a different turn than Peri's. Maybe someday we'll get to read her version. My wife Deniz deserves gratitude for bringing Peri into the world and putting up with me while drafting this novel.

Deep thanks to Shanna McNair and Scott Wolven at High Frequency Press for believing in this work and helping to sharpen its prose. I am indebted to Nami Mun for inquisitive exploration of early drafts and unending encouragement. Crystal Pearl and Ron Morgan were extremely generous with their time and talent in offering feedback on early drafts. Thanks also to instructors at the Stanford Novel Writing Certificate program, including Martha Conway, Lauren Kate, Ron Nyren, Rachel Sarah Smith; and to colleagues Rick Heisler, Mo Henderson, Shella Jacobs, Janice Maloney, Jen McKeirnan, Erica Minetti and Helen Wang. Instructor Jeffrey Ford and peers at The Writer's Hotel provided wonderful feedback and solidarity, including Meg Besser, Scott Branks del Llano, Julie Price Carpenter, David Carrington and Ed Pearlman.

ABOUT THE AUTHOR

Derek Cressman is an award-winning author of fiction and non-fiction based in Sacramento, California. Cressman wrote countless white papers, op-ed columns, fact sheets and reports as well as two books as part of a thirty-year career in public policy advocating for democracy issues such as campaign finance reform and voting rights. In 2019, he published his first novel, *Reality™ 2048*, which was a finalist in the Foreword INDIES Book of the Year and the Eric Hoffer Book Awards First Horizon American Fiction contest. Cressman is a graduate of Williams College and of the Stanford Online Certificate in Novel Writing program.

www.ingramcontent.com/pod-product-compliance
Lightning Source LLC
LaVergne TN
LVHW052303191025
823584LV00008B/10